Cara Colter shares he[...]
British Columbia, Can[...]
than thirty years, an an[...]
horses. She has three grown children and two
grandsons.

Michelle Douglas has been writing for Mills & Boon
since 2007 and believes she has the best job in the
world. She lives in a leafy suburb of Newcastle, on
Australia's east coast, with her own romantic hero, a
house full of dust and books, and an eclectic collection
of sixties and seventies vinyl. She loves to hear
from readers and can be contacted via her website:
michelle-douglas.com.

Also by Cara Colter

The Prince from Her Past

Winter Escapes miniseries

Their Hawaiian Marriage Reunion

Fairy Tales in Maine miniseries

Invitation to His Billion-Dollar Ball

Summer Escapes miniseries

Cinderella's Greek Island Temptation

Also by Michelle Douglas

Tempted by Her Greek Island Bodyguard
Secret Fling with the Billionaire
Tempted by Her Best Friend Billionaire

Summer Escapes miniseries

The Venice Reunion Arrangement

Discover more at millsandboon.co.uk.

AN INVITATION FOR CINDERELLA

CARA COLTER

MICHELLE DOUGLAS

MILLS & BOON

First published in Great Britain 2026
by Mills & Boon, an imprint of HarperCollins*Publishers* Ltd,
1 London Bridge Street, London, SE1 9GF

www.harpercollins.co.uk

HarperCollins*Publishers*, Macken House, 39/40 Mayor Street Upper, Dublin 1, D01 C9W8, Ireland

An Invitation for Cinderella © 2026 Harlequin Enterprises ULC

The CEO's Plus-One Charade © 2026 Cara Colter

Forbidden Cinderella in His Castello © 2026 Michelle Douglas

ISBN: 978-0-263-41933-7

01/26

MIX
Paper | Supporting responsible forestry
FSC™ C007454

This book contains FSC™ certified paper and other controlled sources to ensure responsible forest management.

For more information visit www.harpercollins.co.uk/green.

Printed and Bound in the UK using 100% Renewable Electricity at CPI Group (UK) Ltd, Croydon, CR0 4YY

THE CEO'S PLUS-ONE CHARADE

CARA COLTER

MILLS & BOON

Dedicated to all those people working quietly in the background: the bank tellers, the store clerks, the custodians, the hairstylists, the teacher's aides, the secretaries. You make the world work. I'm grateful.

CHAPTER ONE

"HOW DARE YOU?"

Molly Littleton held the phone away from her ear as insults rained down on her. This was the side of Eva La Lydia people did not see, she mused. Who knew the husky-toned actress could be quite so, well, shrill?

She waited patiently for a break in the rant, and then said, calmly, "I'm sorry, Miss La Lydia, but the nondisclosure agreement is not negotiable."

"How dare you insinuate I would kiss and tell?"

Molly closed her eyes. It was very tempting to remind the up-and-coming actress that she had done exactly that—kissed and told—on her last three boyfriends. Poor Douglas Hampton. The whole world now knew his kiss was garlic-tinged, rated *ewww*, by the actress.

Not that Molly's boss, Liam Westerhouse, would *ever* have garlic-tinged breath. And Molly was absolutely certain a kiss from him would also never be rated *ewww*.

Even though she was all alone in her office, thinking of Liam's kisses made her face suddenly feel hot, as if just by having the thought, she'd been caught in a terribly inappropriate situation.

She opened her eyes, bit her tongue and forced her thoughts in a different direction. As she often did under stress, she glanced around her office, taking in the order and subtle high-end touches with an inward sigh of deep delight.

Her neat desk had the soft, rich glow of solid walnut. The deep, luxurious pile of the wall-to-wall cream-colored wool rug absorbed sound, making her office a sanctuary of quiet in the middle of the world's busiest city. Two iconic black-and-white photos—the originals—were on the wall her desk faced, and depicted the very skyline she could look out on every single day.

She swiveled to those views now, and felt a sigh—arrival—within her. Not something that should be risked by giving into the temptation to give Miss La Lydia a piece of her mind. Or worse, allowing renegade thoughts of her boss's kisses.

The daylight was leaching from the New York skyline, being replaced by the office lights within the Manhattan office buildings popping on, one by one.

Molly still had to pinch herself about how far she had come from a rundown bayou neighborhood—closest big center, Shreveport, Louisiana—to *this*.

Still, evening falling was an urgent reminder of the task at hand and the fact time had run out. There was no way an NDA from Miss La Lydia could reach Molly's desk before the awards event, Innovators on the Move, which was starting in two hours.

She was aware of feeling relieved. Who wanted to expose Liam to *that* for an entire evening?

"Perhaps we can work together another time," Molly lied smoothly.

Her suggestion was met with momentary—and blessed—silence, before the screeching ensued, worse than before.

"I'm nearly ready to go," the actress cried. "I'm being dressed by—" She named one of the best fashion houses in New York.

"I'm really sorry, Miss La Lydia, but without the NDA, we cannot possibly move forward."

She hoped that didn't mean Eva would offer to rush it over. Thankfully, that didn't happen.

"I'll have your job, you rude little snip," Molly heard as she was disconnecting. "I'll be calling Liam personally—"

Note to self, Molly thought, do not trust Francis, from publicity, to come up with red-carpet companion suggestions for their boss again, no matter how much good press and attention for the company and the event that they might generate.

She'd been trying to get that signed NDA agreement for weeks. She should have suspected something was up as the litany of excuses from Eva's assistant had piled up: could you send another copy; it was on its way; in the works; just needed a signature; lost by the building concierge.

Now, Molly was in the rarest of positions: caught out. Her boss would be attending the publicity-generating awards show without a date. It wasn't the end of the world, but it also wasn't how her world worked. She glanced again at night falling on the city, and considered. Who could she ask to step in for La Lydia? Who on earth could be ready for a red-carpet event on such short notice?

She was just scrolling through her business phone when the door to the outer office was flung open and her boss strode in, all energy and confidence, and she felt that familiar sense of a world on snooze coming vibrantly to life, black and white turning to color.

Liam Westerhouse was gorgeous.

Stunningly, unforgettably, amazingly gorgeous.

Today, he was wearing a beautifully tailored suit, light gray jacket, with a crisp white shirt underneath it, knife-creased, narrow-legged slacks. Liam had a gift for always getting the tie exactly right and today it was exquisite—silk that held the multiple shades of the grays of storm clouds. Gold cufflinks winked at his wrists.

The suit subtly accentuated a beautiful build, slender rather than beefy.

And yet there was no mistaking the power in those shoulders, and in the length of his legs. His belly was flat beneath the shirt, his hips narrow.

And as compelling as all that was, it was his face that absolutely took her breath away. He had a mop of golden hair that never failed to look faintly messy, delightfully at odds with the perfectly put-together look of the suit.

That mane of luscious hair framed a face that was chiseled and flawless, with high cheekbones, strong nose, a faintly clefted chin. His chin and cheeks were roguishly whisker-shadowed. Like his untamed hair, the whiskers were an intriguing contrast, as if a secret outlaw wore the suit as a disguise.

But it was Liam's eyes that were his most stunning feature. Well, besides his generous mouth and the intriguing puffiness of his lower lip, which, given her renegade thoughts of earlier, she was simply not allowing herself to look at.

But his eyes! Framed in a fringe of sooty lashes, they might be called hazel, though that word really didn't do justice to the blend of green and gold and brown.

There was always something in them: a spark, a quality of dancing mischief that made her want to smile.

Even now, when she was aware she had let him down.

Before she made the admission of her failure, he stopped, cocked his head and looked at her. Really looked at her, in a way that made her feel seen.

Not, admittedly, that there was much to see. The designer suit—matching jacket and pencil skirt—that Molly had snagged at a high-end thrift store was a nice shade of cream that she hoped blended her in nicely with the carpet. She had left off the splurge item: a brand-new colorful silk scarf.

The scarf didn't go with her plan to notch down her appearance in direct correlation to her growing awareness that she had developed an embarrassing crush on her boss.

Some women might have amped up, but Molly was not that woman. It would just make her whole humiliating awareness of him all too obvious. It could make for awkwardness in the office.

Her office, run to her standards, was a very, very long way from the mail room where she had begun at Liam Westerhouse's company, FIX.

So, disruptions of a personal nature would simply not be tolerated.

Today, Molly had made herself particularly invisible. As well as choosing a beautifully cut but otherwise bland suit (from her collection of equally bland high-end thrift store finds), her dark brown hair was pulled back in her typical stern bun.

Though sometimes she indulged in a "messy" bun, she had never once, not even when she worked in the mail room, worn her long hair loose.

Since coming to work for Liam, she always wore glasses. Today, the pair she had chosen were particularly heavily framed. In addition, Molly had allowed herself only a hint of lip gloss and eye makeup. Just enough to be professional in her upscale office, not enough to draw attention.

And despite all that, there it was, that look in his eye as if he *saw* her, completely. Of course, by now she knew that was one of the many gifts Liam brought to this business.

He made people feel seen and important. And there was not a single thing put-on about it. His skyrocket of success was, at least in part, because of his very genuine interest in his fellow man.

And for Molly, there was nothing like authenticity to up her crush factor. Though his scent didn't help. His aroma was distinctly his. In the very center of all the action and mayhem and energy that made up New York City, Liam smelled of forests, hidden valleys and waterfalls.

She resisted an urge to tuck an escaped strand of dark hair behind her ear and to run a tongue over her lips. Both gestures would probably be a dead giveaway.

Executive assistant, falling hard and fast. Well, she told herself, sternly and firmly, in the he-makes-women-giddy department, she could get in line with the rest of the world!

"Sunday," Liam said, after a moment of studying her. "You look distressed. I hate it when you look distressed."

She'd been working for FIX for eighteen months, and for Liam directly for the last six. She'd come to his attention after she had made a suggestion in the mail room that had upped the efficiency of that department considerably.

At first, she'd been an assistant to his assistant, but Maxine had decided she wanted to devote herself to her new grand-babies, twins with some minor health issues. So, somehow, three months ago Molly had found herself stepping into her predecessor's shoes.

In truth, she had never had a job she loved so much, or that she felt so devoted to. She'd come from a childhood world of absolute chaos, and so bringing order to a complicated life felt as if it was the very thing she had been born to do.

She had referred to herself, early on in her new position, as his Girl Friday, and he had considered it with a tilt of his head.

"I don't like that term," he'd said, after a moment.

"Why? It comes from the name of Robinson Crusoe's assistant on the deserted island. And then, that theme was played on in a 1940s movie called *His Girl Friday*."

"Is there anything you don't know?" he'd asked.

"Of course there are things I don't know!"

"Huh. Who wrote Robinson Crusoe?"

"Daniel Defoe."

"What day did the Titanic sink?"

This was a little game they played often, both of them enjoying it equally.

"April 15, 1912. The vessel sank four days into her maiden voyage."

"See?" he said, with a satisfied sigh. "How do you do that? Oh, wait! You told me. You read. And you know things."

That didn't tell half the story, of course. The full story was a childhood of coming second to her brother, Donnie, in an environment of chronic poverty, chaos and addiction.

And into all that, the discovery of a library and a kind-hearted librarian, Mrs. Deverille. A discovery of the escapes offered the very second one opened a page. Any page. Of any book. And in that small library Molly had learned to read anything she could get her hands on.

"The next time I play trivia, I want you as a partner."

But, of course, as the recent keeper of his schedule, Molly knew Liam's life did not exactly have room for playing trivia and that there was no being his partner—in any sense of the word—anywhere in her future. Or his. Even early on, she'd known not to complicate the best job she had ever had.

"It really only refers to an indispensable assistant, male or female," Molly had told him. "There's nothing derogatory about it."

"No, I disagree," he'd said. "The whole Friday thing. There's something vaguely master to servant about it that I don't like. Are you indispensable? Yes."

The crush had probably started that second of being told she was indispensable, being *seen* as valuable and with something to offer.

No, that was a lie. The crush had probably started the moment she had laid eyes on him, even back in her mail room days. All the women who worked here had crushes on him. It was perfectly harmless.

Until it wasn't.

CHAPTER TWO

THAT'S WHAT MOLLY had kept in mind when Liam had regarded her so solemnly as he weighed in on the nickname Girl Friday.

"My servant?" he had said, then added firmly, "No."

"How about Sunday, then?" she'd kidded him, then as now, eager to hide how he was making her feel behind many layers, humor being one of them.

"Sunday." He'd considered it. "You do work Sundays. And it's in keeping with your ability to pull off absolute miracles. Okay, Sunday it is."

She gave him a little mock salute.

He considered for a moment. "But only if you call me Saturday."

They'd laughed then. That had been the first time in their working relationship they had laughed together, and really, if she looked for the little sparks of her ridiculous crush on him being fanned more dangerously to life, that exchange would definitely rate.

He did call her Sunday. But she only called him Saturday on the rarest of occasions, because it seemed way too familiar. Still, he absolutely would not stand for her calling him *Mr. Westerhouse* or *sir*.

Molly also found the familiarity of calling him Liam uncomfortable, so she settled on *boss*, or sometimes *chief*.

"So, Sunday," he said, "why the look of distress? Not much rattles you."

"Well, we find you without a date for Innovators on the Move. Which begins in—" she glanced at the wall clock "—one hour and fifty-three minutes."

"Ah." He seemed singularly unperturbed. "Who was it supposed to be?"

"Eva La Lydia."

Eva La Lydia was arguably one of the most beautiful women in the world. Her boss, endearingly, wrinkled his nose and grimaced.

"The name alone," he said, with a rueful shake of his head. "Awful. Whose idea was that?"

"The name? Or the arrangement for her to accompany you to the event?"

"The name, even though the origins of the name are probably obscure—"

"Not really. Her real name is Evelyn Lyndall. After being discovered playing Fantine in her high school production of *Les Misérables*, she thought a French take on her name would make her a standout as she pursued her acting career."

He didn't ask how she knew, but of course she was going to do a bit of basic research on anyone he was being paired with.

He pointed to his chest and then her. "See?" he said. "You and me and trivia. We could take on the world, Sunday. Okay. Question two: whose idea was it to set me up with *her* for the evening?"

She was glad she could not take credit for that one.

"Francis Whittaker, from publicity. Miss La Lydia is the star of *Yellow Rock*. Being seen with her would bring plenty of coverage to both the young innovators and to FIX."

"Ah, well," he said, "I'm sure FIX will limp along without the exposure. Sorry about the young innovators having to settle for just me, though."

He grinned at her, and he looked so impossibly charming she had to steel herself against the flutter of her heart.

"I should warn you," she said firmly, determined to keep it

all business, "Miss La Lydia has said she's going to complain to you personally. About me."

"She doesn't have my phone number, does she?" Liam asked, alarmed.

"Not on my watch," Molly said, emphatically.

"Good job, Sunday. What's her complaint?"

"She didn't like my attitude."

"Your attitude?"

Molly consulted her notes. "Rude and snippy, to be exact. She wouldn't sign the NDA, and so I told her the evening was off. She has a record of kiss and tell."

She kept her eyes firmly on her notes. For a few seconds. Then, despite her legendary discipline, she couldn't resist sneaking a peek at him.

And the part of him responsible for kisses.

Would he have kissed Eva? She cast about in herself for questionable motives. Was she guarding him, even subconsciously, from other women's kisses? Was that why she'd called off the evening?

Of course not! It was all about the NDA.

"I take full responsibility," Molly said, "for the evening not turning out. I really should have made sure the NDA was in order, sooner."

"Ha. It sounds as if we dodged a bullet, really."

We.

Molly was aware of this horrible ability she had developed to make something out of nothing.

"How could I spend a whole evening with someone willing to think one bad thought about my Woman Sunday?"

There was that feeling. That wonderful feeling of someone having your back. You could not risk that on something as ridiculous—and hopefully fleeting—as a crush.

"Thanks, boss," Molly said. "Of course, Miss La Lydia would have been great publicity for FIX, as Francis knew when she set it up. She's the It girl, right now."

Again, she saw a slight flattening around Liam's mouth, as if he had known all along that the image the star projected was not at all who she was.

Well, he would know. He had been seen with some of the most beautiful and famous women in the world. None seemed to impress him.

If there was one thing she knew for certain about Liam's personal life, it was that he didn't really have one. His relationship was with his business.

And he was absolutely committed to being single.

Still, that required doing this delicate dance with the media. Publicity was good for the business. They played on Liam's star quality all the time. The fact that he was twenty-eight and single worked in their favor, because women *adored* him.

He'd twice been featured in a very well-known publication as their choice for Bachelor of the Year.

But it was also a balancing act to keep his life private, and to allow him to give most of his focus to what he did best, which was running an incredible business.

Liam, in defiance of his family's traditions and old money, had pursued his own interests and become a mechanical engineer. While he was in university his parents had been killed in a plane crash. He'd inherited an absolute fortune and could have easily given up his education and gone on to live the lifestyle of the rich and famous, acting as honorary CEO for the family business, Westerhouse Group.

Instead, he had completed his education, graduated with a master's degree, and without touching his inheritance, he had founded FIX (Find Innovative eXcellence). It had started small, but he'd discovered a missing component in an aerospace project, and developed a solution that had brought him incredible notice and propelled him toward success.

Since then, absolute brilliance, discipline and energy had created a meteoric rise of the company. Liam brought his incredible abilities, vigour and enthusiasm to finding solutions and creating products in a wide-ranging number of industries, including manufacturing, aerospace, automotive, construction, energy and biomedical.

"So, I can try and find a last-minute for you," Molly volunteered, "or you can go solo. I'm afraid ducking out isn't an option as the company is one of the sponsors and you're one of the presenters."

"Up-and-Comer of the Year." He patted his suit pocket. "I have my speech right here. As per your notes: award goes to Jordan Houston, inventor of Fresh, a portable device that can convert fouled water to fresh and has unbelievable potential in natural disaster areas."

"You make my job so easy," she said.

"No, you make my job easy. I know, by the way, your job is not easy. It's hard. And somehow you make it seem like every day, no matter what I throw at you, is an absolute delight."

Dangerous to bask in his approval! She moved on rapidly.

"So, boss, solo or should I find someone?"

"I'm not really familiar with many of the people in that organization," he said. "I have an unfortunate picture of sitting at a big banquet table by myself, twiddling my thumbs."

She was pretty sure he'd be surrounded by admirers in seconds, though no doubt that could be as difficult as sitting alone.

"It'll remind me of my unhappy younger self," he said. "The little outcast who sat by himself through meals for all my private school years. Though sometimes I just bypassed the mess hall and ate in the kitchen with the cook. She loved me after I fixed the commercial dishwasher that had given her grief for years."

Every now and then, *this*. This precious glimpse of what had made Liam Westerhouse so different from so many others who had been born into the kind of wealth he had been born into.

He was a good role model for someone like her. *You could mine your past for strength and resilience.*

She thought of the latest phone call from her mother and shuddered. Well, maybe not *her* past.

They needed more money for Donnie's latest legal battle. It was not his first one, but it was by far the most serious.

Molly thought about her younger brother. He had been the hope of a family abandoned by their father. In the mess of desperation and bitterness dear old Dad had left in his wake, Donnie had been the rising star, the bright shining one she and her mother had pinned their hopes on.

Her brother was good-looking, had ample easygoing Southern charm and was extraordinarily athletic. The colleges started scouting him when he was still a junior in high school. He was National Football League material and everybody knew he was going to be a star—he was going to put their little backwater bayou on the map.

He was their ticket out. Molly learned only his needs mattered. She was there to serve the king of their household.

And then, he was injured, at a practice. A broken shoulder. A family without medical insurance. Donnie given opiates to control the pain.

Instead of their ticket out, he had completed the Littleton family's spiral downward.

And yet, her mother could not let go of her vision of Donnie. She continued to pour her adoration—and the family's very limited resources—on Donnie. She continued to treat Molly as if her only job on earth was to shore up her brother.

Escape to New York had given Molly the physical distance she so desperately needed, but the mental bonds were harder to break.

Donnie had been caught in the wrong place at the wrong time, according to her mother's latest call, her words increasingly slurred as the call progressed.

He had nothing to do with the armed robbery of Baskin's liquor store. Donnie had only been walking by. He was an innocent victim in the whole thing.

He's going to go to jail, her mother had wailed, *if we can't pay a good lawyer. You should see what you get for free. He'll be in jail for the rest of his life if we have to use the public defender. Do you know what happens to good-looking boys like him in jail?*

Molly wondered what Liam would think if he knew about *that*. What anyone here at FIX would think if they knew the truth about the prim, proper and entirely professional Miss Littleton's ongoing dramas with a family plunged into poverty, desperation and hopelessness that had started when the last auto plant had pulled out of Shreveport, and decades later, showed no signs of ending.

Her mother seemed only to resent the fact Molly had managed to escape it all, as if her abandonment was identical to their father's and as if Molly had left her mother and Donnie to be devoured in an alligator-infested swamp. Though that resentment didn't keep either her brother or her mother from treating her like the Bank of Molly.

And her guilt about leaving them all behind—about loving her new life so darned much—kept her writing the checks.

No wonder she had developed an unrealistic crush on her boss. If ever there had been a girl who needed a fairy tale, it was Molly!

Still, she'd grown up with enough hard knocks that she'd known you could open the pages of a story and escape there, but you had to tread that fine line of not investing in dreams too deeply. Hope, after all, was the most dangerous thing of all.

"Don't you have someone you can call?" she asked Liam, and inserted a light note into her voice as she added, marveling at the fact she was in a position to tease him, "'World's Most Eligible Bachelor'?"

CHAPTER THREE

MOLLY LOVED IT when Liam wrinkled his nose, which he did now, at being reminded he was considered one of the world's most eligible bachelors. "I'm not currently seeing anyone."

Which, of course, as keeper of his social calendar, Molly knew.

In the eighteen months she had worked for the company, and the three since she'd had total reign over his personal schedule, Liam had never been seeing anyone. He seemed more than content to let his staff figure out companions for him when he needed an escort for an event.

These were always, as far as Molly could tell, one-offs. He never asked her to find him a phone number, never requested any follow-up information.

"Married to my job," he'd said to her once, cheerfully. "The best partner ever."

She could see this was true. Liam Westerhouse was married to his job. He worked relentlessly. In his world there were no weekends. He was usually at his office in the morning before she got there, and he was often back there at night as she was getting ready to leave.

Molly had chided him once, that he was working too hard.

"Working?" he'd said with genuine surprise. "I'm not working, Sunday. I'm playing."

His social calendar was jam-packed, but only with events

that benefited or forwarded the cause of FIX or one of the many organizations and charities that FIX supported.

"I'll try and find someone," she said. "So you don't have to sit alone. It's very short notice, though, so no guarantees."

"Maybe I'll just bow out."

She gnawed her lip. "I don't think they could find another presenter on such short notice. I researched Jordan and she really hopes to work for FIX one day. I think she'd be devastated if you didn't show up."

"Probably any representative from the company would do."

"It's pretty short notice, chief."

Liam contemplated that, and then brightened.

"Sunday," he said. "You'd be perfect for the job."

"What job?" she stammered.

"You could do it!" he said. He tried to pass her his notes for his speech. "You've already done the homework. You know about the award winner. You'd be a perfect representative of FIX."

"No," she said vehemently, shifting her chair away from the papers he held out to her.

"Oh—" he gave himself a smack on the forehead "—how thoughtless of me to think you'd be any more comfortable sitting alone than I would be."

"That's not it," she said.

"What is it, then?"

"Really? I'm a nobody. From Liam Westerhouse and Eva La Lydia, to me?"

He looked stunned by that. He cocked his head and narrowed his eyes. It felt as if he was seeing her differently than how he normally did.

"A nobody?" he said, something dangerous in his tone.

"I mean not a celebrity. Not a person of note."

"You are not a nobody," he said, that same dangerous note in his voice.

She thought of her mother and brother. If only he knew!

She realized she felt like an imposter. Even though she had spent countless hours taming that telltale touch of the South from her voice, poring over magazines to figure out how to look "right" for an upscale office, investing money in pedicures and manicures—things scorned in her childhood neighborhood—she still had this awful feeling someday she was going to be caught.

"Never mind," he said, and he seemed to be in rare ill humor. "Just cancel it. I'll make it up to the kid getting the award. She could come for a tour of the company. I'll take her for lunch or something."

She thought of Liam's jam-packed schedule. Where was she going to fit that in? She could feel a little headache gathering between her eyes, right over the bridge of her nose.

"How about if I go with you?" she said, impulsively.

She reminded herself she was not impulsive. There was always a price to be paid for being impulsive.

"Like pretend to be my date?" he asked, astonished.

"No, no, nothing like that!" She was blushing wildly.

"Oh," he said, snapping his fingers. "Like my plus-one."

"That sounds like an unfortunate dress size," she said.

He laughed.

As soon as Liam laughed, Molly was aware her intent in offering her services for the evening had not been completely pure. It wasn't about finding a lunch slot in a tight schedule. And it wasn't just about being helpful in a new way, either.

No, she wanted to spend more time with him.

She was being greedy for his company, pure and simple.

And she, of all people, should know about the dangers involved in wanting *more*.

"*Plus-one* is just a phrase people use," Liam said to her. "It just means a kind of no-strings-attached companion for an event."

"Oh," she said. His having to explain it to her just reminded her more how she had never really been in the mainstream, not like the sophisticated people he generally hung out with.

Liam cocked his head, considering. "Sunday, it's an absolutely brilliant suggestion, no matter what we call it. You don't have to give a speech; I don't have to eat alone."

She felt compelled to clarify. "I'll just be your assistant, as always."

"Exactly! But people won't know that. It'll look like you're my date—"

"Plus-one," she inserted, and earned his grin.

"And as a bonus, with none of the complications that come from a real date."

"Complications?" she said, uncertainly.

"You know. To kiss or not to kiss."

The very question that she had wondered about for his date with Eva! It was an unfair invitation to look at his lips, again. The downward swooping of her stomach told her that far from being brilliant, this was possibly the dumbest idea she'd ever had.

"You know," she said, weakly, "maybe I didn't think it through."

"How very unlike you," he said, that lovely mouth quirking upward, again, in that hint of a smile a Girl Sunday—or a plus-one—could live for.

"Agreed," she said, and his smile turned to a laugh at her sullenness.

"I'm sorry," Liam said. "Did you just realize you had other plans?"

It just went to show, Molly thought, that while she knew practically everything there was to know about him, Liam knew next to nothing about her. Wasn't it evident that she did not have other plans? Wasn't it evident that work—and a good book on her bedside table—were her life?

The consequences of her wanting more were just beginning to sink in. The truth was the less he knew about her the better and this impulsive invitation was opening territory she did not want opened.

Besides, it would be more than evident to anyone who saw them together she was outmatched.

That no matter how much time she spent on her accent, no matter how carefully she selected clothes from the thrift store, no matter how much money she spent on manicures and pedicures, she could not belong in the world he moved in so easily—a world of money, sophistication, power.

"It's not that I have another plan," she said, though how she wished she had a handsome man and tickets to a Broadway show to fall back on. "It's just I'm not dressed for an event like that, and I don't live close enough to go change."

As if she had a dress that would work for a function like that, even if she did live close enough to go change.

"Where do you live?" he asked, puzzled.

See? This was the door she had opened. One ill thought-out statement and she had invited this peek into her personal life that had not happened in the time since she'd become his assistant.

"I have a little place in Marine Park."

"Marine Park?"

"Brooklyn."

"Isn't that a long commute?"

"It's not bad. Forty-five minutes. I like the subway."

"What?"

This was the problem with sashaying over the line into the personal. Now she had to avoid telling him that every single thing about New York was a miracle to her, from having a tiny, peaceful basement suite, to riding the subway with other people who were on their way to ordinary jobs that they totally took for granted.

He considered that, and then asked, carefully, "Do you need a raise?"

Sometimes, despite how humble he usually was, despite his

being the boy who had eaten in his school kitchen with the cook, being raised with a lot of money showed. He couldn't believe anyone in the world who had a choice wouldn't live in Manhattan. He was obviously incredulous—even though he was trying to hide it—that anyone enjoyed the subway.

Had he ever even been on the subway?

She resisted the temptation to ask. "No, I do not need a raise!"

"Are you sure? Because you have been putting in a lot of hours on the weekends, too."

"I'm sure." The truth was she would probably pay him to work at his company if she had to and she was already stunned by the amount of money she was making. FIX was inordinately good to all its employees. In fact, she could have a small place in Manhattan if she wasn't bankrolling her current family disaster.

There was that deliciously sexy upward quirk of his mouth again.

"There you go, Sunday, the one-in-a-million person who would say they don't need a raise."

He looked so genuinely appreciative of her.

Don't preen, she ordered herself. If there was one thing her childhood had taught her, it was to not get distracted from dealing with the crisis at hand.

"Anyway, I don't have anything to wear, and I don't want to embarrass you, so—"

"Embarrass me? Oh, Sunday. You could be wearing a flour sack dress and everything you are would still shine through."

She winced at that, though not the shining-through part. The flour sack part. Because Liam Westerhouse didn't have any real clue what a flour sack dress was. She, on the other hand, had a worn picture tucked in her top bureau drawer of ancestors wearing those dresses, staring into a camera, defeated, and resentful of their horrible circumstances being captured on film.

He eyed her thoughtfully for a moment, and then waved a hand at her. "Clothes are easy. If having something to wear is your only worry, let's go get you something."

Of course not being dressed appropriately was not her only worry. *This* was her worry: stepping into more uncharted territory with her boss. Once the line between personal and professional blurred, was there any putting it back?

It felt as if, if she now invested in this plan that she had very stupidly suggested—here were the consequences of impulsivity—she could wreck the perfect life she had maneuvered her way into, disturb the precious balance she had so carefully created and controlled.

And wasn't that the very legacy she was trying to outrun?

Littletons had a special gift for snatching defeat from the jaws of victory, for turning blessings into curses.

She knew she had to back away from this.

Say no, Molly told herself. Go home to her tiny, cozy apartment, her book and a fussy African violet she had named Winspear. Well, probably not the book, tonight. Liam had a trip to Québec City coming up next week and she had not taken care of the final details.

She knew something about Liam that hardly anyone knew. He *loved* chocolate. And so somehow this had become one of her things: Before he left on a trip, she researched all the local chocolatiers and made sure a selection of the very best the region had to offer was available in his hotel room. She always did it on her own time, as it didn't really fall under the purview of her duties. She paid for it herself. It made it feel like her gift to him, a way of expressing some of her pent-up feelings without saying a word.

He didn't seem to have caught on that she was behind the chocolate. She had begun waiting with anticipation for his return, because inevitably, he would say, "Sunday, you've got to try this."

Thinking of the interesting evening ahead of her, Molly glanced at her watch and made another excuse.

So much easier, somehow, to safely indulge her secret crush from a distance. "I'm pretty sure most of the shops are on the brink of closing."

His phone was out of his pocket in a flash. "I have a friend."

Oh. *Now*, he had a friend. But five minutes ago, when he'd needed someone to go with him to the awards dinner, *nada*.

"I'll ask them to stay open for an extra hour. What do you say?"

Liam was really offering her a kind of Cinderella experience. And though she was a long way, physically, from her roots, the girl of rags and ashes lived on inside her.

A girl who had longed, powerfully, for fairy tales.

Really, she was living a fairy tale. Dream job. New York City. Distance from her crazy family. Little apartment. Even her plant was thriving. It was all so blissfully domestic. Normal. Except for that one part.

Secretly in love with her boss.

She had to kill this tiny, persistent longing for more. That was one lesson she needed to carry from her hardscrabble childhood. Don't wish for too much. Don't dance with boldness. Don't take chances.

There was safety in invisibility.

Say no, Molly ordered herself.

Instead, of its own volition, her shoulder lifted as if it was the most casual of decisions, as if she wasn't playing fast and loose with the very thing that had given her happiness—her career.

She heard herself say, as if she was one of those breezy, fun-loving girls capable of being impulsive, "Sure. Why not?"

Fifth Avenue was buzzing as Molly and Liam made their way down a crowded sidewalk. It was early spring and New York was shaking off the gray winter doldrums.

Coming from a small town, she loved this delicious combination of energy and anonymity.

Not that it was so anonymous with Liam at her side. In a city where no one looked at each other, it seemed everyone looked at him.

Some people, of course, would recognize him.

But it was more his sheer presence that attracted so many glances, and a few boldly inviting gazes.

Liam didn't appear to notice, taking her elbow on occasion to guide her through the worst crush of the crowds.

And then he was holding open the door of a boutique aptly named Second Chances. As the door closed behind them, Molly felt the hush, in sharp contrast to the bustle outside.

She had walked by this business many times and even allowed herself to wonder about going in, but she never had. It was not just a boutique but a complete makeover service.

She slid Liam a look. Did he think she needed that? A complete makeover?

Of course he did! No one wanted a plus-one, even a fake plus-one, who wasn't quite up to standard.

The entry lobby was beautiful—a subtle pay station at its center, with a lighted wall of extraordinary before-and-after portraits behind it. The transformations people experienced here were nothing short of stunning.

The motto was etched on the desk in silver relief.

Don't change who you are, ever. But embrace every single thing you were meant to be.

She wasn't sure that bold statement included young women from the wrong side of the tracks in Louisiana.

For a moment, she considered bolting out the door. She could feel the ground shifting under her feet. She could feel something coming; she could smell it the way an animal can smell a storm coming on the wind. And it was the thing she hated the most.

Change.

Almost as if he sensed her discomfort, Liam ever so lightly touched her arm. The perfect "plus-one" touch. Without a word that touch said, *Hey, we're in this together. I got you.*

The change wasn't coming, she realized. It wasn't a flash of lightning off in the distance. With that light touch, it was *here*. The storm was breaking.

CHAPTER FOUR

LIAM SENSED SOME CHANGE in Molly almost the second they walked through the door of Second Chances. He slid her a glance, trying to figure out what the shift was.

She looked, really, as she always did. She was wearing one of those box-like suits she preferred, and sensible shoes. Her dark hair was scraped back into a stern no-nonsense bun, which for some reason accentuated how glossy it was, and how it was completely untouched by artificial color. The color of her hair reminded him, suddenly, of melted dark chocolate.

Those glasses made her look endearingly earnest and owlish. But just as for some reason her hairstyle made him more aware of how glossy those strands were, the glasses that he suspected were intended to make her seem serious always made him aware of how stunningly blue her eyes were.

There hadn't been girls at his private school, but Liam had come to see Molly's type later in university. The ones who hugged huge piles of books against their chests, avoided eye contact and seemed most at home in the library.

He certainly had not given a thought at the time to what valuable employees those studious, seemingly intent-on-being-invisible young women would become.

From those first days, when Molly had come into his office under the wing of Maxine, he'd seen what her gift was.

Complete competence.

Molly simply radiated reliability. In a very short time he'd come to find her indispensable, with her razor-sharp intelligence and her amazing organizational skills.

He'd never seen her caught out, never seen a challenge upset her or defeat her.

She was imminently trustworthy. Was that why he'd blurted that out about eating in the kitchen with the cook? He was not sure he'd ever shared that with anyone before.

But now he was aware that something had happened as soon as they walked in the door of this boutique. At a glance, it wasn't that noticeable. He saw her studying the pictures behind the desk and realized, for the first time, that this wasn't just a boutique. It was some kind of makeover place.

Was that the cause of the fine tension around her mouth and in her eyes? Was that why her shoulders were ever so faintly hunched forward, as though she wanted to disappear? He noticed her arm was stiffly at her side, but that she was rubbing her index finger against her thumb together nervously.

"Hey, I didn't know about that," he assured her with a nod toward the pictures. "I just thought it was a place to pick up a dress."

Despite his clumsy attempt to make her realize he approved of her just the way she was, the smile she gave him seemed strained.

He realized Molly Littleton, his Woman Sunday, his executive assistant extraordinaire, was a duck out of water.

A man came out of an alcove off the main reception area.

"Mr. Westerhouse," he said, extending his hand, "a pleasure. I'm Christopher."

"I appreciate you staying open. We've had a sudden shift in plans and my assistant wasn't sure her current outfit would work. This is Molly Littleton. I've pressed her into extra duties tonight. She's unexpectedly attending an awards dinner with me, with a cocktail event to follow, so she needs to choose a dress."

"We'll have something perfect," Christopher assured them smoothly.

Molly did not look reassured. "I wouldn't even know what I'm looking for." Her voice seemed high and uncertain.

Liam stared at her. His Molly? Who could handle anything? His Sunday, who had just put some full-of-herself starlet firmly in her place, felled by a dress?

"Ask her anything," Liam suggested, trying to find familiar ground to put her at ease. "She's my superpower. A walking encyclopedia."

Christopher played along, guiding Molly toward the boutique area. "When was America discovered?"

"Too easy," Liam said, following close behind them as if he might have to prevent a full bolt toward the door.

"*Discovered* has become a slightly contentious term," Molly said, and she did sound relieved and grateful to be on more familiar footing, "but Christopher—oh, possibly your namesake—Columbus landed in the Americas on the island now known as the Bahamas in 1492. He was thought to be the first European but actually his arrival was predated by several centuries by the Viking explorer, Leif Erikson."

Liam wagged his eyebrows at Christopher. "See?"

Christopher tilted his head at Molly. "I could swear I hear the faintest trace of the South in your accent," he said.

Any confidence being back on familiar footing had given Molly evaporated. She had a sudden deer-in-the-headlights look.

Again, Liam was aware how different she was outside of the office environment. She was so sure of herself in that realm, radiating confidence and certainty and utter competence.

He had never detected any kind of accent in his assistant. He thought she would confirm or deny Christopher's observation but instead she was silent. It occurred to him part of the reason Molly was so good at her job was that she seemed most comfortable staying in the background.

It also occurred to him how very little he knew about her personally. Though he'd found out two new things about her today—three if you counted Christopher's observation about her accent.

Molly didn't like the spotlight. Really, he should have known that from the understated way that she dressed at the office.

But, even more surprisingly, he'd discovered she wasn't motivated by money. She'd vehemently turned down his offer to compensate her more.

These observations were hitting him like a breath of fresh air. In other words, Molly was the absolute antithesis of every other woman who had been his plus-one in the past few years.

And certainly the antithesis of Charlotte Weeby, a woman he had narrowly escaped marrying.

Charlie. What some people would call a gold digger. He felt that familiar rush of anger, not so much at her for betraying him, but at himself for being so naive, so blind to who she really was, so desperate for love...

He snapped himself out of that train of thought.

All the more reason that Molly was absolutely perfect to be his plus-one. He wondered, a bit guiltily, if he'd been so enamored with how she'd performed her job that he had really failed to see her more deeply.

Well, here was his chance to make it up to her. What woman didn't love an all-expenses-paid shopping trip?

Apparently Molly. She looked terrified by the array of choices displayed on the racks of clothing in the boutique they had entered. She moved to a rack, hesitantly, and turned over a tag.

Her look of terror deepened.

"Of course I'm paying," he said, stunned that she would reach any other conclusion. Again, the opposite of anyone else he'd gone out with.

A look flashed across her face: something proud and obstinate.

"You don't need to buy me a dress, chief."

"It's a business excursion," he said. "Completely unexpected."

The stubborn look deepened on her face. "Working in the office is business, too, and I don't expect you to provide me with a wardrobe."

The truth was he'd provide her with a thousand wardrobes if it guaranteed her happiness as his employee.

"When I asked you to go to our office in Los Angeles last month," he said reasonably, "did you buy your own ticket?"

She looked suddenly worried, as if maybe she *should* have bought her own ticket.

It was everything he could do not to hit himself in the forehead with his fist.

She turned away from him and squinted at the dress selections. She did that little thing where she gnawed on her lip while she thought about it.

When had he come to love that *thing* so much?

"Okay," she said. "Once. And then I'll have something to wear. You know. In case."

She was blushing.

"In case?"

"You know, in case it ever came up again. That you needed me to play your plus-one."

"Sunday, you're giving me a headache. Could you just pick a dress?"

"Speaking of brand-new worlds," she said, nervously. "Where do you begin?"

Now that it had been pointed out, he could hear the faintest of accents, and he found it unsettling that it hinted at parts of his seemingly straightforward assistant that he knew nothing about.

And whatever that was, in that faint accent, it suddenly seemed mysterious, and dangerously sensual.

"I think you'll find your size in this section," Christopher said.

Liam watched, bemused, at his unflappable assistant being

so flustered over this. A dress. She plowed her hands into the rack, flipped through a few dresses, then yanked one out.

She held it up in front of her. "I'll try this one."

Liam stared at the dress, aghast. It had large patterned purple flowers all over it and a lace collar. It reminded him of something the mother had worn on a reality television show he had watched once—only once—who had had far too many children. He slid Christopher a look.

His ever so competent assistant was now staring at her choice, looking as if she knew what a terrible mistake the dress was and did not know how to back down. Oh, geez. Was her lip trembling?

"You'll have to try on more than one," Christopher said smoothly.

She turned back to the rack like a prisoner being forced to choose her own punishment and began reluctantly, and a bit frantically, sorting through more dresses.

"Why don't we each choose one for you?" Christopher suggested, easily. "You, me and your boss? And you can try them all on, and see which one you like best."

Each choose one? Liam was going to choose a dress for Molly? He hoped she would say no, she was quite capable of choosing her own dress. But he did not get off the hook that easily. She actually looked relieved by Christopher's suggestion!

The moment seemed surreal, as Liam stood at her shoulder, thumbing through the choices.

Surely he had stood this close to her before? Why hadn't he ever noticed her scent?

Spicy. Mysterious. Sensual.

Just like some place in the Deep South that he hadn't known about.

Liam felt as if the weight of the world was on his shoulders as he carefully skimmed through the dress selection. The choice suddenly seemed fraught with complications.

He did not want her to think there was anything wrong with the way she was.

He did not want to choose something inappropriately sexy. Or horribly dull, either.

"This one," he said decisively, finally settling on what felt like a very safe choice. Some memory of his mother getting ready to go out tickled. *You can never go wrong with the basic little black dress.*

He held up a very plain dress for Molly's inspection. The look on her face was wounded, as if he had chosen a nun's habit.

She snatched it from his hand, and added it to the hanger she already held aloft, far away from her, as if the clothing items were fish that smelled bad.

Christopher, thankfully, had the most experience at this. He carefully picked a dress in bronze, and then he relieved Molly of the other two and led her to the fitting area. Molly trailed him.

Liam wasn't sure what he was supposed to do, which for a decisive man was not a comfortable situation to be in.

She shot him a look over her shoulder and the faint pleading in it—*how on earth do we find ourselves here*—made him ever so reluctantly follow her.

What was he supposed to do? Surely not weigh in on her choices? Somehow the plus-one thing, which had at first glance seemed like such a perfect solution, had become unexpectedly complicated.

Liam sighed and sat down in a deep chair that Christopher motioned him toward.

But wasn't that the nature of charades, even ones that were extremely well-intentioned?

Unexpected complexities arose. It was the way of them.

CHAPTER FIVE

"YOU'RE NOT GOING to the gallows," Christopher admonished her, in an undertone, as he tucked her into a spacious change cubicle with the dresses. "Most women would *love* this."

As the door clicked closed behind him, Molly contemplated how she would absolutely love to be *most women* right now. But she simply wasn't. She never had been. She'd always been an outsider in *that* world of matching your fingernail polish to your lipstick, of giggling over boys, of knowing what was trendy and of being comfortable and familiar with the phrases of the day.

Like *plus-one* for instance.

She thought she had found a place at FIX where her inherent unusualness was a good fit. Maybe even her strength. Now, her world felt horribly off-kilter. In jeopardy, even.

She put her back against that door and took a deep breath.

She was panicking. For goodness' sake, it was a dress, not trying to find a lifeboat aboard the *Titanic*. On April 15, 1912.

Still, her boss, yes, the very one she had a secret crush on, was right outside, settling onto one of those sofas. She was grateful for a real door. Not a flimsy curtain.

Was that what was causing the sensation of panic? That she was going to be standing in her underwear just a few feet from him, separated only by an insubstantial door?

Or was the panic because Christopher had noticed her accent. So what? It wasn't as if he'd sent out an announcement card: *trailer trash*.

No, maybe it was because she'd slipped up and suggested the plus-one thing might happen again.

Had she sounded happy?

Of course she hadn't sounded happy! So far, this new experience with her boss felt like her worst nightmare. To add to the sense of being overwhelmed, which she had felt from the moment she walked in the doors of Second Chances, shopping for dresses with her boss—him insisting he would pay—all this just felt way too weird and way too intimate.

And this change-up in her routine was too catastrophically sudden, especially for someone who liked planning as much as she did. It was a plunge from her regular life into *this*—modelling dresses for a fake date with her boss—in the blink of an eye. It was like falling through ice into a lake when you thought you were on solid, dry land.

Molly glanced at her watch and gulped. They were now one hour and thirteen minutes from the awards dinner. One hour and three minutes if they arrived at least ten minutes early, which, of course, they should.

There was no time for self-doubt. No time for rumination. She had to approach this as a soldier on a mission, a soldier with orders from her commanding officer.

Taking one final deep breath, Molly discarded her clothes. She caught a glimpse of herself in the mirror. Her underwear was pristinely clean, of course, but she was aware it was both worn and extremely utilitarian. She was pretty sure she'd had this bra since high school.

She blew her limited clothing budget on outer trimmings, and even pre-used designer items were expensive, particularly when you were trying to keep your brother out of jail.

No one—except Winspear—was ever exposed to her undies, anyway.

When had she started thinking of Winspear, her African violet, as if it was a roommate?

That, along with the picture she cut in her worn undies—

her extraordinarily well-put-together boss sitting mere feet away, his underwear no doubt as extraordinary as he himself was—left Molly with a clear evaluation of herself.

Pathetic.

And now, she had allowed a totally inappropriate thought about Liam's underwear, and even as she mentally forbade herself to go down that road, a little voice inside her insisted on asking—

But what do you think? Boxers or briefs?

She pulled on the first dress with just a little more force than might have been absolutely necessary. It was her choice, the purple one. As she yanked it over her head, her hair pulled partly out of its bun.

She glared at her image in the mirror. The dress was like a bride's choice for a bridesmaid she didn't particularly like.

The shoes were so wrong. She kicked them off.

Standing there barefoot, with her falling-down hair, and the dress settling around her like a *flour* sack, she looked every inch the girl from the trailer park trying with a pathetic desperation to fit in where everyone knew she didn't belong.

"This one won't work," she called. Was she going to cry?

"The purple one?" Christopher asked, knowingly. "With the collar?"

"Yes."

"Try on the bronze."

She didn't want to try on another dress! She wanted to go home and water Winspear and open her file on Liam's upcoming trip. There were things to do, comforting things, like double-checking with the pilot and making sure the hotel had upgraded the suite.

Still, they were on a time frame, so screwing up what little courage remained, Molly did as she was told. The dress slid on over her head like a whisper and fell down around her, to her feet. She wrestled with the long zipper for a bit, and with every inch it went up, Molly became aware she had never worn anything that *felt* like this dress. As if it was hugging her.

She turned and stared at herself in the mirror, stunned. Her sense of being pathetic vanished.

Was she really that superficial? The entire way she felt about herself could be fixed with a dress?

Well, a gorgeous dress, but nonetheless... The dress shimmered, its V-neck delicately sensual, rather than overtly sexual. It was formfitting to the waist, where it snugged in hard, before it flared out in a cloudy dream.

Her hair suddenly didn't look messy. It looked—did she dare say it—slightly chic. Even the bare feet didn't matter.

She reminded herself that this was what Second Chances did, what Christopher did every single day.

This business, and its consultants, turned ordinary people into the best version of themselves, the version they might not have even known was there.

She felt transformed, indeed a Cinderella story—barefoot trailer park girl to princess in the wave of a wand. But what no one ever said was how discombobulating a Cinderella experience was. How much it made you aware of *pretense*, the underwear just underneath it probably being a more true reflection of who she was.

Still, there was no denying it felt a bit like the dress in the dance scene of *Beauty and the Beast*. Transformational.

"Well?" Christopher called.

It felt exquisitely bold to let this startling version of herself step out of that changeroom.

Christopher stepped back and tapped his chin, assessing, but it was Liam she was watching. He looked up from his phone and his mouth fell open.

The look on his face both thrilled her and terrified her.

A boss couldn't look at an employee like that! It was the precise reason she'd been dressing down for months.

Because that look—that she probably would secretly revisit

for the rest of her life—could cause complications of the worst kind in the workplace. It was the kind of look that could make a woman hope for things she could never have.

Still, a part of her that was not rational gloried in his gaze. A man's frank appreciation of a woman.

But rational had always saved her, and while she could enjoy this moment, her enjoyment had to be brief. She couldn't live in a place like this and maintain the most important thing of all.

Control.

Liam seemed to reach the exact same conclusion because he snapped his mouth shut and looked back at his phone. "You dress up pretty good, Sunday."

"Thanks, chief."

"The Oscars, yes," Christopher decided with a reluctant sigh, "an awards banquet, even an upscale one, no."

And so Molly's moment as Cinderella drew to a reluctant— but blessed—close.

She went back into the cubicle and took off the dress. She put on the final choice, Liam's pick.

When she turned to face herself in the mirror, she was shocked to see Liam's choice for her was even more stunning than the Cinderella gown had been. Because the dress that had looked uninteresting, possibly even dowdy, on the hanger, looked incredible on.

It was the simplest of dresses, a sleeveless sheath. There was no plunging neckline and it ended modestly just above her knee.

And yet it was a dress that celebrated sensuality, but ever so subtly. It was sophisticated, and made her feel exquisitely— and powerfully—feminine.

She took a deep breath. There it was again. She could taste it on the air.

Change, a storm at its beginning stages, when it could seem so benign, even exhilarating.

She stepped out of the change room and avoided Liam's

gaze. Christopher nodded his approval. "Obviously, the one. Let me go find shoes and accessories to match."

He was gone in a flash, but the truth was she had barely registered him.

She finally built up her nerve enough to meet Liam's eyes. There was that look again, even more intense than it had been with the bronze dress. It was a look that could melt bones. He masked it quickly, looked back at his phone again.

"You look great, Sunday," he offered, the faintest hoarse note in his voice.

Christopher was back. He set impossibly high heels on the floor in front of her and secured a simple strand of pearls around her neck.

She stepped into the shoes, and Christopher sighed with satisfaction.

"Perfect," he breathed. "Classic. Audrey Hepburn, *Breakfast at Tiffany's*. Well, almost perfect. The hair! Have we got time for a quick visit to the salon side?"

She glanced at her watch. "Fifty-one minutes," she said to Liam. "Forty-one, if we arrive ten minutes early."

He lifted a shoulder. "Or forty-six if we arrive five minutes early."

The best possible thing happened. Their eyes met. She felt the way she felt in the office. Connected. On the same page. A team with common goals and a common understanding of how they would arrive at them.

They laughed.

Christopher whisked her quickly to the salon side.

A stylist, Ramone, freed her hair from the bun that was much the worse for wear for all the dresses being pulled on and off over her head.

"Oh, my," he said. "Why would you wear all this glorious hair like that? I don't have time to cut it, much as I would like to. I'll just quickly style it. I don't even need the iron."

He took Molly's hair and wound it around his fingers, fluffing and spraying as he went.

The result was an extraordinary cascade of big looping curls.

"Give your head a shake," the stylist said.

It took Molly a full second to realize he meant it literally. She shook her head, and her hair swayed and danced in a sensuous wave before falling naturally to the curve of her shoulders.

Hair completed, the stylist opened brand-new makeup packets and continued to work. Molly really did need to give her head a shake at what was emerging. Her cheeks looked sculpted.

And her lips! They looked full and faintly pouty…and like lips that invited kisses.

"Close your eyes," Ramone said. "Last thing. There. Presto, done."

Molly reached for her glasses.

"You are not putting those back on! They fall in the same category as the way you wear your hair. As in, why?" The stylist set them playfully on the end of his own nose, and his expression became bewildered.

"They're not even prescription!" he said, accusingly. "You don't need glasses!"

He looked as if he was going to toss them out, but Molly rescued them.

"Why?" the stylist asked her again.

"Because I want to be taken seriously," Molly said, defensively. "I want to look like a professional. Not like—"

She stared at her reflection in the mirror.

"A supermodel?" Ramone suggested.

"What have you done to my eyes?"

Her eyes suddenly seemed to take up her whole face. They looked huge and a turquoise shade had emerged in them.

"Just added a little something. Your natural lash is great, but everybody can benefit from a little enhancement."

In the life-is-full-of-surprises department Molly would have never guessed she would be wearing false eyelashes by the end of the day.

Or that she'd like them!

She reminded herself, but without too much sincerity, that she didn't like surprises.

She really did look like a supermodel. She really did need to give her head a shake now!

In fact, a stranger looked back at her. An utterly gorgeous stranger.

Should she ask Ramone to tone it down? She didn't feel like herself. She felt like she was pretending to be someone else.

But really? There was no time now for a redo, and in a way she *was* pretending to be someone else.

"Embrace it," Ramone said, softly, as if Molly had spoken all her doubts out loud.

Why not follow that well-meaning advice? Why not embrace this alter ego, this hidden side of herself; why not give herself the freedom to play with it?

Why not brush off that sense of *not good enough* that clung to her like a greasy scent of cooking that had gotten into her clothes?

She was pretending tonight, anyway. She was pretending to be Liam's plus-one. She was always way too serious. Why not, for once in her life, have fun with it? Why not embrace it? Why not dance with it?

Just until the clock struck midnight?

What harm could come from it? Just once. It occurred to Molly that was very likely what everybody who played with matches said.

CHAPTER SIX

MOLLY GLANCED AT her watch.

Christopher appeared at her side, made a face at the watch, whisked it from her wrist and put it in the black clutch that he handed her. He pried the glasses from her grip and put those in the bag, too. Then, he helped her out of Ramone's salon chair and pushed her gently toward the front lobby where Liam was waiting, looking out the front window, rocking back on his heels.

"We have two minutes to be five minutes early," he said, and then turned to look at her.

For a moment, he looked utterly stunned, his composure completely gone. She had not been aware that some of his suave confidence was a mask, until it slipped.

And what she saw underneath it was even more compelling.

One hundred percent pure man.

Something powerful, raw and vulnerable at the same time in his face.

"Sunday," he finally asked. "Is that you?"

"To be perfectly honest, I'm not sure."

"What did you do to your hair?" he croaked.

"Oh—" she touched it self-consciously "—it's just down."

"What happened to your eyes?"

"False lashes. I believe the legs of a thousand spiders were harvested to create this look, so I hope you appreciate their sacrifice, poor things."

He smiled at that.

She opened up the handbag Christopher had given her, and took out the eyeglasses. She settled them on her face. Even if they weren't real, she felt so much better wearing them. The fake glasses made her feel as if she was herself.

"Whew," he said. "You are *my* Sunday. I think. I have to make absolutely sure."

She cocked her head at him.

"What's the capital of Bolivia?"

"It actually has two capitals. La Paz is the administrative capital, while Sucre is the constitutional capital."

His smile deepened, and somehow they moved closer to what they really were, as the unguarded expression left his face.

"Um, boss, we have to run," she said, peering in her purse at her confiscated watch. "We literally now have one minute to be five minutes early."

"Maybe for tonight," he said, "you should call me Liam."

"All right," she said, and then after hesitating just a second, "Liam."

She couldn't believe the way his name came off her lips. Good grief. All husky and sensual, somehow.

Despite the fact they were running late, they both stood there for a moment, contemplating how such a small thing felt like a momentous shift.

But then *her* Liam was back. Despite her using his first name, one hundred percent her boss.

Confident.

Suave.

In control.

But once you had caught a glimpse of the other, could you ever forget it?

"Can you run in those shoes?" he asked her.

"I doubt it," she said.

And just like that his hand was in hers, and they were running out onto Fifth Avenue, dodging through an indulgent early evening crowd, sharing laughter over her absolute clumsiness in the unfamiliar shoes.

They arrived, breathless, at the venue. Liam let go of Molly's hand.

Her hand in his, as they had navigated the crowds, was even more unsettling than her amazing transformation. If he resisted looking at her, though, which was difficult, and didn't take her hand again, it was going to be much easier to think of her as his always faithful assistant, just filling in, helping him out for the evening.

A single photographer stood outside the venue, glancing moodily at the sky. Liam followed his gaze and realized it looked as if it might rain. The front steps were completely empty, which reminded him they were running late. The attendees were all already inside.

"Not much of a turnout from the press corps," he said to the photographer, who lifted his camera to his eye in a rather desultory way and took their picture. He surveyed the result in the window at the back of the camera and then tucked the camera in his bag.

"Innovators on the Move?" he said, dismissively. "Non-event. Except for Eva La Lydia. She sent out a blanket text saying she'd had a last-minute change of plans. I'm sure there's a swarm outside Lucali's at the moment. She hinted Douglas Hampton might be with her."

"Oh," Molly murmured. "Good old garlic breath."

"I mean, sorry, Mr. Westerhouse," the photographer said, "but that trumps a two-years-ago 'Bachelor of the Year.'"

"Ah," Liam said. Despite the missed publicity opportunity for both the Innovators and FIX, his relief at not being with Miss La Lydia was immense. He hadn't liked the fact she'd been rude to Molly and he liked her even less now that he knew she kept the paparazzi on speed dial.

"Why did you stay?" he asked the photographer.

A lifted shoulder. "Always the chance of getting the surprise shot. Or scoop. Who are you?" the photographer asked Molly, looking at her with sudden and faintly predatory interest, as if she might be that scoop.

Liam actually felt Molly shrink beside him. There was that deer-in-the-headlights look again. He nodded at the photographer, put his hand on the small of Molly's back and guided her into the safety of the building.

Inside, particularly once they'd been shown to their seats, Molly relaxed and looked around with that curiosity that was inherent to her.

He appreciated Molly even more as the evening went on. Because, while some people would find the awards part of the function exceedingly dull, she did not. At one point, she leaned over and asked him for his phone.

"I accidentally left mine at Second Chances," she whispered.

He unlocked his phone and handed it to her unhesitatingly, which he realized was an unconscious measure of his trust in her.

She opened an app, and when he glanced over, he was very relieved to see that despite the startling new look, there was *his* Sunday, totally engrossed in making notes about people being given awards, and the products or techniques they had developed.

Again, Liam was grateful Eva was not here. Even knowing next to nothing about her, he was familiar with the type. He suspected by now she would have been fidgeting in her seat and plotting how to draw attention to herself.

He got up and gave the award, and when he came back to his seat Molly was beaming at him.

"That was amazing," she said. "You hit all the right notes. Look at Jordan! She's just so happy."

He was a successful man. He received awards and accolades and attention all the time.

Why did the look on Molly's face eclipse all of those?

Because in a world where you could not trust much, and where things did not always end up being as they appeared, his Woman Sunday was one hundred percent authentic. Which was ironic, given that she was *pretending* to be his date tonight.

"You want to get out of here?" he asked her when the awards show drew to a close. There was a cocktail meet and greet after, but it occurred to him he'd imposed on his assistant quite enough for one day.

"Oh, no," she said. "I think you should go talk to Jordan." She still had his phone. She consulted her notes. "And I want to talk to James McPherson about his hydrogen energy research. And also Lucy Williams about that camera she developed. I hope she has a prototype with her."

Despite how glamorous she looked, Liam was inordinately relieved that this definitely was his Sunday: earnest, enthusiastic, serious, all business.

"Can I get you a drink?" he asked. "Wine? Cocktail?"

"Oh," she said, and something flashed in her face that he didn't quite understand. "I don't drink."

"Not at all?" He had thought a bit of alcohol might help her relax in this new environment.

"Well," she laughed uncomfortably. "You know. Water."

Always so literal, dotting every *i* and crossing every *t*, making sure there were no misunderstandings.

"I meant alcohol," he clarified.

Again, that look on her face. He was momentarily reminded that there were many things about Molly Littleton that he didn't know.

"Oh," she said, her light tone not matching the look in her eyes. "I've just never seen anything good come out of it."

He cocked his head at her, intrigued. First of all, he could hear the accent he had never noticed before. Barely, but there.

And like the barely discernable accent, this disclosure hinted that his straightlaced assistant had experienced a life he knew nothing about. Was that deliberate on her part? Or a lack of interest on his?

A healthy lack of interest, he told himself sternly; he did not *need* to know a single thing about Molly Littleton's personal life.

And yet, still, he probed, tentatively, keeping his tone deliberately light. "What does that mean? Spiked punch at the high school prom?"

"Exactly!" she said.

He felt the oddest little shiver along his spine. His one hundred percent trustworthy assistant had just lied to him.

Her eyes lit up. "Look. It's Frank Beltane. He's the one who has that idea about the dog-walking apparatus."

And just like that, she was gone.

Had she really been that enthused about spotting Frank? Or had she literally stepped away from the conversation?

He watched her get Frank's attention, watched the man's face light up at being buttonholed by such a beautiful woman, but then, within seconds they were engrossed in an earnest conversation, as if they had known each other for years, not seconds.

His discomfort over her lying to him eased. He could be wrong, after all. He was seeing her in a new way, and it might have made him extrasensitive to nuances he'd never noticed before.

Or maybe she'd had—as had most people—a terrible experience with drinking. Who wanted to tell their boss about ending up in a bad situation because of inexperience and bad choices brought on by drinking?

Though it must have been very bad for her to never drink again.

Making way too big a deal of it, Liam told himself, and deliberately rolled his shoulders to release some unexpected tension from them.

Possibly bringing his own bad experiences to the table.

He'd nearly gotten married once, to a woman who was not one single thing that she had claimed to be or that he had thought she was. He could still feel the wound of it.

That was what had made him hypersensitive to the possibility Molly had lied to him. His own baggage, not hers.

And really, wasn't all his baggage what made Molly the perfect companion for the evening?

It was *never* going anywhere. She was too valuable an assistant—the best he'd ever had—to risk it all going down the tubes over the fact he'd noticed tonight she was beautiful as well as extraordinary at her job.

CHAPTER SEVEN

LIAM WAS SOON surrounded by people wanting his attention, and he turned his energy, deliberately, to that, listening, asking questions about ideas, digging deeper. This was at the heart of everything he did: digging through mountains of coal for the diamonds he knew were there.

Still, he was aware his legendary focus was just a touch off. As the evening went on, Liam was constantly keeping track of Molly, watching her out of the corner of his eye, seeing how people reacted to her.

Considering her initial discomfort when they had gone to Second Chances, he had expected she might be a little more clingy, but she had found her groove, and he dismissed any remaining niggles of apprehension he'd felt earlier. Watching her interact with people, Liam felt newly appreciative of how lucky he was to have her.

And yet by the end of the evening, that appreciation was faintly tinged with something darker. Molly had an absolute swarm of young men around her.

It isn't jealousy, he told himself sternly.

Worry, maybe. Professional. That someone would spot her spellbinding combination of brilliance and efficiency and try to steal her from him.

But no, that wasn't it. Not exactly.

He realized he felt protective of her. Molly was indeed smart and efficient, but there was also a naivete about her that was in stark contrast to the sophistication of New York.

Again, it was that side of her he hadn't noticed before. In the office, a very contained environment, that didn't show at all.

But in that dress shop, it had been so apparent that she was a duck out of water and that her strengths in the office didn't really transfer to other worlds. He was keeping a sharp eye on her because he didn't want her to get bowled over by her popularity. Be taken advantage of.

You're such a hero, he chided himself, as he went and rescued Molly from a young innovator who was getting way too close to her.

"I think it's time to go," he told her.

He saw the relief in her eyes, the flash of annoyance in the slightly inebriated young man's. Liam raised an eyebrow at him that sent him scuttling off for cover.

It took a while to leave—stopped so many times on the way—but finally, they made it to the door.

As they left the building, the storm that had threatened earlier had broken. They stood under an overhang at the front door watching water sluice off the roof.

"You seemed to really fit in," he ventured, peering out at the rain.

"Oh," she said, with a happy laugh, "it was like a nerd convention. Of course I fit in. But I have to say, my feet are killing me."

And then she bent over and slipped off the shoes, dangling them in her hand and squinting at the sky. "I'm going to make a dash for it, boss."

"A dash for it? In your bare feet? And where do you think you're going?"

"I'll grab the subway. Of course, not in my bare feet. What do you think I am, a hillbilly?"

For a moment she looked as if she wanted to clap her hand over her mouth, but instead she bent and put the shoes back on, wincing as she straightened.

"I don't care how much you love the subway," he told her

firmly, "you are not taking it home at this time of night, dressed like that. You'd be soaked before you got across the street."

She glanced down at herself as if she'd forgotten, totally, how she was dressed.

"Fine," she said. "I'll call a rideshare."

"I'm calling the car for you."

"It's nearly midnight. Don't get Paul out of bed. I'm comfortable with the rideshare."

He wasn't. But how far did he push the protector thing without seeming overbearing and as if he did not trust her competence?

But then she stared down at the bag she was carrying and frowned.

"I just remembered, I don't have my phone. Can I borrow yours again?"

And then the frown morphed into total alarm.

"What?" he asked.

"I don't have my purse," she stammered. "I just have this one Christopher gave me. It's not just my phone. I don't have any money—or my credit card—to pay a rideshare."

"Oh, for pity's sake, Sunday. Do you think I wouldn't pay for you to get home?"

He looked at her outfit. Despite the fact they were standing in the scant protection of the overhang, it seemed to be reacting to the dampness in the air, clinging to her.

He was distressed to notice how his assistant was quite curvy.

And her luscious hair, beginning to curl wildly about her face, was very sexy.

He wasn't putting her in a rideshare or a cab.

"I think the best thing would be to call Paul, after all," he said.

"Yes, I think that would be best," she said. "Thank you."

But before he could fish his phone out of his pocket, she closed her eyes, rocked back on her heels and groaned.

"Feet?" he asked, sympathetically.

"Worse. Boss, I don't have anything from my purse, including my house keys."

He let that sink in. "Do you want me to get you a hotel room for the night?"

"You know I'm something of an expert at booking hotel rooms, right?"

"I hadn't thought of it, but now that you point it out, it's part of what you do to make my life so seamless, isn't it?"

"It is," she said, sadly. "And this is what I know about hotels: Without ID it would be easier to get into Buckingham Palace or Fort Knox than to get a hotel room."

"But surely if I go in with you—"

She shook her head, and her hair cascaded down around her shoulders. He knew it would be the wrong time to laugh at her dilemmas and he tried to stifle his smile, but she squinted at him dangerously.

"Is there something about the fact I'm going to be sleeping in an alley tonight that you find amusing?"

"Well, you have to see the irony. The woman I count on to fix *everything* has been given an unfixable problem of her own."

"Oh, yes, very funny. Ha ha."

He couldn't help but notice she was starting to shiver.

"You know, even though I've come to count on you to solve every problem and it's probably made me quite lazy, I can still pull a solution to a dilemma out of the hat when I have to."

"And? Your solution?"

"You'll come home with me, of course."

It was a humiliating ending to what had been such a good evening. Pretending to be Liam's plus-one had not been nearly as challenging as Molly had thought it was going to be. After her initial discomfort in the dress store, it had really been quite fun, and certainly stimulating.

She had learned a great deal on topics she had known nothing about previously, and she always enjoyed that. It had been like gathering information at a living library tonight.

Molly *loved* learning. She loved that black-and-white world. She liked adding to the formidable arsenal that her brain kept of *facts*, those wonderful immutable things that did not have any kind of emotional complexity attached to them.

Not like being asked why you didn't drink.

Not like being invited home with her boss. A dumb mistake had put her in a very awkward predicament.

It grated on the perfectionist in her. She was a detail person. She could ferret out the potential for disaster, for every single thing that could go wrong; she prided herself on putting out fires before they started.

Except, as Liam had pointed out, just a little too gleefully, in her own life.

"Don't worry," he said, "there's nothing inappropriate about it. I host guests all the time."

She *knew* that, because she was the juggler who kept all the balls in the air.

"You know Maria and Paul have a suite in my apartment."

Of course they did. She knew that. She knew he had staff live with him. She often liaised with both Maria and Paul on logistical matters: deliveries, dinner guests, overnight stays, transport.

"So, we'll be chaperoned," he said. And then laughed again. "A chaperoned charade."

"Don't be ridiculous," she snapped at him. "We don't need a chaperone. I trust you completely."

His eyes flitted to her hair, and then her lips. Finally, he met her eyes. "Good," he said, a little hoarsely.

"It's just awkward."

"Ah well, really, Sunday? What's life without the odd little surprise thrown in?"

Stable, she thought, *safe*.

And maybe just a little bit dull. She sighed. "Thank you for your generous invitation. I have no choice but to accept."

"Gracious," he said.

"Nothing personal. Just caught out."

"The thing you like the least. The rain's letting up a bit. Should we walk, or should I call Paul?"

It would be utterly ridiculous to call Paul. They could walk to his apartment before the poor man got out of bed.

"Walk," she said.

Unfortunately, every step was pain. Though she tried bravely to hide it, Liam noticed, stopped and guided her to a step they were passing by.

"Sit down."

Was he going to call Paul after all? So silly, only a few more blocks. Still, she was not sure how she could make it.

He crouched in front of her and slipped one shoe off her aching foot. She looked at the top of his head, and had a sudden irresistible desire to touch those tawny locks. She tucked her errant hands under her thighs.

"Sunday," he said, unaware of the terrible battle being waged within her, "you've got a really bad blister on the back of your heel. The strap must have been rubbing."

It was a sign of a life bereft of human touch that his hand felt so blissful cupping her foot. She pulled her foot away hastily. She didn't want him to notice her rough, calloused soles.

"I don't like my feet being touched."

He lifted an eyebrow. "Ticklish?"

She'd let him think what he wanted.

He slid off her other shoe. "I'll just look," he assured her. "This foot has a blister, too, only it's right here."

Despite his promise not to touch, his finger gently stroked a raw place on the side of her big toe.

The combination of pleasure and pain made her draw in her breath.

"I'll go barefoot the rest of the way," she offered, quickly, drawing her foot out of his hand. *Like a hillbilly.* She didn't say it out loud this time, though.

"You're not going barefoot in New York City!" he said.

A *hillbilly* who hadn't worn a real pair of shoes until she was six years old. And then, they were only for school, not to be worn casually.

When she went to the spa now, the pedicurists almost always gathered wide-eyed around her feet, chatting among themselves in a different language.

But you didn't have to speak their language to know that no amount of emery boarding could fix that! Her hardscrabble previous life was etched into the hardened soles and thick calluses on her feet. New York City was nothing compared to places where she had dug her toes into Red River dirt.

Unfortunately, while the soles of her feet were as tough as shoe leather, the rest of them, unusually wide because of her early shoelessness, didn't fit most real girl shoes.

Liam still crouched in front of her, turned now, his back to her.

"It's only a few blocks," he said, and reached around and patted his back invitingly. "Hop on."

Her boss was going to piggyback her through the streets of New York? Of course she had to say no. She had to suck it up and put those shoes back on.

It was so unprofessional!

And so sweet.

In fact, it was entirely and utterly irresistible.

Still gripping her shoes by their straps in one hand and her purse in the other, Molly stood up behind him and put her palms on his shoulders. She could feel the springy strength of his muscles, the beautiful broadness of him underneath the custom tailoring of his jacket. Hesitantly, one at a time, Molly slid her legs around his waist and put her arms around his neck, her shoes and purse dangling under his chin. Her dress hiked up past her thighs.

His arms locked behind him, supporting her bottom, and he eased to his feet. The rain was a bit harder, now, but she could feel the heat rising off his back, scorching her inner thighs.

That hair that she had wanted so badly to touch was tickling at her face, and the damp was releasing a scent from it that was as crisp and clean as freshly laundered linens.

The rain started with a vengeance then, and he snugged her in tight to his back and stepped forward. His strength was easy and unselfconscious. After a moment, juggling her weight while she soaked up the unexpected and sweet ecstasy of this physical closeness, he broke into an easy lope.

"If you want to go faster," he said. "You don't have to slap me in the face with your shoes and purse—the more traditional *giddyap* will do."

She tightened her grip, but the shoes were still bouncing around, and he exaggerated his head bob, pretending to dodge them, and yelling, "Ow," every time one grazed him.

"Giddyap," she said, feeling crazily inebriated, as if she had imbibed after all. She swatted him with her purse, and he complied with a surge of speed.

Molly began to laugh at the total wonderful absurdity of what was happening. And the absolute unexpected intimacy of it, too.

At this moment in time, they were not a boss and his assistant.

Not the CEO and his plus-one.

Nothing about this felt like a charade. In fact, it felt like one of the most real things she had ever experienced.

They felt like any normal guy and his girl caught in a rainstorm in New York City.

His laughter, deep, rumbling, a total letting go, joined hers.

And then they were charging together through a New York night, dodging in and out of late-night pedestrians, and through puddles and across streets, the peals of their laughter a private delight in a public world.

Molly felt something in her, always tightly wound, always in control, let go, completely, wildly, ecstatically, as she clung to Liam tighter.

As she surrendered, it felt as if his strength, and his aroma, filled every part of her, parts that she hadn't known were empty.

She wondered, ever so briefly, if it spoke to a life devoid of even simple pleasures, that this moment had a peculiar shine to it.

That it rosc easily to the top of the best moments of her entire life.

CHAPTER EIGHT

LIAM SET MOLLY DOWN on the sidewalk in front of his building. Molly was soaked. Her glasses were so wet that looking through them gave the sense the world had turned into a large impressionist piece of art, all the lines and colors wavering and blurred, utterly vibrant.

Her dress clung stubbornly, stuck to her thigh where it had ridden up when she had accepted that invitation to climb on his back. She was trying to yank it down when he turned to face her.

Molly straightened, and drank in the sight of him. Like her, he was utterly soaked, his jacket and slacks clinging to him, his shirt nearly transparent. She could make out the hard lines of his chest and belly underneath it, even the dark circle of his nipple.

He was the one who had been running, carrying her; he should have been the one who was red-faced and breathless.

But it was she who could barely breathe, who could feel her heart threatening to leave the confines of her chest. Her thighs, the only dry place on her, were burning from the heat of such intimate contact with him. It felt as if they might burst into flame.

"Cold?" he asked when she shivered. He took her arm, and guided her up a few wide, shallow steps to the protection of the portico around the entrance to his building.

She was about as far from cold as you could get. On the

other hand, Liam was smiling easily, his eyes still holding the spark of the laughter they'd just shared.

He didn't look at all how she felt, which was entirely discombobulated.

In fact, he looked as if he piggybacked women through the rain-soaked streets of New York at a casual lope every day of his life.

His hair was wet to the scalp, slicked to his head, and it had turned a darker shade of gold. She watched a raindrop—or maybe a single bead of sweat—slide out from under a lock of that hair, run down his temple, over his cheek and then zigzag crazily toward his lip.

She stared as that drop found his upper lip, and his tongue reached out and flicked it.

As it turned out, she hadn't been as far from cold as you could get. There had been some wiggle room, because she felt a bolt of heat run through her that felt as if she had been struck by lightning.

He reached, casually, for her glasses, and slid them off her nose. Wordlessly, he slipped a corner of his shirt out from under his waistband—the only part of him that was dry—and wiped the water from her lenses, before he carefully placed them back on her nose.

It was a good thing she was so wet, or she was pretty sure she would have spontaneously ignited. It probably spoke to a very pathetic life that it was just about the most romantic thing that had ever happened to her.

She turned away from him hastily, and made a pretense of studying his building.

It was right across the street from the south end of Central Park, and even a relative newcomer to New York, like her, knew this was the toniest address in a city of very posh addresses. This historic sandstone building was iconic. A rare apartment had come available in this building a few days ago and been snatched up. It had made the news for breaking New York's record per-square-foot price.

"Come on," he said. "Let's get in before you shiver to death."

A uniformed doorman appeared and held open the door for them.

"Mr. Westerhouse. Miss."

Not a ripple of *anything* in that man's face that hinted if there was anything unusual about Liam showing up with a barefoot girl on his back at nearly midnight, both of them soaked to the skin.

"Thanks, Mike," he said to the doorman. "Have you had a good night?"

She had always liked this about Liam. No matter who he encountered, he had that gift for making them feel seen and appreciated.

She needed to remind herself of that. It was the way he was in the world. From acknowledging the doorman to wiping water off a pair of eyeglasses, it wasn't *personal*. He was naturally considerate. It would be a terrible invitation to disappointment to take it any other way.

Liam led her through the lobby, and the feeling Molly had had of being deeply connected to him fled. She was very aware of the differences in their worlds as she tried not to gawk at everything.

She kept her mouth firmly shut, but the entrance area was utterly spectacular, with huge, crystal-dripping chandeliers dropping from an intricately patterned plastered ceiling. Hardwood, laid in herringbone, was covered with gorgeous area rugs. Deep couches faced each other, with a backdrop of huge arched windows that looked out toward Central Park on one side of them, and a huge gas fireplace, lit, on the other.

It looked like she imagined a living room in a palace would look.

"Does anyone ever actually sit here?" she whispered, awed.

Liam looked at the area as if he'd never noticed it before.

"What would they do here?" she asked. "I mean it looks as if it would be a very nice place to spend an afternoon with a book, except it's a little public. I mean, don't they have their own apartments for that?"

He looked amused by her, and she felt gauche.

"It would be a beautiful place for a wedding reception."

Now why had she said that? And why had she sounded so wistful, getting "hickier" by the moment.

"I think people just wait here. Like to meet friends or to wait for a car. I'll pay more attention and report back to you, Sunday."

"Thank you," she said, solemnly. She begged herself to stop digging in deeper, but she had to add, a little primly, "Because that seems like an extravagant waste of very expensive real estate."

He laughed then. "A missed opportunity for building income," he said. He was teasing her, but it made her acutely aware this world was as foreign to her as the face of the moon.

At the elevator bank, she looked back and saw the prints of her wet bare feet tracking across the shiny floor, next to his shoe prints.

Did someone come behind her and clean that up?

Liam was untroubled by such questions, apparently. He slid a card from his pocket and tapped it against a wall-mounted keypad. The doors instantly whispered open.

"Good timing," she said. "Just as if it was waiting for us."

"It was," he said, as they stepped inside. "It's private. It only goes to my floor."

A private elevator, one they were dripping puddles of water in. Again, he seemed untroubled, while she fought an urge to find a rag or a paper towel and look after it. The rich scent of wood polish came off the glossy walls and combined with the rich aromas of him.

Her feeling of being in a movie, or a dream, only intensified as the elevator doors whispered open again at *his* floor.

Nothing in her whole life—not even the rich, subtle, tasteful decor at the office, or the palace-style ambience of the lobby—could have prepared her for the exquisite poshness of his apartment.

With a tilt of his head and a gesture with his arm, he invited her to step out of the elevator ahead of him. She found herself in a wide entry mezzanine, the marble floor deliciously cold and smooth beneath her bare feet. She avoided creating a puddle on a subtly faded rug with deep colors and an intricate tapestry pattern that looked as if it belonged on a wall in a museum, not on a floor.

She could see the mezzanine opened up to a living room, softly lit, even though no one was in it. Banks of windows faced the darkened park, and two exquisite sofas faced each other over a coffee table that held a stunning bronze sculpture. At odds with the ultrasleek, sophisticated decor, somehow the piece, a cowboy on a horse, couldn't have been more perfect.

Molly was aware of feeling one hundred percent paralyzed as Liam pried her hands off her shoes, glared at them for a minute, and then put them, with a touch of ceremony, in an empty wastebasket under an antique entry table.

"I think those cost the earth," she said, uneasily.

"It doesn't matter what they cost," he said. "It matters what they're worth. Which is zero, given the injury they've caused you."

"Still," she said. "Maybe a secondhand store?"

"What kind of person are you? Would you really inflict that kind of misery on someone else?"

Then, discussion over, he tossed his elevator card on the entry table, stripped off his coat, threw it on an upholstered bench.

Her focus shifted off the shoes. Was she going to go into that gorgeous room? With this gorgeous man whose shirt was sticking to him? And then what? She could stare at him admiringly while they soaked—and possibly ruined—the buttery leather of those couches?

"I don't have anything to change into," she realized out loud. "And no pajamas, no toiletries. Nothing to wear tomorrow."

She looked down at her soaked dress glumly. She wondered if the beautiful garment was completely ruined. She looked back at Liam, who cocked his head at her, registering her discomfort.

"Normally, I have this amazing assistant who could solve all that in a—" he said, and snapped his fingers.

He was trying to put her at ease.

She was fighting a desire to bolt.

And then a woman, graying hair, in a neat bun, and a sturdy skirt and matching blouse, came around the corner.

"Luckily," he said, smiling, "we have Maria, who is nearly as good as you at solving problems and putting out fires. Molly, Maria. Maria, Molly."

Molly felt relief surge through her as Maria came and took her hand.

"Finally, we meet Miss Sunday," Maria said.

Of course, Molly had dealt with Maria many times, though they had not met yet.

Maria was to Liam's personal life what Molly was to his professional one.

Her relief, she realized, was mostly because of Maria's innate warmth. It was like being greeted at the door by a beloved grandmother.

It eased some of her sense of being somewhere that she didn't belong. That she would never belong.

"Molly finds herself without her house keys—" Liam filled Maria in "—so she'll be staying the night. She doesn't have, um…anything."

"Come with me," Maria said, and Molly found herself being led in the direction Maria had come from.

Again, she tried not to gawk at the gorgeous paintings and decor in the wide hallway.

Just past a state-of-the-art kitchen, Maria opened a door to a room, and Molly went in to find herself in an opulent guest suite.

"The bathroom is through there," Maria said. "Have a quick hot shower. It will take the chill off. There's a robe on the back of the door. Come out to the kitchen when you're done. I'll have hot chocolate."

Molly thought she should refuse, that she shouldn't impose on the hospitality of Liam and his staff any more than she had to.

It was so late. Maria probably would like to go to bed, though there had not been a flicker of anything but welcome in her lovely crinkled face.

On the other hand, Molly was here. She was probably going to be in a situation like this once in her entire life.

Why spoil it? Why not just enjoy it all as the spectacular, unexpected gift that it was?

"Hot chocolate sounds amazing," she said. And it did.

Speaking of amazing, that also described the suite she found herself in. It was stunning with its huge bed, tone on tone decor and wall-to-wall windows that looked out over the sky-line of the city.

She wanted to go look out that window, but she was aware she was dripping onto the thick carpet, and suddenly a shower felt like the best idea ever.

The water pounding down on her rain-chilled flesh was just what she needed. She stepped out of it, finally, when she realized the hot water was *never* running out. She found a robe—luxuriously thick and pristinely white, as if it was brand-new—on a hook behind the door. She pulled it on, and then towel-dried her hair, squeezing the water from it.

A bit self-consciously, she stepped out into the hallway and made her way to the kitchen. Somehow, she had thought she was going to be alone with Maria there, but Liam was there already, sitting at a small kitchen table, talking animatedly with the older woman.

His freshly showered aroma filled her nostrils. He had on a T-shirt and a pair of string-tied pants. It was the most casual she had ever seen him. She tried not to stare at his arms. She'd only seen him in long sleeves previously, sometimes rolled up at the cuff.

Seeing the lovely bulge of his biceps made her think what a shame it was to keep those arms covered up!

Coupled with the fact she was in a housecoat, the moment was infused with an intimacy just as powerful as riding on his back had been. She was not sure how much more she could handle of her boss tonight!

"Actually, I'm going to bow out of the hot chocolate—"

"Nonsense," he said. "Sunday! You haven't lived until you've had Maria's hot chocolate. Plus, I was just bragging you up. Maria. Ask her anything."

Maria came and put a thick mug on the table. Steam rose from it, and it was topped with a mound of thick cream and chocolate shavings. The aroma was an enchantment.

Molly was drawn to that table like a magnet being drawn to steel.

"Some cooks use a secret ingredient in apple pie," Maria said. "Do you know what it is?"

Molly took a sip of the hot chocolate. She closed her eyes. "Ambrosia," she said.

"Well, I do like a good Ambrosia apple for pie, but that wasn't what I meant."

"Oh, and I was referring to the hot chocolate. Ambrosia are known to be good pie apples, because they're so sweet and hold their shape while cooking. Their lower acidity can mean less sugar is needed."

"You bake!" Maria said, as if this was an accomplishment equivalent to a moonwalk.

"Oh, no, sorry, I didn't mean to give that impression. I read a story once called 'Apple of My Eye,' and some of the details stuck."

"Ah," Maria said, clearly not seeing reading as quite the same kind of accomplishment as baking.

"Anyway, I think occasionally amaretto or rum are considered a secret ingredient—flavor enhancers—in apple pie."

Maria went back to looking impressed. "Spaghetti?"

"Sometimes cinnamon."

Liam lifted a shoulder and grinned. "Told you."

Maria shot Liam a look, patted Molly's shoulder and then left them alone.

Alone.

"Hey," Liam said. "Do you want to take this out on the deck?"

A deck in New York City. In a housecoat. With the world's best hot chocolate and the world's best-looking man, who was unselfconsciously showing off his unexpectedly lovely arms.

Tomorrow she could let her life get back to normal.

Tonight she was embracing every sweet surprise that life gave her. She followed Liam through his extraordinary living room and a patio door that slid silently open to the deck.

Decks were rare enough in New York City, but this one was huge, its flagstones wet and shiny, the rain bouncing off them.

But they didn't even get wet, as there were deeply cushioned lounge chairs under a roofed pagoda structure.

She settled into the chair, her feet stretched out before her. She pulled the housecoat belt tight around her. Her every sense seemed to be extraordinarily heightened. She took a sip of the hot chocolate and closed her eyes.

"I *love* Maria," she said. What she really meant was that she loved it all.

"She was in charge of the school kitchen at my private school, and Paul was in charge of the garages."

He hesitated, and Molly held her breath, turning slightly to look at him.

He looked unusually pensive, not the laughing man who had carried her through the rain-washed streets.

Something different was happening here. It was evident from his silence and his facial expression—Liam was debating something.

"They saved me," he said, quietly.

Molly could feel something exquisite unfolding inside her. *This*, this moment felt like they were moving into new territory. He'd alluded earlier today about an unhappy childhood and now it seemed he was going to say more.

She felt the trust in the confidence he had just shared with her, and his trust felt as much a gift—maybe more so—than everything else that had happened tonight, including the surprise piggyback ride.

CHAPTER NINE

LIAM DIDN'T KNOW why he had said that.

He and Molly had an astounding working relationship, but before today, he rarely revealed anything about his personal life.

Why would he jeopardize what they had by introducing new elements? He could feel the vulnerability in it.

He ordered himself to back up, to back away. He was under the spell of something and he needed to break out of it.

But he didn't. His legendary discipline failed him. He *wanted* her to know this other side of him. He felt compelled to tell her.

Well, if you were going to tell anyone, why not Molly? She radiated trustworthiness. Even now, she didn't press, at all. Waited. Silently. A promise of some kind of acceptance of him in that silence that he could not resist.

"Even before I went to private school, I'd found my way to the kitchens and garages of the various places we called home, though I use the term loosely. None of them were actually *homey*.

"Except in the kitchens and the staff quarters, the garages. There was warmth there that I craved. All the staff always made a fuss over me. When I started tinkering with mechanical things, I got a lot of approval for it.

"Maybe the first approval of my life. I don't actually know why my parents had a child," he said, slowly. "They both seemed equally baffled by this small, noisy, energetic creature in their household. I didn't really fit into their lifestyle. They off-loaded caring about me. There were nannies, and it seemed as soon as it was a possibility, off to private school I went.

"I didn't fit in at private school any better than I had at home. I wasn't interested in the things that interested my schoolmates, especially sports. I was intensely interested in how things work. And so I found my way to the kitchens and garages of the school, and the fact I hung out with *the help* made me a target of a lot of bullying.

"Maria and Paul really did save me. Always welcomed me. Always made a fuss over my strengths. I felt, in all the world, as if they *saw* me. And even better, that they liked what they saw.

"It disappointed my parents immensely when I went into mechanical engineering. It wasn't a prestigious degree. I was supposed to get an MBA, as I was expected to step up and be the CEO of the family businesses.

"They died in a plane crash before I finished college. Maria and Paul were there for me when that happened. Grief is even more complicated when you suddenly realize you are never going to get the moment you waited your whole life for.

"But Maria and Paul gave me what my parents never could. They've been there for me ever since. Both of them should be retired, but they just won't hear of it. I actually bought them a condo in Florida, a few years ago, because Maria's always complaining about how cold winter in New York is."

He chuckled softly, "That lasted about a week. They hated it. They arrived back here with their suitcases. Maria told me she had to have a purpose getting up in the morning. Imagine, me, being someone's reason for getting up in the morning. It's humbling.

"At least she doesn't complain about the weather, anymore."

Sometime, while he told all this, Molly's hand had crept into his, and in that touch, acceptance and encouragement.

Somehow, he had wanted to tell her about his relationship with Maria and Paul, and instead had revealed way too much about himself.

He glanced at Molly. He braced himself for pity in her eyes. Pathetic to have told her this poor little rich boy story, unloved by his parents, bullied at school, turning to the hired help to have his needs met.

But when he looked at Molly, he saw no pity in her steady gaze at all. There was a look of tenderness so deep it could overwhelm a man.

"Now I understand why you're the way you are," she said, softly. "The gift you bring to everyone is that you see their intrinsic value. It's amazing to see someone turn challenges into strengths. It's hopeful. Thank you for telling me."

It occurred to him his lovely assistant was prepared to see him through rose-colored glasses.

And nice as that was, he needed not to read too much into it. In fact, he needed to get things back on track.

The track that he had knocked them off.

He removed his hand from hers. Liam wanted to coax Sunday back; he wanted, suddenly and almost desperately, for things to be the way they had been before.

"So," he said, "what was the most exciting part of tonight, for you?"

She looked taken aback at his sudden shift.

"Can I only pick one?" she asked.

"Okay, two," he conceded.

"Um, you go first."

He had to guide them back to familiar territory. He couldn't risk this relationship—best thing that had ever happened to him, his Woman Sunday—to these kinds of distressing deviations from their norm.

"Okay," he said, pensively. "I thought the widget that controlled air flow to cooling mechanisms on big machines had potential. And of course, Jordan's invention, Fresh, was simply amazing."

For a moment, his unflappable assistant looked completely flummoxed.

"Oh," she said, after a moment, "the most exciting thing from the awards function."

What had she thought he meant?

"Can I see your phone?"

He handed it to her, and she scanned through it. He was close to accomplishing what he wanted, bringing them back to familiar ground, so now was not the time to notice how adorable she looked, the light from his phone reflecting off her glasses and the teeth her tongue was caught between.

"I'm going in a different direction than you," she said. "I liked the all-natural insecticide made out of geraniums. What an incredible way to turn something so abundant into a product *after* its original purpose has been fulfilled."

"I agree, in principle, but it's problematic. How would you possibly collect all the used geraniums? And creating and marketing a one-off product is difficult. She might be better to take that idea to a company that's already producing insecticides or beauty creams."

"Okay, my second favorite was the virtual reality one."

"For swimming pools," he recalled. "That was a good idea. Creating underwater images that could make it seem as if you were swimming with sharks."

"Or on a coral reef. Or in a completely imaginary underwater world."

Just like that, they were themselves again. Even though she was in a housecoat, even though he'd confided something to her that he never told anyone, the awkwardness was gone, and they were fully immersed in the amazing and infinite world of ideas.

When she yawned, he finally realized it was way too late for this.

He got up, and she got up. They stood looking over the New York skyline and then they turned and he found himself looking at her.

"You know," he said, "I think this went amazingly well. What would you think about doing it again? I mean, stepping in as my companion, my plus-one, again sometime? It's so comfortable."

Did she look strangely disappointed by the suggestion?

"Of course," she said. "Whatever works for you, chief."

Somehow his relief at having such a reliable easy-to-be-with companion for events was short-lived.

Because Molly took a deep breath. She stood up on her tip-toes and her lips brushed his cheek.

All that work he'd done to get Sunday back, to get them back on familiar ground, disappeared like mist before a hot sun.

"Thanks for a really fun night. Especially the piggyback ride."

He realized maybe continuing this plus-one charade wasn't going to be quite as comfortable as he thought.

Molly spun away from Liam, but not before registering the shock in his eyes that she had kissed him.

Good heavens! A benign little *thank-you* for what had been a very fun evening. And an unexpectedly exciting one, too.

Though it showed what different pages they were on, that she thought the most exciting thing about the evening had definitely been the piggyback ride.

Well, until she had kissed him and felt the scrape of his whiskers under her lips.

And meanwhile, Liam thought the most exciting part of the evening was some widget that did something she could barely understand.

She found her way through the apartment back to the beautiful room, and she slipped in and closed the door behind her, leaning into it, thinking of her lips grazing his cheek.

Thinking of him telling her those things about his younger days, entrusting her with confidences that just deepened her sense of falling for him.

So unprofessional! It was an evening of mistakes compounding on each other in that awful way that mistakes tended to do. Forgetting her purse at Second Chances cascading into a series of unpredictable events.

Not one of which she would change.

She noticed a brand-new overnight bag had been set carefully on her bed, and she went over and studied it. It was gorgeous, actually—deep red leather, with beautiful stitching, one of those bags sophisticated people used as carry-ons.

She opened it.

It felt like Christmas morning. Brand-new pajamas. A pair of plain black yoga pants and a white V-necked T-shirt for tomorrow. Socks. Comfy loafers. Some plain underwear, cotton panties, a pull-on, one-size-fits-all sports bra. A toothbrush and toothpaste. She'd even been provided with a rudimentary makeup bag filled with little pots of eyeshadow, a mascara tube, lip gloss, a compact with blush in it. Surprisingly, there was a mini–first aid kit, and when she peeked inside it, everything that was needed for blister-aid was there.

And if she hadn't told Liam she didn't like her feet being touched, would he have looked after the foot first aid? The very thought made her shiver. She made herself focus on the delights she had found in the bag.

It looked as if Maria had guessed her sizes perfectly.

Molly put on her new pajamas, and climbed between the crisp linen sheets. She had read, of course, about thread counts and Egyptian cotton.

Until you experienced it, it was way too easy to dismiss such luxuries as all hype, as just people with too much money finding new and exotic ways to spend it.

But nestled into those sheets, the bed deeply comfortable, the apartment silent around her, she wondered if she had ever felt quite so safe.

She fell asleep instantly.

When she woke, though, to the morning light filtering through the bedroom window, the feeling of safety was gone. Molly contemplated the awkward intimacy of being in her boss's house, her lips still feeling oddly *changed* for having scraped across his cheek.

Her predicament was really not much different from last night. She still didn't have her purse, so she was going to have to find something to do with herself until Second Chances opened. She didn't even have her phone to find out what time that was!

Well, one thing—he wasn't seeing her in her pajamas.

Except he'd already seen her in a housecoat, so that barn door had already been left open. Still, it wasn't too late to start doing some damage control. Walls had come down last night. For both of them.

It was tempting to want them to stay down, but no, that was completely unacceptable.

He wasn't dealing with her dirty laundry, either. She stuffed the pajamas from last night in the bag. She went and gathered the dress off the bathroom floor. It was a mess, worse because she had left it in a heap. She wasn't sure it could be saved, but maybe it could, with careful hand laundering. And she *was* one of the few people left on the planet who had an iron and knew how to use it. The dress joined her new pajamas in the overnight bag.

She showered, put on her new clothes, scraped her hair back extra severely. She looked in the full-length mirror and it made her happy that she could pass for any other woman in NYC on a Saturday morning. She dressed her blisters and gave into the temptation of a slight dusting of makeup.

She opened her door to find a bag on the handle.

She peered in it.

All her things she had left at Second Chances were there, her purse on top. She went back into the room, closed the door and sank on the bed.

This was what *she* did. She solved problems. She put out fires. She looked after others. It was astonishing to find herself in the position of the one being looked after.

Actually, it made her want to weep.

Since she felt like weeping, anyway, she pulled her phone out of the bag and braced herself for messages—probably increasingly hysterical when Molly couldn't be reached—from her mother.

The phone was one hundred percent completely dead.

Finally, she gathered herself and left her room.

She heard a clatter of dishes and followed the sound to the kitchen.

Maria was busy. She turned and smiled at Molly.

"You're up. Did you sleep well? What can I make you for breakfast?"

She seemed, embarrassingly, to know what was on top of Molly's mind.

Where was Liam?

"Liam's left for the gym already," Maria said.

Of course. Molly knew that. It was right there on the schedule she looked at every day. Saturday at 6 a.m. he went to the gym. Why had she thought today was going to be different?

Did she seriously think he would feel as eager to see her again as she had been to see him?

"Waffles? French toast?"

There was no excuse to stay here! Molly had her keys. She had her wallet. She could stop and pick up a bagel anywhere along the way home.

But it was hard to give up this feeling of someone looking after her for a change.

"Waffles would be lovely."

Maria busied herself mixing batter and heating what looked to be an ancient waffle maker.

"Thank you for finding all those things for me," Molly said, as she dug into the delectable homemade treat a little later. "It couldn't have been easy in the middle of the night. And having my stuff returned before the store even opened."

"Things?" Maria said, genuinely puzzled. "What things? What store?"

CHAPTER TEN

"You know. The items I found in my room last night. Pajamas." Molly gestured down at herself. "What I'm wearing. And my stuff that I forgot at Second Chances."

"I'm sorry, I don't know what you're talking about."

Startled, Molly realized that Maria hadn't provided her with these emergency items. Which meant her boss had. Liam must have been arranging a delivery while she'd been in the shower last night.

And he must have been up at the crack of dawn pulling strings to get her stuff out of the closed store.

Maybe Liam didn't need her nearly as much as he said he did.

It seemed he was quite capable of being a Man Friday, all by himself.

An hour later, she said goodbye to Maria and did a final check of her room: towels neatly folded over the shower bar, tub and sink left spotless, bed made.

With a sigh, Molly realized it wasn't just hard to give up being looked after, but hard to say goodbye, period. It wasn't just the luxury, it was the *feeling* she had here of deep serenity, of a world that unfolded in an orderly manner all the time.

It was the sense of being safe somehow, deeper than anything she had ever felt before.

Still, she made herself shut the door firmly on the bedroom

she'd been provided, and she went to the front mezzanine where they had come in last night.

Her hand on the elevator button, she took one more look around, as if she could memorize the beauty of this space and tuck it away inside her for those times when chaos came.

And with a family like hers, those times were inevitable.

Her eyes caught on the wastebasket, tucked under the entry table. The shoes from last night were still in it.

The reason for the piggyback ride. Her very own glass slippers, really, that had carried her into her unexpected night in this Cinderella world. Whether it was the poor girl in her, or whether she planned to have them bronzed, she wasn't sure. But she could not bear the thought of those shoes being tossed away.

She fished them from the wastebasket and zipped them inside her new bag.

The subway brought her crashing back to the reality of life. Even though it was Saturday, it was crowded. She couldn't find a place to sit. She stepped in gum. The man beside her smelled bad. Another snored loudly from his seat.

Just yesterday, she had *loved* the subway, the quintessential New York experience.

Unfortunately, her brush with lifestyles of the rich and famous also tainted how she felt about her space.

She stepped in the door of her tiny, beloved basement suite and waited for *that* feeling. Being home.

Just yesterday she had *loved* this space.

Now all of it—her secondhand finds, the tightness of the space, poor Winspear sitting in the light of the one tiny window—seemed faintly tawdry.

And that was *exactly* the problem with experimenting with a station above your own in life. It was exactly as her mother had warned her—about getting *ideas*.

It planted the seeds of dissatisfaction. It made a person

greedily want *more*. Molly thought of how hard it had felt to leave the quiet sanctuary of Liam's apartment this morning.

She had an awful flash memory of her father drinking, before he'd disappeared from their lives forever.

Drink after drink after drink.

There was *never* enough to soothe his sense of not having or being enough.

She drew in a deep breath, ordered herself to stop it, immediately. There were things to do. The dress to save, shoes to clean. Winspear to look after.

Chocolates to arrange for Liam's trip.

She fell on the last task with the enthusiasm and focus of an underfed dog who had been thrown a bone.

After a while, she remembered to plug in her phone. As she had guessed, there were many messages from her mother and several missed calls.

She listened, with a sinking heart, to the messages. The lawyer needed a ten-thousand-dollar retainer.

People, Molly realized, thought ten thousand dollars was a lot of money, until they had a legal problem.

Her phone rang. It was her mother, and she didn't want to talk to her, didn't want all that shrill desperation to take the shine of her evening with Liam away from her.

Stressed, she checked her bank account. Not enough, but it would have to do. She sent it.

She got a text from her mother within seconds.

Not an ounce of gratitude.

When can you come up with the rest?

Molly deliberately turned her phone back off. She'd never been so happy to see the inside of her office as she was on Monday.

It had become her sanctuary. She could not risk everything

this place gave her because she was having extremely complicated feelings about her boss.

Whom, despite knowing better, she couldn't wait to see.

And he did not disappoint. As soon as Liam came in the door, she felt something in her go calm, as if everything in her world was going to be alright.

If Liam felt any awkwardness at Molly's unexpected stay at his apartment, it didn't show at all.

She pulled the red leather bag out from under her desk. "I'll return this to you."

He squinted at it, then waved his hand. "Oh, no need."

He asked after her feet. If the memory of piggybacking her blazed through his mind the way it did hers, it didn't show.

After assuring him her feet were fine, she moved on quickly, wanting to get his focus away from her because it was just too easy to bask in his caring.

Briskly, all business, Molly briefed him about the week.

"You leave for Québec City early Wednesday evening to sign the final agreement with Maple You Do, Maple You Don't on Thursday. It'll be a day of meetings, leaving early Thursday evening. I've sent your itinerary to your phone but here's a printed copy for you. And here's the booklet."

She'd gotten in the habit of preparing a briefing book for him when he went on any trip, even a short one. This time she'd included notes about the maple syrup industry, a bit of the history of Québec and Québec City, and a bit of background on the small family business that had grown too fast and needed exactly the kind of help FIX provided.

She'd left out anything about Québec's amazing chocolate industry. That would be her surprise to him when he got there.

He thumbed through the book, pleased, and then looked up at her. "It's definitely a poster child case of what I always wanted FIX to be, a company that helps other companies be the most they can be with just a few simple changes to their operating efficiencies and marketing.

"You've put a lot into this booklet, for a visit that really amounts to less than twenty-four hours."

She could feel the heat rush to her cheeks. "I'm sorry," she stammered. "You're right. I spent much too much time on it."

It occurred to her she was getting way too used to running the show.

Too big for her britches, her mother would say.

"Have you been to Québec City before?" she asked.

"Yes."

"I'm mortified," she said. "I should have really checked that before I spent so much time on preparing—"

"Sunday, stop. I don't feel like you wasted your time. Or mine. These advance preps you do for me are invaluable. Don't change a thing."

But she knew she would. Already she was noting, *less time researching short trip destinations. Check if he's been there before.*

"You loved putting this briefing together, didn't you?"

Oh! The last thing she wanted was for her *loves* to be so transparent.

"I did," she admitted. She shouldn't elaborate, but she did. "I read a book about a little girl, set in Québec City in the 1700s. It's been on my bucket list since then."

He cocked his head at her. "Really?"

"Really."

"Well, that's an easy one to fulfill. Is your passport in order?"

"Yes, it is." She'd applied for a passport when she was sixteen years old. Silly, really, a girl from a backwater with no hope of ever going anywhere. But having that document had felt as if she had a secret key that could open whole worlds to her.

And now look! Still…

"Oh," she said, embarrassed. "I wasn't hinting."

Had she sounded as wistful as she felt? She was really becoming much too transparent to her boss.

"Of course you weren't hinting! But the more I think about it, the more I like the idea. Sunday, clear your schedule. It'll be a kind of combination assistant and my plus-one. I mean, one day isn't much, but we'll manage to squeeze in a traipse through the Old City. Bring good walking shoes. See? You'll need that bag again, after all."

Of course, that was truer than he knew because she certainly didn't have any appropriate luggage for a business trip.

On a private plane, a voice inside her squealed.

It caused a disturbing sense of weakness in Molly that her boss could make dreams come true so casually, in the absolute blink of an eye.

In her world, dreams were something you hankered after, *forever*, bracing yourself inwardly for the unlikely possibility of them ever materializing.

What was she going to do now? Say no?

"It's only for one day, Molly. You'll be home safe in your own bed by Thursday night."

He hardly ever called her Molly, and especially not with that aching note of gentleness in his voice, as if it was evident to him that she was such a creature of habit that this change in plan was throwing her for a loop.

It wasn't really a weakness to give in, Molly told herself. Liam was her boss, after all. He was telling her how it was going to be. She couldn't really argue with him.

"I'll book an extra room," she said, keeping her tone as professional as possible, when inside her doubts gave way to something completely different.

In fact, a little renegade voice was singing—*singing*—in her. *Québec City. And Liam.*

Of course, she had known eventually there would be a trip she accompanied him on. Maxine had travelled with Liam several times a year.

Somehow Molly had expected she would be *ready* for it. That she would have weeks or even months to prepare and plan.

On Tuesday night, she could barely sleep she was so nervous and excited. She got up three times to check that she had put her passport in her purse. Then she lay awake going over every possibility. She'd only been on a plane once before, on that trip to Los Angeles. It had made her feel queasy. What if she got sick, this time? Plus, this time there was an extra challenge. She'd never crossed an international border before, but she'd watched reality television shows about it.

What if her brother's latest brush with the law put a red flag beside her name? Or her father's ancient history came back to haunt her? What if she was questioned in front of Liam?

What if they said she couldn't enter Canada?

That little doubt that was never far away—*you aren't good enough, you're an imposter*—flared to life.

She got up and looked at the outfit she had laid out. It had to be appropriate for a day at the office and the later afternoon trip.

She had chosen a dark jacket and skirt, a plain blouse and flat shoes that would be good for walking if they did have a short opportunity to see Old Québec. She only kept the blouse and shoes as she laid out a new outfit.

She traded out the skirt for pencil line black slacks and the jacket for a gray hand-knit sweater. Very grandmotherly, a more trustworthy look for the customs officials. Then she traded out the blouse for a patterned one that might hide stains better if she spilled coffee during turbulence or worse, got sick on herself.

She double-checked what she had packed for Thursday, another plain skirt and solid-colored blouse. The flat shoes should be good for both days, and comfortable for walking.

It was a nerve-wracking day at the office, partly due to her lack of sleep. She was glad Liam was off-site today, because she'd had enough trouble concentrating. For some reason, every little noise, even the phone ringing, made her jump, and she wouldn't have wanted him to see that.

She hadn't been able to eat because her stomach was so butterfly-ey. Molly finally stepped onto the FIX private jet early Wednesday evening. She had outwardly—she hoped—tamed her anxiety, but inwardly she was a mess.

Coming off the loading bridge, she paused at the entry door to the cabin. She could barely hear the crew member's warm welcome over the buzz in her ears.

Molly was suddenly aware there were some things you could never prepare for. Being on a private jet was one of them.

She definitely did not belong here. But still, she took it all in, like an awed visitor being given a glimpse of the crown jewels.

Like the interior of Liam's apartment, the interior of the jet oozed an atmosphere of calm, luxury and wealth.

Stepping into the cabin was like stepping into a very posh living room. A deep, creamy leather couch faced a highly polished cabinet with exquisite wood grains. A bar, she deduced.

Farther along, four leather reclining-style seats faced each other, forming a conversation group. Behind that was a dining table, and then a door, slightly open to reveal a sumptuous bedroom.

Liam arrived, coming in the door behind her. He practically bumped into her, as she was glued to the spot.

"Hey, Sunday. You made it," he said. "Pick a place to sit. The recliners are the most comfortable if you're going to read. This sofa is the best for watching a movie or television. A screen pops out of that console."

She contemplated the fact that people watched television while travelling hundreds of miles an hour at thirty thousand feet. She had not even looked at the screen on the back of her seat on that first flight to Los Angeles.

This seemed even more surreal, almost too much to handle.

She turned and stared at him, paralyzed, hoping she would find something in his familiar face that would calm the anxiety inside her.

"Sunday! I didn't picture you as a nervous flyer, somehow."

Oh! Again, she did not like the fact that Liam seemed to be getting better and better at reading her. And if it was only flying! It was all of it. Crossing a border. Being out of her depth. This was not the office, which had become such a comfort zone.

This was a brand-new world, and a brand-new way of being with Liam, and Molly felt hopelessly out of her depth.

CHAPTER ELEVEN

MOLLY'S SENSE OF being an absolute bundle of nerves was not diminished by Liam's presence. In fact, she felt it would make her seem incredibly unworldly if she admitted to her boss she was quite the newbie to air travel.

Before that trip to LA, the longest trip of her life had been by bus from Louisiana to New York, her newly acquired diploma from Mrs. Michael's School of Business laid carefully, so as not to get folded, in the bottom of her worn suitcase.

She'd found out, and quickly too, when she'd started applying for jobs, that her diploma was laughable.

Where she came from, Mrs. Michael's was considered an institute of higher education, not to mention an affordable one.

Attending Mrs. Michael's was bound to give her highfalutin ideas about herself, according to her mother.

Molly had been lucky to get on at the mail room at FIX. It was really nothing less than a miracle.

And she would have to say the very same thing about her, Molly Littleton, being on board a private jet in any capacity.

She wondered what her mother would think about this.

She'd want more money—that's what she'd think about it.

Molly made her way, unsteadily, as if they were already in the air, to the group of recliners, sat down, squeezed the armrests.

"I knew you'd pick reading," Liam said, taking the seat beside her. "Do up your seat belt. Don't recline until after we've taken off."

"Aye, aye, chief," she said, and her nerves calmed ever so slightly, though she knew relaxing totally was out of the question. And she was right. From the thrust of takeoff, to all the strange sounds and the little bumps, it felt to Molly, this time, as it had last, as if flying was completely unnatural.

Liam's parents had *died* in a plane crash.

How could he be sitting there, calmly opening his briefcase and accepting a coffee from the flight crew?

She herself did not accept coffee. Or snacks. Despite choosing an outfit that took in the possibility of accidents, Molly had a sense of needing to maintain control over every element that she possibly could. No splashing coffee cups for her! No admittedly delicious smelling meal to add to her stomach turmoil.

She actually felt worse when they finally landed than she had when they'd taken off. To her, this was the most terrifying part of the trip.

She felt like a spy she had once read about crossing Checkpoint Charlie from East Berlin to West Berlin right after the Second World War, the lives of dozens of people riding on his successful crossing.

"Where do we clear customs?" she asked Liam. Her voice sounded tiny.

"Oh, they'll come to us." He didn't even look up from what he was doing.

Sure enough, when the sealed door was opened, the cabin crew welcomed officials from Canada Customs on board.

The man and woman chatted with the crew for a moment, then made their way back toward Liam and Molly.

Nothing good in her entire life had ever come from people wearing uniforms! She had been raised with a good healthy suspicion of all authority figures.

She felt as if her heart was going to beat out of her chest as she passed her passport, slightly damp from her sweating palms, to the border official.

"Is everything all right, miss?" one of the officials asked.

Checkpoint Charlie. Checkpoint Charlie. Breathe. Smile.

"Yes," she said, "everything's fine."

"I think she's scared of flying," Liam said, passing them his own passport.

"Ah, well, you're safely on the ground now. *Bienvenue au Canada.* Welcome to Canada. Enjoy your stay."

"That's it?" she whispered to Liam, when they turned and left. After all her inward rehearsing of answering questions calmly and articulately, she wasn't sure which feeling was more acute: Relief. Or disappointment.

He gave her a look. "What were you expecting?"

She lifted a shoulder. "A few questions, maybe. Some *interest*."

"Huh, you don't look like the type they are interested in."

Was he saying she didn't look interesting?

"What are you hiding from me, Sunday?"

It felt as if her heart stopped beating in her chest.

"What?" she whispered.

He squinted at her appraisingly. "Ah," he said. "International jewel thief."

And then he grinned. She realized he wasn't sniffing out some truth about her family; he was *teasing* her.

"America's Most Wanted, Top Ten," he guessed again and then sighed dramatically. "It's always the ones you least suspect."

A long way off, and too close at the same time.

"I just thought at the very least, I'd get my passport stamped," she said, trying to keep it as light as he was keeping it.

"If we ask them, they will," he said, with an indulgent smile.

"No," she said hastily, "it's fine." She was not inviting more scrutiny from Canada Border Services! With her passport back in her hand, she considered the fact it was official: She, Molly Littleton, had been admitted into a foreign country. Welcomed, in two languages!

Liam was looking at her closely. "You've never crossed a border before, have you?"

"Only my second time on a plane," she admitted. What had happened to not telling him that? As if he couldn't tell!

"Wow," he said. "Almost a vir—"

He stopped abruptly. "You did great, Sunday."

He had, very wisely, decided against a comment on virginity. Instead, he had paid her a small compliment. Small as it was, it felt like wind lifting sagging sails. For the first time she allowed excitement to outweigh the anxiety.

For the most part, every single adventure she had ever been on was inside the covers of a book. If you didn't count her family shenanigans, which were never the kind of adventures anyone in their right mind would sign up for.

Real adventures were more nerve-racking than she'd expected. But if she had to venture outside her comfort zone, could she have been assigned a better guide than Liam?

Liam watched Molly as the limousine whisked them away from the airport and into Québec City.

She'd flown twice.

She'd never been in another country.

Now, she was craning her neck. Even though evening darkness had fallen, she was trying to see everything.

"Look," she breathed, "there's one of the gates into Old Québec. Did you know it's the only fortified city north of Mexico?"

"I didn't," he said.

"This is one of the oldest European settlements in North America," his living, breathing encyclopedia told him. "Old Québec is a UNESCO World Heritage site."

When they got out of the car at the hotel, she turned and stared across the street.

"I can't believe we're staying right here," she said. "This

is what I wanted to see the most. The Parliament Building of Québec."

Not the shopping, he thought wryly, not the world-class restaurants. No, the parliament buildings.

He followed her gaze. The structure did look magnificent, especially lit up at night.

"It was inspired by the Louvre Palace in Paris," she said, with a sigh. "There's a tour, if our schedule permits. After our meetings tomorrow. I mean, I'd go on my own time, of course."

He could tell her to go while he was in meetings tomorrow, but he couldn't bring himself to do it.

"No, I'd like to see it, too."

Which surprised the hell out of him, because he'd been to Québec City many times and it had never once occurred to him that he would like to take a tour of the Parliament Building.

He realized, suddenly, it had nothing to do with the Louvre-inspired buildings, as magnificent as they were.

It was about *her*, somehow.

It was about Molly.

Liam had travelled the entire world. He moved in circles where people had everything. They had private planes and helicopters and estates. Sometimes they owned multiple estates and homes situated everywhere on the globe. They had stables full of horses and garages full of cars.

And they had done everything. They had experienced the most iconic beaches in the world, been to the rainforests, gone on safari in Africa, helicopter-skied in the Rockies. They had dined at every five-star restaurant in every major city on all five continents and shopped at the most exclusive stores on the planet.

He knew those people. That was his world. That was the world he'd grown up with and the world he still lived in.

Nothing thrilled. Nothing excited. The people in the small circles of the extraordinarily wealthy weren't exactly jaundiced by new experiences, but bored? Maybe.

Even as a kid, he'd been different. He'd found things interesting that other people overlooked. How things worked fascinated him. He'd come to find his satisfaction in the endless frontier of new ideas rather than in collecting things, in testing the limits of experiences.

As for the parliament buildings, he was not going to miss Molly experiencing the world with such freshness and such wonder.

She was, he realized, looking extra plain today. She wore no makeup at all, and her hair was pulled back sternly. She was wearing a gray sweater that looked like something someone would wear who owned a cat and crocheted doilies in their spare time.

The outfit, thankfully, hid all those luscious curves he had seen the night they'd gotten wet together.

And yet, despite that, despite what he suspected was a deliberately toned-down appearance, she was radiating a soft beauty.

He could feel her energy reaching across the chilly night and filling him with an odd warmth.

Looking at her face as she gazed toward those parliament buildings, it occurred to him that she looked as alive, somehow, as he had ever seen her.

If he saw Québec City through her eyes, whatever that was shining so softly from her was going to be contagious. He was going to feel brand-new in some way he had not felt before.

And he just wasn't sure if that was a threat.

Or a promise.

It was only for one day, he told himself.

"Are you hungry?" he asked her, realizing suddenly she had eaten nothing on the plane.

"Absolutely starving."

"Have you ever had poutine?"

"What?"

"Ah, *finally* something you have never heard of."

"What is it?"

"A Québec staple. French fries, drenched in gravy and cheese curds."

"Well, that sounds perfectly horrible."

"Doesn't it?" he said, pleasantly. "It's caught on in other places, now. You can even get it in New York. But it's never the same as having it here. My favorite is duck-duck. The french fries cooked in duck tallow and the poutine topped with duck meat."

"It's sounding worse and worse," she said, with the cutest little wrinkle of her nose.

Liam, he warned himself, *do not start seeing Sunday as cute.*

But it was too late for that. After getting caught in the rain with her last week, he was never going to see her the same way again, anyway.

"I've never had duck," she said, pensively.

That word *virgin* popped into his head again.

"Well, let's make it a complete day of firsts, shall we?"

She looked doubtful.

"Duck is very prevalent in Québec culture and cuisine," he told her.

She still looked unconvinced.

"Sunday! Trust me."

A man could live for the look that lit up her eyes in that moment.

CHAPTER TWELVE

"OF COURSE I trust you!" Molly said to Liam.

He glanced at his watch. Québec was in the same time zone as New York. There should be plenty of places to eat that were still open. And so they checked in and dropped off their bags.

The concierge recommended a restaurant just blocks away, in the Old City, renowned for its duck-duck.

And so, walking past the lit parliament buildings and under an archway in the thick stone wall that surrounded Old Québec, Liam was aware of beginning an amazing journey of witnessing Molly as she discovered brand-new things.

She did not disappoint!

Of course, Old Québec was an absolute enchantment, certainly one of the most beautiful cities Liam had ever been in, but its beauty deepened around him as Molly noticed everything with complete wonder. Cobblestones, dates on buildings, the flowers in window boxes.

He held open the door for her of the restaurant that had been recommended.

"*Bonjour. Bienvenue.*" They were greeted by a lone waiter who seemed to also be acting as the maître d'.

"*Bonjour,*" Molly offered haltingly, and then she won over the waiter completely by adding, just as haltingly, "*Comment allez-vous?*"

He beamed at her, then switched seamlessly to English.

"I am wonderful," he said. "Is there any other way to be on a beautiful spring evening in Québec City?"

No, Liam realized, as they were shown their table, there was absolutely no other way to be.

"Especially," the waiter said, pulling out chairs for them with flourish, "if you are lovers."

Molly's eyes went very wide and her mouth opened and then snapped shut, as she looked at Liam helplessly to correct the misinterpretation.

"Just business associates," Liam said to the waiter, who looked pleased, as if he might have been fishing for this very information.

After the waiter left, Molly deliberately looked at everything but Liam.

Again, no detail went unnoticed: the ancient hardwood floors, the blackened timbers of the roof, the depth of the sill of the window they were seated at.

"Oh, my gosh," she said, touching the stone, "the wall must be three feet thick."

The waiter doted on them—Liam was pretty sure he was flirting shamelessly. Liam noticed, faintly amused but mostly annoyed, that despite her downplayed appearance the man was like a moth, drawn to her light.

And indeed, Molly was radiating happiness.

Liam wondered, *did that mean she'd been unhappy before?*

Liam realized this was the second time he'd been with her that she had attracted male attention. He'd practically had to chase that guy off her at the awards dinner, too.

It occurred to him that these young men were seeing something about Molly that he'd missed.

He found himself studying her.

It hit him like a bolt of lightning. Yes, there it was.

It wasn't just her wonder, or her curiosity.

It was passion.

Burning right below the surface of her reliable Sunday self.

"What?" she asked him, self-consciously taking a sip of her water.

With relief, he realized it wasn't passion, after all.

"You still have the eyelashes on," he said.

That was it! Men were suckers for things like that.

"Oh," she said, glumly. "I think they attached these things with construction glue."

She seemed totally unaware she was being flirted with by the waiter. Liam consulted with her over the menu.

"Poutine, for sure."

"Don't order two," she said and did that wrinkled nose thing. He hoped the waiter didn't see it, because it was as compelling, somehow, as her eyelashes.

"Could I just try yours? I don't think I'm going to like it. I'll have the meat pie."

He contemplated that. Being with a woman who was conscious about wasting things, who didn't order one of each item on the menu and take a single bite simply because he could afford it.

That's what Charlotte had been like. It was good to remember her, the woman who had so charmed him that he had nearly married her.

It was good to remember Charlotte as Molly was suggesting eating off his plate, which seemed extraordinarily intimate.

"Get your own," he said. "You're going to like it."

When the waiter came back he ordered.

"Two poutine," the waiter repeated, with approval. He pronounced it poo-tin.

"It makes me nervous. I haven't had it before," she confided.

"What? A virgin!"

He effortlessly used the word Liam had avoided earlier.

"You will not be disappointed," he promised Molly with a fiendish wag of his eyebrows.

"I don't know. I'm being talked into it against my better judgment."

"Ah," the waiter said smoothly, "sometimes overcoming judgment is the best way in life, yes?"

"Oh," she said, very vehemently. "No!"

She *still* didn't know the waiter was flirting. Liam caught his eye and raised a warning brow.

The man lifted a shoulder, as if to say *but you said you're just business associates*.

And that was true. Were these feelings of protectiveness within the realm of that relationship?

Thankfully, Molly didn't notice the wordless interchange between Liam and her new admirer.

She had her phone out. "The last tour of the Parliament Building is at 4:30 tomorrow afternoon. What do you think? Will we be done meetings by then? Can we squeeze it in? Should I book?"

He suddenly didn't want her to *squeeze* anything in. He wanted to keep that look on her face forever.

She was the best assistant he had ever had. Why not show his appreciation of her? Good Lord, the waiter was doing a better job of appreciating her than he was.

He'd surprise her with an extra day in Québec City. They could go sightseeing together on Friday.

"I'll look after it," he said.

She put away her phone and gazed up at the ceiling. "Can't you just feel it? All the years? All the people? Life unfolding over the centuries. Love and sorrow?"

The thing was he *could feel* it.

There was that passion again. He was kidding himself that it was the eyelashes. Though they did do incredible things to her eyes.

The poutine arrived. She stared at it, her expression horrified. Liam saw it through her eyes.

Okay, definitely not the most visually attractive dish in the world. In fact, it looked like something that hadn't agreed with the cat.

But she was aware of the waiter hovering and of course, so was he. The look he gave him did not move him along.

Both men watched as she picked up her fork.

She toyed with the topping and then took a deep breath. She speared a french fry covered in goopy gravy and white chunks of curd. Dark duck meat clung to the top of it. She regarded her fork with dismay, then closed her eyes and popped the morsel in her mouth.

The startling combination of flavors registered. The look on her face, Liam thought, should really be reserved for private moments. Very private moments.

Her eyes flew open.

"*Mon Dieu*," she exclaimed.

The waiter chortled with delight, while Liam looked at the tiny little gravy spot that graced her bottom lip. Her tongue darted out and flicked it.

Mon dieu, indeed, he thought.

"I'll have whatever she's having," the waiter said, paraphrasing a very famous line from a movie. He moved away, pleased, as if that line was invented by him, and he had cooked the dish himself.

Molly looked after him, a tiny frown playing across her lips, her brows dropped.

"Was he…" she whispered, searching for words and turning back to Liam, wide-eyed.

"Coming on to you?" Liam asked dryly.

She looked every bit as horrified as she had when the dish had first been set in front of her.

But then she giggled.

And he found the humor in it, too.

And then they were both laughing, and he realized she was not the only one drenched in happiness.

"I loved that," Molly said, the following afternoon, after the tour of the parliament buildings was done. They were standing on the front steps. Their hotel was a two-minute walk away. They would go get their things and then it would be over.

She looked out over Québec City. *Au revoir*, she thought, but she didn't say it out loud. She knew all her longing would be in that phrase, naked for Liam to see.

Coming here, this spontaneous trip, had been such a gift. The dinner last night. The meetings today. It had been amazing to see Liam at work outside the office. He had never once made her feel like just an assistant or even introduced her that way.

He had coaxed her opinions out of her, made her feel like a contributing member of the team.

To see him in action had made it clear why he had enjoyed such success at what he did.

"I guess we should go get our things and head for the airport," she said. "I scheduled the flight for seven. If we call for a car—"

"I cancelled the flight."

"What?"

"And extended our rooms for one more night."

"What?" she asked again, her voice a whisper this time. Her longing had been naked after all. But what was astonishing was that it had influenced him.

"I rescheduled the flight for the same time tomorrow and kept the hotel rooms," he said.

"You knew about this this morning," she said. "That's why you told me to leave my bag in my room."

He laughed. "You absolutely hate spontaneity, don't you?"

Well, yes, she did, but she could also feel everything she believed starting to shift uncomfortably within her. Like, for instance, her belief—*good things don't happen to people like me*.

"I can't just whisk you away when you've hardly seen any of it. It's on your bucket list, after all."

Molly had to turn rapidly away from her boss. She was going to cry. He had extended the stay for her and for her only.

She had never had anyone do anything quite so special for her before.

"If we're staying an extra day, I'll have to rearrange your

appointments for tomorrow," she said, after she had gathered herself.

"No worries. I already looked after it."

"Do you need me at all?" she asked.

"Of course I do, Sunday. That's what this is all about. To let you know how much I need you. And appreciate you."

She still had her face tilted away from him, but he crooked his finger under her chin and turned it to him.

"Are you crying?"

"Of course I'm not crying!" she said, lifting her glasses and taking a swipe at her eyes.

He frowned, pressed a gentle finger against the corner of her eye, regarded it thoughtfully. "Wet," he deduced.

"Well, maybe a little. I'm easily overwhelmed."

"That's a side of you that doesn't show at work."

"Because that's a controlled environment."

"This is why you don't like surprises," he said.

She wanted to tell him she had very little experience with *nice* surprises. On the other hand, she did not want him probing that dark corner of her life, a place that—if she could not leave it entirely behind her—at least she did not have to show to others.

CHAPTER THIRTEEN

THANKFULLY, AFTER gazing at her quizzically for a moment, Liam took Molly's cue to move on.

"Do you have enough clothes?" he asked her. "For an extra day?"

"Oh." This was what spontaneity did. A cascading effect of more and more problems to be solved as a result.

"I can make do."

"I can't," he said. "Let's go get a few things and then go for dinner."

Everything in his world was so fluid and uncomplicated. Money might not be able to buy happiness, but it seemed to be able to buy just about everything else. It would be too easy to get used to this, to want it.

She had to keep her defenses up. She just had to!

But when they stopped at the first little boutique they came across just inside the walls of the Old City, she realized her defenses had been crumbling for a long time. And shopping together—again—was just the nudge needed for them to be completely destroyed.

"Do you know we were doing exactly this a week ago?" she said. "Shopping?"

He grinned at her. "How about that? It's our plus-one-iver-sary."

She found herself smiling back at him.

"And this—" Liam held up a red plaid lumberjack-style

shirt "—would be the perfect way to celebrate. This would look good on you."

He was teasing her, again. It would all just be so easy to get used to—the light banter, shopping together, a life of *nice* surprises.

She knew it couldn't last. She knew she shouldn't be *playing* with something that meant so much to her—her job, her relationship with her boss. Loving him from afar had felt quite safe before and ever so predictable. These rapid developments since last Friday should be regarded with her customary caution toward change.

On the other hand, the changes were already in motion. She was aware she was as helpless to stop them as she would be standing in front of a moving train with her hand up.

For once in her life, could she stop ferreting out the potential for disaster? Could she stop anticipating impending doom? Could she just go with it? Relax and enjoy?

Tentatively, Molly plucked a shirt off the rack. "Oh, look, there's a matching one for you."

"Let's try them," he suggested, and in unison they pulled the beautifully made woolen shirts over their business clothes.

He regarded her thoughtfully, laughter making the colors spark in his eyes like gold dust catching the light.

"Not quite there," he decided, and he looked around the store. "Aha!"

He snatched a fur-lined aviator-style hat from a loaded shelf. He plopped it on her head, and tied the string tightly under her chin.

Then, he turned and got a similar fur-lined cap for himself, and did the same thing.

He looked outrageous, adorable and completely unselfconscious in his hokey tourist version of a *Québecois*.

He took out his phone, and they hammed it up for selfies.

"Those photos are top secret," she told him, after he put the phone away. "I don't want anyone in the office to see that."

"To see Miss Littleton having fun?" he chided her mildly.

"Exactly!" But then she couldn't help but add, "Do you think people at the office perceive me as uptight?"

Unspoken: *Do you?*

"I don't think I've ever heard anybody say anything that wasn't pure admiration of your organizational skills and memory. Though, once, Smith, in accounting, said you reminded him of his small-town librarian."

"And a higher compliment could not be paid! That's what I always wanted to be when I was growing up."

"Really? Why?"

"From the first moment I stepped in a library, I was in love. Even before I understood about the worlds hidden within the covers of books, I found the order was so appealing, the calm, the quiet."

"So what got in the way?"

She already felt she'd said way too much. Wasn't the natural question that might be asked *why* did she need order so badly? Calm? Quiet?

She was not sharing the hard fact that life got in the way of her dream. A degree in library arts was as far away for her as a trip to the moon. Mrs. Michael's School of Business had been a bad enough budget stretcher, never mind a real live university.

But she wasn't sharing any of that with Liam.

"It's a dangerous field," she said, and then she leaned in and whispered to him, "Men have fantasies about librarians."

It was uncharacteristically bold, but who wanted to be seen as uptight all the time? Besides, there was something about wearing a fur-lined aviator cap that gave her the courage to step out of her self-imposed mold.

Liam reared back from her, stunned. And then he shouted with laughter.

"They do, indeed," he said. "Just ask the waiter from last night."

"Why would he have thought I was a librarian?"

"Not a librarian, precisely. The *type*."

"What type is that?"

"You know. Glasses. Hand-knit sweater, don't-mess-with-me bun."

Since that was *exactly* the fade-into-the-background look she'd been trying for, why was she slightly offended?

"But I think people suspect there is a layer to you that you keep hidden. And it intrigues."

That was somehow both reassuring that she wasn't a complete frump, and at the very same time, hit too close to home.

She took off the shirt and the hat. "I suppose we'd better find something more suitable," she said.

A half hour later, purchases wrapped in brown paper, Liam insisting on carrying them, they made their way back to the hotel.

"I'll knock on your door in, what, half an hour? Is that enough time?"

When the knock came to her door, she opened it and Liam was standing there looking not like himself at all in jeans and a button-down shirt rolled up at the sleeves. His hair was still wet from the shower.

She was wearing the casual slacks and blouse she had bought. Against her better judgment, she had let her hair down, and she was glad she had because of the way his gaze lingered there for a moment.

The only other time she'd seen Liam casual was a week ago, in his pajamas.

It occurred to her that his charisma, that aura of confidence he carried himself with, had nothing to do with thousand-dollar suits.

It still oozed off him even when he wore very casual jeans.

And he was eating chocolate. Eating chocolate was a very sexy look on him.

"Did you get some of this?" he asked.

"No."

"You have to try it. I wonder why you didn't get any? There was a basket of it in my room."

See? She did have secrets, and maybe more of them than she wanted.

But this one delighted her. That she gave him secret gifts and he had no idea they were from her.

"Let's go get some dinner," he said.

"You're ruining yours with chocolate."

"There's something you need to know about life. Chocolate does not ever ruin anything."

He broke her off a piece and handed it to her. She popped it in her mouth. It was exquisite. It felt oddly and wonderfully sensual to be sharing chocolate she had secretly given him, as if it was infused with a magic potion.

That promised the most illusive thing of all. The thing money could not buy.

Happiness.

Molly turned rapidly away from Liam, needing to focus on anything but how something so simple as a shared piece of chocolate could turn into an enchantment.

"I'll just grab some of the guidebooks in the room. Over dinner we can figure out an itinerary for tomorrow."

"No," he said. "Absolutely not. No plan."

She turned back to him. "No plan?" she asked, nervously. Really, for her it was like saying no life jacket as you boarded a rickety ship.

"Sunday! That's what you do all day every day. Let's be spontaneous. Let's just do whatever comes up and whatever we feel like doing. Let your hair down."

He didn't mean it literally, of course, but his eyes did go to her hair.

"Which I see you've already done," he said.

She wished she hadn't, because for a heated moment, she could imagine his hands in her hair, loosening the pins...

She bit her lip. Letting her hair down, figuratively or literally, seemed downright dangerous.

She could have easily gone back to the same restaurant—

oh, how she loved the familiar—but Liam did not seem eager to go back there.

He had *not* been jealous of the attentions of the waiter, she told herself, but letting her thoughts go there showed the absurdity of allowing undisciplined ideas to invade your mind.

She deliberately flicked her hair over her shoulder.

"I'm in love with the duck-duck," she said. "Are you sure we shouldn't go back there?"

Something flickered in his face. The woman in her liked it. The waiter *had* brought up some feelings in him.

"They'll have it other places," Liam said smoothly. "Let's avail ourselves of as many different things as possible."

She accepted another piece of chocolate from him and let the hotel door click closed behind her. She was pretty sure his gaze flicked to her as she slowly put that piece of candy in her mouth.

So they ended up in a different restaurant, still quaint and charming, history oozing out of its thick stone walls and black-timbered roof.

The meal was exquisite. And breathtakingly expensive.

Still, when it was over, she asked the waiter for the bill.

"What are you doing?" Liam asked, astonished.

"I'm paying."

"What? No, you're not."

"I am, Liam."

"But why?" he sputtered.

"Because I'm celebrating our plus-one-iversary. And I wanted to give you something I bet you never get."

Liam stared at Molly.

It was easy to stare at her with her hair down. It was like catching a glimpse of a secret side that was mind-blowingly different from his buttoned-up assistant.

It was more like *his* Sunday that she was one hundred percent correct.

This was what he did not get, ever: someone else picking up the tab. There was an expectation, always, and particularly with women, that since he was wealthy beyond what people could imagine, he *should* pay.

He remembered her eyes sparking with tears outside the Parliament Building, and he was stunned to feel some kind of that same raw emotion clawing at him.

How had she found her way, unerringly, to his vulnerability, his weariness of people's expectations of him?

"Are you okay?" she asked with a frown.

"Yeah." He passed his hand over his eyes. "You were right," he said. "It's totally unexpected. And you were right. It never happens to me."

"I don't want you to feel used," she said, gently.

"I would never feel that from you."

"But you have felt it."

Molly. Maybe this was part of why she had become the world's best assistant. She read things. She picked up on things others did not. She was deeply, and terrifyingly, intuitive.

She saw a vulnerability in him that no one else had ever seen.

"Oh, yeah," he said. He went to get up. It was time to go. The waiter had not returned with the bill.

"I nearly married her," he said, and somehow he was sitting back down instead of getting up. Even though he begged himself not to say anything else, he just kept talking. "Her name was Charlotte. Weeby. I met her shortly after my parents died.

"I was feeling so unanchored. We may not have been the most lovey-dovey of families, but they were still my touchstone.

"I realize now I was looking for something. Looking so desperately that it blinded me. She seemed to be from a family very like mine. She came from my world. She fit in." He smiled; aware it might have a hint of bitterness in it. "She was good at spending money. Really good. My money. I was so crazy for her, she could have asked for the moon and I would have figured out a way to pull it out of the night sky for her.

"She was planning the wedding of the century. At some point, I might have registered it was unusual that her parents weren't kicking in anything. But I put it down to me being old-fashioned and continued paying the bills.

"The budget was pretty much unlimited, and she exceeded it. But it seemed to make her happy, so I was happy."

He stopped.

"And then?" Molly probed gently.

"A business associate warned me her family was on the very edge of financial ruin. They'd thrown her out to me like bait for a fish. And it had worked. I was completely hooked."

"I'm so sorry," she said.

"Foolish doesn't even begin to say how I felt at being duped. At *wanting* something so badly that I could overlook every single warning sign, every single red flag."

"And you've been wary ever since," she guessed quietly.

Again, that feeling, of being seen, of raw emotion clawing at his throat.

"Hence, you being my plus-one being so perfect," he said, trying for lightness of tone.

She smiled, not the least fooled. It was a smile of such tenderness that a man could lose himself in it.

"Hey, Sunday," he said, needing desperately to get back on familiar footing. "What was the building date of the parliament buildings?"

She told him the day they had started construction and the day they had finished.

"Are you going to remember everything they said on that tour?"

She nodded.

"Forever?"

"I'm afraid so."

"Is it a photographic memory?"

"If it has a name, I suppose that's what it is."

"When did you start noticing people were impressed by it?"

"Oh." She looked uncomfortable. "I mostly tried to hide it. I was accused of showing off. A lot."

He looked at her. The bill came, and she paid it, her tongue caught between her teeth as she figured out the tip.

"My abilities don't extend to math," she said, as if she had failed in some way. She passed the waiter the bill and her card.

He realized everybody had a secret pain that they carried, a disappointment, a stinging hurt.

And there was only one cure.

Scary as it was.

Each other.

CHAPTER FOURTEEN

LIAM FOUND HIMSELF wanting to drag out the evening, just to spend more time with her. Telling her about his failed relationship had made him realize how much he trusted her. It was a good feeling to trust someone. Heady.

He had the entirely inappropriate thought that he should ask her if she wanted to celebrate their plus-one-iversary by going dancing.

For an astonishing moment, he could picture her: letting go, her hair down, swaying in front of him.

What was he doing?

Being completely unprofessional, that's what. It was one thing to reward her for being the best assistant in the world with an extra day in Québec City.

Going dancing would be something else entirely. Inappropriate, a terrible breach of the employer/employee balance.

An erasing of some very important boundary between them.

As they walked back to the hotel through the enchantment of Old Québec, it seemed as if it was alive with romance. Where had all these young couples come from? So in love?

Or was he just in a frame of mind where he noticed those things whereas he had not so before?

Just as he could picture what she would look like dancing, he could suddenly picture his hand in hers, and *exactly* what that would feel like. Just as he steeled himself against that desire to take her hand, fate intervened.

She tripped over one of the uneven cobblestones.

He darted in front of her, catching her before she fell, righting her.

And there they stood, chest to chest, a delicate gorgeous blush rising up her cheeks, her amazing blue eyes wide on his, her scent tickling his nostrils, the streetlights casting a glow on her face and her lips and her hair.

"Oh," she said. "Sorry. Clumsy."

"It's not you," he assured her. "It's the cobblestones. Romantic, but hazardous."

Had he really called *stones* romantic? He had, but the coupling of romantic and hazardous should really provide a cautionary reminder to him that he was *not* going down that road with Sunday.

Still, he did not let go of her hand when they resumed walking. Because, he told himself, the stones *really* were hazardous and if chivalry was not dead he had an obligation to protect her.

It had nothing to do with the fact he had been one hundred percent wrong when he had foolishly thought he could imagine how her hand would feel in his.

Because how it really felt was better than anything a man could imagine. Her hand in his was a perfect fit—small, warm, soft—and yet there was unmistakable energy and strength there, too.

He let go of her hand—recognizing his own dangerous reluctance to do so—once the cobblestones were behind them. He buried his hands deep in his pockets and did not even dare to take them out to wish her a formal good night at her hotel room door.

The next morning, Molly's hair wasn't down, but it wasn't in her usual style, either. She had it in a messy bun. The change in style made him aware of how innately sexy she was, and also grateful for the fact she seemed eager to keep that part of herself under wraps.

Thankfully, Liam felt he had spent what remained of his

evening acutely aware of how alone he felt, at the same time fortifying himself with a careful review of what was and was not appropriate between an employer and his employee.

They started their day at a bakery that was not in the Old City, but that was very close to their hotel and that Molly had wanted to try. Despite his saying *no itinerary*, he was pretty sure she had spent the time after he'd dropped her off looking up the must-do's of Québec City.

"Look what it's called," she said, stopping below the sign and smiling at him as if she had prepared the best surprise in the world.

He glanced up at the sign. "Epi-Fanny," he read out loud and looked askance at her.

She laughed. "Liam! Epiphany!"

She so rarely called him by his first name. The way it made him feel when she did was an epiphany in itself.

He could feel the part of him that wanted to rigidly adhere to rules waver. And then waver some more, as he was laughing, too.

He didn't have to be uptight. He just couldn't take her hand! Still, they could just have fun. Wasn't that the idea of this extra day?

The laughter felt as if it was the foreshadowing of a perfect day, a feeling that was validated when Epi-Fanny had the most amazing display of croissants he had ever seen, including chocolate-filled ones.

They left the bakery and found Rue Saint-Louis and followed it through Porte Saint-Louis, the gate into the Upper Town of Old Québec.

Liam's concerns about what was and wasn't appropriate evaporated as they gave themselves over to exploring the twisting, hilly cobblestoned streets. They steadily made their way downward toward the Lower Town.

They went in and out of shops. They explored the Ursuline Monastery, which had been founded by a group of cloistered nuns in the 1600s. It had grown to be almost a city within the city with its churches, a school that still operated, living quarters and chapels.

In defiance of an icy wind blowing up off the St. Lawrence River, they took smiling selfies on the Promenade des Gouverneurs, the iconic copper-roofed turrets of the Fairmont le Château Frontenac soaring in the background.

From the Château, they took the steep staircases down and down again to the Lower Town and the most famous street in the Old City, the Petit-Champlain. Just off Petit-Champlain, they had French onion soup for lunch at a dark tavern, a hole in the wall, that Molly had found out was the oldest existing tavern in North America. Like so many other places, it had incredibly thick stone walls, deep sills, a roof blackened from the days the huge fireplace had worked.

"You can feel it here, can't you?" she asked with at least as much reverence as she'd had when they toured the monastery. "The crush of bodies, shouts, laughter, the drunken arguments, of so many men who would have been congregating in this city. Soldiers. Fur traders. Builders."

He could feel it, as she painted that picture. And he could *see* her so clearly. She was deep and she was sensitive, and somehow he did not want her to know how moved he was by that.

He raised an eyebrow at her. "Also the best French onion soup I've ever eaten."

She laughed, but if he had intended a light response to her serious observations to keep a comfortable distance between them, he'd miscalculated. Her laughter, and how it lit up her face and made her extraordinarily beautiful made Liam feel more connected to her, not less.

After a thorough exploration of the Lower Town, they rode the glassed-in tram that connected the upper and lower part of the Old City. Again, his sense of connection to her deepened when he realized watching her face was a complete delight as the tram emerged from its station, and a panorama unfolded one frame at a time: first the jagged, steep rooftops of the lower city, and then the wide swatch of the St. Lawrence River, a ferry chugging down it, and finally the more modern buildings that dotted the northern shore.

Molly probably would have gone down all those steps just to ride the tram again, except for the distraction of the scents coming from a gourmet popcorn shop with thrown-open windows that drew them in.

They tried samples. He, predictably, chose chocolate, even though the maple syrup and pecan was tempting. But Molly was letting her wild side out.

As they sat on a bench, he watched her happily munching on her ghost pepper and bacon flavor, noticing her hair was coming down, figuratively and literally.

But the problem was, so was his!

In the afternoon, despite legs aching from all the walking and hill climbing, Molly insisted they see the Citadelle de Québec. The National Historic Site was located atop Cap Diamant. It had sweeping views of the Old City, dominated by the Château Frontenac.

Molly told him it was known as the Gibraltar of North America. A more somber mood came over them as they took the tour of the star-shaped fortification that enclosed 300 years of history. That early history was particularly bloody.

Finally, they stood on the windswept Plains of Abraham.

"It's hard to believe," Molly said. "It's so peaceful now."

Indeed, it was a sweeping and beautifully maintained park, where people walked the curving paved pathways with their dogs.

But from the look on Molly's face, she did not see the people walking their dogs. As in the tavern she was connecting with something else. She saw young soldiers hunched against the same cold wind that blew now, filled with the terror of young men who did not know they were part of history in the making.

The battle that occurred here shaped the future of Canada and changed the course of history for all North America.

She drew in a deep breath.

"Hey, are you okay?" he said, as she turned her face away from him.

Her shoulders were shaking.

"What's wrong?" he asked. He found himself, despite his resolve to have a no-contact kind of day, touching her shoulder.

"I'm not sure. This ground," she said, her voice tremulous. "This beautiful place was fertilized with the blood of young men. It's still here, right below the surface."

As she had been on the Parliament steps, Molly was embarrassed by her emotion. She swiped her eyes with her sleeve. But it seemed as if the more she tried not to cry, the more unable to control it she was.

They had squeezed so much into today. He thought they had probably walked close to twenty miles.

She was exhausted, obviously. He wasn't aware how high her guards were until he saw this.

He saw that her exterior of calm control—the person who knew so much and could fix anything—protected her from a world that could be callous and hard.

Liam saw how very sensitive Molly was.

He felt as if he *saw* her. Completely.

Just as she had seen him yesterday, when she had paid for the evening meal at the restaurant.

He stepped into her, wrapped his arms around her, pulled her into his chest. He wanted her to know he accepted her exactly as she was.

Maybe even cherished this rare look into another person's soul.

As if she understood the message that needed no words, she gave herself over to him, her weight sinking against his, her sobs silent, but heaving her whole body.

He could feel the warmth coming off her as she melted into him, could feel her soft curves against his own hard lines.

It felt perfect, just as holding her hand had.

He was aware there were some things money could not buy.

A person revealing their authentic selves. Opportunities to stand in the light of someone else's trust.

Holding Molly, Liam felt he had never been more of a man than he was in that moment.

Molly had grown up in an *I'll give you something to cry about* world. She'd gotten more and more proficient at hiding her sensitivity.

So what had gotten into her? You could not *cry* in front of your boss! And yet she had done it, not once, but twice, in less than twenty-four hours!

Her outburst of emotion on the Plains of Abraham had taken her completely off guard.

But not as off guard as Liam's reaction.

With his arms wrapped solidly around her, and her nose pressed against his chest, her tears wetting his shirt, she felt the way she had felt when she had fallen asleep in his apartment. Safe.

Only this was a deeper kind of safety. Because she had revealed something about herself that she had always thought was a weakness.

And instead of feeling mocked for it—as she always had been in the past—when his arms folded around her, she felt something she was not entirely sure she had ever felt before. *Cherished.*

That feeling of being cherished only deepened as they left Québec City. On board the plane, he gestured to the bedroom.

"You take it," he said.

"Oh, I can't."

But he gave her a look that brooked no argument, and she found herself in a deeply comfortable bed. Even though the linens were fresh, she was certain she could catch the aroma of him.

Lying in his bed was nearly as wonderful as being held in his embrace. Tomorrow, she told herself firmly, everything would go back to normal.

She would be back in her little apartment, back in her office where everything would be under her control again.

Where her desire to keep her love for her boss secret would not be tested over and over and over.

He woke her up gently as they approached New York. Molly sat at the airplane window watching the lights of the city, clinging to the fairy tale she had lived for just a while longer.

Then Liam was putting her in a car.

"Got your keys?" he teased.

Oh, how she wished she didn't! See? There was that greedy part that had had a taste of good things and now wanted them to go on endlessly.

Well, she had the rest of the weekend to get herself together. To marshal her resources and rebuild her walls.

She thought she had succeeded.

She had even managed to get the remainder of the false eyelashes off by the time she was at her desk Monday morning.

She had worn her dowdiest suit. She had scraped back her hair in her sternest bun. She was determined to put the magic behind her.

But her every vow disintegrated when Liam appeared at her desk.

"I've had this idea," he said.

"Yes, chief?"

"Could you be my plus-one forever?"

CHAPTER FIFTEEN

MY PLUS-ONE FOREVER. Molly felt as if she was going to melt into the earth. What was Liam saying? What was he asking? Her imagination went wild, as her heart went mad, beating so hard and fast she thought he might be able to see it.

"It wouldn't be that onerous," Liam promised.

She came back to earth with a thud. Oh. Of course, her boss was just suggesting a continuation of the arrangement they already had.

He was wrong about it not being onerous, of course. While that might be true for others, there was some complexity to Molly's situation. First of all, she was in love with her boss.

It might be just a bit *onerous* keeping that under wraps.

"It would be the odd outing that required a companion," Liam said, rushing into her silence. "For instance, the CEO of Blue Cloud and his wife have asked me to join them for dinner and an NHL playoff game next weekend. Second Chances has asked me to come to the opening of their new location. There's a cocktail party for Hamish Peterson's birthday coming up. That kind of thing."

Just like in Québec City, all those outings would require her leaving the comfortable fortress of her office, where it was relatively easy to keep the defenses in place.

Plus, there was that thing Liam didn't know. She was a poor girl from the wrong side of the tracks.

She didn't even know which fork to use if there were options.

And he wanted her to sit across the table from some of the most successful and sophisticated people in the world and hold her own?

"Of course, I'd make sure you were compensated for the extra hours."

That confirmed that for Liam, this was strictly a business transaction.

"And you could have a clothing budget. I mean, the New York Friends of the Hudson Charity Gala is coming up at Grand Ballroom at the Manhattan Center. I know the kinds of things women wear to balls."

"A ball?" she said, weakly. *Like Cinderella?*

"It's one of the biggest events on the New York social calendar. Fundraiser. Red carpet."

To avoid looking at him, Molly opened his schedule on her computer.

"You've already asked Leanne Doherty," she said. Leanne Doherty was a pop star who could fill a stadium with tens of thousands of screaming fans. "I have it all here. Corsage already ordered—"

"I'll speak to her," he said. "She won't care."

Molly considered that. *She* was being chosen over Leanne Doherty.

It would be easy to be swept away by all this. What he was suggesting was downright dangerous. To her heart! To her composure! To her career! Deciding to say yes to this could have truly disastrous consequences to the cozy, safe life she was building for herself.

That safe, cozy life reminded her of the circumstances she was trying to leave behind, but she still had obligations. She had to try and help her brother as much as she could. How could she, in good conscience, say no to the extra money?

Molly told herself *that* was the nudge, and not the fact she could not resist the opportunity to spend more time with Liam.

At a ball, something within her sighed.

She tried, one last time, to be rational. Nothing about her life had prepared her to step into Liam's world in any capacity other than as his very competent assistant.

On the other hand, people could learn anything, couldn't they? Look at how she had taken to being his executive assistant, as if she'd been born to do this job.

How could she say no, especially given how pleadingly he was looking at her, as if she, and she alone, could save him from a horrible fate, like death by firing squad?

"I guess we could give it a try," she said, uneasily.

"I knew I could count on you, Sunday. Here."

She stared down at what he had given her. It was a gold credit card with the company name on it.

"Why don't you go see Christopher?" he suggested.

Molly felt a wave of relief. Christopher was *exactly* the person she needed to see.

Christopher greeted her like a long-lost friend. He actually hugged her.

"How was the awards dinner?" he asked. "Was the outfit perfect?"

"Except for the shoes," she said.

"There are sacrifices involved in being beautiful."

"I need your help again." She confided in him about her upcoming challenges with her boss.

"You're making my dreams come true." He stood back and gazed at her appraisingly. "Something's different. You're glowing."

"I am? I can't think why. I mean I had a trip to Québec City."

"Québec City! I love Québec City! And was Mr. Westerhouse on that trip?"

She blushed crazily. "Nothing happened."

Well, nothing and everything, and from the look on Christopher's face, he *knew*.

"Never mind," Christopher said. "I had a little crush on him myself by the time you two left here."

She laughed at that.

But then she wasn't laughing, because Christopher said, "The question is what are you going to do about it?"

"Nothing!" she said. "It's entirely inappropriate."

"Huh. One of those girls."

"What girls?"

"The ones that don't believe they can have what they want."

"Well, I can't."

"Well, why don't we give you the look of someone who can and just see what happens?"

"I don't want you to turn me into someone else," Molly said, slowly.

"It's not like that, at all. I look at it as uncovering who you really are."

"Um, about that."

"Yes?"

"You know how you heard that accent?"

"I still hear it."

"That's who I really am. I might need a little more than a few items of clothing. I don't even know what fork to use."

"Oh," Christopher sighed. "Remember that TV show a few years ago? Where gay men took a straight guy and sorted out everything from his whiskers to his wardrobe?"

"I have no idea what you're talking about."

"Oh, dear, I'm dating myself." He laughed. "True on so many levels. The whole concept of Second Chances is exactly this—like polishing a rough stone and finding a gem underneath. Not that I think you're a rough stone, exactly. But let's see what Ramone's doing. We'll start with your hair. You want to get a man's attention? Change your hair."

"I don't want to get a man's attention," Molly protested. "I just want to be presentable."

"Nonsense. What you want is to be the absolute best you can be."

She settled in Ramone's chair.

"I remember you," he said.

"You do?"

"Of course, he does," Christopher said. "Molly! You're memorable."

Ramone took her hair out of the bun and let it cascade down around her shoulders.

"I can do anything I want?" he asked.

"Well, within—"

"Anything you want," Christopher interrupted her.

Ramone put a band around her hair, took out a pair of scissors and cut it off. He held up the hank to her shocked eyes.

"Look!" he said, pleased. "Enough to donate to a wig-making charity."

And then he went to work with his scissors, and when he was done, Molly stared at herself stunned.

Her hair fell in a thick, gorgeous, healthy wave to her shoulders. She was not sure what technique he had used, but her hair swung every single time she moved. It framed her face in a way that made her feel as if she had a brand-new face.

But he wasn't done. He tut-tutted over her removed eyelashes, and carefully applied new ones. And then he got out his makeup kit and *taught* her.

"See how a line here makes your cheeks hollow out? You see how this makes your lips look fuller? You see how you can make your eyes look twice as large?"

When he was done, she stared at herself.

"And these?" Ramone said, picking up her glasses off his counter. "Belong right here." And he tossed them in his trash can!

Molly looked at her reflection. It was exactly as Christopher had promised. It was the best of her. It was the best she could be. She did look ready to accompany Liam Westerhouse anywhere!

Christopher whistled his complete satisfaction and then whisked her out of the chair into the clothing part of the boutique.

In seconds, Molly was wearing a pair of calf-length black trousers that she thought might be a little too tight.

"No, no, they show off your ass-etts," Christopher said happily. He coupled the trousers with a gorgeous tailored pale pink blouse, silk, and thankfully the shirttails drifted down over her ass-etts!

"Buttoned up like this for day, buttoned down like this, with this scarf, for night. Ta-da! And then these!" He dangled a pair of stilettos from his fingers.

"No!"

"Just try them," he wheedled.

So, she did.

"Worth any kind of pain?" he asked her.

And, of course, they were.

He helped her choose several more outfits that could go from office to evening wear. All of them had the most subtle hint of sexy to them, almost as if highlighting her ass-etts was completely accidental.

"There's going to be a ball, too," she told him. "We're going to attend the Friends of the Hudson Charity Gala."

"Oh," Christopher breathed. "I've always wanted to be someone's fairy godmother—"

He waited for her to laugh, and she did.

"And you get to be my Cinderella!"

Molly laughed again. Somehow, he was making this so much fun.

"I'll source out the perfect dress. Oh, I can't wait to start looking."

"I liked that bronze one I tried on before."

"How exciting this is! The bronze dress was perfection."

She felt herself gulp at the enormity of the challenge she was taking on by stepping into Liam's world. On the other hand, she was nothing if not an overachiever.

And she wasn't going to just be content to be Liam's plus-one. With Christopher's coaching, even if it was a charade, she planned on being the best plus-one in the world!

Taking on this new role was terrifying, and yet there was no denying it was exciting, too. But the thing was, it was a *role*, a part she was playing: worthy companion.

And yet, somehow, being a worthy companion to Liam felt the same as being responsible for his chocolates and buying him dinner that night.

She wanted to do it, and she wanted to do it perfectly, like a secret gift to him.

But it didn't hurt her confidence one single bit that she looked so sophisticated, sexy, beautiful.

"Act as if you deserve anything you want in the whole world," Christopher advised. He looked at his watch. "Oh, closing time. Let's go have dinner. I want to know every single thing about you."

Well, maybe not everything, she thought, but still she accepted his invitation, and he began, gently and sweetly, coaching her on which fork to use.

They had the most pleasant evening together, and he walked her to the subway after.

"You own it!" he called after her.

She swished her hips playfully at him.

"Just like that!"

She wore the narrow trousers and the pink blouse into the office the next day. She applied makeup the way Ramone had showed her.

She wore the shoes!

"Hey, Sunday—" Liam came through the door as she was standing at the filing cabinet.

She turned toward him. "Morning, chief."

He stopped in his tracks. He visibly gulped. "What have you done to your—" his eyes swept her "—your hair?" he croaked weakly.

"Oh, it's just a haircut." She owned it by giving her head

the most subtle shake. Her hair cascaded over her shoulders. And then, she *owned* it walking by him to her desk and putting just the tiniest swish in her hips.

She sat at her desk.

She glanced up at him.

Bingo.

Except that Liam seemed to avoid the office after that! Or maybe she was imagining things. He did have a very busy schedule. He was around ravishingly beautiful women all the time. He wouldn't be afraid of that, would he?

The new look would be a colossal backfire if her boss started avoiding her because of it.

She insisted on meeting Liam downtown for the dinner and hockey game, as she didn't want him picking her up at her very humble house.

Christopher had coached the outfit, and she was dressed in comfortable shoes, for once, go-anywhere snug jeans, a button-down silk shirt and a jacket. Liam was standing outside the restaurant waiting when she arrived. Her awareness of him—he was gorgeous, even in a ball cap and casual slacks—was sharpened by his absence from the office this week.

She scanned his face, worried that things were changed between them, but no, there was that easy grin, as he came forward.

It faltered for just a moment as he took her in, and her heart stopped for a moment, as he seemed to contemplate the appropriate greeting. She hoped, foolishly, of course, for even the most casual kiss on the cheek, and he seemed to be thinking about it, but instead, he put his hands in his pockets and rocked back on his heels.

"Sunday! Have you been brushing up on all things hockey?"

"I focused more on Blue Cloud."

He laughed. "Of course you did." And then he was holding open the door for her, and his hand touched the small of her back for one delicious moment as he guided her in.

She was glad for her research as she met Grant Purdue and his wife, Katherine. As it turned out, the CEO's favorite topic was his business, so any awkwardness she felt was soon erased by the fact Mr. Purdue had the single-mindedness and focus of many extremely successful people. As in Québec, she enjoyed seeing Liam in this setting, comfortable, at ease, gracious, asking all the right questions, thinking of ways to involve Katherine in the conversation.

The hockey game was loud and boisterous and Molly was soon genuinely engrossed, not so much in the game, as in Liam's response to it. Again, she was seeing a different side of Liam—so enthused about *his* team—and she loved this glimpse into yet another side of him, a kind of boyish, playful side.

As the crowds thinned in front of Madison Square Garden, the Purdues grabbed a cab and she and Liam saw them off.

"How was that for you?" Liam asked, when they were gone.

"It was fine. I had fun, actually."

"Did you?" He was watching her closely.

"Didn't you?" she asked, startled. *What had she done wrong?*

He sighed. "I grew up with people like that. I find them very tiresome."

"Oh." She was relieved it was *them*, not *her*. "But you were so charming!"

"Was I?" His mouth quirked upward, and she felt herself blushing that she had noticed that about him, but hardly anything about their companions.

"I grew up with that," he said, quietly, and she realized she was being entrusted with a confidence. "I grew up with women who had to let you know, in the first five minutes of meeting them, that they had a Hermès purse, worth half a million dollars—"

Molly gasped. "Her purse was worth that?"

"Oh, of course, she didn't say, precisely. But when she told the little story about Grant being shocked at the price of it, you were supposed to *know*. Grant is not the kind of guy who would be shocked at the price of anything."

She couldn't help herself. She giggled. She was pretty sure it was some kind of shock, herself. "Sorry, chief, next time I'll research Hermès handbags. Half a million? Seriously?"

"Seriously."

"She brought a bag like that to a hockey game?"

"She did."

"But where was the bodyguard?"

They both chuckled over that, but then she became serious.

"You know I'm out of my league, don't you?" she whispered.

"Ah, Molly," he said, "that was my world. One where people decided whether or not they liked you based on what you had, not on who you were."

She saw that Liam was not so much being critical of the Purdues as telling her something about his world, sharing a confidence with her.

"It must have been very lonely for you, growing up like that," she told him softly. "Being genuine in a world that isn't."

He smiled at her, a man who had been seen. He said, softly, "I can't tell you how refreshing I find you, Molly. How real. I was watching you watch the hockey game."

So, they'd been watching each other watch the hockey game.

It was a silly thing to do, but she'd done it once before, and she could not resist, now, even if it jeopardized everything.

She stood on her tiptoes. Her intention was to brush her lips against his cheek, just as she had before. A quick thank-you. A quick, *I see you, Liam*.

But somehow, he turned his head, at exactly the wrong moment, or the right one, depending on how she looked at it.

And she tasted the cool softness of his lips. He didn't pull away from her. He tasted hers.

The whole world felt as if it shifted on its axis.

He pulled away from her, startled. He looked as though he might apologize, but he hesitated just long enough for her to say, "I'm going to grab a cab, Liam."

"I'll call a car."

"No, I'm fine."

And then she was dashing away from him. When she glanced over her shoulder, for a moment it looked as if he would follow.

Instead, his expression pensive, he watched from a safe distance as she got in the cab and it pulled away.

Over the next while, she joined Liam for half a dozen small engagements: cocktails with associates, an opening for one client, and a product launch for another, a lunch program charity event.

At first, she was worried questions about her were bound to be asked, not just by the new people that she was meeting but by Liam.

But she quickly found that most people, like Mr. Purdue, found the topic of themselves quite fascinating, and she became adept at deflecting curiosity about herself.

With Liam it was harder, because he was genuinely interested, so she developed a strategy of answering his questions with anecdotes that usually involved books.

Where was she from? A small town in Louisiana that had the *best* library. And then, without naming the town or its dreary circumstances, she'd described the first book series she ever read, *Freddy the Pig*. She had tossed in a full description of Mrs. Deverille and he would seem enchanted, and unaware she had really told him nothing at all.

Had she had a pet growing up? Of course she hadn't had a pet! The family could barely feed themselves. But she had told Liam only about a book, *Because of Winn-Dixie*, that was almost as good as having a pet.

Did she remember who she had gone to senior prom with? Oh, she hadn't gone to senior prom (never mind no money for the dress) because she'd been reading *Wuthering Heights* at the time, and she had found Heathcliff far more fascinating than any of the boys she could have gone to prom with.

"Heathcliff, huh?" Liam had responded, and they'd both laughed.

They didn't kiss again, but it was there between them, a sizzling temptation that sharpened everything—a glance, an accidental touch of a hand, a shared laugh.

As she navigated people's questions, and all the new environments she found herself in, Molly could feel her confidence blossoming. For the first time in her life she felt a growing ease in social situations.

Of course, she had a secret weapon.

It would be easy to say it was her very own fairy godmother, Christopher. He provided her with the most dynamite wardrobe and fashion advice that any fake plus-one had ever had. Whether she said her duties would entail a hockey game or an opera, Christopher always had the perfect solution.

Christopher had taken her completely under his wing.

She didn't even know how she had longed for this her whole life until she had it.

Christopher became her friend. And her confidante.

But it wasn't Christopher's influence that was building her sense of herself. It wasn't that at all.

It was the way her boss looked at her, especially when he thought she wasn't looking. It was the surge of energy she felt when they accidentally touched. It was the sense of *knowing* him on newer and deeper levels.

It was a life tingling with potential.

With dangerous, wonderful, terrifying, amazing possibility.

CHAPTER SIXTEEN

LIAM WATCHED MOLLY against the dazzling backdrop of the Metropolitan Opera House. He was aware that ever since Québec City, a door had opened in her, and as they spent more and more time together in so many different situations, she was stepping through that open door. With a new verve and a new confidence.

It wasn't just the new haircut, the lack of eyeglasses, the way she was wearing her makeup.

It wasn't just the new wardrobe—and he wasn't sure if he was happy or sad that all those wonderfully frumpy grandmother sweaters had been dumped.

No, it was in the way she moved.

And the light in her eyes.

There was a compelling new confidence in her, and he couldn't help but notice that it seemed to grow every time she was his plus-one.

Suddenly New York seemed very much like his Québec City experience with her, though, of course, the two cities could not be more different.

Québec was quaint and enchanting. New York was high energy, glamorous, sophisticated. And yet the sense of discovery was the same: as if he was seeing his hometown in a brand-new and exciting way now that he was exploring it with Molly.

He had been going to the Lincoln Center for the Performing Arts since he was a child. In the Lincoln Square neighborhood on the Upper West Side of Manhattan, it was a sixteen-acre property that housed over thirty indoor and outdoor facilities, and hosted five million visitors a year.

But now, attending the performance of *La Bohème* at the Metropolitan Opera House with clients, it felt as if he was seeing the utterly magnificent building for the very first time.

He cast a glance at his plus-one. He was fairly certain that was the same black dress she'd worn to the awards night, but even that looked different on her tonight than it had before because of the new way in which she carried herself.

"Those aren't the same shoes, are they?" he asked, in an aside after he'd introduced her to the clients. "Am I going to be piggybacking you home?"

"Well, I hoped," she teased him.

When he'd told her about this event, she said she'd never been to an opera before. He thought she might be bored with it, but from the first moment she was the perfect plus-one. She engaged with the couple they were with; she had—of course—done her homework on both of them. She probably had a file on her phone named *Rod and Belinda Miles*.

There was no dress code, so every style was there, from people who were casual in jeans, to people in the very best designer clothes money could buy.

And he saw Molly could hold her own against any of them! This thought that Molly could fit in anywhere was reinforced by her interaction with the clients, a lovely older couple from England.

He watched her with them. They were totally charmed. She was so genuinely interested in their lives, curious about the details of where they lived.

Rod was regaling with her a tale about a very bad pony named Henry, and then she and Belinda were commenting on the dresses other women were wearing, heads together, as if they had been best friends since high school.

They entered the theatre and found their seats and Liam was aware of loving the curiosity she brought to it. The wonder.

Of course, she had done her homework on the opera, too, and was sitting forward in her seat, with that earnest expression he had come to love.

Once the performance began, the earnestness dissipated, and Molly was absolutely entranced. Liam found himself watching her face more than the opera. During *O soave fanciulla*, the duet between the poet, Rodolfo, and seamstress, Mimi, in Act I, she was rapt, her face soft with longing as the two protagonists fell in love.

By Act IV, where Mimi succumbs to tuberculosis, Molly was crying, silently, huge tears slithering down her cheeks.

He put his arm over her shoulder and gave it a squeeze.

But somehow his arm remained there.

And then the realization struck him.

It wasn't Molly who had changed since Québec. No, her appearance might have changed, and certainly she seemed more confident, but the essence of her was unchanged. Solid, funny, sensitive, thrifty, reliable, brilliant.

It was he who had changed.

She had opened his heart in ways it had never been opened before. For the first time since Charlotte, he felt trust.

He thought back over the last few weeks.

Molly had always been smart and that shone through, still, but now some of the reserve she'd always had was retreating.

Liam had noticed the benefits of their outings with her as his plus-one were spilling over into the office.

The feeling that they *knew* each other just kept growing. They had lively discussions about so many different things.

His sense of respecting her, and seeing her completely as his equal, kept deepening. Sometimes they completed each other's sentences.

But if comfort was increasing at one level of their relationship, he was also aware tension was running on a parallel track.

An awareness of each other sizzled right below the surface.

A tension that was stoked by the little intimacies that were necessary to a successful plus-one relationship.

Him taking her hand to help her out of a car.

Or putting his hand on her back to guide her through a doorway.

The way their eyes met when someone was speaking, and the same thought occurred to them at the same time.

The opera was over. Liam helped Molly put her jacket back on, watched as she pulled her hair out from under it, and it cascaded in a rich wave around her shoulders. She looked at him and smiled, and he could still see the tears sparking in her eyes.

The truth hit him like a shock from an electrical wire. He could feel its power staggering him.

"What?" Molly, ever sensitive, asked, as he put his hand on her back and guided her out of the crush of people.

He had never been more grateful than when the couple they were with begged off, and got in a cab back to their hotel.

"You know what day it is today?" he asked Molly, as people leaving the opera flowed around them, as if they were an island in a sea.

"Day?" She cocked her head at him.

"It's another of our plus-one-iversaries. Four weeks today since you officially became my plus-one."

She laughed.

That laugh. When had it come to be the music he lived for, the sound he wanted to hear…the word blasted, shockingly, through his brain—

Forever.

The truth was, he was in love with her. He could no longer imagine a life without Molly in it.

"You can't have an anniversary every week. It derives from the Latin *annus*—"

"I love it when you talk dirty," he teased her and was rewarded with a little smack on his arm.

"Which means year, not week or month."

"Well, I happened to know that, which is why I avoided calling it an *anni*versary, and called it a plus-one-iversary instead."

This was a complete lie, of course, and she seemed to know it. Still, he thought, you could celebrate the gifts life had given you every single week. Every single day. Every single hour.

Maybe it was just the power of the opera still with him: its poignant reminder of the power of love, but also the reminder of the fragility of life.

He could have argued with her about whether or not you could have a *versary* of some sort every week, but suddenly words seemed too small to say what he wanted to say.

Instead, he kissed her. As soon as he tasted the sweetness of her lips, he knew he had waited his whole life for this moment.

And everything she was was in the way she kissed him back.

"I'm going to call Paul," he said, unsteadily, reeling from the power, the invitation, the total giving of herself in the way she kissed him back.

"I have a better idea," she said.

He had never quite heard that tone in her voice: sultry, sexy, pure feminine sensuality.

She leaned into him; her hand squeezed his arm as she stood on her tiptoes and whispered in his ear.

"My feet hurt."

"Would you please throw those shoes in the garbage?" he whispered, hoarsely.

"Oh, no," she said. "Because how else would I get you to carry me home?"

Home.

She slipped off her shoes, and he turned his back to her. The crowds had largely dispersed now, not that it mattered.

It felt as if he and Molly were all alone in the world.

She climbed onto his back. He could feel the strength in her legs as she wrapped them around his waist.

He snugged his arms around her calves, felt her own arms around his neck, the sweet crush of her curves against his back.

If he had hoped that carrying her would dispel some of the energy throbbing within him—and her—he'd totally miscalculated.

By the time he reached his building and set her on the ground, it was obvious they were both nearly on fire with need.

That thing that had been crackling in the air between them had suddenly burst into flames.

This was what happened, he thought, when you tried to ignore the warnings; the snapping and crackling of dangerous things needed to be addressed *before* it *became* something that was out of control. A plan needed to be in place before the full power of the storm struck.

He knew that. He'd been fixing things his entire life.

Too late, a voice in him whispered. Much too late now.

Because there was a place in every man where logic no longer served. There was a place in every man where nature overcame reason. There was a place in every man where the exquisite madness of the moment overcame the need to have plans and contingency plans and backup plans and projection plans.

There was a place in every man that was absolutely powerless against the forces that were enveloping him.

There was no point in fighting.

"Good evening, sir. Miss."

For some reason, it was Mike's greeting that snapped him out of the spell he'd been under. Had he really thought he could bring her home? And what? Sneak her into his bedroom like a teenage boy sneaking in his prom date?

What would Maria think?

She'd practically raised him. She would expect him to be a better man.

He expected himself to be a better man!

He could not have Molly thinking he would take advantage

of his position. They talked so easily together, but this was one conversation they had not had.

He needed to broach it with her. He needed her to know he could not rush blindly into an intimate encounter with her, driven by lust.

He needed her to know he respected her, completely, and that he knew who she was. Newly confident, yes, but his old Sunday was also there, right beneath the surface. Careful. Responsible. Dependable.

He could not live with himself if he did anything to jeopardize the way she felt, not about him, but about herself.

Liam didn't feel as if he should just begin this very serious conversation that needed to happen between them out of the blue, without thinking carefully about his long-range plans.

"Mike, would you have Paul bring the car around? Molly needs a ride home."

She looked, understandably, stunned. She wouldn't look at him as she put her shoes back on. All that confidence was draining out of her like water swirling around the drain in a tub.

"Molly." There was so much to say. He needed to reassure her.

"Please don't say anything," she whispered.

"Look, I'm your employer. There's an imbalance of power. It's—"

She turned to him, her eyes flashing. "I asked you not to say anything."

Her fury was better—so much better—than the defeated look of seconds ago. And yet it also showed him the pure passion, the fieriness that was right there, below that calm surface.

He could have changed his mind, right there.

He wanted to throw rational thought to the wind, scoop her up in his arms, draw that passion from her, unleash it.

Thankfully, the car drew up before he gave into the temptation.

Did he kiss her goodnight? Wasn't that the exact question

he'd hoped to avoid when he'd come up with the brilliant, superflawed idea that Molly would make the perfect plus-one?

He didn't have to make the decision, because Molly cast him a look so heated he was rather stunned to find he was still intact—not a little pile of ash—as the car pulled silently away.

He'd done the right thing.

Why did he feel so terrible?

Because she hadn't felt saved. She felt rejected.

Liam had messed up, and he knew it. He'd hurt the person he least wanted to hurt in the whole world.

Look, buddy, he told himself as he got on the elevator, feeling as lonely as he'd ever felt—and he had felt plenty lonely in his life—*you better figure out what you want. Pronto.*

He couldn't sleep. He paced his room.

He thought over that stunning discovery he'd made as he had helped her put on her jacket tonight.

It was true. Liam was head over heels in love with his plus-one. He couldn't imagine his life without Molly. It felt as if it would be a landscape bereft of joy and meaning, desolate, lonely, hopeless.

He texted her.

Somehow he had to let her know.

He opened the conversation with, Hey, hope you're home safe. Thinking of you.

She did not respond.

He could feel his whole body tensing, waiting for her to say something, anything, but the minutes ticked by, and she didn't.

Annoyed with himself, he shut off his phone.

And then threw it across the room.

He stood at the window and considered his options. No, *their* options. Had she been thinking of this, too? She was brilliant. She had to know she couldn't keep working for him under these circumstances.

He wondered what her preference would be. A transfer to another department while he courted her? On the other hand, as CEO of the company, no matter which department she worked in, he had authority over her.

Of course, he had a million connections in the business world. If she wanted, he could put all of those at her disposal, so that she could choose a job at a different company while their courtship unfolded.

And yet, as he considered those options, he felt the emptiness, already, of not seeing her every day, of her not being a part of every decision, everything that unfolded at work.

He turned from the window, deep in thought.

He had made the right choice tonight; of that he was certain. There was, and always had been, an innocence about her.

He had not spoken one word of commitment to her, and he'd nearly taken her to his bed.

Really? What did that amount to? A tawdry office affair, leaving both of them without honor.

He needed to slow this train down.

But even as he thought that, he wondered if it wasn't too late.

CHAPTER SEVENTEEN

"AND THEN he kissed me," Molly whispered to Christopher, who had just met her for lunch.

"He kissed you or you kissed him?"

"Christopher. Kissing is kind of a mutual thing!"

"I want to know who instigated it."

"Well, he did. But I'm the one who took it entirely the wrong way."

"How can you take a kiss the wrong way?"

"Oh! I threw myself at him. I invited myself back to his place. I behaved like a completely wanton tramp."

"Stop it!" Christopher warned her sternly.

"Anyway, in front of his building he came to his senses, and he called a car and sent me home. Rejected me. And now he hasn't been at work all week."

"So, he's had a change in schedule."

"I keep his schedules!"

"You need to see this differently."

"There is no way to see it differently," Molly said, glumly. "I came on to my boss. He rejected me. It's so humiliating."

"Molly," Christopher said, gently, "he did the right thing. You know that, don't you?"

"No," she wailed, "I don't."

"In a world where honor has become an old-fashioned word, he behaved honorably."

"I'm quitting my job," she said. "I can't face him."

"No, you are not quitting your job," Christopher said. "And yes, you can face him. Don't you dare back up. Don't you dare go back into hiding. You go after what you want."

"But I want him," she whispered.

"Exactly."

"And he doesn't want me."

Christopher snorted. "Not wanting you and behaving honorably are two entirely different things."

Molly contemplated that. Could she interpret Liam's behavior as chivalrous, rather than rejection? It was true—she had seen, over and over again—that he had qualities of honor and decency.

"Christopher," she said, slowly, "are you suggesting it's my turn to take charge? To let Liam know he's not the boss in all areas, and he's not going to call the shots?"

"See? What a bright girl you are!"

"He hasn't cancelled the gala," she said, pensively. "I could make *my* intentions known."

Christopher gave her an approving grin. "We need to change directions with the dress."

"But I love that bronze dress."

"Well, yes, it's very pretty, in a kind of princess-style way, but you don't want the gown of an innocent young girl all starry-eyed to be at the ball. You want the dress of a mature woman who knows exactly what she wants and how to get it. A dress a man, no matter how formidable his discipline is, is not going to be able to say no to."

"No such dress exists," she said, though she did have to admit what he was describing was exactly what she wanted.

In fact, it felt as if the ball was going to be the moment that all this plus-one stuff had been leading to all along.

"I'm sure I saw that exact dress in a window on my way here. Call in sick," he said. "We're going dress shopping."

Molly had never called in sick a day in her life. But Liam wasn't at the office anyway.

"Okay," she said.

She let Christopher guide her down Fifth Avenue. It was hard not to be intimidated. Saks, Tiffany & Co., Bergdorf Goodman, Swarovski, Harry Winston…

And then they were standing at the window, looking at *the* dress.

She could see why it had caught Christopher's attention. Floor-length, a formfitting solid mossy green overjacket, with wide lapels and three-quarter sleeves, was buttoned at the waist, but then flared open, framing an even more formfitting, floor-length underdress.

The fabric of the sleek underdress was the same as the jacket, but only glimpses of it could be seen. Woven on top of it were embossed vines and subtly glittering flowers in an array of subtle shades—blues, darker greens, turquoises, whites.

"That is the most stunning dress I've ever seen," she breathed.

"Exactly," Christopher said.

She gulped as she looked up at the name on the store. Even in the sea of exclusivity that was Fifth Avenue, that name stood out.

"I can't afford anything in here," she told Christopher, balking as he held open the door.

"Nonsense. You have a clothing budget."

This was true. In fact, Liam had specifically mentioned this event when he'd given her that credit card for clothing purchases.

But somehow she didn't want Liam paying for the dress whose sole purpose was to overcome his reluctance and seduce him.

She went through the door Christopher held open. She looked around. She felt sick. This was not the kind of place she belonged. She turned to leave.

Christopher's hand stopped her.

"You walk in here as if you own the place," he told her quietly. "You walk in here a woman one hundred percent worthy of anything they have. Because you are."

She realized there was an underlying message here. It wasn't just about being worthy of the dress.

It was about being worthy of Liam.

It was about leaving her insecurities behind her.

As it turned out, of course Christopher knew everyone in the clothing business in New York.

She found herself being ushered into the fitting room as if she was an old friend of high standing.

She looked at the dress. A price tag was ever so subtly tucked in the sleeve. She should have been aghast.

But to her, it was more than apparent the dress was worth every penny.

"No underwear!" Christopher called.

She gulped. Of course that was true. A dress that clung like this one left no room for lines and bunched-up underwear.

Moments later, she stepped into the dress, sliding it up over her naked skin.

She was pretty sure she had never felt anything quite as sensual as the silk. She reached back. There was a nearly invisible zipper that went from below the small of her back all the way up. As she pulled it, the dress molded to her as though it had been painted on.

Christopher had to help her with the last few inches of it and with each inch that the zipper moved up, the dress became…more.

More beautiful. More fitted. More sensual.

They stepped out into the multimirrored foyer of the change area. The dress was extraordinary. The simplicity of the cut offset the embossing, which caught the light and sparked as if fire was hidden within the fabric. The dress was held up by the thinnest of spaghetti straps at her shoulders.

Oddly, she did not feel at all like a shy girl from the sticks.

She felt as if the dress had been made to bring out the woman in her.

Christopher drew in his breath. "Oh, my."

He walked around her, tucking and pulling and then sighed with absolute satisfaction. "Put on the jacket."

She did, and he buttoned it at her waist.

"Walk," he said.

She did as he asked, and the jacket flowed out and around her, floating on the air behind her, revealing only the lower part of the dress. Somehow, with the jacket, the dress was even more sexy because it whispered rather than shouted at her sensuality.

"Do you see what it does?" he asked reverently. "It hints, it compels, it begs you to take off that jacket. There's a coat check at the Grand Ballroom. You leave that jacket there. No chickening out!"

She bought the dress. And, though it was way too expensive, a beaded clutch that complemented the dress beautifully.

Within seconds of paying for her purchases, her phone pinged. She didn't even look at it. She already knew what it was.

Her credit card company warning her she'd gone over her limit. Thankfully, she'd been spared the humiliation of having her card refused.

"Should we stop at Tiffany's?" Christopher asked. "A little diamond choker?"

"I can't even afford groceries for the next month, never mind a diamond choker."

"Worth it," he said.

"Worth it," she agreed. But inside, reality was setting in. She was going to have to call Donnie's lawyer, and say she couldn't make a payment this month.

The dress in the bag straightened her spine, though.

It was okay, she told herself firmly, to put her wants ahead of those of others for once in her life. It was okay for her to have a life!

It was worth every single penny she had spent on that dress—and the missed payment to the lawyer—when she saw the look on Liam's face.

She hadn't seen him for just over a week, since last Friday's fiasco. At Christopher's insistence, he had helped her get ready at Second Chances, which was closed for the day.

Ramone had stayed late, too, and he upswept her hair, sewing a single gardenia into the sophisticated chignon he created. He did her makeup.

Then, Christopher insisted on helping her into the dress. He stood back admiring her when he was done.

"Don't cry!" she implored him.

"What kind of fairy godmother doesn't cry?"

"But if you cry, I cry…"

"Don't you dare! The makeup." He crooked his elbow and they walked together out to the front lobby of the store.

"I'll give you a few pointers while we wait," Christopher said. "So in a dress like that you walk like this."

She burst out laughing as her tall, somewhat bulky, friend walked delicately through the lobby.

"What are you laughing at? Are you missing the smoking sensuality? You do it."

Playfully, she followed his advice, adding a lot more drama than was necessary. But Christopher approved of the drama.

The odd thing was, she didn't really feel as if she was pretending; she felt as if a secret side of herself was rushing to the surface, demanding to be seen after being kept in hiding for so long.

"He's here," Christopher hissed at her, as they watched Liam's long, sleek black limo—not Liam's usual private car—draw up to the curb in front of the building.

"Okay," she said, "I'm ready, I'll go out—"

"You most certainly will not go out!" Christopher said, as if he was a protective father vetting his daughter's prom date. "You will wait right there. Mr. Westerhouse will come in for you."

Christopher positioned her in the front lobby, as if he was the maid of honor getting the bride ready at the altar. He fussed for one last second over the fall of the coat and the dress.

Liam came through the front door. Molly's awareness of him was even sharper for not having seen him for a week.

Her world shrank down to one thing. Him.

CHAPTER EIGHTEEN

LIAM WAS DRESSED FORMALLY, in a three-piece black tuxedo, the streamlined jacket closed with covered buttons. Below the bowtie, the deeper V, typical of a tux jacket, showed off the immaculate, brilliant white of a tailored shirt. The ensemble was completed with highly polished black dress shoes.

"Oh, my," Cristopher said under his breath.

Indeed, Molly thought, dressed like that and with those chiseled good looks, Liam looked like James Bond.

He'd even managed to tame his hair tonight, and it added to his look of intense sophistication, a man who would be utterly composed in any situation.

And yet, when his eyes fell on her, he did not look composed. At all.

He paused for a moment, taking her in, and then, regaining himself quickly, he crossed the floor to her, gazed down at her with the most beautiful expression she had ever seen.

Utter and totally unveiled longing.

"Molly," he said, his voice hoarse, "you look absolutely ravishing."

"Thank you," she said, and felt the deep certainty of a woman coming into herself. And not because of a dress, either. But because she knew what she wanted.

"I want to apologize for the other night. I think I may have given you the wrong impression," he said, softly.

The old Molly would have wondered if he meant he had pulled back because their feelings for each other were so different.

But the new Molly could see the truth in the way he was looking at her.

"No worries," she said. "Let's not talk about it this instant."

There. Who was in charge now?

He cocked his head at her, as he considered this new set of rules, beginning with her deciding the direction of the conversation. A little smile tickled his lips.

As if he *approved*.

"Here," he said, and put something in her hands.

She glanced down at the long, narrow velvet Tiffany box, and slowly opened the cover.

It was a diamond choker.

Her eyes flew to his.

"A little bird told me," he said, and he slipped the choker from its box, and she turned her back to him, felt the caress of his hand on her naked skin as he fastened the choker. That caress solidified her sense of being a woman, of being the one who could set what happened next in motion.

She caught Christopher's eye. He was smiling.

Own it, he mouthed.

Liam escorted her outside, waved off the chauffeur and opened the door for her himself. She had never been in a limo before.

They soon joined a long line of limos in front of the Manhattan Center. She tried not to press her nose against the window, but she was so curious about who was getting out of the cars.

One by one, those cars disgorged the elite of New York City onto the red carpet. Anybody who was anybody—actors, musicians, writers, athletes, business people—was here tonight.

Throngs of people, cell phones out, were piled deep on either side of the velvet cords and the army of security guards that held them back.

There was a formula for arriving: the car stopped, each couple went up the red carpet, sometimes stopping to greet fans. Then they paused at the top of it, smiled and waved, answered a few shouted questions from the assembled paparazzi and then went into the building.

"You know what I'm figuring out?" Molly said, as they sat in their car without moving for fifteen minutes. "Being famous makes everything take a long time."

Liam laughed.

Molly said, "Guess who just got out of the car in front of us? Mickey O'Donnelly."

"Be prepared for a really long wait then, because there's nothing that man likes more than attention."

Molly looked at Liam with surprise. He rarely said anything bad about anyone, that confidence he'd shared with her about the Purdues being the only exception she could think of.

But he was right. Careless of the cars lined up behind them, Mickey, star of a new action miniseries, greeted dozens of fans and then proceeded to hold court on the front stairs, shamelessly posing for photos, utterly ignoring the woman he was with.

But Molly was thankful for the attention he garnered. In fact, she was grateful for the whole A-list, because Liam, thankfully, barely rated in this crowd.

She was right. The frenzied paparazzi calmed as she and Liam made their way to the front entrance of the Manhattan Center. She was so grateful for those last-minute instructions on how to walk, Christopher's mouthed *own it.*

They turned at the top, and she remembered Christopher's advice. Liam's hand resting lightly on her waist gave her a boost of confidence.

"Who's your lady friend, Mr. Westerhouse?" a single voice called.

For the first time since she'd accepted this invitation, a shiver of apprehension went through her. She had wanted to draw Liam's attention tonight, and in fact she had pursued that goal with a certain singleness of focus that had excluded thoughts about how unwelcome the attention of strangers would be. She certainly didn't want the press interested enough in her to start looking for more info.

She answered. "My name is Sunday."

She could feel Liam's eyes on her, but she didn't look at him. She didn't want to see the question in them.

"Sunday?"

"Just Sunday," she said.

"Oh, a one-name thing like you think you're like Cher or Madonna."

The remark was faintly cutting, and she realized how hard a shell celebrities must have to develop. However, she thought the slight sting—and the note of dismissal that went with it— were well worth it to keep her anonymity.

She remembered Christopher's instructions, and taking a deep breath, she allowed Liam to help her out of the jacket at the coat check. There was no missing the light in his eyes sparking deeper as he took in the full, no longer subtle, sensuality of her dress.

But she had already determined the dress was not what was making her feel sensual. It was *him*. But more, it was herself, and a desire to explore the almost mystical compulsion she was feeling to have Liam know all of her.

As much as she had always dreamed of a ball, she suddenly wished them away from here. To some place quiet, and private, where they could discover, fully, the sizzling mysteries leaping in the air around them.

On the other hand, what if she was reading this all wrong? What if Liam turned her away again?

She forced herself to focus on the setting, rather than her partner, and she had to try not to gawk.

"Look at the ceiling," she breathed.

Liam's lips twitched.

"What?"

"You're surrounded by some of the most famous people in the world, and it's the ceilings that get your attention?"

"Well, speaking of getting my attention, I think that lady over there might have a Hermès bag."

He laughed, as she had hoped he would, and some of her tension dissipated.

There was to be a silent auction before the ball began, and they went around and looked at the items. Liam began to introduce her to some of those people. Only a few weeks ago, Molly might have been intimidated by this, but she found the more she met people, the more at ease she felt.

Suddenly, Mickey O'Donnelly was right in front of them.

"Liam, isn't it? Westerhouse. We've met before."

"Yes, we have," Liam said, and her eyes flew to his face at the cool note there. Mickey didn't seem to notice it at all.

He turned to her and gave her the full wattage of his famous smile. He leaned in way too close to her. She could smell the booze on his breath.

"And you are?" he asked, not giving Liam a chance to introduce her. "Besides the woman I've waited my whole life to meet?"

"I'm Sunday," she said, putting out her hand.

She was alarmed to find her whole hand enveloped in a rather large, sweaty one. Suddenly she was being yanked toward the man.

"You can be my Sunday, my Monday, my Tuesday—"

She tried to get her hand out of his. He held on tighter.

"Wednesday, Thursday…"

She was being pulled up against his massive chest.

"Let her go," Liam said.

Mickey ignored him, "Friday, Saturday…"

Suddenly Liam's hand had slipped between them and was

placed firmly on Mickey's chest. When Mickey ignored Liam's second command to let her go, he followed up with a none-too-gentle shove.

Mickey let go of her hand, and she fell away from him, gasping, feeling like a fish that had escaped back into the ocean in the nick of time.

The two men faced each other.

"How dare you?" Mickey said. And then he lunged right at Liam, his head down, like a bull charging.

Liam stepped easily out of his way, but the famous actor crashed into the waiter behind them and women screamed and glasses shattered.

Mickey turned unsteadily back to Liam. His date had his arm, pleading, but he shook her off and made another run at Liam.

This time Liam, caught by the crowd, didn't sidestep aside in time, and the two men went down on the ground, Mickey on top. Mickey proceeded to pummel Liam.

Maybe the ladies of the red carpet thought the answer to this unexpected turn of events was to shriek their dismay, but Molly had cut her teeth on drunken brawls. She was not going to stand by screaming or whimpering while Liam was being hurt.

She threw her clutch on the floor, took off one shoe and leapt onto Mickey's back. The poor zipper on her dress simply wasn't made for a wrestling match. She heard the back of it split, and then she felt a cool breeze in exactly the wrong place. But in the heat of the moment all she cared about was getting this horrible man off Liam. She hit him across the head with her shoe. He reeled back from the blow, shook her off him and then he rolled off Liam and got to his feet. He stared at her. Then offered a hand.

"Holy ker-schmole, you got a punch." He smiled crookedly, the smile he was famous for. "You can be my January, February, March…"

She ignored his hand, and Liam was up and offering his. She ignored that, too, reaching behind herself and trying to hold together her split dress.

In what moment of madness had she decided fashion overcame practicality and forgone the underwear?

In a flash, Liam took in her dilemma, whipped off his jacket and crouched down beside her, wrapping it around her.

His scent clung to the jacket, and calmed her in this sea of chaos.

As Liam helped her to her feet, and handed her her purse, there were suddenly security people everywhere. Molly noted, uneasily, every single person in the ballroom now seemed focused on the kerfuffle, and every single person had a phone out.

Although it was probably the least of her fashion problems, her hair was out of its chignon. The gardenia had fallen out, and was getting trampled by the press of people.

Liam took her elbow and ushered her, limping because she only had one shoe on, through the crush of people. It seemed every single gala attendee had their phones out.

With his other hand, Liam had his own phone out, too, and was calling for a car. He, thankfully, seemed familiar with the layout of the place, and led the way to a side exit. Finally, they were out in the fresh air.

She realized she'd dropped the shoe somewhere.

"Sunday," he said, "you can't seem to keep your shoes on."

She was grateful to him for teasing her about *that* instead of the much more obvious fact that she had just shown her fanny to the most elite gathering in New York City. Even now, she could feel a breeze, finding its way through his jacket, to her backside. She should be utterly mortified, and yet looking at him, she felt herself focusing on the strong sense of connection between them.

She felt as if she could *sail* through any challenge life presented her with, as long as Liam was by her side.

He looked at her for a long time. If she hadn't seen the absolute truth in how he felt about her in his torn shirt and with bruised cheek and swollen lip—the cost of protecting her—it was right there in his eyes.

She reached up, ran her thumb gently over his bruised cheek, his swelling lip.

"Are you okay?" she asked him.

Instead of answering with words, he kissed her thumb. The jolt that went through her was as shocking as if she had touched an electrical wire. But she didn't move away from it. She left her thumb there, on the soft beautiful swell of his lip.

His tongue came out of his mouth and flicked her thumb. Who could have predicted being scorched by lightning was so fantastic?

Their limo pulled smoothly into place, and she pulled her hand away from his face. She was trembling.

And she knew it wasn't from the encounter inside, either. The chauffeur was out, holding the door open for them.

"Let's go home," he whispered, his voice hoarse with need, as he laid his forehead against hers.

"Yes," she whispered back. "Let's."

CHAPTER NINETEEN

MOLLY REMEMBERED, as they arrived at Liam's building, that she had made all the arrangements for Maria and Paul to go see their grandchildren in Minnesota this weekend.

They were no longer chaperoned. And it was no longer a charade. She and Liam were completely alone here.

Not a word had been spoken between them since they got in the car, but sometimes silence spoke louder than words, and their joined hands, his thumb making circles in her palm, made the awareness between them sizzle. And behind that awareness was need, naked and powerful.

A need to know each other on a new level, in a completely different way.

When they got off the elevator in his apartment's foyer, he looked down at her, his eyes darkened with tenderness. He slid his jacket from her, his hands skimming her shoulders, as he went. He let it drop to the floor.

"Molly, did you want…are you?"

He stopped, the most composed man in the world, completely unsure.

She took the uncertainty from him. She put one hand behind the strong column of his neck and drew his lips to her own. She nibbled delicately around the swollen part, but if he felt any pain, it did not show in the ravenous way that he met her lips with his own.

With a sigh of surrender, he lifted her right off the ground, cradled her to his chest, strode through his silent apartment to his bedroom. He set her down on her feet, and closed the door.

They stood, for a suspended moment, looking at each other, not taking in the havoc that had been wreaked on them and their clothing, but taking each other in, recognizing each other, acknowledging a hunger that would not be refused any longer.

He kissed her again, taming the ferocity of his hunger, imbuing that kiss with tender welcome, and then with growing need, and then with passion.

Molly answered him from the deepest part of her being. Every single thing she was feeling was pouring out of her and into him, as their energy surged around them, and then melded.

Without taking her lips from his, she reached for, and found, the buttons of his shirt. One by one, she freed them. He lifted his lips from hers, and took the smallest step back from her. He shrugged out of the shirt.

It seemed to her that Liam, shirtless, was a work of art, the most beautiful she had ever seen. She closed the small distance he had opened between them and touched him. His skin was warm, flawless, silky. She ran her hand over the extraordinary masculine surfaces of his mounded pectoral muscles, down the line of his taut belly. Then she trailed her lips over every inch that she had just touched with her hand.

He put a single finger under her chin and eased her lips away from his chest. His eyes locked on hers, he found what remained of the zipper in her dress, and lowered it. When he could lower it no farther, he cocked his head at her.

"Molly—" his voice was so hoarse "—you need to be sure. One hundred percent—"

She answered by putting her hands on each strap of the dress and sliding them from her shoulders, revealing inch by inch just how sure she was.

The fabric whispered down her, cool air touching her skin, even as his eyes branded it. The dress caught at her waist, and Liam moved to her, and tugged it the rest of way down.

She stood before him, completely unclothed. Peripherally she registered the rather shocking fact she felt absolutely no shyness and certainly no shame.

She felt a simple delight in herself, and her body, and the way his eyes worshipped that. She stepped into him, not so much bold, as sure. Her hands found the button on his trousers and flicked it open. And then the zipper. She slid the fabric down.

Once, she had conjectured, in a moment that had felt so entirely wanton at the time, boxers or briefs.

Black boxer briefs.

Again, the sheer beauty of his body left her feeling breathless with the need to know more, to be more, to open herself to the miracles of sensation, of completion, of exploring the ancient secrets that men and women had been compelled to discover about each other since the beginning of time.

He lifted her to him, again, skin against skin.

He laid her on his bed, skimmed off the shorts and came to the arms she held open for him. He laid himself, with exquisite control, on top of her, holding his weight off her, casual about the strength it took to do that, comfortable with it.

His lips sought hers, and he stoked the fire between them, careless of the bruising he had sustained. His tongue danced with her lips and her tongue, and then his head dropped and he anointed her with the fire of his need.

"Liam," she whispered, a plea for completion. "Liam."

And then they joined in the age-old ritual of creation that encompassed the past and celebrated the future. Molly was aware, in some deep part of herself, that *this*, this ecstatic joining of a man and a woman was where every other act of creation sprang from: every song, every piece of art, every fashion designer dreaming a dress out of nothingness, every single thing in the whole universe seemed as if it must spring from this single source, this explosion of life's longing for itself.

A man and a woman's deepest longing, one that lived within

them, largely without their awareness, suddenly and deeply satiated.

Not a single word was spoken between them. What were words in the face of such immensity, in the face of having been part of the sacred dance of life?

They fell asleep in each other's arms.

CHAPTER TWENTY

LIAM WOKE UP with the light spilling in his bedroom window, just as Molly's hair was spilling across his chest. He could feel her breath, warm puddles of the life force, on his skin.

He was not sure if he had ever felt like this before.

One hundred percent a man, her protector, her companion, the other half of her soul. She awoke ever so slowly, and he watched, entranced as she stretched and sighed, and rubbed her nose, and seemed as if she might go back to sleep.

And then her eyes flew open, and she took him in.

A man could live forever wanting what she gave him in that sweet smile of welcome. He had the most delicious sense of being seen, completely.

They made love again.

This time without ferocity or frenzy, a slow unfolding, a delight of discovery. And then they were in the shower together, that lovely, playful intimacy snapping and crackling in the air between them.

Wrapped in thick robes, they finally made their way to the kitchen.

"Waffles?" he asked her after he'd made coffee. He couldn't stop sneaking looks at her. Molly, with wet hair, wrapped in a housecoat, sipping coffee.

It felt so wonderfully and amazingly intimate, the kind of simple moment a man wanted to capture.

"You don't know how to make waffles," she teased him.

"The toaster kind!"

They were laughing. It wasn't that funny, but pure delight was shimmering in the air between them, looking for ordinary things to attach itself to, so it could express its joy.

It occurred to him that he needed to tell her. She couldn't work for him anymore. They'd have to make some choices together about how to move forward. It never seemed as if there was an imbalance of power between them, but it was there, nonetheless.

Technically, he was her boss.

Still, he didn't want to move away from the lightness in the air between them by introducing other elements.

Not yet. He would go with that feeling he was having, of everything being all right. That nothing could go wrong with his world.

Not now.

"Actually," he said, "Maria has the waffle maker that she brought from the old country. It's one of the first things I ever fixed for her, and it still needs constant attention. Worth it though. Should I try it? Do you have a waffle recipe stored in that prodigious mind of yours?"

She looked thoughtful. "I don't. But who needs a mind like mine, when we have the internet? It's making me redundant. I'll just go grab my phone and we'll find a recipe."

She was gone a very long time.

When she came back, there was a look on her face that struck pure fear into him.

Just moments ago, he had thought nothing could go wrong with his world. Had that been like throwing a challenge before the gods?

"Molly? What is it?"

She sank into the kitchen chair. He saw she had his phone, too. She pushed it across the table to him.

"It's gone viral," she said.

Puzzled, Liam picked up his phone. He was shocked by the number of messages on there. Hesitating, he opened one.

There it all was, captured forever.

No wonder she looked so distressed! Her dress ripping open not just in front of the attendees, but now, thanks to all the social media platforms, in front of the whole world.

"Molly, it'll die down. Someday, you'll think it's funny."

"You don't understand, Liam. They're asking questions about me. They want to know who the mystery woman Mickey O'Donnelly and Liam Westerhouse were fighting over."

"So?" he said.

Her voice was very small.

"There's something I haven't told you."

It came out, slowly, her voice cracking with shame. A father losing his job and his pride and abandoning Molly, her brother and her mother to descend into despair and desperation. The brother who was going to fix it all, and instead carried them further into the pit of poverty and addiction. Her brother was in some kind of serious trouble with the law.

"I ran away from it all," she told Liam, "when I came to New York. I never told you, at first, because what boss needs to know his employee's sordid past? And then…after I started being your plus-one, it just felt as if it would blow it all up, if I told you. As if you wouldn't be able to put distance between us fast enough.

"I was so happy. I didn't want to risk the longest streak of happiness I'd ever had. Donnie, my brother, has been charged with a crime," she finished. "That's what's going to come out."

Liam stared at her, stunned.

How could she not know none of that would have mattered to him?

What mattered was that she hadn't told him. She hadn't trusted him. Even now, she was telling him because she was afraid the media would get to it first, not because she wanted to.

While he had given her every single thing he was, she had thought…what? That he was such a superficial snob that where she came from would change the way he thought about her?

In that moment, he felt two extraordinary sensations; side by side. The first was wanting to comfort her, to take her pain from her, to let her know it was okay.

But the second was the stronger of the emotions, and it won. It was a feeling of complete betrayal.

And of being fooled in some way that made him feel he also couldn't trust himself.

Because he had thought Molly, with all her wonder, was the most authentic person in the entire world.

Which, he reminded himself, was really his pattern, wasn't it? Choosing women who were very good at keeping things from him?

He thought now of how she had answered so many of his questions. He didn't really know her, at all. What he knew was which books had been present during the major events of her life. At the time, he'd thought it was adorable. He'd asked after her family, and there had been mention of a brother.

Think Huckleberry Finn, she'd said.

Now, it turned out, Huckleberry Finn with a dark side. *Molly* with a dark side, a side that was quite willing to be deceptive.

It made it hurt even worse that he had been so sure about Molly, so utterly convinced that she was the one he could spend forever with.

Now, his whole sense of what was possible was shimmering before him, an oasis in a desert, shimmering before a blistering sun.

Disappearing.

Just a mirage, after all. Just the charade it had always been.

CHAPTER TWENTY-ONE

MOLLY SAT SILENTLY as the car Liam had ordered for her whisked her through the streets of New York. She was trying very hard not to cry.

In the end, they had not had waffles. She had said she thought she should go, and part of her had hoped Liam would try to stop her.

Would tell her, no, everything was going to be okay.

Instead, she recalled the look on his face with a deep shudder. And felt completely shattered, the antithesis of how she had felt when she had woken up in his arms this morning.

Her whole body had still been vibrating from what had transpired between them. She had realized she had never in her entire life felt like this: so alive that she could feel her life energy coursing through her.

So alive that she could feel the air on her naked skin, smell the tang of Liam in the air, hear every single sound that came through those open patio doors.

After they had made love, she had been in a heightened state of awareness, as she took in *everything* about him. She took in the broadness of his shoulders, the beautiful expanse of his flawless skin, stretched silkily over smooth, hard muscle.

His hair was rumpled, the way she liked it best of all, and she couldn't resist reaching out and touching it, again and again.

But then that moment, when she had gone in search of her phone and found it. Found both of them, actually, their screens blinking away with incoming messages.

Her breath had stopped in her body, as she opened her phone.

Text messages. From Christopher. From people at the office that she barely knew.

From her mother.

The ones from Christopher seemed like the safest bet. She opened them.

Omg, girlfriend, what happened?

And then he'd sent her a link. After link. After link.

She and Liam and Mickey were going viral. All of it. Including her dress splitting open. Her backside was going viral.

But the worst part was the conjecture.

Who was the mystery woman these two men were fighting over?

But, as was the way with her life, just when she thought it was the worst part, no, it could get worse yet.

Because this was the part she had not revealed to Liam. She'd opened the texts from her mother, almost hoping that the abundance of them meant there was some new family catastrophe unfolding.

But no, her mother, who lived on the internet late at night, was also sending her clips from the night before.

Only hers were captioned quite differently from Christopher's, and it was obvious as the messages went on that she'd had more and more to drink.

Your name is Sunday, now? Like what, you're ashamed of us?

You've been holding out on me. Dating one of the world's richest men?

How'd that happen? Like Pretty Woman?

You're living that life, and you couldn't help us out with the lawyer this month?

You haven't asked him for a loan to help your brother?

I googled that bobble you're wearing. It's worth fifteen grand. If you pawn it, it would go a long way.

Everybody wants to know who you are. I wonder how your sugar daddy would feel if he knew you're just pond scum?

Trust Molly to notice her mother had misspelled bauble! Still, she had known then she couldn't wait. She had to tell Liam right away. She couldn't ignore her mother's threats any more than you could ignore a venomous snake.

She'd been aware, as she made her way back out to the kitchen, that this was exactly the problem with allowing yourself to be ruled by emotion, by letting yourself believe in dreams, by *owning* it, as Christopher had insisted she do.

The problem was, she hadn't owned all of it.

Now, the whole world was going to be trying to find out who the mystery woman was. Her mother did not appear to be above blackmailing her with her secrets about her family.

This was the part Molly, who had thought through everything her entire life, had—blinded by love and dreams—not thought through.

That *who* she really was could hurt him, and damage the reputation of the company. Of course, she should have told him sooner.

But she had wanted it not to matter, even as she knew all along it did.

As Liam had become more and more open with her, she had become more and more secretive with him. There was an aspect to *pretending* to belong in his world that had been very freeing.

It was like she had believed, by putting on pretty clothes and being exposed to Liam's world—private jets, travel, culture—she could leave behind that little girl who had hidden out in the library to get away from the chaos of her family life.

She had convinced herself that confiding in your boss about your personal life—especially your past personal life—would be completely inappropriate.

Sometimes, though, accompanying him, sitting with some of the most successful people in the world, hadn't she been struck by the utterly terrifying thought: *What if they knew?*

Wasn't that why she'd given the one-name response to the inquiry tonight?

She'd made the biggest mistake of all.

For a moment in time, she'd *believed* Christopher when he had told her she could have anything she wanted.

She couldn't.

She had felt that acutely when she had seen the look on Liam's face after she had told him the truth.

Wrapped in his jacket, in her torn dress, he had walked her through the lobby and to the door.

He didn't kiss her.

There was something terrifying and remote in his face as he said goodbye, opened the car door for her and put her inside.

Driving away from him, Molly understood, suddenly, the addictions that had held her family in its grip for generations, because she had wanted to turn and kiss that remote look off his face with every fiber of her being.

But she knew the one last taste could be enough to lead to a sensation—powerful, unfightable—of never being able to get enough.

Of never being able to live without him.

In the back of the car, Molly turned off her phone and she did not turn it back on. She was exhausted. She stumbled into her apartment and went directly to bed. But sleep evaded her. Finally, the tears came. She wept.

During the past few weeks, as Liam's plus-one, for the first time in her life, she had felt like maybe, just maybe, she had caught glimpses of everything she'd ever dreamed of.

A sense of being cherished.

Valued.

Safe.

But now that her past had come back to haunt her, she was in the grip of a family curse that precluded happiness. She'd foolishly ignored the lessons that her life had given her.

Believing in dreams hurt.

Hope for a different life only caused pain.

You couldn't really *ever* leave your past behind you.

But those feelings left her with a deep down sense of despondency. A hopelessness that no amount of hiding in her house, trying to soothe herself with ice cream and movies and playing games on her tablet was going to solve.

She was going to have to find a different job, and fast. She couldn't go back and face Liam. She didn't have a penny in savings thanks to her brother and that torn dress that she'd hung in her closet, despite the fact it was beyond repair.

She knew she had to pull herself together, and at lightning speed.

But the truth was, she didn't even have the strength to turn on her phone, not even as a future in homelessness loomed in front of her.

Homelessness. That went very well with the family narrative, actually.

The third day after the fiasco, there was banging on her door. Surely, not the landlord? She hadn't missed the rent yet. That inevitable event, and eviction, was a full two weeks away!

For a moment, her heart *hoped*.

Liam, come to rescue her, the maiden in distress riding away with the knight on the white charger, like the final scene in *An Officer and a Gentleman*.

How could she *still* believe such nonsense?

She went and threw open the door.

Christopher stood there.

"What? How on earth did you find me?"

"That is no way to greet your fairy godmother," he reprimanded her cheerfully. He took in her appearance—horrible—with a sympathetic glance, and marched by her.

He took in the whole apartment and sighed.

"An African violet?" he asked. "Seriously, Molly?"

"What is wrong with an African violet?"

"You might as well have a business card, *no life*."

"I don't have a life," she wailed. The tears came as Christopher guided her to the couch.

She told him every detail of her sordid past—growing up in poverty, her father abandoning the family, them investing in the dream of Donnie only to have it crushed by his injury. And now, her once star brother might be going to jail.

"I've always been terrified of anyone finding out," she admitted. "Especially Liam. And now, because of what happened at the gala—because I got too big for my britches—I had to tell him."

"How'd he take it?" Christopher asked, as if looking at her wasn't quite a big clue.

"He didn't say much. But the look on his face—" She sniffled. "Please tell me it's all dying down."

"Oh, not at all," Christopher said, cheerfully. "It's gaining steam. The mystery woman that Mickey O'Donnelly and Liam Westerhouse were fighting over. I *love* Mickey O'Donnelly, by the way. I may never forgive you for laying the boots to his face."

"After all I just told you, the thing you can't forgive me for is attacking Mickey?"

"Molly—" he was suddenly serious "—all that stuff you told me is about what happened to you. Stuff happens to everyone. It's not who you are."

"It's part of who you are," she said, stubbornly.

"Maybe the best part," he said to her. "The part that makes you strong and resilient."

"I somehow doubt Liam will see it that way. If the story is still gaining traction, it will reflect on him and the whole company. I'm an imposter and a charlatan and…"

"Oh, darling," Christopher said, "stop it. In time, you're going to see this as the best thing that ever happened to you."

She gawked at him.

"Molly, you can't get your sense of value from someone else, no matter who they are, not even a gorgeous someone else like Mr. Westerhouse. What interests *you*?"

"I don't have any interests!" she wailed.

"Exactly," Christopher said, sagely. "As if the African violet didn't tell me that."

"Quit disparaging Winspear!"

"Oh! You've named that dreadful thing. This has all happened in the nick of time. You were going to make that man your whole life, weren't you?"

Molly thought back over the months that she had come to work in Liam's office. She realized she already *had* made him—her work for FIX—her whole life.

"That can't work," Christopher told her. "I know your type exactly."

"What type is that?" she asked, feeling slightly defiant that Christopher thought he knew so much about her.

"The type who thinks your dreams rely on another person. First your brother, now Liam.

"The type who thinks you can earn your way to love. It's a kind of subtle neediness that will rot a relationship from the inside out. You have to bring *wholeness* to love."

"How do you know all this?" she asked him, feeling deeply the truth in every single thing he was saying.

"The school of broken hearts," he said, without any kind of self-pity. "Give me your phone."

She went and found it. When she tried to power it up, it was completely dead. He plugged it in and asked for her password.

He scanned her messages. "Look, forty-three messages of increasing panic from your fairy godmother. Just as many from your mother. My goodness! She's perfectly awful. Ah, here we go. *Boss.* Oh, look, it's not nearly as bad as you thought. He wants to talk. Molly, you're tormenting the man."

Tongue between his teeth, he tapped in and read out loud, *"Darling, I'm going to need a bit of time. I'm not sure how long. I hope you'll wait for me. Love you forever. Molly."*

"You can't send that—"

CHAPTER TWENTY-TWO

"OF COURSE I can send it." Christopher grinned at Molly and pushed a button—very theatrically, too.

"Liam will never believe that's me! *Darling*?" she scoffed.

"He'll think it's you. What else would he think? Aliens kidnapped you and are using your phone?"

"Love you forever?" she asked, mortified.

"It's true, isn't it?"

She started to cry again. "Yes."

"Let me dig through your cupboards and find something for lunch." Christopher fussed. "When's the last time you ate? Go do something with yourself. Brush your teeth. Have a shower. You won't believe how much better you'll feel."

Though she was reluctant to take his advice, she did, and she did feel better, as she made her way back into her small kitchen to find Christopher. It even felt like a relief to have someone managing her life, instead of her doing the managing all the time, trying to keep so many balls in the air.

Christopher held up a can of tuna, accusingly. "Is this what you eat?" he asked.

"Sometimes."

"Oh, my goodness. I hope you don't open the can and stand at the sink with a fork."

Her silence was all the answer he needed.

"Good grief, Molly! How you treat yourself is how others will—"

Another knock came at her door, loud and insistent.

Molly's heart stopped. Her eyes flew to Christopher's. She only really knew two people in New York—a pathetic life, as Christopher had pointed out—so it seemed like there was a good chance it might be the other one at her door. That would be the fastest response, ever, to a text, almost as if he'd been waiting for it.

And if Christopher could find out where she lived, so could Liam. All he had to do was open her personnel file. Not even any detective work involved.

"Don't you dare run to that door," Christopher told her, setting down the unopened can of tuna. "You stay right here."

"Oh, my," she heard him say, and then two sets of footsteps crossed her living room floor. She closed her eyes. Her heart was beating way too fast.

She opened them. Her heart plummeted to the bottom of her feet.

"What are you doing here?" she asked Mickey O'Donnelly.

He dangled a shoe off his pointer finger. "Delivering the glass slipper."

Wrong prince, she thought, sadly. In what world did Mickey O'Donnelly show up at a woman's house and she was disappointed?

She folded her arms over her chest. She noticed his world-famous grin looked forced. In fact, he looked tired. She ordered herself not to feel any sympathy for him.

"How did you find me?"

He lifted a shoulder. "Private investigator."

"That's a lot of trouble to go to."

"It was important to me. I wanted you to know how sorry I am. For the way I behaved. As you probably guessed, I'd had way too much to drink. I'm a pretty decent guy when I'm sober," he said, hopefully.

"Yes," she said, "isn't everybody their best selves when they're sober?"

Mickey gave her a wounded look that she wasn't falling all over herself over his legendary charm. He cleared his throat.

"A long time ago, Liam Westerhouse dated one of the women I'd been seeing. She tossed me over for him, actually. And when that went nowhere, she wouldn't give me the time of day, after. She said Liam had showed her how a woman should *really* be treated."

How well she knew that, Molly thought.

"I guess I had a bit of a bee in my bonnet since then. So, when I saw him again, after having just blown three whole months of sobriety, I thought, *oh, I'll make a play for his girl, see how he likes it.*"

"Dumb," he said, contritely, "really juvenile."

She felt a blow to her already tattered ego that Mickey had not, in fact, been blown away by her beauty the other night. She should have known other circumstances were at play.

Christopher was standing in the doorway, regarding Mickey with the funniest little smile on his face.

"Anyway, I know it's really not enough to say sorry. I mean, a drunk like me has said sorry to a million people in a million different ways. But I'm sober right now, three days in—and I'm trying to make amends."

"That's so nice." Christopher spoke up when Molly remained churlishly silent. "And I have the perfect way for you to do it."

Mickey turned and looked at him, and something flashed like fire between the two men. It was obvious to Molly, in that second, that she wasn't the only one who kept secrets, ones that felt as if they would be absolutely life-shattering if they were revealed.

"We were about to go for lunch," Christopher said smoothly. "Weren't we, Molly?"

She nodded mutely.

"You can buy," Christopher told Mickey.

Over the next few days, Molly found herself being relegated to plus-one again as she accompanied Christopher and Mickey, Mickey highly disguised behind a ball cap and oversize sunglasses.

The man, America's heartthrob, was hiding a secret that he thought could destroy his career.

But what Molly could clearly see was that keeping the secret was destroying him. And wasn't that exactly what her secret had been doing, too?

She realized she truly loved Liam, but how could she ever know if he'd truly loved her, when she'd never given him a chance to know who she really was?

She had hidden her whole life. In the library, in books, even in coming to New York, she'd been hoping to outdistance what she came from.

But now she saw there was only one answer.

It was so obvious to her that Mickey needed to come out.

And so did she.

Liam glared at the stack of crumpled chocolate wrappers on his desk. He loved chocolate. Why did it all taste like dust?

He went out to the outer office.

His new assistant, Destiny or Deirdrehe, couldn't seem to remember to save his life—looked terrified. Why was she terrified of him? He was a reasonable man.

"Did you find out where the hotel in Québec City got that chocolate from?"

"I called them, Mr. Westerhouse."

He didn't ask her not to call him that, because what if she started calling him *chief* or *boss* like Molly had?

Molly, who he missed more, not less, every single day that passed.

He'd swallowed his wounded pride after she'd left his place that morning. He'd seen he was really making it all about him.

What about her? What about that poor kid who'd grown up like that, who'd found refuge in quiet libraries and in the brilliance of her own mind? He'd texted her. He'd said they needed to talk. Actually, he'd texted her several times.

And been ignored.

And then, finally, that grating, un-Mollylike message.

Darling, I'm going to need a bit of time. I'm not sure how long. I hope you'll wait for me. Love you forever. Molly.

Darling? Wait for me? Love you forever?

But, that clear message: Don't call me, I'll call you. Now, if he pursued her, would he be stepping all over a clearly set boundary?

Was he still her boss, which would only make it worse if he bulldozed through the boundary she had set? She hadn't come to work. And she hadn't said she was quitting either.

He *hated* this. He hated his life not being in order. He hated not knowing what was coming next.

It felt like Sunday's biggest betrayal, not that she had withheld the truth from him, but that she had now abandoned him, as if he had somehow been the one who'd disappointed her.

And maybe he had. Okay, she hadn't revealed much—make that anything—about herself, but had he asked? Had he shown interest in her beyond being ecstatic about someone who kept his life in order?

Now, without her, he recognized just how much order she had brought to his life and on how many levels. Because now it was as if it was falling to pieces in every possible way. Every day felt like a torment. It had been six days—nearly a week since he'd had her in his bed. What was she waiting for?

"The hotel says they don't provide chocolate to guests."

"But—" He stopped. It occurred to him that the spectacular chocolate samples had started appearing in his life at about the same time Molly had appeared in his life.

"Oh," he said, "check the accounts for that trip then. It'll be listed as a business expense somewhere."

Ridiculous, of course, to use resources to track down something so petty.

But it didn't feel petty. It felt like anything that could relieve the pain he was in had to be sought out, no holds barred.

Three hours later his new assistant informed him, apologetically, as if it was her fault, that there were no records of chocolate purchases anywhere among the Québec City bills.

"You can check yourself," she said, placing copies of bills carefully down on the corner of his desk. "It's four o'clock. Can I go for the day?"

A clock-watcher. Oh, face it. He was looking for things to dislike; he was itemizing all the ways she wasn't Molly.

"Sure," he said. "Go."

He did not want to look at those bills. But he did. Reliving every bite of poutine, every tour, every single purchase. Every glorious moment had now become a torment.

His new assistant was right. There was no chocolate to be found on the bills.

He went very still. It meant Molly had purchased it herself. For him. Giving to him long before he'd known it.

Loving him, or so he might have thought. Her last text message had actually confirmed that.

Love you forever. But she needed time. How much time?

He fought down the feeling, *I can't live without her.*

He didn't even know her, he reminded himself bitterly. Liam had *trusted* her with every single thing about himself.

And she had given him nothing but the names of books.

And now she seemed to be getting on with her life. This morning, some paper had a picture of her playing Frisbee in Central Park—across the street from where he lived…what kind of new torment was that—with two men.

Oh, she looked as if she was having the time of her life. The paper claimed one of the men was Mickey O'Donnelly, of all people.

To him, that seemed like pure conjecture. The man in the baseball cap and oversize sunglasses could be anybody!

As if he didn't feel slapped down enough, why would Molly be with Mickey O'Donnelly? How was it possible their paths had crossed again?

Why would she be so quick to forgive the actor for pounding the living snot out of the guy who had come to her rescue? Her hero, really.

It occurred to Liam, stunned, that he was *jealous*. And not a benign little *oh, I wish it was me* jealousy, either.

It was fists clenched, jaw tight, smoke coming out of his ears jealousy.

Still, did it matter who it was? While he was trying to down enough chocolate to put him out of his misery, Molly Littleton, *his* Sunday, looked as if she was having the time of her life. Without him.

He heard the outer office door open. Melody or Bambi or whatever her name was must have forgotten something.

Or worse, someone was coming to see him, and she was not there to redirect them. Away from him.

Away from his obvious misery.

Away from the fact he was way off his game.

The new assistant was *not* working out. People couldn't just drop in and see him. Molly had known that intuitively.

Molly.

And there she was, standing in the doorway of his office, looking just like *his* Sunday, except no glasses.

But this was between them now: a night spent together; her confession of deception; his choosing not to call her; her not coming back to the office; her demanding space; her being photographed with Mickey O'Donnelly, of all people.

He hated it that his well-ordered world now felt like a confusing hot mess of emotion, and like he could never return to those days when Molly was his Sunday.

And his sun.

"What are you doing with Mickey O'Donnelly?" he blurted out.

"Hello, Liam."

Yeah, yeah, manners and all that crap. He glared at her.

She tilted her head at him. He could see something in her blue eyes that made him feel calmer than he had felt in days.

Like he'd been outrunning wild beasts in the forest and found himself inside a cottage, his back braced on the door.

The irony, of course, was that she had brought these wild beasts into his well-ordered life.

He remembered sitting on the plane with her after they'd landed in Québec City, teasing her about being a jewel thief or on America's Most Wanted.

It's always the ones you least suspect, he'd said to her.

How true that was proving to be. His reliable, ordered, dependable Sunday bringing him this absolute chaos of emotion.

"Still playing plus-one," she said.

"You're Mickey O'Donnelly's plus-one?" he rasped out.

"Not exactly. I'm not actually the one with Mickey O'Donnelly."

Liam went very still. He thought of that picture he'd seen this morning, of the three people playing on the spring green lawn of Central Park. The other man, now that he thought about it, seemed vaguely familiar to him.

"Oh," he said, his relief so stunningly intense that he thought he would cross the room and kiss her.

But suddenly, he realized, he could not.

He could not be the boss; he could not take charge. He had to let the dynamic shift between them. So he made himself stay where he was.

"You bought the chocolate," he said. It was the most ridiculous thing he could say. Not *where had she been?* Why had she done this to him? Did she know he loved her? Did she mean it when she said she would love him forever? Could she torment him like this if she knew that?

"Yes," she said, closing the door quietly behind her. "I did."

"Why?"

"I loved you," she said.

Loved? Past tense. He tried not to let his panic show.

"I loved you in secret," she said, softly. "My whole life has been about secrets. It's funny, how I sincerely thought keeping them was protecting you. And me. And the exact opposite was true."

He thought back on that moment at the gala when she'd given her name as Sunday. How he thought she was being clever.

But, looking back on it, really, shouldn't he have seen the sudden tension in her? The fear? Why could he see it so clearly now when he'd missed it entirely then?

"Can I tell you my secrets?" she asked. "All of them?"

Something in him stilled. He didn't feel betrayed that she had kept them from him. He dropped all comparison of this situation to anything that had happened to him in the past.

He saw the incredible—and fragile—gift she was holding out.

"I thought you'd never ask," he told her. And he went around his desk to her and took her hand and led her to the sofa.

Of course, she had told him all this in his kitchen that morning, but now she confided the worst of it to him.

Her mother was threatening to blackmail her.

Her mother. He digested that.

"Oh, Liam, I know it feels as if I didn't trust you. But it's worse. It's that I didn't trust myself, or life."

And why would she, he wondered, with a mother like that?

"When I came here, I made work everything. I don't even have a life. I can't bring that to you. Not only a bad past, but a boring person who doesn't even have one interesting thing in her life. Except Winspear."

"Winspear?"

"My African violet, since I'm revealing every pathetic detail."

He threw back his head and laughed. "Violet Winspear! That's so clever."

"You can't possibly know who Violet Winspear is!"

"Of course I do! My mother read romance novels voraciously, always hiding them under pillows as if they were porn. I think those little books saved my mother's life, actually."

"Mine, too," she said. "The library. The boxes of books purchased at garage sales and secondhand stores.

"But that's the problem, Liam. I can't come to you like *this*. I know everything you like. I don't even know what I like."

"You like making me happy."

"You know it's not enough, don't you?" she said, sadly. "I have to find myself, Liam. I have to go out and figure out how to make myself happy before I can come to you. I need to put myself in charge of my own adventure. Maybe take a rock-climbing course. White water rafting. Find some friends. Do some travelling. I cannot make you my whole world. In time it would destroy us both."

He thought of his mother, so much in the shadow of his father. What had she been looking for in those romance novels that she had felt she needed to hide?

"Molly," he said, slowly. "What if you don't have to take that journey to yourself alone? What if we both go?"

"I don't understand."

"I like making you happy, too. Could we both find out who we are, together? You've tried the solitary path. I've tried the solitary path. It seems we both have just gotten more and more lost. Let's be lost together. Let's see if we can find a new path together."

"I'm still not following."

"Let's discover the world and each other as if it's all Québec City, as if it's all just a great adventure waiting for us to discover it."

Tears were coming to her eyes. His beautiful, sensitive Molly. He took one teardrop on the tip of his finger and placed it on his lips.

"And I promise," he told her softly, "if you're not completely happy in thirty days, I'll completely refund your misery."

And then her arms were around him, and she was crying against his chest, and he could feel her absolute trust in him, and his in her.

Her lips found his, and his found hers and a world that had gone gray burst into an amazing rainbow of colors.

And so it began.

It wasn't so much a courtship as a season of discovery. They explored New York together, bringing to it the same wonder they had brought to that trip to Québec. They saw Broadway shows, but also went to tiny little clubs tucked into brick walls that featured comedians and musicians and plays no one had ever heard of. They ate at five-star restaurants and from street stands, and in out-of-the-way diners. She invited him to ride the subway, and she made tuna casserole in her basement suite. They played cards after, some silly children's game that made them both laugh until they cried.

They went out with friends, and doubled with Christopher and Mickey. They took spontaneous trips.

But to him, the best was when they did nothing at all. When they strolled Central Park or took a picnic there, when they sat out on his deck with hot chocolate, when they listened to music, holding hands with their eyes shut.

It all confirmed what he already knew.

He was ready to sign up as Molly's plus-one. Forever.

He took her back to Québec City, that place where he had first fallen in love with her capacity for wonder, and where he had let her coax out his own.

He proposed to her on the ramparts of the Citadelle, in the middle of a blizzard, with the ghosts of history blowing around them.

Some might have thought it was a strange place to propose, but he had chosen it on purpose. Those ramparts, which looked down on what had become one of the most beautiful places on the planet, represented something.

They represented suffering and sacrifice and turmoil and conflict.

But they also represented the depths of human spirit rising out of challenges. When the challenges subsided, as they always did, didn't they leave in their wake beauty and strength and resilience? Didn't laughter seem sweeter and flowers seem brighter after the storms had passed?

Didn't the simplest of truths arise? That love was the survivor?

When all else had passed, love remained. Love carried light through the darkness, and it would, always, rise again, as surely as the sun rose after the night.

He knelt in that blizzard before her, and without him saying a single word, Liam knew that Molly understood.

All of it.

"Molly, will you be my wife? Will you let me love you all the days of my life? Cherish you? Protect you? Laugh with you? Create with you?"

And she said yes, her voice given to a wind that would carry these feelings—*hope, belief, love, dreams*—into the hearts of their children and their children's children, and a future her *yes* was shaping, and that would go on and on, beyond where they could ever see it.

EPILOGUE

IT WAS THE wedding of the century. Even in a city that knew no bounds when it came to purely opulent events, this one stood out.

It was as if a Royal wedding had come to New York City.

The cathedral was one of the most well-known in the city. With its soaring towers and detail work of the neo-Gothic style, it took up a full city block. All roads into it had been closed, the barricades opened up only for the long, endless line of limousines that pulled up in front of the sweeping granite steps.

The guest list included business people, icons of film, royalty, sports figures. Liam had never seen such a gathering of so many accomplished people from so many different fields where the atmosphere was so benign.

He had heard no sniping. Nothing competitive.

Everybody just seemed so genuinely happy, so enchanted by the whole idea of happily-ever-after. Even the few selected members of the paparazzi who stood outside had put away their normal jaundiced expressions and just looked as if they were embracing the possibility that fairy-tale endings could happen.

Anybody who was anybody was spending a beautiful autumn day at this wedding and the reception for twelve hundred people that would follow.

Liam glanced at Molly.

She was absolutely glowing. The stress of getting this event ready—a challenge to even her superhuman organizational skills—had fallen away. There was not a sign of the effort involved in tracking down three thousand missing pure white gardenia plants.

There was not a sign of dealing with temperamental everybody: chefs, guests, wedding party members, relatives.

Of course, it might not be the wedding that was causing all of that glow.

Liam rested his hand, lightly, on Molly's baby bump. She gave him a look that was complicated—excited, terrified, content—before she covered his hand with her own. All the activity in the church seemed to still as both of them waited to feel the baby—their baby—stir beneath their fingertips.

Christopher had so badly wanted Molly in the wedding party, and for Liam to be seated in the front in those three aisles reserved for family and the closest friends.

But, no, the baby was already three days overdue.

Their baby, Liam thought, again, with wonder.

"Olivia, if it's a girl," Molly whispered.

"No! She'll get called Olive," he whispered back. "Sunday, shouldn't we have settled this by now? Our first failing as parents. Baby born, no name."

She patted his hand reassuringly, "Maybe we'll just know when we meet him. Her."

Molly, his superorganizer, hadn't even wanted to know the gender of the baby. He hadn't even been able to persuade her by saying it would make it easier to plan the nursery. No, she insisted it was going to be a surprise, the thing she had once hated most of all.

"I don't see why you've chosen this, of all things, to be relaxed about," he groused good-naturedly.

"It's entirely your fault," she said. "Being loved has made me feel, shockingly, as if I don't have to be in control of everything."

"Huh." There was no arguing with that.

"Shhh," she said, her attention now fully on the front of the church.

The two men, Mickey and Christopher, who had become Liam and Molly's best friends in the world, both were standing at the altar now.

Ready to say yes to forever.

He thought of how chance worked in people's lives. What if Mickey had never tackled him that night? Never had a reason to find Molly after, to offer his amends, never met Christopher?

Was it just chance, he thought, sliding his beautiful wife another glance. It seemed like so much more. Coincidence didn't quite say it, either. Serendipity?

Whatever it was, sometimes, it seemed like two people were meant to be together and the universe found a way to make that happen, against all odds.

For themselves, Molly had chosen quite a different kind of wedding. Even though she'd been well aware she could have had all of this—no. They had been married on the deck of his apartment, with only a few people in attendance. Maria and Paul, of course, her mother, and her brother, Donnie, Christopher and Mickey.

The reception, in the front lobby of his building, had been like the best block party ever. The neighbors had come. The staff of the building, and of FIX. He was pretty sure even strangers had wandered in off the street and joined the revelry.

It was at his and Molly's wedding where, once again, there had been a meeting of chance, that divine collision of circumstance and coincidence.

Mickey O'Donnelly had rescued Molly's brother, Donnie. With seeming total ingratitude for the lengths that had been gone to to have his legal problems concluded with no jail time, her brother had been running, drunk and mostly undressed, through Central Park.

Had Mickey recognized a kindred spirit? Had he seen that

Donnie wasn't trying to wreck his sister's big day? Had he seen, even then, the supreme talent that so often went hand in hand with supreme damage?

Had he simply been protecting Molly?

Or was it part of this thing called *amends* that he was so determined to make to the world for every bad thing he had ever done?

Whatever it was, he'd asked Donnie if he wanted a part in his latest film venture. That was two years ago. Donnie's good looks and natural charisma had done the rest. Well, and Mickey's introducing him to twelve-step programs.

In the super small world that was celebrity, it probably was not so surprising that Donnie was at this wedding with Eva La Lydia, whom Liam had overcome his dislike for when he recognized her as his own catalyst toward his destiny.

What if she'd signed that NDA?

What if Molly had never volunteered to become his plus-one? Would they have found their way, anyway? Or would she have continued to secretly send him chocolates, and would he have continued to be oblivious?

And then, of course, there was Liam's mother-in-law, sitting next to Molly looking very queen-like in her pink suit and gloves, and a little box hat with a veil over her eyes.

He'd overheard her telling someone on the church steps before they'd come in that both her children were so successful because of her firm and consistent parenting.

She had said it with a completely straight face!

But his mother-in-law really was a lesson in what could happen to people when the desperate edges were removed from their lives. When they found safety, and every day wasn't a hardscrabble fight toward survival. She was actually nice. Sometimes.

Suddenly, he felt Molly, her shoulder against his, stiffen. He could almost feel the ripple of shock that jolted through her, even though she was silent.

"What?" he whispered.

"My water just broke," she whispered back, mortified.

For a moment, he felt pure panic.

But then he remembered what a big part the universe played in everything, whether a man acknowledged that or not.

This moment, right now, had been planned since the beginning of time. The seeds that would be this baby had been sewn into Liam and Molly since the day they both had been born.

There was something about being a small part of such an immense plan that was both humbling and reassuring.

This was why Molly had wanted to sit at the back of the cathedral, instead of accepting Christopher's pleas to be in the wedding party. She had refused that invitation, just in case she had needed to make a quick exit.

Never underestimate the power of a woman's intuition, Liam thought.

He shrugged off his jacket, and wrapped it around her as she rose. It was a way tighter fit than it had been at the gala!

They edged out into the aisle. Molly was trying desperately not to attract attention.

She might have saved herself the trouble, because Christopher, mid-vow, stopped and swiveled toward them.

For a moment both he and Mickey looked as if they would abandon their places at the altar to run down the aisle and be with their beloved Molly and the child they already considered themselves uncles to.

But Liam raised a thumb to them. *It's okay, I got this, my friends.*

Christopher, never, ever afraid to be himself in the world, called, "Remember, if it's a boy, name it after me."

Ha. Christopher was not even on the short list of the pages of names Liam and Molly had been compiling.

But as it turned out, all those boy names were completely unnecessary.

Because five hours later, a baby wrapped in a pink blanket was set in Liam's arms. Looking into the squalling face of his baby girl, the hours of agony that had preceded her arrival were erased.

She was in an absolute fit of rage at being brought into the world. She had no hair, her skin was splotchy and her features were worthy of an extraterrestrial.

And Liam was not sure he had ever seen anything quite so beautiful as his daughter.

He had certainly never felt anything like the warrior rising within him, who silently vowed he would lay down his life, if the need ever arose, to protect this child.

Liam slid onto the bed beside Molly. It was really quite laughable that he thought himself any kind of a warrior after what he had just witnessed his wife go through.

Exhausted, she leaned her head against his shoulder and touched the round miracle of that cheek with her small finger.

A tiny hand escaped the blanket and caught his own finger, grasping it with astonishing strength.

The baby went very quiet. Her eyes, the color of slate, fastened on his face, and she took him in, solemnly, as if she already knew what she was in his and Molly's world.

Safe, in the very center of it.

Love made manifest.

He had been stoic throughout, calm, the perfect coach, maintaining a strong face, knowing it was the least he could do in the light of his wife's courage.

But now the enormity of the love in the room hit him, and he began to weep, silently, the tears saying what no words in the world could ever be able to say.

Molly's lips found his cheek.

"Grace," she whispered.

The name had not appeared on any of their extensive lists.

Liam thought of how he had been trying to name that force that had guided so many lives, nudged unlikely people toward each other.

He had tried chance and coincidence and serendipity, but now he saw what it really was.

Grace, that force that hummed quietly and steadily, unacknowledged, in the background of a person's life. Grace, that powerful, invisible force guiding a man who was stumbling toward that place his heart had always longed for.

When he looked at his daughter, he could not imagine any other name belonging to her.

"Hello, Grace," he whispered, through his tears. "Welcome to this surprising, beautiful, crazy, amazing journey called love."

* * * * *

If you enjoyed this story, check out these other
great reads from Cara Colter

The Prince from Her Past
Cinderella's Greek Island Temptation
Invitation to His Billion-Dollar Ball
Their Hawaiian Marriage Reunion

All available now!

FORBIDDEN CINDERELLA IN HIS CASTELLO

MICHELLE DOUGLAS

MILLS & BOON

To Mum, who continues to read my stories
with the same gratifying enthusiasm she always has.
I love you, too!

CHAPTER ONE

Sadie stared out of the window as the car wound up the side of the hill towards Enzo's castle. Every now and again she'd catch a glimpse of it: *gobsmacking*. Apparently the view of the castle from the water was extraordinary. However, as she was an average everyday Cinderella and not some society princess with a private yacht, Sadie wasn't going to be fortunate enough to see it from its 'best side'. Not that she was here for the scenery. She was here for the attics.

The thought made her dance in her seat. *You're here for the attics* amongst *other things*.

She did her best to rein in her excitement. She couldn't get too carried away with the attics. Her first priority was Enzo. She was here for him. She'd promised Chelsea.

She grimaced. It was nine years since she'd spent any quality time with him, though. When she'd pointed that out, Chelsea had said, 'But the two of you were always on the same wavelength.'

That was not how Sadie remembered it. She'd *thought* they'd been on the same wavelength. But…she'd been wrong. It had devastated her at the time, but she'd survived. At eighteen, she'd thought herself such a grown-up, but she'd been nothing more than a child.

Oh, God, what if things were…awkward? She scrubbed a hand over her face. *Stick to the plan.*

Pulling in a breath, she did what she could to slow the

racing of her heart. Good advice; she'd stick to the plan. She would not start obsessing over Enzo like some starstruck teenager. She would keep the past firmly in the past. *And* she'd be cheerful.

Besides, it wasn't as if she hadn't seen Enzo at all in the last few years. There'd been Chelsea's wedding. Nothing untoward had happened then. She hadn't immediately started crushing on him. She hadn't followed him with her eyes all evening. She hadn't started wishing and hoping.

Because, after one obligatory 'How are you?', 'Great! How about you?' conversation, you studiously and strenuously avoided him.

Scrunching up her face, she again glared out of the window. All of that stuff was ancient history. She was an adult now and she would behave like an adult. Enzo was going through a challenging time and she'd do whatever she could to help. That was all. Because Chelsea had asked it of her. And she'd do anything for her best friend—her *pregnant* best friend. The fact it had also provided her with the perfect escape from Australia was neither here nor there.

A familiar wave of heaviness settled over her at the reminder of what she'd left behind in Melbourne. Her mother was home. Verity Beckett was back, twenty-seven years after dumping Sadie with her grandparents and heading out into the wide blue yonder, never contacting them again.

Until now. The thing she'd always hoped for as a child had finally happened. But, instead of the bright-eyed, smiling woman she'd secretly imagined, swooping in with big hugs and lots of laughter, Sadie been confronted with a hard-eyed woman with a calculating smile.

What a mess!

No brooding. It was what it was. Time to focus on the future.

Squaring her shoulders, she lifted her chin. She was on an

adventure. She was embarking on the first step in her new life away from Australia and her family. That was the Mediterranean Sea down there. She was on the Italian Riviera—*her*—and she wasn't going to let anything spoil this holiday. And, as an expert in repairing antique toys, she was going to enjoy mending a few from the castle for Chelsea and her unborn baby.

Shaking her head, she huffed out a laugh. With everything that was happening in her life, she wasn't going to have time to crush on Enzo. She'd be too busy spending her spare time working on the toys, applying for jobs and planning this new life of hers.

A moment later, she gave another excited shimmy. While they might not be the only reason she was here, those attics were still more than a cover story—she *would* get a chance to explore them. Which meant, amid all the jollying and cheering up she'd promised to do for the unsuspecting Enzo, she'd also get to go treasure-hunting.

A view of the water below emerged as the trees thinned. Still and blue on the late-afternoon air, it looked like something from a travel brochure. Craning her neck, she tried to keep it in view as long as she could. Chelsea had told her the beauty of the Ligurian coast would knock her sideways. Maybe it wouldn't be so hard to drag herself away from the attics after all.

The road curved and the view disappeared. Forest rose up all around them—a forest full of dark pines, like something from a fairy tale. Like the wood Hansel and Gretel had found themselves lost in. Or where the Beast had his castle in *Beauty and the Beast*.

That reference had her wincing. Enzo might be scarred after his accident, but it didn't mean he'd become a growly, snarly beast, despite what Chelsea said. A grump, perhaps, but not a beast.

She pressed her hands together. If he was grumpy, then she'd be the opposite. She'd be bright, breezy and enthusiastic—a breath of fresh air. She'd be the perfect epitome of some guy's little sister's best friend: bright and bubbly, familiar and uncomplicated. Chelsea and Enzo might only be step-siblings—Chelsea's father had married Enzo's mother when Chelsea had been fourteen and Enzo eighteen—but they adored one another. Chelsea called him 'the brother of her heart'. And Chelsea was the sister of Sadie's heart.

Wrought-iron gates in an imposing fence of grey stone swung open, and Enzo's castle came into view. She craned her neck to try and take it all in. When Chelsea had told her it was a small castle, she hadn't realised a small castle wasn't literally *small*. Nor had she envisioned how imposing or beautiful it would be, with its stone walls rising from a paved courtyard to soar into the gentle early-evening sky.

Guido, the driver, directed her to huge double doors, then he and the car disappeared round the side of the house… *uh, castle*. The doors were flung open before Sadie could reach them and a woman Sadie would put in her early fifties beamed at her.

'You must be Miss Sadie Beckett. I'm Luisa Belotti, Signor Lorenzo's housekeeper. Signora Chelsea, she has told me all of your favourite things to eat and I am looking forward to… how do you say it…cooking up a storm?'

Sadie couldn't help but laugh at the warmth of the welcome. 'I'm pleased to meet you, Signora Belotti. I fear I'm going to be totally spoiled for the next fortnight.'

'You must call me Luisa.' Luisa led her inside. 'We want you to feel at home while you are here. It will be nice to have another person to fuss over.'

'Then you must call me Sadie. I…'

She came to a dead halt in the entrance hall, an enormous, whopping room that was all stone and dark wood, with a fireplace that could seat half a dozen people inside of it. How on earth did one feel *at home* in this?

The housekeeper smiled. 'It is impressive, *vero*?'

'Just…wow.'

'Now, would you like to go up to your room to freshen up or would you prefer to see Signor Lorenzo first?'

'Enzo,' she said promptly.

'Excellent. That will give Guido time to take your bags up to your room. And you must be eager to see Signor Lorenzo. I understand it has been quite some time.'

'Ages and ages.'

As she followed Luisa up an impressive set of stairs, Sadie's stomach tightened. She ticked off all the things she knew about Enzo these days: his property developing company was one of the most successful in all of Italy, making him wealthy beyond anyone's wildest dreams; he dated cruel women, if the scathing critiques Chelsea treated her to were anything to go by; and five months ago he and his latest girlfriend had been badly injured in a dreadful car accident.

She pressed her hands together. She had no reason to be nervous. Enzo might've retreated from the world over the course of the last few months, but, considering all that had happened, that was understandable. She didn't doubt he'd host her warmly enough. She was his little sister's best friend. They had *history*. And, luckily, she was no longer the starry-eyed girl she'd once been.

Luisa led her through several large reception rooms to a magnificent drawing room. Light poured in at the wall of windows that arced in a graceful curve to form a grand version of a bay window.

Sadie came to a dead halt again. 'No way! You *have* to be joking me!'

Sadie's feet automatically took her across to that bay of windows to drink in the view with a greedy gaze. A manicured lawn and a strategically wild garden gave way to a view of the Mediterranean that currently reflected the colours of the twilit sky—all soft blues, pinks and silvers. In the still air, it looked as smooth as a mirror.

'No joke.'

The familiar voice had her stomach clenching, but she resisted the urge to swing round. Staring at the view, she smiled.

Enzo used to tease her about her obsession with *Pride and Prejudice*. Would he remember?

'Tell me the truth. When did you first know that you'd fallen in love with Mr Darcy?'

She changed voices. 'I believe I first mistook it from seeing his beautiful grounds at Pemberley.'

'You know that isn't a direct quote?'

'Don't be pedantic. I'm paraphrasing.' Swinging round, she determinedly kept a smile in place and moved across to where he stood in the shadows—tall and solitary, his hands resting on a cane. Luisa quietly retreated out of the room.

Before Sadie could reach him, though, he adjusted the walking stick in such a way as to prevent her from reaching across and hugging him or giving him a peck on the cheek. She fought to keep her eyebrows from shooting up. Instead, she thrust her hand at him, forcing contact. 'Hello, Enzo.'

He had to move the stick from his right hand to his left. Scowling, he shook her hand—a perfunctory single pump practically over before it had begun—but she kept hold of it and moved in a step closer to stare up into his face.

A jagged scar zigzagged across his forehead from his hairline to bisect his left eyebrow. Her stomach clenched up tighter than a lid on a pickle jar. He'd been lucky not to lose an eye! A succession of scars peppered his left cheek. She felt as if her heartbeat were being pressed under glass. 'Hellfire and brimstone,' she murmured, releasing his hand.

Only this time it was he who held her hand captive and refused to let it go. Dark eyes flashed. 'Pretty, isn't it?'

She glowered back. 'Damn it, Enzo, but yes! How can your scars make you look even more beautiful? How is that even possible?'

Her hand was abruptly released and she had to set her legs to stop from falling. He moved the cane back into his right hand, becoming scarily aloof again. 'Stop being ridiculous.'

'I'm not.' And she wasn't. 'A mere mortal like me can only gaze in awe and envy. Mind you, if I had to go through a horrific car accident to win such beauty, I'd give it a hard pass. I'm truly sorry about your accident, Enzo.'

His glare didn't abate. 'Do you know how truly grating your "cheerful" Aussie accent is?'

'I absolutely do,' she said, amping up the cheer factor another notch. Chelsea hadn't been exaggerating when she'd said he'd turned into a grump. If he'd ever spoken to her like that back when she'd been a lovestruck teenager, she'd have died. 'When Chelsea said you'd become bad-tempered, I didn't believe her. I told her you'd always been kindness personified.'

If possible, his scowl deepened. 'You should've believed her.'

'Clearly, but it's going to take more than a bad temper to scare me away.'

He'd started to turn, but he swung back, his frown deepening. 'Why?'

'I have one word for you.' She pointed ceiling-ward. 'Attics!'

He rolled his eyes.

She sent him the cheeriest of cheerful smiles. 'That, and the fact I'm no longer madly in love with you.'

He nearly dropped his cane. She grinned. In fact, she grinned so hard he ought to be blinded.

Scowling, he led her into an adjacent room—away from the windows with their amazing view, away from the pretty marble fireplace and all the beautiful things. Trailing behind him, she silently pointed to the windows and all the things. *What was wrong with sitting in there?* But he didn't turn round; didn't see her unspoken questions.

This new room was smaller and darker, but that didn't mean it was actually small. Despite the fact it had vaulted ceilings and a fireplace, it lacked the character of the drawing room. It lacked warmth. It lacked…charm.

Was this where he liked to sit? No wonder he'd grown so grumpy and gloomy. She made a silent note to hunt out some colourful cushions and throw rugs to quietly brighten it up. What the room did have, though, was a big-screen TV and a bookcase full of DVDs, which gave her an idea.

He gestured for her to take a seat on the sofa as Luisa returned with a tray of coffee and *petits fours*. 'To tide you over until dinner time,' she said with a smile in Sadie's direction, before promptly departing.

'Chelsea told me you'd be obsessed with the attics.'

She poured him a coffee and handed it across. He sat in a big battered armchair that somehow suited him. She selected a pastry with care. 'She made me promise not to hole myself up there for the entire fortnight.'

His lips twisted, though she didn't understand why. She bit into the pastry—oh, god, it was so good—before gesturing in the direction of the view and the sea. 'With that right on the doorstep, I suspect my promise won't be as hard to keep as I thought it might be.'

A sceptical eyebrow rose, and again she didn't understand what he had to be sceptical about. Actually, it was more than scepticism… Cynicism, perhaps? 'So today you get me on my best behaviour where I don't pester you to immediately show me the attics. That happens tomorrow.' It took a force of will to keep her voice steady and upbeat. 'And speaking of manners…' She set down her coffee and pastry. 'Thank you for having me here, Enzo.'

'I was under the impression I didn't have a choice.'

She stared into those dark, dangerous eyes and frowned—while a wholly disassociated part of her marvelled at the breath of his shoulders. She might've had the biggest crush known to man on Enzo years ago, but she'd never properly *appreciated* those shoulders.

'Look, I know that Chelsea can be…persuasive in her persistence, but—'

'Let's cut the pretence, Sadie.'

What pretence?

'I know my family have sent you to report back on my health, my state of mind and my future plans.'

Just like that, his cynicism made a horrible kind of sense. She could see all too clearly why he really thought she was here. It was lucky she no longer had those stars in her eyes, because they'd have taken a nosedive into the depths of a cold, dark sea right about now.

'You *know* that?' She feigned shock. 'Then I guess you also know, besides sending a detailed report back to your family, I've been instructed to cheer you up and take your mind off your troubles. And, as Chelsea and I thought you'd probably outgrown kites and skateboards, we figured me seducing you might do the trick.'

Because he thought *that* was what she was here for—to seduce him when he was in a weakened state and his defences were down. Did he honestly think Sadie had no pride? A hard ball of something fiery and fierce settled in the pit of her stomach. 'But why stop there, we said, chortling up our sleeves. Why not seduce you into marriage and then I could have the honour of looking after you forever, because… well…looking after a grumpy, entitled man has always been my *one true dream*.'

Best of all, she delivered it with the biggest of cheery smiles.

* * *

Sadie drew out the words 'one true dream' with a mockery that stung. Enzo closed his eyes and pinched the bridge of his nose. Heat prickled his face, his neck, his ears. His skin might be naturally olive, but he doubted it hid the way he flushed.

Not that he deserved the comfort of hiding his embarrassment or shame. Sadie hadn't deserved the bitterness he'd flung at her. Neither did his family. Why couldn't they just leave him alone, though? Why did they have to disturb his peace and solitude?

An invisible eyebrow rose inside him. *Peace?* Okay, fine, just solitude, then. He didn't want anyone disturbing his solitude. Especially not someone who'd started flirting with him the moment she'd arrived.

Had she been flirting, though?

She'd quoted Jane Austen at him! She'd intimated that she'd taken one look at his castle and had fallen *in love* with him.

She was joking.

He wasn't laughing.

Except… He rubbed at an ache that stretched through his chest. While once upon a time she might've had stars in her eyes where he was concerned, there were no stars in her eyes now. *That* was a good thing.

He frowned, halting mid-rub. There were no stars in Sadie's eyes, but nor was there pity or revulsion.

'So why don't we begin again?'

He started, realising he'd let the silence stretch too long.

'Hello, Enzo, it's nice to see you.'

She toasted him with her coffee, but he shook his head. 'Why don't we start with me apologising?'

Her hair was cut into a bob that bounced an inch above her shoulders, and she made a movement that sent it swishing, the dark strands catching the light. 'Absolutely! I'm good with that.'

The breezy bounce of her hair and good-natured satisfaction almost made him smile.

'Go on, then.' She set her coffee cup down and rubbed her hands together. 'Make it good.'

He did smile then; he even huffed out a laugh. He needed to work on that, because he didn't doubt that Sadie had been sent here by his family. And if he wanted her to give them a favourable report…

'Sadie, I apologise for my rudeness and for insinuating you were here for some nefarious purpose. I humbly beg your forgiveness.'

She seized her coffee cup again. 'Not bad. A six out of ten.'

He stiffened. 'What was wrong with it?' He'd always been a ten-out-of-ten guy.

'You didn't mean it.' Her distracting hair swished some more. 'Oh, you meant the bit about the rudeness.'

'I meant it all!'

She surveyed him over the rim of her coffee, infuriatingly calm. 'You still think I'm here for nefarious purposes.'

He did his best not to focus on that infuriatingly distracting hair. 'I do not think you're here to seduce me.'

Despite her assurances, he knew how angry and ugly his scars looked. He also knew that some women didn't care what a man looked like—not when that man happened to be as rich as Lorenzo Lombardi. But Sadie wasn't the kind of woman who'd pounce on a man when his defences were down. Sadie wasn't the kind of person who took advantage of anyone.

How do you know? You've had next to nothing to do with her for the last decade.

He knew because he knew Chelsea. He knew what a support Sadie had been to Chelsea when they'd been at boarding school together. A person didn't change that much. A person didn't go from being kind and caring to being only interested in all they could get. Chelsea wouldn't continue to talk about her with so much warmth, wouldn't continue to love her so much.

'But you do think I'm here to spy on you.'

Her eyes narrowed, and for no reason at all perspiration gathered on his top lip. 'Not spy. To check up on me.'

Tempting lips pursed.

Tempting? *What the hell...?* Maybe all of this solitude was sending him loopy. No amount of lecturing could stop him from watching in fascination as those very pretty lips un-pursed.

'Heaven forbid your family should be worried about you.'

Her words released him from the temporary spell. 'Are they worried?' He was no longer in hospital, no longer in a critical condition, no longer damaged beyond recognition. They should be relieved.

'I am, so they must be! I wasn't before landing on your door step, but to now find you so...malcontent.'

What did he have to be content about?

Financial security, the roof over your head, the fact you're alive?

He scowled.

'Naturally everyone was worried when the accident happened, and immediately afterwards. Everyone was beside themselves.'

Had she been beside herself?

'But, as soon as you were declared in a stable condition, my worry eased. I figured you'd have a tough and painful road ahead, but I also knew you to be strong and resilient.'

He felt neither of those things.

'So, when Chelsea started fretting and being a worrywart, I blamed pregnancy hormones.' A frown lodged in her eyes. 'Thankfully, though, she does actually want the toys she's sent me here to retrieve restored, and thankfully I've been itching to get inside your attics for as long as I've known about them, or she'd have come here herself.'

What the actual...? He swore.

'Exactly! Because this—' she pointed at him '—would not do a pregnant woman much good.'

'Dominic wouldn't have let her come.'

Sadie stared at him for two beats before seizing a huge strawberry and popping the entire thing in her mouth. He had a feeling she'd done it to stop from saying something... stinging, harsh, something she'd have to apologise for later.

She dabbed her mouth with a napkin when she was done. 'Chelsea and Dominic might be a loved-up duo, but he's not the boss of her.'

'That's not what I meant.'

'Are you sure? Because it's what you said.' Leaning forward, she peered at him with narrowed eyes. 'It's not a side of you I've ever considered.'

Something ugly shifted through him. 'Scales falling from your eyes?'

'Thick and fast,' she shot back cheerfully.

He was *not* his father or his grandfather. 'I am not some sexist jerk who thinks women should love, honour and *obey*, Sadie. I chose my words poorly. In saying Dominic wouldn't let Chelsea come, I merely meant he'd have tried to talk her out of it.'

Admittedly that might've been easier said than done, and he suspected the twist of his lips acknowledged as much. 'Barring that, he'd have come with her.' As a comfort and support, and to shield her from her stepbrother's bitterness.

'And you think that would've helped allay her worry?'

Not one iota. *Damn it.* He needed Sadie to send his family a good report. He didn't want them worrying about him, nor did he want them descending on him *en masse*. 'I'm sorry, Sadie. I'm cranky about everything, and have clearly been on my own too long. My manners have grown rusty.' He grimaced. 'It's been difficult to let off steam when I can't exercise. And one can't yell at the staff.'

'Especially when good staff are hard to come by, or so I'm told. I expect trying to replace staff who've walked out would be an utter bore.'

Her teasing nonsense had some of his tension easing. 'Beyond the pale,' he agreed. His father had yelled at the staff and Enzo refused to follow in those footsteps. 'You're the first person to breach the castle walls since my accident, I'm afraid, and that's made you a convenient target for all my built-up crankiness.' He hauled in a breath. 'I'm sorry. I'll try and do better from now on.'

'Okay, you just upgraded yourself to an eight out of ten.'

He tried to smile but it felt more like a wince. 'I'll keep my fingers crossed that the attics make my bad behaviour worth it.'

Her light laugh was balm to his bruised soul. 'I'm sure they will, and I'll upgrade your apology to an eight-point-five if you promise to show me them first thing tomorrow.'

'Done.' It seemed the least he could do.

She glanced at his leg, a question in her eyes. He bit back something surly. 'I've orders to exercise it. The stairs will do nicely. The doctors would approve.'

She let out a breath he hadn't realised she'd been holding. 'Okay, good.'

He stretched his bad leg out in front of him, tried not to wince at the aches and twinges and found a smile from somewhere. 'An eight-point-five isn't so bad.'

Her eyes danced. 'You're getting the hang of this "being an amiable host" gig. In another week, you'll be back to your usual charming self.'

He had to grit his teeth. Was she being deliberately irritating? Unclenching his jaw, he said, 'Speaking of being a considerate host, I'm sure you'd enjoy a chance to see your room and freshen up for dinner.' In roughly two hours' time…

Surely that would give him enough time to shore up his defences and don a pleasant face?

On cue, Luisa appeared to show Sadie to her room. With a grin and a twinkle, Sadie followed her out. He found himself staring after her and shaking his head. He might need longer than two hours.

The grilling started at dinner. Expecting it, Enzo gritted his teeth and held his own in the tit-for-tat that ensued.

'When did the plaster come off your leg?'

'Three weeks ago. How are your grandparents?'

'Oh, muddling along, you know?' She gestured to his leg hidden beneath the table. 'You have exercises you have to do?'

'It's called rehab, Sadie. Exercises to increase strength and flexibility.'

She bit her lip. 'Does it hurt?'

He retorted with, 'Like the blazes some days,' and then wished he hadn't when her face fell.

'I *am* sorry, Enzo. It's so unfair.'

She had no idea how unfair, but he shrugged. 'It'll pass. The leg will get stronger.' He didn't want—or need—her face going soft like that.

As if sensing his discomfort, she became brisk again. 'Have you had any after-effects from the concussion?'

He gritted his teeth harder. 'No. And, Sadie, this is information my family already knows. You won't need it for your dossier.'

She gave a jaunty shrug. 'I like to dot my i's and cross my t's.' Spearing a piece of Luisa's excellent gnocchi on the end of her fork, she waved it through the air. 'Besides, this isn't for some fictional report. I'm asking because I'm curious and because I…care.'

She hesitated over that last word and he wondered why. He might've been a beast earlier, but they'd known each other a long time. If their positions had been reversed, he'd have cared about how she was doing too. If Chelsea asked him to check up on her…

Rolling his shoulders, he changed the topic. 'Where are you working now?'

'For a big auction house in Melbourne that specialises in antiques.'

'And you're working as a toy restorer?'

She gave a silent scream. 'I know! Crazy, isn't it?'

It was actually kind of perfect. Except… He fought a frown. 'I thought you wanted to open your own doll hospital?'

Her gaze promptly snapped away. 'So did I, but there's so much more variety at the auction house. Oh my God, you should see the treasures that come through.' She clasped a hand to her heart mock-dramatically. 'It's bliss.'

He fought a frown. She was lying. But *why*?

'Owning your own business is great in theory, but in practice…' She shook her head. 'Speaking of business, though… Yours?'

'Booming.'

Had she chickened out of setting up her own business?

'And is it true you've not seen your ex-girlfriend since the car crash?'

The question caught him off-guard. His hands clenched about his cutlery so hard, the ancient silver made divots in his palms. The ache in his fingers echoed the ache in his chest, and his leg. Somehow he kept his voice steady. 'Correct.' Thank God. He never wanted to clap eyes on Claudia again.

'The heartless piece of scum.' Sadie slammed her cutlery down. 'That narky collection of lark's vomit!'

He blinked at the inventive insults.

She tossed a few more into the mix—something about smelly toads and worms in compost heaps. Her shoulders deflated, though. 'I'm sorry she broke your heart, Enzo.'

Hold on. What? She'd broken his leg, not his heart.

'You deserved better.'

They were in agreement there. Before he could set her straight, though, she leaned across the table towards him and the gold flecks in her hazel eyes caught the light from the chandelier above and held him temporarily spellbound.

'Are you truly worried about how you look now?'

The words doused him in icy reality. He pulled on a mantle of forbidding hauteur. No one had dared ask him that question, and he hadn't thought Sadie would have the nerve to ask it either. A trickle of reluctant admiration filtered through him. He stamped it out. He thought it brave… Nonsense, it was rude! Except it didn't come across as rudeness. It came across as concern.

She raised her hands. 'I know, I know—skating close to danger, on thin ice et cetera… It's just…' Her hands twisted together. 'One of the reasons I'm here, Enzo, is to, um…' She moistened her lips. 'To prepare you for the surprise birthday party Chelsea is planning to throw for you here in…um… four weeks' time.'

Chelsea was doing *what*? He shot to his feet.

Sadie pointed a finger at him. 'And you can't let on that you know.'

Enzo didn't say a word. He turned on his heel and stormed out.

CHAPTER TWO

SADIE SWEPT INTO Enzo's gloomy living room at eight a.m. the next morning and let out the breath she'd been holding. He hadn't put in an appearance at breakfast and she'd wondered if he'd spend the entire day avoiding her. But here he was, looking admittedly stormy and scowling, but most definitely present in the flesh.

A sigh welled through her. That flesh might be a bit battered and bruised, but what she'd said yesterday still held true. Those scars—even as fresh and angry as they were—not only *didn't* detract from Enzo's magnetic masculinity, they enhanced it.

His face had always been impossibly beautiful. It could've been used in scientific textbooks to illustrate beauty's principle of symmetry. In marring that ideal of perfect symmetry, his scars gave him an uncompromising ruggedness that only enhanced his other...advantages.

She gazed now at the imposing height, the broad shoulders, deep chest and muscled torso, and another sigh welled through her. Enzo still had the power to make a grown woman weak at the knees. She braced her legs and refused to allow them a single tiny wobble. *Ahem.* She wouldn't allow them *two* wobbles; one was understandable.

Instead of focusing on his advantages, she focused on his scowl. 'Let me guess—you're not a morning person?'

His jaw tightened. 'And a good morning to you too, Sadie.'

'Oh!' She feigned shock. 'After the way you stormed away last night, I didn't think we were bothering with manners any more.'

Dark eyes narrowed, but she merely beamed. 'But it's a new day, the sun is shining, manners are once again flavour of the month and it feels as if anything is possible!'

Closing his eyes, he rubbed a fist across his brow. She suspected he was counting to ten.

'Headache coming on?'

His eyes snapped open. *Uh-huh.* She probably deserved that glare, but she refused to tremble beneath its force. Enzo might be cranky and out of sorts and, if what Sadie thought was true, nursing a broken heart from the dastardly Claudia; he'd gone deathly pale when she'd mentioned Claudia's name last night. But buried beneath all of that was the kind heart she remembered from her teenage years.

More importantly, buried beneath all that grumpiness was the brother Chelsea adored. And, as Chelsea was the sister Sadie had never had, she'd do whatever she could to uncover him again. But a more softly-softly approach might be called for.

'Perhaps you should take some paracetamol.'

'Already loaded to the hilt.'

She crossed her fingers and held them up for him to see. 'Hopefully it'll kick in soon and give you some relief.' When he didn't say anything, she tried to contain an excited wriggle. 'So the fact you're actually here… Does that mean we can head straight up to the attics?'

He shook his head, not in refusal, but a kind of bemusement.

'If I say pretty, *pretty* please with a cherry on top?'

'As it appears I'll get no peace until I do…' He hitched his head in the direction of the stairs. 'Follow me.'

She kept her tone deliberately light. 'Are you really expecting peace while I'm here, Enzo?'

They were halfway up the first set of stairs and he swung round so fast she feared his bad leg wouldn't hold him. She shot her arms out ready to catch him.

The mouth that had opened—no doubt to utter something cutting—closed again. '*What* are you doing?'

'Getting ready to catch you. I didn't know if your leg would cope with you spinning around like that.'

His jaw went slack. 'Sadie, if I am in danger of falling, get out of the way. I'd squash you flat!'

'I'm stronger than I look.' And he wasn't going to do any additional damage to himself; not while she was here. She'd never be able to look Chelsea in the eye again. 'I reckon I could prop you up long enough for you to get your balance again.'

He muttered something under his breath in Italian.

'But you didn't lose your balance; you didn't fall over.' She patted him on the shoulder. 'Good for you.' Which sounded patronising, when she didn't mean it to, but she was so darned relieved he hadn't hurt himself…

Oh! The heat from his shoulder collided with her palm in a scorching, dizzying wave, and she reefed her hand away. Enzo's shoulder was rock hard and agonisingly tempting beneath his shirt.

What the hell? No way! She wasn't going to tread that same old, tired road again. She could admire his masculine beauty, but that was where it stopped.

'The girl I used to know was kind of quiet and shy.' She glanced up to find Enzo glaring at her.

'While the guy I used to know would never have glared at me like that.' She waggled her eyebrows. 'Looks like none of our expectations are coming true. More surprises are probably hovering on the horizon just out of sight. Energising, isn't it?'

Nothing—not even the smallest of smiles. She planted her hands on her hips. 'So you not only broke your leg in that car accident, but your sense of humour too, huh?'

His eyes narrowed.

'Never mind, I expect with some concerted rehabilitation it can be resurrected.'

'You're relentless, aren't you?'

'Like water torture.' With a wink, she slipped past him to skip up the rest of the stairs. 'Come on, slow coach, the attics await!'

He followed, grumbling, but she swore she glimpsed a brief smile.

'Turn left at the top,' he instructed.

'What's on this level?'

'Bedrooms, mostly.'

They climbed another set of stairs. 'My bedroom is on this level.'

She glanced over her shoulder. Had he deliberately placed her on the floor that was furthest from him and the rest of the house—or, rather, castle?

Glancing up, he hesitated. 'Your room isn't as large as the rooms on the second floor, but it has one of the best views of the sea, and I thought you'd like it.'

Things inside her turned gooey. *No melting...* 'The view is out of this world. And, Enzo, my bedroom is enormous and perfection in every way.' He'd taken the trouble of giving her a room he thought she'd like. The old Enzo was still there, even if he was trapped under something heavy.

They continued climbing to the next floor. 'The old servants' quarters are on this level, and then...' Enzo led her to a half-staircase with a landing and two doors at the top. 'The attics.' He gestured at the doors—one to the left and the other to the right. 'Which one do you want to go through first?'

'This one on the...right!'

Enzo pushed open the right-hand door and ushered her inside. She stood just inside the doorway to clasp her hands beneath her chin, her gaze wandering over the assorted boxes and items of furniture that greeted her. Three big dormer windows flooded the room with light, ensuring it was neither dank nor dark.

'I thought you'd be rifling through boxes and pulling off dust covers by now.'

'This is a moment to be savoured. In this moment, anything feels possible. I don't yet know what delicious treasures might be found.'

'There won't be anything of value. My father picked the attics clean years ago.'

'Pfft, what did your father know? He was an idiot. And look!' With a laugh, she pounced on an old-fashioned paddle ball, the rubber string still intact. Swinging round, she sent the rubber ball arcing towards him, pulling it back at the last moment so as to not hit him.

To his credit, Enzo didn't even flinch. Dropping it back into the box, she emerged with a Rubik's Cube. Without warning, she tossed it to him and he caught it without dropping his walking stick.

'What the hell, Sadie?'

She slid him a grin. 'The accident didn't affect your reflexes. *That* needs to go in my report.'

This time he finally smiled properly, as if he couldn't help it, and it sent a bigger surge of adrenaline through her than the attic had done. Enzo's problem was he'd been left to his own devices for too long. He needed a bit of convivial company to jolly him up and get him out of his own head for a bit. Admittedly, he had a lot of reasons for feeling down in the dumps, but brooding didn't do anybody any good.

'Well, I'll leave you to explore and—'

'Oh no, you don't.' She'd noted the way he'd started to

lean more heavily on that cane of his. 'Please sit here and keep me company.'

Pulling a dust cover off what looked like an old dining-room chair—its embroidered seat now a little worse for wear—she tested its strength then patted its seat.

'I don't need a rest, Sadie.'

'Which is just as well because, eventually, we're both going to have to trudge down all of those stairs again. But I have no ulterior motive, other than the fact that I might need your manly muscles to help me move some boxes.'

To her surprise, he did as she bid. 'I'll stay if you answer a question for me.'

'Deal!'

'What really happened with your doll hospital idea?'

She tried not to fidget under that piercing gaze. 'Like I said last night, nothing, really. It just seemed a bit risky.'

She recalled the looks of horror on her grandparents' faces when she'd outlined her plan to them, and swallowed. They'd lost no time pointing out all the reasons it would be too risky, too challenging, too *ambitious*. She stuffed down the sigh that rose through her. 'I put it on the back burner, and decided to get some experience in the workforce first.'

'It wouldn't have been a huge outlay to start up a business like that.'

It still would've taken all she'd had.

'If you need a backer, I'd be happy to invest in your business.'

She swung back, probably with her mouth unflatteringly ajar, wondering if she'd heard him correctly.

'You have what it takes to make a business successful, Sadie.'

Did she?

'A specialised, in-demand skill…and passion.'

That word filtered through her: *passion*. How long had it

been since she'd truly embraced her passions rather than try to diminish or ignore them? And how long had it been since someone had truly believed in her, shown faith in her, the way Enzo just had? And he hadn't seen her in years.

'Sadie?'

She shook herself. 'Bless your boots, Enzo. That's such a generous offer.'

'But you're not going to accept it?'

She shook her head.

'Because of your pride?'

Because her life was in flux; because she'd packed up all her things in Australia with no plans to return any time soon. But she didn't want to talk about that. She didn't even want to think about it. 'Because, while I'd be prepared to risk my own money, I'm not risking anyone else's.'

'I have a lot of money. I can afford to lose some.'

She stared down her nose at him. 'Are you boasting?'

'Just stating facts.'

That made her laugh. Simple fact of the matter was, she'd lost her nerve for starting up her own business. If she'd been truly passionate about her doll hospital, she wouldn't have let anyone talk her out of it.

Something inside her threatened to lift its head and come back to life, but she patted it kindly and told it to go back to sleep.

'If you change your mind…'

'Thanks, Enzo, that's kind of you.'

She wouldn't change her mind, though, and she hoped he'd let the matter drop. Her shoulders might've actually sagged when he said, 'So, how are you going to do this? Is there a method to your treasure hunting or are you all magpie randomness?'

'I have a treasure map!' She pulled out her phone with a flourish. 'Courtesy of Chelsea. I need to find the piano with a bust of someone important-looking balanced on top.'

'Galileo, perhaps?'

She followed his finger to where it pointed. 'Aha! I need to keep it on my left and take eight steps towards a 1950s pram before then turning right at the trunk made of alligator hide.' She followed Chelsea's instructions. 'Now, somewhere here there ought to be a box full of linen, and behind that… eureka! Here's the tan suitcase.'

She held it aloft like a trophy and then trudged back to where he sat. Grabbing a little wooden stool, she plonked herself across from him and set the suitcase between them. 'Buried treasure duly found.'

'Chelsea hid it for you to find?' He gaped at her. *'Why?'*

'Because…fun.' She spread her hands. Didn't he ever do anything just for fun?

At the word fun, he scowled again. 'Look, Sadie, about this party…'

She leapt up to poke about some bits and bobs nearby—including a vanity case and a men's jewellery box. 'The one that Chelsea is throwing for you?'

'What other party would I be referring to?'

Mischief shuffled through her. 'Oh, your mother hasn't mentioned the ball she's giving to raise funds for homeless women? She's counting on your attendance. It's not until November, though. And your stepfather has organised a box at…let me think…is it AC Milan or Inter Milan? Anyway, there's some huge football day out. Then of course there'll be the baby shower once Chelsea's littlie arrives.'

'Very funny. I actually believed you for a moment.'

She set the vanity case and jewellery box beside the suitcase and sat on the stool again. 'What gave me away?'

'Stephen hates football. Cricket is what he loves—a game I truly don't understand. But back to this party Chelsea has her heart set on—it *cannot* happen. You need to find a way to stop it.'

'I see no need for that. Why would I want to spoil her fun? Why would you?'

His jaw clenched. 'It's *my* birthday!'

She gestured to the suitcase. 'You own whatever's inside that suitcase, but you don't seem to begrudge its contents to Chelsea. She said you'd told her to take whatever she fancied from up here.'

He glanced at the suitcase and his frown deepened. 'I told her to take anything she wanted. Why did she leave it behind?'

'Her email answers that. Here, listen to this…' She scrolled down to Chelsea's initial message. '"Enzo told me to help myself to anything I wanted, and as soon as I saw these I wanted them with my every atom. But I didn't want to jinx this pregnancy, not after finding out what had happened to Mum. So I gathered them up, put them in the tan suitcase and hid them, not wanting to count my chickens".'

'When did she do this?'

'The first time she visited the castle. So, when was that… two years ago?' That was when Enzo's horrid father had died, leaving him this not-so-humble pile of rocks.

His stare remained steady. 'What did Chelsea find out about her mother?'

Sadie wasn't sure it was her place to say. Chelsea hadn't sworn her to secrecy or anything. Actually, she was surprised Enzo didn't know already.

'Sadie?'

'She found out her mother had had several miscarriages. One before she was born and two after. She found these—' she pointed at the suitcase indicating its contents '—before she and Dominic married.'

'And before becoming pregnant.'

'Exactly. But unlike her mother she hasn't had an early-stage miscarriage. She's nearly five months gone and in the best of health,' she added, because there were new shadows in his eyes and she wanted to eliminate them as soon as she could. 'She's in the hands of an excellent doctor who's aware of her mother's history. She's being monitored carefully and coddled appropriately. There's no reason why her pregnancy won't go full-term.'

He blew out of breath. 'Good. Right.'

That was the moment Sadie saw what he held in his hand— that Rubik's Cube she'd tossed to him earlier, except now it was solved. Reaching out, she took it and turned it over and over in her hands—each side was a perfect square of colour. 'How did you do that? I could never figure these out.'

'It's just a puzzle.'

She handed it back to him. 'If you're clever enough to solve a Rubik's Cube, Enzo, then I expect you also have the smarts to convince everyone you're having fun at a party you don't really want.'

Except the energy it would require of him and the unwanted intrusion into his solitude left Enzo feeling unutterably heavy. He didn't *want* to celebrate anything—least of all another journey around the sun.

'There's a bit more in Chelsea's message you should probably hear.'

He glanced back at Sadie. She had a smudge of dirt on one cheek, but both her cheeks glowed with good health, and her eyes shone. Was it because she loved attics? It seemed such an innocent thing to love. Maybe he'd spent too much time in the company of women who had left him feeling jaded— women like Claudia—but it was hard to trust in anything as innocent as someone's enjoyment in exploring the contents of attics that didn't belong to them.

There was no denying Sadie's enjoyment, though. Her eyes sparkled, and every now and again she'd shimmy as if she couldn't help it. But was that enjoyment innocent? Did she somehow mean to profit from his attics? And, if she did, did he care?

He cared nothing for these things per se. If he'd needed the space, he'd just as soon have carried everything down to the incinerator and burned it. So if anyone he knew wanted the contents of his attics, shouldn't he be happy just to let them take it?

Recent events, though, had burned the generosity from his soul. He now found himself hungering to punish anyone who wanted to take advantage of him. Another part of him hated himself for this attitude, for his suspicions.

Sadie isn't trying to take advantage of you.

She was at the castle with an ulterior motive.

Sì, to help you.

He didn't want help. He didn't want company. He didn't want a party! He wanted to be left alone to recover his strength, to process all that had happened and to solder the broken bits of himself back together. What he didn't want was sparkling eyes, glossy hair and lips so pretty they made him wonder what it would be like to kiss them.

Again...

His chest clenched. He'd never forgotten the kiss he and Sadie had shared all those years ago.

Not relevant!

He shook himself impatiently. After recent events, he'd sworn never again to embark on a serious relationship. He wasn't going to give any woman the power or opportunity to pull a Claudia-sized tantrum on him. He wasn't going to give any woman the chance to ruin his life.

How do you feel about unserious relationships, fleeting flings, temporary hook-ups?

He blinked. His mouth went dry. In the next moment, reality hit. He was not going to *hook up fleetingly* with his stepsister's best friend. *That* had the potential to lead to trouble. His mother had suffered enough domestic disharmony at his father's hands to last a lifetime. He'd sworn never to do anything to disrupt her current happiness. She deserved to enjoy her hard-won peace.

'Enzo.'

He started at the sharp note in Sadie's voice.

'You were miles away.'

And, from her look, wherever his mind had been, she hadn't considered it either pleasant or happy.

Welcome to my life.

'I apologise for my inattention.' If memory served, she'd wanted to tell him something—no doubt something he didn't want to hear.

Instead, she leapt to her feet. 'Come on; today is for fun. Let's take our treasure downstairs and admire it properly.'

It was the last thing he'd expected. 'But you've hardly looked at anything.'

'Not true.' She gestured to the bounty at their feet. 'I'll get to work properly tomorrow. Like I said, today is just for fun.'

'Isn't there anything else you want to take downstairs?' He could carry more than the suitcase.

'Well, as tempting as I find that beautiful treadle sewing machine over there, it's far too heavy for us to carry downstairs.' Her smile widened and she bent down to pat the suitcase. 'Besides, I expect to find plenty in here to keep me occupied.'

She handed it to him, before gathering up the vanity case and jewellery box. Had Chelsea given her treasure-map directions to them as well?

At the last moment, she settled them on top of a box that she hefted into her arms. 'How's a girl supposed to resist a miscellaneous box of odds and ends, I ask you?'

Suppressing a smile, he ushered her out of the door. It

wasn't until they were standing on the landing and facing the door opposite that he realised what her earlier revelation also indicated. 'If you knew that Chelsea's so-called treasure was through the right-hand door, that means you also knew the toy collection is through the left one.'

'Rumbled!'

He pointed. '*That* has to be the attic you're actually dying to get inside.'

'It is.'

'Then why…?'

Her hands were full of box, but one finger uncurled to point at the suitcase. 'Enzo, there are toys inside that. Chelsea wants me to restore them for her children—as long as I have your permission to do so.'

Of course she had his permission.

'*That's* why I'm really here. What's behind the left-hand door will satisfy professional curiosity. It can wait.'

Not just professional curiosity but her own personal curiosity too, he imagined. Sadie had been obsessed with antique toys ever since he'd known her. It occurred to him now, though, that he didn't know why. And why the hell hadn't she pursued her dream to open her own doll hospital?

He glanced at the closed attic door and then at the suitcase he held, and his lips twisted as he twigged what she was up to. 'You're putting Chelsea's needs before your own.'

She frowned at whatever she saw in his face. 'I'm not sure what you're getting at. I'm going to enjoy—'

'It's a little heavy-handed, don't you think—all of this leading by example? It must be wearing.'

She blinked.

'I am *not* having a party, Sadie. I won't have my house invaded and me paraded like a circus exhibit. If Chelsea persists with the idea, then I'll vacate the premises and she and whoever she invites can party without me.'

He turned and started down the stairs, swearing he heard her mutter, 'Selfish pig,' under her breath. He didn't give a flying fig what she thought of him. Nevertheless, the insult burrowed under his skin to prickle and burn.

He swung back, his hand gripping his cane so tightly, his fingers started to ache. 'What she should be doing is looking after herself and preparing for the arrival of her baby!' Not jumping on a plane from London and hiking it across to his isolated castle.

'Has it not occurred to you that might be exactly what she's doing in throwing this party?'

'Don't be daft! She's doing it out of some misplaced sense of responsibility!'

'I see.'

Ice dripped from her voice. In the past, he'd considered her quiet and shy, but never icy. Beneath her reserve she'd always been as warm and comforting as *risotto alle Milanese*—his favourite dish. For reasons he couldn't fathom, this new iciness infuriated him.

'Why are you really here, Sadie? What are you hoping to gain by rifling through my attics?' He barely recognised the mocking fury in his voice, but he couldn't stop the hot rush of words. 'Are you hoping to win kudos and a healthy commission from your auction house for an as-yet-undiscovered treasure?'

She didn't utter a single word of protest, but her mouth had gone thin and she eyed him, the suitcase and his stick with a wariness that cut him to the quick.

'Do you mind if I get past?'

He immediately pressed himself against the wall to let her slip by, his heart slugging against his ribs while nausea churned in his gut. He forced himself down the steps after her, keeping a reasonable and respectable distance. The accusations he'd flung at her had been vile. And the *way* he'd flung them at her...

She was halfway along the corridor when he finally made it to the bottom. 'Sadie.'

She halted and turned, but she didn't move back towards him.

'I know I sounded fierce just then. But…' His heart thundered. 'You have to know I'd never hurt you.'

Her eyes flashed. 'No. I *don't* know that. I don't know you at all any more, Enzo.' Her face fell. 'What happened to you?'

He remained silent, but a chasm opened in his chest. Had he truly frightened her? If he had, it'd be unforgivable. What the hell kind of person was he in danger of becoming?

'I know you're in pain.' She pointed to his leg before touching a hand to her chest above her heart. 'But that's no excuse for directing your anger at me. Certainly not with the kind of force you just did. Your accusations are not only unfounded, but unforgivable.'

Her words stabbed him like knives, each of them finding their mark.

'Chelsea is one of the most important people in my life. Your family have never been anything other than welcoming and kind to me. To think I would ever seek to profit from that financially…' She lifted her chin. '*No!* That's more a reflection on you than me.'

True; all of it was true. A hard, cold lump the size of a gravestone lodged in his chest. He was in danger of turning into his father. Not in a million years would he have thought himself capable of that.

'But you haven't just insulted me, you insult Chelsea too. "Some misplaced sense of responsibility"—that's what you called it. She loves you, Lorenzo, with all of her heart. She considers you her brother. *Some misplaced sense of responsibility.* Is that how you feel about her?'

'No,' he croaked. He adored Chelsea. He'd walk over hot coals for her.

He set the suitcase down and braced a hand against the wall, concentrating on his breathing, concentrating on stopping the corridor from swaying. Selfish and self-absorbed, was what he'd become.

'Do you need help down the stairs?'

He shook his head. He didn't deserve her help. The corridor stopped swaying and he forced himself upright. 'Sadie…'

'Me coming here was a terrible mistake, but it's one I can rectify.'

She turned on her heel and disappeared down the stairs.

Enzo limped back to the attic stairs, lowered himself down to them and dropped his head to his hands.

CHAPTER THREE

STOMP! STOMP! STOMP!

Sadie followed the clifftop path down to the beach at its base. Slamming hands onto her hips, she glared at the crescent of golden sand, at the soft sapphire sea and the inviting shade beneath the pine trees that fringed this exquisite beach—all of it utterly glorious.

Sadly, she wasn't going to get to enjoy any of it. Spinning on her heel, she stomped back up the path—*thump, thump, thump.* By the time she'd reached the top, some of the oomph had gone out of her fury.

Okay, enough with steps for one day. Would anyone notice if she melted onto the soft grass and stared at the sky for a while to catch her breath and give her legs a chance to recover their strength? It was only the thought that Enzo might be watching from one of his castle's many windows that prevented her from doing any such thing. Gritting her teeth, she forced her legs across the lawn in the direction of the terrace.

The terrace was a paved expanse that ran the full length of the castle. Curving gently, it formed a generous semi-circle at the castle's rear. Planters of various sizes were dotted about, filled with colourful flowers, screening hedge plants and several strategically placed pencil pines, all of which helped to demarcate and complement the different seating areas on offer—large and small, open and private—all sharing that enviable view.

It was only when Enzo stood from one of the tables that she realised he'd been watching from much closer quarters than a window above. On the table in front of him sat a jug of water, moisture condensing its sides. Her mouth fell to its knees and begged for mercy. Who knew stomping could be such thirsty work? But, rather than race over to pour the contents of the pitcher down her throat—or over her head to cool her overheated flesh—she halted and folded her arms.

'Sadie, will you please do me the kindness of joining me?'

She had a flight to book and bags to pack.

'Please give me an opportunity to apologise to you properly...' He hesitated. 'And comprehensively.'

That final word emerged reluctantly, as if he'd had to force it out. *Good.*

He poured a generous glass of water, ice tinkling temptingly, and set it in front of the other chair. 'It's a hot day, and you must be thirsty after your walk.'

With a huff, she stalked over to the table, reached for that alluring glass and took a long, satisfying drink before sitting. *For Chelsea.* 'Just so you know, I'm doing this for the water, not for you.'

'Noted,' he said, though she suspected her childish gibe had him fighting a smile.

If he laughed at her, she'd get up, walk away and leave—end of story. She'd always known she wasn't good enough for the likes of Enzo Lombardi and his peers. At unbidden moments his mother's words still sounded through her and they still had the power to make her flinch.

Sadie is not from our world. This has to stop. She doesn't have the resources to negotiate the world you come from.

These days, though, she didn't have to put up with such snooty attitudes.

Enzo's not like that.

Of course he was. Chelsea wasn't like that, though. Chelsea was an utter sweetheart. At the thought of her friend, her heart sank. Was she really going to let her down? She hitched it back up. She wasn't—*Enzo* was.

She took another sip of water while Enzo remained chafingly silent. She lifted her glass in his direction. 'Just so you know, I'll be leaving as soon as I finish this.'

Which meant he had the time it would take her to drink half a glass of water to properly and comprehensively apologise. She crossed her fingers beneath the table and hoped that he could manage it.

When Enzo had yelled at her just then on the attic stairs, his face contorting with fury, it had been like a knife to the heart from the boy she'd once adored. She knew her girlhood crush on Enzo had been nothing more than immature longings and fantasies—insubstantial and not based in any kind of reality. But one of the things she cherished from those long-ago memories was the fact that Enzo had always been kind to her. He'd always treated her with respect.

Until that stupid kiss at that stupid ball when she'd been eighteen. A kiss that had burned itself on her brain. A kiss she'd never been able to forget. His subsequent withdrawal had been the exception to the rule—and even then he hadn't been unkind, just…aloof. But this morning it had occurred to her that maybe it was all his former kindness that had been the exception, and some silly, long-ago part of her heart had broken.

She'd wanted to leave and never see him again, and now she could. Draining her glass, she set it on the table with a decisive click and rose. 'I'd like to say it's been a pleasure, but we both know that'd be a lie. Goodbye, Enzo—'

'Oh God, don't leave. I'm sorry. I'm struggling to find words to explain myself. I can't find any that will…that are halfway polite. Damn it, Sadie, I don't recognise myself when I look in the mirror any more. I *hate* what I see!'

His chest rose and fell as if he'd been running, and his eyes flashed, but he held her gaze. A lump lodged in her throat.

'I didn't know vanity was one of my besetting sins and...'

And...?

'I'm angry with myself for being so shallow.'

She turned his words over. She'd never considered him vain, though clearly that was the interpretation he'd arrived at, and had found himself wanting as a result.

'The thought of having a party where people are going to look at me as less than I was, as an object to be pitied, feeling sorry for me... I can't stand it.'

'That's not vanity, Enzo,' she said slowly, shaking her head. 'That's pride.' And that was something she could understand.

He scratched a hand over his jaw, a jaw currently darkened by an intriguing stubble. 'Will you let me pour you another glass of water? Or half a glass?' he added when she didn't immediately answer.

Her thirst was nowhere near quenched, but she refused to capitulate quickly or easily. 'Half a glass.' She took her seat.

He dragged in a breath. 'I knew you were coming to the *castello*, and I thought I was prepared, but I didn't realise someone intruding on my solitude would have such an impact on me.'

'Impact how?'

'I thought you'd be as quiet and reserved and shy as you always were. But you're not.'

He'd thought she'd be easy company—as in, easy to ignore. Had he expected her to be soothing and sympathetic? He'd have loathed her sympathy and viewed all attempts at being soothed with suspicion. She sipped her water. 'You thought I'd tiptoe gently around you like everyone else has done.'

'I suppose I did.'

'You've had plenty of people coming in to mop your fevered brow. You're on the road to recovery now and no longer a patient. I didn't think you'd appreciate it if I came in all softly-softly and treated you like you weren't capable of looking after yourself.'

'*That* would've been appalling.'

She spread her hands, silently asking what was the problem, then?

He scowled. 'Instead you came in all demanding, turning everything on its head, and *impossible* to ignore.'

'*That's* why you lost your temper and shouted like you did?'

He rubbed a hand over his face, grinding back an impatient sound. 'I did *that* because you wouldn't listen to me. I said no to the party—told you I didn't want one—but you blatantly ignored me.'

Her heart started beating too hard.

'My fear since the accident is losing my autonomy.' His lips twisted. 'When I was lying in a hospital bed, my leg in traction and my mind groggy from the concussion, in my more lucid moments I wondered if I'd ever be independent again. The thought that I might not be had me wanting to die.'

Her hand flew to her mouth.

'And, when you didn't listen to me, it felt as if I was losing control—in danger of once again forfeiting my autonomy.'

His words not only took the wind out of her proverbial sails, they left her becalmed. She'd made him feel worse when he was already struggling with his self-image, and she hated herself for it. 'I'm sorry, Enzo. Truly sorry. I didn't mean to make you feel that way.'

He stared back. His jaw clenched. 'How do you do that?'

Do what?

'Give a ten-out-of-ten apology just like that.' He snapped his fingers. 'And I'm not looking for an apology. I know you didn't mean to make me feel like that. If I'd been in a better frame of mind, I'd have bitten my tongue and counted to ten. Instead I yelled at you like a damn brute. And the look on your face…' He forked a hand through his hair. 'I'll never forget it. I'm sorry I frightened you. I promise to never yell at you again or—'

He broke off, breathing hard. 'Sadie, I hope to God you know I'd never lay a finger on you; that I'd never hurt you.'

'Of course I know that!' And she did. It'd been her own foolish heart and memories she'd fled from, not him.

His eyes narrowed, as if he didn't quite believe her. 'I acted like a bully.'

She'd had to deal with bullies most of her life. The girls at boarding school had made her life an absolute misery. If it hadn't been for Chelsea, she didn't know what she'd have done. That quiet, vicious bullying that had let her know she'd never belong, never be one of them, never be enough, had been relentless and awful. To be so constantly undermined…

Enzo might not think her good enough, might not think she belonged in his world, but he'd never say such a thing out loud. His temper had shocked her, but she hadn't felt bullied, and nor had she felt afraid for her well-being. 'You know what I think? I think your life these last few months has been too fraught, too heavy and dark. You need to learn to cultivate a sense of insouciance again.'

One corner of his mouth hooked up. *'Insouciance?'*

'What? It's a beautiful word. And so much more exotic than "equanimity" or plain old "balance".'

'Is that what you are these days—insouciant?'

'And bright and breezy.'

'Whatever it is…' his lips relaxed into a smile '…it looks good on you, Sadie.'

His gaze was full of warmth and appreciation and she found herself wanting to bask under it. Their gazes caught and held for a fraction too long. With a jolt, she dragged hers away. 'Flatterer.'

'Flattery is better than intimidation.'

'See, you're getting the hang of it already. Keep this up and we'll have you bright and breezy and insouciant in no time at all.'

But would they? She recalled the expression on his face when she'd mentioned Claudia's name last night—how haunted and lost he'd looked, how pale and tense he'd gone. It had made her stomach churn. 'Do you want to know how I got over my crush on you, Enzo?' she blurted out, apropos of nothing.

He blinked, but then his gaze sharpened. 'I'd very much like to know.'

Hers had been a schoolgirl crush, while whatever he'd felt for Claudia had been far more mature, but maybe she could say something to help him find a path out of his heartbreak. 'My life was on the point of change that last summer I spent with your family.'

'You were heading off to university.'

She'd spent several weeks each summer with Chelsea's family whilst at boarding school. They were warm, idyllic days just hanging out with Chelsea—and often Enzo as well—swimming, sunbathing and playing tennis. By the time she went to university, she hadn't had to deal with the mean girls from boarding school *and* she'd been able to indulge her love of history and art while discovering other things she'd also come to love. 'I threw myself into the experience.'

'What do you mean?'

'I mean, I wasn't there to simply tick off a list to achieve a qualification. I *loved* what I was studying—I had a new passion to focus on.'

'I can see how that would be helpful.'

Did he, though? 'I joined clubs.' Fun people had actively enlisted her. It had been so inclusive. 'The hockey club, the history club, a book group… And I worked two part-time jobs so I could afford to move out into a shared house.' She'd made herself too busy to brood endlessly about Enzo.

'Independence is a great experience.'

'It meant I could stay out as late as I wanted.'

He huffed out a laugh. 'Meaning you dated.'

'Of course I did.' More importantly, she'd become her own person.

'And it helped?'

She slid him a mischievous grin. 'Depends on which dates we're talking about.' She was quiet for a moment. 'Before university, I always saw my life as a bit grey. Spending the summers with your family was the one bright spot in my life.'

He frowned. 'I never knew that.'

'Why should you? What I'm trying to say, Enzo, is that, when I had the opportunity to, I surrounded myself with all the things I loved that brought me energy and enthusiasm and filled my life with colour.'

He stared at her for a long moment. 'So…you're not-so-subtly telling me that I should surround myself with colour?'

Surely it was better than grey?

His face went tight. 'Your teenage crush is a different beast from what I've had to endure in recent months.'

'I know, but…'

'It's naïve to think that I can simply snap my fingers and—'

He broke off, breathing hard, and it was all she could do not to cry. Because, whatever else this Claudia had been, she hadn't deserved this man's love.

'But I do not wish to argue with you again. Let's agree to disagree.'

So much for trying to help. 'Fine, but here's something else for you to chew over: you *do* have your independence; you *haven't* lost your autonomy. You have the kind of money to take your life in whatever direction you want. That has to feel liberating.'

He stared at her. 'I…'

Enough already. 'I accept your apology, Enzo. Thank you for explaining all of that to me.'

He eyed her warily. 'And you'll stay?'

She hesitated. 'The party…?'

His gaze snapped away from hers and he stared out at the horizon, his mouth a grim line. He really didn't want a party, did he?

'And by "party" I mean a small and intimate affair with only family and close friends—not thrill-seekers coming to gawk.'

He grimaced.

'Enzo, do you really think it unreasonable that your family want to celebrate the fact that you're still here to celebrate with?'

'What if I promise to think about it?'

'That would be both generous and good-natured of you.' Reaching across, she filled her glass to the very brim. 'Thank you. I'd love to stay.'

Enzo closed his eyes and let out a breath. Sadie was going to stay. From now on he needed to be more careful, more measured. A party might be anathema to him, but so was worrying Chelsea, especially when she was pregnant.

He had no doubt that Sadie would've made light of the incident, would've assured Chelsea all was well and probably just said something along the lines that he was fine and simply needed more time to adjust or something. But Chelsea would've read between the lines. If Sadie had left, it would've sent Chelsea into a tizz. She'd have insisted on coming to see him. On top of everything else, he'd have had an over-protective, eagle-eyed little sister to deal with as well. One who read far too much into everything he did and everything he said.

His temples started to throb. It'd be preferable for Sadie

to stay for her allotted two weeks. She could send favourable reports back to Chelsea on his progress and welfare, while he came up with a way to gently extricate himself from the party. He'd be careful to make sure Chelsea never knew that Sadie had told him about it either. He wouldn't betray Sadie and cause trouble between the two women. They meant a lot to each other and he had no intention of messing with that. But he had no intention of having a party either.

For the next two weeks Sadie could poke away in the attics to her heart's content. He'd find things to keep him busy during the day and all that would be required of him would be a few hours with Sadie in the evening—a bit of conversation… Maybe Sadie would like to watch TV or read a book, and then he could pretend to watch or read too. Not ideal, but not the end of the world. And temporary—*very* temporary. He could muster the resources to grin and bear it.

He glanced at Sadie from the corner of his eyes. Time to don his 'good host' manners and show her some additional reasons why staying here—temporarily—could be just the ticket. Sadie going home relaxed and rested would convince Chelsea more than words ever could that all was well at the castle.

He knew she'd seen the beach… 'Have you stumbled upon the pool house yet?'

Her gaze swung from where she contemplated the view, and the summer sun picked out the amber flecks in her eyes. She'd once described her eyes as a muddy green, but there was nothing muddy about them. The cool green and that startling amber had him thinking of shady forest groves or of diving into a still sea to swim in a forest of kelp.

'You have a pool?'

'Not just a pool, a pool *house*—an entire entertainment complex.' He did his best to stop his lips from twisting.

'Who needs a pool when…?' She waved a hand towards the sea.

'Come and see.' Maybe then she'd realise.

Draining the contents of her glass, she stood and gestured for him to lead the way. He took her to a building on the other side of the garden, and the expression on her face when he led her inside had him biting back a smile. The sun flooding through the arched windows at this time of day, and bouncing off marble, crystal, cut-glass and gold-gilt furniture, could be a bit much.

The light danced on the water of the thirty-foot pool, as it did on the tiled fresco of mermaids that decorated its base, while the individual pendants of the three chandeliers that hung above it twinkled with a narcissistic brilliance. The furniture arranged around the pool's perimeter—all glass, white leather and gold gilt—likewise gleamed with an indulgent lustre. The entire enterprise boasted extravagance, excess and wealth.

He loathed it.

The view through the wall of glass, however, was unparalleled.

They watched a sleek white yacht glide by on the turquoise water below and only when it had passed did Sadie turn to him. 'This looks like something from a movie set.'

'It's been used in two Italian films and a French one.'

'I suppose the benefit of this is one can swim all year round if one wants. Because, of course, it's heated?'

That last was phrased more as a question than a statement, and he nodded.

Her eyes lit with sudden mischief. 'And one could have some rather fine parties here.'

He was *not* having a pool party.

'What's through there?' She pointed to two doors in the far wall.

Striding across, he opened the first one. 'Ladies and gents shower rooms.'

She shrugged, as if to say, *of course*.

He led her through the other door to a games room with a full-sized snooker table as well as a poker table, and then opened the door beyond it.

'Sleeping quarters!'

Yes; because apparently it was sometimes easier to fall into the nearest bed rather than make the effort to go back to the castle and climb a flight of stairs. Or, if one had been his father or grandfather, one could smuggle the mistress of the moment in to stay there while their wives remained oblivious in the castle.

'Oh, this would've been a dream as a teenager. To be able to have a pool party-slash-sleepover here… What fun!'

Was that what she'd wished?

'Especially when one has a fully stocked kitchen at one's disposal,' she said when he led her through another doorway into the catering kitchen. 'This is industrial-sized!'

'And, given some of the parties that have taken place here, necessary.' He led her back out to the pool.

'Life in a castle is lived on a grander scale, huh?'

If one were his father and grandfather, absolutely.

'And yet here you are, rattling away on your own.'

'*Sì*, I am a poor little rich boy indeed, am I not?'

She rolled her eyes. 'My heart bleeds.'

He found himself fighting a smile. 'Besides, I'm not alone. You're here.'

'I don't count.'

He blinked. 'Why on earth not?'

'Because I'm a trespasser—uninvited and unwanted.'

'Sadie, I…'

'Oh, don't worry. I'm over our earlier spat. I'm here to do a job, that's all.' Shaking her head, she started walking beside the pool. 'I don't belong in this world.'

What on earth…?

'But it's fun to get a peek behind the curtain.'

She sent him a grin that momentarily knocked the air from his body. He took an involuntary step back. Why did her smile have that power? Was he still suffering the effects of the concussion? Had he locked himself away for too long? Maybe it was time to get back to work.

'And yet…'

He shook the troubling thoughts away to find her with her hands on her hips and her back to the pool as she surveyed the view again. 'And yet what?'

She waved a hand at the view. 'This pool house is extraordinary, but it's nothing on that.'

He imagined the expression on his father's and grandfather's faces if they'd heard her words and grinned.

'Oh!' She swung back, darted a glance at his leg. 'The pool must be great for therapy.'

He stiffened, his hands clenching around the cane. 'I don't *do therapy* here. I can manoeuvre the stairs down to the beach quite nicely, thank you.'

Not that he had. But she didn't need to know that.

'Oh, okay.' But then she sent him a comical hangdog look. 'Please don't make me go back down there now.'

His eyes narrowed. Did she doubt his ability, despite what he'd said?

'You might be used to negotiating the insane number of stairs in this place, but I'm not yet stair-fit. The trek up to the attics and then down to the beach have done me in.'

He had to laugh then, because she obviously meant it, and just like that everything was fine once more. He needed to stop being so touchy about his mobility. 'Then how about lunch instead?'

'Yes please.'

'And then we can investigate the treasure you brought down from the attic.'

'You're describing my perfect afternoon.'

Just as well. He had a lot to make up for.

* * *

Sadie halted when they reached the drawing room, setting the tan suitcase on top of a table. Enzo's lip curled. He loathed this room, filled as it was with memories of his father and grandfather—of shouting, smugness and casual cruelty.

He opened his mouth to suggest they move to the adjoining room when she said, 'The light's fabulous in here. Do you think we could…?'

She gestured to the table and then the bay windows. With a shrug, he'd helped her move it across to rest beneath them, where she'd get the full benefit of the natural light. He swore she held her breath as she unlatched the suitcase. It was more entertaining watching her face than seeing what she pulled forth.

She surveyed the lined-up treasures, lowering the suitcase to the floor. 'Your sister has a good eye.'

'Of course she does.' Chelsea was superior in every way.

'So let me explain what we have here.' She mentioned the names and brands of the teddy bear, clockwork robot, jack-in-the-box and toy dog. There were a couple of dolls and Dinky cars, and a spinning top too. 'Restored, these would be in huge demand on the open market. Some, like these two—' she indicated a Sweet Baby doll and a Barbie doll '—are vintage, but quite common, so they wouldn't fetch as much if you wanted to sell them.'

He didn't want to sell them. They were Chelsea's to do with as she pleased.

'How much would you charge to restore this lot?'

'I'm not charging you!'

'But—'

'Chelsea is my dearest friend in the world. While you…'

He found himself holding his breath.

'You, Enzo, have allowed me to storm your castle, and are letting me stay in this extraordinary place—' she gestured at the view '—to have the holiday of a lifetime.'

Her words had a funny lump lodging in his chest.

'It'll be an honour to restore these toys. A labour of love.'

'Noted,' he said, 'And greatly appreciated. But, for curiosity's sake, what would you normally charge?' *If* she had her own toy and doll hospital.

She cocked her head to one side. 'Well, let's see...' She touched each item lightly, making mental calculations, and then gave him a sum that had his brows lifting. 'I know it's expensive...'

'Nonsense! One should pay handsomely for your kind of expertise. I'm glad these things can be restored for Chelsea's children to enjoy. I'm glad you're making a living doing what you love.'

Her eyes went suspiciously bright. 'Thank you.'

Clearing his throat, he backed away, seeking an excuse to absent himself, to go and do something far away from her. Because a teasing, sassy Sadie was one thing, but a soft Sadie was an altogether different proposition. Instinct told him to retreat before he...what? He wasn't going to do *anything*.

A long-ago memory resurfaced, but he resolutely pushed it away. He definitely wasn't going to kiss her, and it would do no good to revisit that particular memory.

'Before you rush off...' Sadie dragged in a breath that had him halting. 'I'm under strict instructions from Chelsea to make sure it is in fact okay for her to take these things.'

'Of course it is!'

'Just so you know, this lot is worth a small fortune.'

She named a sum that had his eyes widening. 'Toys are worth that much?'

'These ones are. And, while we're on the topic of money, that's a vintage Goyard suitcase there and worth at least two thousand euros.'

He shook himself. 'Whatever these things are worth, Sadie, I want Chelsea to have them. She'll cherish them, and her children will cherish them, and that's as it should be.' He shifted and frowned. 'She wanted you to make sure...?'

'She'd rather die than have you thinking she was taking advantage of you.'

'She—?'

'I know, I know! I told her you'd never think that, but she's seen plenty of other people take advantage of you, and she's determined to never do anything that will make you feel like that.'

Would it really be so bad to have a party?

Rolling his shoulders, he shook off the thought. He wasn't having a party, but... 'I'll ring her.'

Striding away, he pulled his phone from his pocket and dialled. Since Chelsea had moved to Europe last year, he no longer had to calculate the time difference.

'Enzo!' Chelsea's voice and the excitement in it reached him down the line, making him smile. 'It's great to hear from you! How are you?'

'Very well. The toys you want are apparently worth a small fortune.'

'Oh, God—'

'But I do not care. They are yours, and I don't want to hear any arguments.'

They talked for a little while and laughed. He should've taken the initiative to ring her sooner. He should ring his mother too.

'Enzo, can I ask you a favour?'

His stomach screwed up tightly. He *didn't* want a party. 'You can ask.'

Chelsea laughed. 'Hedging your bets, huh? I don't think it's a huge favour. It's just...can you make sure that Sadie doesn't bury herself in the attics for the entire fortnight?'

He bit back a sigh. 'I will do my best.' But it wasn't any of his business how Sadie wanted to spend her time.

'It's just…'

His every sense went on high alert at the sudden strain in her voice. 'Yes?'

'She'd probably kill me for telling you.'

'Not literally. Go on.'

'Well, Sadie's recently had some unsettling news. Her… um…her mother has returned.'

What the hell? Sadie's mother had abandoned her as a baby and left her to be raised by her grandparents. And now she was home…

He forked a hand through his hair. Chelsea and Sadie had become the best of best friends at boarding school in Australia. His stepfather Stephen was Australian and had travelled a lot for work. It was how he'd met Enzo's mother. After his first wife's death, he'd sent his daughter to the very best schools.

Sadie's background had been very different. She'd been one of a handful of scholarship students—awarded full board and tuition due to academic excellence. Chelsea had felt cast adrift at boarding school and had been still grieving the death of her mother. Sadie had…

He swallowed. As Chelsea told it, Sadie had saved her, had made her feel less alone, and had made her laugh again. Sadie had made her see the future could be a happy place.

She taught me to dream again.

That was why Sadie had always been off-limits to him. Because she meant as much to Chelsea as the rest of their family did. If he ever did anything to hurt Sadie, Chelsea would never forgive him. It could create the ugliest of splits, which would break his mother's heart, and he couldn't bear that thought.

But Sadie's mother had come home… 'Has Sadie actually seen her?'

'Yes. It didn't go well.'

'So you sent her here?'

'Two birds, one stone,' she whispered. 'I really do want those toys restored and I knew that would be something she'd love to do. I hope you don't mind me imposing like this, Enzo.'

'No, it was a good thing to do.' Sadie's mother had come home… As he rang off, he found he didn't mind Chelsea sending Sadie here. Not now. Not one little bit.

CHAPTER FOUR

SADIE DIDN'T SEE Enzo until dinner time. No doubt he was avoiding her which, God forbid, suited her just fine. They both needed a time-out after that ugly spat. Some people could take that kind of thing in their stride, but she wasn't one of them. She suspected Enzo wasn't either.

Funny, but she hadn't grown up with anyone yelling at her as a child. Her grandparents were gentle people, kind enough in their own way, though joyfulness hadn't featured large in their lives. If she was being bluntly honest, joy hadn't featured in their lives at all.

Until recently. And that had only brought home to her how short she'd always fallen in their affections. It was hard to love someone with her whole heart only to have them not love her back in equal measure or even a half measure. That was the way to a broken heart. It wasn't just some gorgeous guy who promised someone the world and then ran away at the first sign of trouble who could break one's heart. One's family and friends could break it too. And it was almost a relief to realise that after so long.

Which was why, from now on, she would wrap her heart in bubble wrap, cotton wool and shock-absorbent rubber and place it in a big, steel box with a whopping great padlock. She hadn't been enough for her mother. She hadn't been enough for her grandparents. And, other than Chelsea, she hadn't been enough for the girls at the boarding school either. Nine years ago, she hadn't been enough for Enzo. She wouldn't let anyone else make her feel 'not enough'.

The guys you've dated over the years haven't been like that.

She'd mostly dated nice guys. None of them had set her world on fire, though. She'd not been able to envisage a future with any of them. Maybe at some indefinable point in the future she'd meet someone who would change her mind. But love wasn't on the agenda for the immediate future. Creating a life she loved needed to be her top priority. A life with strong foundations. A life that wouldn't let her down.

'Are you still going over what happened earlier?'

Enzo stood in the doorway of the dining room, surveying her with those dark eyes of his, and she sent him a swift smile. 'Nope, just off with the fairies.'

'They're bad fairies, then.' He took a seat. 'Are you sure I don't need to apologise again?'

'Positive. Besides…' she grinned '… I think you've had enough practice for one day. I was just reflecting on the fact…' Gah! What was she doing? She was supposed to be bright, breezy and *insouciant*—not earnest and serious.

'Yes?' That raised eyebrow assured her she wouldn't get away without an explanation, and what the heck? The truth was better than making things awkward between them again.

'You were reflecting on…?'

Luisa entered with their plates. Sadie stared at the vision of tuna on a bed of finely sliced crispy potatoes and the side of buttered steamed vegetables that were placed in front of her. She lifted amazed eyes to the other woman.

Luisa winked. *'Bon appétit.'*

'This looks like heaven.' Seizing her cutlery, Sadie pointed her fork in the direction in which the housekeeper had disappeared. 'She's wonderful.'

'Agreed. As you were saying…?'

She laughed. She could manage some teasing mixed in

with the seriousness. 'Never fear, I will reveal all. I just have to try the tuna first.'

She did, and it was perfection. Closing her eyes, she relished the taste and texture. This was her favourite meal. When she opened them again, she found Enzo gazing at her with the same expression he'd had in his eyes when she'd examined Chelsea's selection of toys. Her mouth went dry. It was the same expression he'd worn the night he'd kissed her when she'd been eighteen—heated, hungry, wolfish.

An answering heat unfurled deep inside her but, unlike nine years ago, she knew this sensation was lust, not love. She knew the difference now and maybe…

Oh, God. Do not be tempted!

Dragging her gaze away, she did her best to quench the heat with two undeniable facts. The first was that Enzo didn't want to feel that heat; she could tell he resented it. The second was the fact he was nursing a broken heart. She had no desire to be anyone's rebound fling. She was worth more than that.

Oh, and there was a third reason for good measure: she would never be enough for Enzo. Ever. And she was through with all that. Enzo came from a completely different world and, as his mother had once pointed out, she would never fit into it. She didn't have the resources to deal with more failure at the moment. She'd left her family; had quit her job. She was moving to Europe to start a new life. *That* was enough.

She glanced across to find Enzo raising an impatient eyebrow that had her wanting to pelt him with the warmed bread rolls. 'You were reflecting on…?'

'Patience isn't your strong suit, is it?'

He blinked.

'And, now that my reflections have been built up to a fever pitch of expectation, you're going to find them terribly anti-climactic. I was merely pondering the fact that you'd deliberately kept your distance this afternoon, and that I was glad of it. It gave us both a chance to regroup.' She shrugged. 'Which in turn had me reflecting on the fact that neither of us are the kind of people who can easily shrug off a shouting match.'

His lips twisted. 'From memory, you didn't do any of the shouting.'

'Regardless, it's still not a "water off a duck's back" thing for us.' She sliced into her tuna. 'Don't you think it's strange when we've had such different upbringings? My grandparents never shouted at me. Occasionally the teachers at boarding school would raise their voices, but no one yelled at us in "sergeant major" fashion.'

The other girls hadn't shouted at Sadie either. Their spite had arrived in quieter and crueller ways.

'Whereas you had a very different experience. Your father and grandfather lost their tempers on a regular basis.' Part of her grieved for the small boy who'd had to bear all that anger.

'*Sì*. A week rarely passed without a temper tantrum from one of them. All of that drama is exhausting. That's why such behaviour now is anathema to me.' He hesitated. 'It's one of the reasons my behaviour this morning appalled me. Theirs is not an example I wish to emulate.'

The tuna promptly lost its flavour. Sadie swallowed her current mouthful, and it settled in her stomach like a lead weight. 'Enzo, you're *nothing* like them.'

'Actions speak louder than words.'

She slammed down her cutlery. 'Five months ago you went through an extraordinarily traumatic event. Then you holed yourself up here in your castle without anyone to talk to. That's a recipe for volcanic outbursts, not an indication you've inherited genetic character flaws. Your father and grandfather were selfish men, but you're not.' She wished he'd look at her. 'But that doesn't mean you're not allowed to be angry sometimes. That's impossible for anyone.'

'The way I choose to unleash that anger is entirely my responsibility.'

She doubted he'd had much choice. The anger and frustration must have built and built until it had taken him entirely off-guard. He'd just…exploded. And, while she might've found it confronting, she hadn't feared for her safety. It had still been Enzo shouting, and Enzo wouldn't hurt any woman. It had probably done him the world of good to get some of that out of his system.

'Anyone would feel angry in your shoes. There was no rhyme or reason for your accident.'

His gaze snapped away and something in her chest faltered. There hadn't been a reason…had there? According to Chelsea, Enzo couldn't remember the crash. The accident had occurred on a particularly dangerous piece of road. The authorities had said it was lucky the car hadn't gone over the cliff—a thought that chilled her to the bone.

Not remembering must plague him. Claudia's injuries hadn't been as severe, but she'd been dozing at the time, and hadn't been able to shed light on what had happened. Knowing Enzo, he probably felt responsible for her injuries too.

Chelsea's scathing critique of Claudia's abandonment of Enzo in his hour of need went round and round in her mind now and she wanted to bury her face in the snowy white linen of her napkin. Had Enzo's scars really appalled the other woman so much? How could she be so insensitive, so heartless?

Sadie had noticed his pallor when she had mentioned her name…

Don't think about that now.

'You've had to endure a great deal of pain, and the frustration of a slow recovery—and you're not a naturally indolent guy—so that's been a challenge in itself.'

Those disturbing lips twitched. 'Is that a polite way of calling me impatient?'

'I wouldn't dream of calling you any such thing!'

He huffed out a laugh. 'If I recall correctly, that's exactly what you just called me.'

The tension in her chest eased a fraction. 'All I'm saying is you've suffered a terrible accident that's turned your whole life on its head. In your place, anyone would feel angry.'

'That doesn't excuse my earlier behaviour.'

'Look, Enzo, you've apologised and I've accepted your apology. Will you please stop wallowing?'

He choked on a spear of asparagus. 'You really aren't a gently-gently person any more, are you, Sadie?'

'Oh, if I were dispensing with the gently-gently approach...' She rested her chin in her hand. 'Has it not occurred to you that your outburst might in fact be an indication that the way you've been dealing with your situation isn't in fact the best way?'

His eyes immediately narrowed into a glare. She did her best to shrug *insouciantly*. 'I understand the urge to bury yourself away from prying eyes, but surely that has an end date?'

'Does it?' Dark eyes skewered her to her seat. 'Are you here to provide me with therapy, Sadie? Is that the role you see for yourself?'

Oh, and there was the anger lurking just beneath the surface. 'Afraid I'm not qualified.' She held his gaze. 'Do *you* think you need to see a therapist?' When he remained silent, she added, 'Or do you just need to stop feeling sorry for yourself?'

It was entirely possible she'd gone too far, but for some reason she was starting to feel angry herself, so she didn't care. 'Self-pity *is* an emotion I've a lot of experience with, though. I spent all of my teenage years in a haze of "woe is me".'

'Nonsense!' he growled, throwing his napkin down beside his plate. 'You never came across as self-pitying.'

'Guess I hid it well.'

Crossing his arms, he raised an eyebrow. 'Why did you feel sorry for yourself?'

She shrugged. 'The girls at school made it clear I was an outsider—that I wasn't one of them.'

At the age of twelve, Sadie had won a full scholarship to a prestigious girls' boarding school in rural Victoria—five hours from Melbourne. She'd been so excited and so quietly proud of herself.

And then had come the reality.

Her grandparents were solid, working-class people—her grandmother a housewife and Pop a train driver. The other girls at school, though, had been the daughters of pastoralists, industrialists, politicians, vice chancellors of universities, High Court judges—the crème de la crème of Australian society.

Some of them had been the progeny of single mothers—not all had come from happy homes—but nobody else's mother had dumped them with their grandparents as a baby and ridden off in the sunset, never to be heard from again. When the girls from school had found that out they'd dubbed Sadie 'UP': the unidentified package at the baggage claim; lost property.

Pushing away the remembered misery, she lifted her chin. 'I didn't fit in anywhere. If Chelsea hadn't told them to back off before claiming me for her BFF, I don't know what I would've done.'

Enzo stared at her with something like horror. For a horrible moment she wanted to hide from all she'd revealed. 'No matter how much I wanted to go back to my old school, I had to stick it out, because my grandparents were overjoyed to no longer have the day-to-day care of me.'

He started. 'Oh, come, Sadie. That has to be an exaggeration.'

'Of course it is.' She winked at him, aiming for levity again. 'As my grandparents don't do joy, they couldn't do *over*joyed, right?'

He snorted. 'Not what I meant.'

'I was a teenager, Enzo. Hyperbole was my default setting. And, while I know my grandparents must love me in their own way, they shouldn't have been lumped with me in the first place. So, while overjoyed is an exaggeration, their poorly disguised relief was not.'

Even now that knowledge had the power to wound her. She'd always been a duty to them rather than a source of pleasure or delight. They'd never been unreasonable, they'd never been unkind, but beneath their kindness had been weariness and sadness. They'd missed her mother. They'd *wanted* her mother. Sadie hadn't even reached the heights of being a poor substitute.

'So, to my mind, I wasn't wanted at school, I wasn't wanted at home…and don't get me started on my mother.'

He stared at her for two beats. 'None of this was obvious on your holidays with us.'

From the ages of thirteen to eighteen, she'd spent several weeks over the summer with Chelsea and her family at their mansion on the Mornington Peninsula, with its spectacular views of the rugged coastline. Their kind of wealth had been previously unknown to her. There'd been a huge swimming pool, tennis courts and an extraordinary games room. They'd swum, gone for long walks and had simply hung out. Those summers had afforded her the time simply to be—nothing had been asked of her, nothing demanded, except that she have fun. Chelsea's family had been every bit as kind and warm as Chelsea herself. It had all felt so magical.

'Those holidays were my respite, a chance to breathe freely.

I swear they gave me the strength to deal with the rest of the year.'

'So how did you manage to drag yourself out of this miasma of self-pity?'

'Started focusing on the things I did have. I had a best friend, and that's no small thing. I buried myself in the things I loved as much as I could—big, fat fantasy novels and fixing things.'

'Like broken toys.'

'I have a knack for it.'

His brow puckered. 'How? Why?'

'Ah, well, that's down to Mrs Aberglasslyn—my grandparents' next-door neighbour. She owned a doll hospital and restored all manner of toys. I was probably six the first time I snuck over to peep inside her workshop.' She'd thought it a wonderland. 'Rather than chase me away, she welcomed me in and showed me what she was working on.'

She smiled at the memory. 'We became firm friends and over the years Ada taught me all that she knew.' A decade older than Sadie's mother, Ada had been the other godsend in Sadie's life. In her late sixties now, she'd retired to the coast. Sadie visited from time to time.

She glanced back at Enzo, who'd remained quiet for too long. 'I told myself that saying, that this too would pass. I knew that one day I'd be an adult and then I could shape my life however I wanted.' Had she, though? Or had she fallen into patterns that wouldn't create waves because that was what she was used to doing? Such as not pursuing her dream to open her toy repair shop, which she also thought of affectionately as a doll hospital, as that was her speciality.

Enzo remained deep in thought and she pushed her own disturbing thoughts away to reapply herself to her meal.

'So...' Enzo glared at his plate. 'This party idea that Chelsea has concocted—it's supposed to force me out of the doldrums?'

Carefully finishing her food, Sadie reached for her napkin and dabbed her mouth. 'I wish a party could make you feel like your old self again...' She shook her head. 'But the party isn't for you, not really, though I don't think Chelsea realises that.'

'What are you talking about?'

'The party is for your family, Enzo. So they can assure themselves that you are in fact okay and on the road to recovery.'

She waited for him to swear, to explode. He did neither. He did pale, though, and she berated herself for her bluntness.

Dragging in a breath that made his nostrils flare, he shook his head. 'Can we change the subject?'

'Excellent idea.' She was supposed to be cheering him up—not making the doldrums even more doldrum-y!

The party isn't for you... The party is for your family. The unalloyed truth of Sadie's words sank into Enzo's bones. Maybe it would be selfish of him to deny them this party, but to have to be cheerful, to put on a show to put their minds at rest... The thought exhausted him. He'd have to field questions—questions that until now they'd refrained from asking.

When will you go back to work?

Do you plan to return to Milan?

Are you starting to feel better?

He didn't know the answers to any of those questions. And there were other questions he dreaded even more.

Have you remembered anything about the accident?

Have you spoken to Claudia?

Lying about the accident didn't sit well with him, but telling the truth was unthinkable.

Fact was, it wouldn't just be a party. It'd be a thinly veiled inquisition. And maybe right now wasn't the best time to consider the pros and cons of a party, when his leg was aching from his exercises and the unaccustomed activity, and his mind was aching from the discovery of how alone Sadie had felt growing up—and the fact her mother had returned.

Sadie clapped her hands. 'After dinner, why don't I grab that box of stuff I brought down from the attic and you can open the jewellery box and vanity case?'

'You haven't gone through it yet?'

'They're *your* things, Enzo. I couldn't do it without you, even though I'm dying to see what we'll find.'

'You've my permission.'

'I opened the suitcase. It's only fair you share the thrill of discovery. Gird your loins, though, it could all end in disappointment. But it's still exciting, don't you think?'

He scratched a hand through his hair. When was the last time anything had *properly* excited him? Did getting out of hospital count? Before that…he couldn't remember.

Sadie took his silence as acquiescence, which was how he found himself standing at the little dining table after dinner, in front of the bank of windows in the detested drawing room with the jewellery box in front of him. Sadie shook out a piece of black velvet from her work bag and spread it beside the box. Folding her arms, she stepped back and simply waited.

Strangely, he found he didn't mind. In fact, maybe even the thinnest thread of anticipation lifted through him, even though he knew nothing of value would be inside—his father and grandfather had sold the family jewels and expensive artworks long ago.

He lifted the lid…to reveal a beautiful, ornate necklace. Lifting it out, he set it on Sadie's piece of velvet, along with a matching brooch and earrings.

'I know a "man of quality" should be able to recognise real diamonds when he sees them, but I haven't a clue.' He couldn't stop his lip from curling. 'As my father knew quality, though, it leads me to suppose these are mere replicas.'

She snorted. 'Your father knew diddly squat.'

He bit back a grin. 'He could tell a genuine diamond from twenty paces.'

'What your father saw were dollar signs. He didn't see beauty.'

Her words made him still.

Reaching for an eyepiece, she bent down to study the necklace. Her dark hair caught the setting sun and for a brief moment it gleamed like walnut silk. 'These pieces might be paste, but they're undeniably beautiful.'

He dragged his gaze from a face alive with animation, and also undeniably beautiful, and swallowed. *'Sì.'*

'Also, it's an exemplary specimen of paste jewellery and I'd date it from the mid-1800s.'

'So this is…?'

She straightened. 'Nearly two hundred years old. What your idiot father couldn't see is that this piece would fetch thousands at auction.'

He smiled at the casual way she hurled insults at his father, but also at the knowledge this piece had bested the older man. 'I don't think I'll sell it.'

'No, it's probably freighted with family history.'

Which promptly made it lose some of its glitter. His family history was nothing to be proud of.

'I bet there's an interesting back story.'

Probably 'interesting' as in awful, he thought, but he left that unsaid. He didn't want to diminish the sparkle in her eyes or her enjoyment in their treasure hunt.

She gestured to the box again. 'What else is hiding in there?'

He opened the two drawers, but they were empty. 'Looks like that's it.'

She frowned. 'May I?'

He immediately stepped aside and gestured for her to take his place. She hefted the box in her hands, as if assessing its weight. Setting it back down, she ran a hand across it slowly, and then stilled. Glancing up at him, she gave a silent scream. 'Give me your hand.'

He did and immediately felt the warmth of her hand, the softness of her skin.

'Feel that?'

His attention snapped back as she ran his finger over a slight depression in the wood. 'I…yes.'

She moved her hand from his to clasp both hands beneath her chin, practically dancing on the spot. The warmth of her hand lingered and that cute smile had heat gathering beneath his breast bone. Damn it! Sadie Beckett was adorable. When had that happened?

She's always been adorable.

'What are you waiting for, Enzo? Press it!'

He couldn't help laughing at her impatience, but that thread of earlier anticipation had grown thick enough now to knit into a sweater. He depressed the button and a secret compartment sprang open to reveal a man's yellow-gold pocket watch. Lifting it out, he set it gently on the velvet beside the paste necklace.

They both bent over it, their heads nearly touching, and her scent filled his senses—something fresh, floral and utterly enlivening. The air whistled between Sadie's teeth. She glanced across at him. 'Now *this* is a find. It's…'

Her words stumbled to a halt and those hazel eyes blinked, as if surprised to find she and Enzo had drawn so close. But then, oh, so slowly, they drifted down to his lips, the gold in their depths sparking. His gaze lowered to her lips—plump, soft, inviting—and heat gathered in his veins, snapping parts of him alive with a fierce hunger. It'd be so easy to…

Sadie snapped upright. Her gaze jerked back to the watch, but a pulse pounded in her throat, betraying her agitation. He stepped back and the sheer difficulty of it had him breathing heavily. While Sadie hadn't flinched at his scars, that didn't mean she wanted him near her. It didn't mean she wanted him to kiss her. And, if he did kiss her, there was every chance she'd only kiss him back out of pity.

That thought doused him as affectively as an ice-cold jet of water. He was careful not to direct any of his anger and loathing at her, though. It was time to stop lashing out like an angry animal. He might find her captivating, and the thought of losing himself to pleasure for a short time held a seductive power that shocked him. But when he'd been lying in a hospital bed, reeling at all Claudia had done, he'd sworn he was done with relationships; with thinking he might one day find the kind of love his mother had found with Stephen. It wasn't worth the risk.

He attracted women who were reasonable and kind on the surface, but who, when they couldn't mould him into what they wanted, threw the kind of temper tantrums that made his blood run cold. He'd had to deal with outbursts, fits of pique, sulking and dreadful insults. He'd had flowers and jewellery thrown at him.

And then there'd been Claudia. Enough was enough. He'd rather be alone than replicate the kind of relationship his parents had shared.

Pulling himself into tight straight lines, he gestured at the watch. 'Treasure?'

'Yes.'

She'd immersed herself in examining the watch again, as if that fraught moment was already forgotten. He rolled his shoulders and fought a frown.

'This is rare—an antique LeCoultre; Swiss. Highly sought after, if in working order, and worth a lot of money.'

Someone had hidden this watch, probably from the thieving greed of the likes of his father, which inclined him favourably towards it. 'Does it work?'

She wound it, and they held their breaths…but nothing happened.

'I'd love to try and fix it.'

'Feel free.'

She sent him her 'school ma'am' look. 'You're far too free with your things.'

'They're just things. Have you ever fixed an antique watch?'

'Sure, but—'

'There you go, you're the expert.' He took the watch, relishing the weight and heft of it. The gold warmed in his hand, and fitted there as if it belonged. 'It'd be nice to see this working.'

When he turned it over, Sadie pointed. 'Who's "Felix"?'

He searched his memory banks, but came back blank. 'My grandfather schooled me on the names of my forbears.' He'd insisted Enzo learn to recite them at the age of twelve. And he had enforced his decree with a heavy leather strap until Enzo could recite his Lombardi lineage perfectly. 'I've no recollection of a Felix.'

Acid burned his stomach. Behind their cultured façade, the Lombardis had been nothing but a bunch of raping, pillaging thugs.

'Maybe these will give us a clue.' She gestured to the box. 'It's filled with old diaries.' She gave one of those excited shimmies. 'Aren't you eager to dip inside them and learn what your relations were really like?'

He knew enough already. But he refused to spoil her fun. *Her mother has returned.* He could only imagine how that had turned Sadie's world on its head. If he could provide her with a distraction or ten for the next fortnight, he would.

'Nope, but knock yourself out.' He pointed to the vanity case. 'I already know what's in that.'

Her eyes brightened. 'What?'

'Take a look.'

As expected, her eyes lit up when she sifted through his grandmother's collection of scent bottles. 'So pretty,' she sighed. 'You should have these on display somewhere.'

'If you find somewhere appropriate, then feel free.' The memories he had of his grandmother, at least, were dear to him.

Sadie turned back, eyes wide and lips parted, which had things clenching up inside him he didn't want. Turning on his heel, he moved into the adjacent room and sat down in his battered arm chair. If she wanted to interpret that as him needing to rest, so be it. It would be preferable to the truth—that he needed the distance.

She followed him and he raised an eyebrow. 'Now, tell me what you'd like to do this evening.'

She sat on the edge of the sofa and nibbled her bottom lip. 'Well, I couldn't help noticing you have an excellent DVD collection, including a bunch of old films I've never seen before. And I was wondering...'

He could watch a film with her and then excuse himself for the evening. It'd be low key, with little asked of him but it'd provide a big tick in the 'good host' column. 'Choose your poison.' Seizing the remote, he pointed it to the big-screen TV.

She rubbed her hands together. 'Audrey Hepburn and *My Fair Lady*, here we come. I'm in the mood for comedy—a lot of comedy—and it's supposed to be fun.'

Which sounded good to him. Sadie was probably in dire need of light-hearted fun. That was tonight taken care of. Now for tomorrow...

'How's this for a plan—tomorrow we have a session in the attic for an hour or two, before heading down to the beach for a swim?'

She stared at him as if he'd given her the moon. He had to fight an urge to puff out his chest.

'*Sì.*' He nodded. 'That looks as if it meets with your approval. And then, if you wish to return to the attics in the afternoon, you can do so.'

'It sounds like heaven, Enzo.'

No, it didn't. But it was the best that he could manage in the circumstances.

SADIE OPENED THE attic door the following morning and stepped inside. Chelsea had sent her photos, of course, but they hadn't prepared her for the reality of standing here amid the Lombardi family's toy collection.

'Oh, Enzo.' She clasped her hands beneath her chin and reminded herself to keep breathing. 'This is *amazing*!'

Even with her attention glued to the scene in front of them, Sadie was aware that Enzo stared at her with a mixture of bemusement, amusement and a touch of impatience…spiced with a hint of affection. Which seemed a lot of reaction to take in, when ninety percent of her attention remained firmly glued to the collection.

Why hasn't it all *your attention? This collection is a once-in-a-lifetime find!*

She rolled her shoulders. *Shut up.* Enzo had always been impossible to ignore. And, even though she no longer had a crush on him, no longer harboured any silly girlish dreams involving knights and white horses, he was still the main reason she was here.

Instead of focussing minutely on Enzo, she made herself take preliminary stock of the room. A central aisle ran down its length, while display cabinets branched off to form horizontal rows either side.

She started down its length. 'This is extraordinary. Not just a collection, but a *museum*.'

'You haven't examined anything yet. You can't…'

But Sadie had stopped listening. She halted. Her hand lifted to wrap around the ridiculously firm flesh of Enzo's forearm to drag him to a stop too. She stared at the item beneath the dormer window at the end of the row and her heart expanded. Forcing her fingers to release him, she sashayed down the aisle towards it. *'Hubba hubba!'*

'Did you just say…?'

'Enzo, meet the object of all my dreams, the true hero of my heart.' She gestured to the wooden rocking horse that stood there in solitary nobility, before kneeling down in front of it.

'The hero of your heart is… *Black Beauty?*'

She stroked a reverential finger down the horse's nose and touched its mane. 'Except this one is a dapple grey.' And it was in the most excellent condition.

'I thought Mr Darcy—'

'The perfect name!' She beamed up at him from where she kneeled. 'Enzo, meet Mr Darcy. Mr Darcy, Enzo.'

He rolled his eyes. 'Sadie…'

'I fell in love with a guy not too dissimilar to this one when I was seven years old.'

She watched Enzo rest his back against the display case behind him, moving his walking stick from his right hand to his left. Was his leg giving him gyp?

'Did you?'

How would he make it down the steep path to the beach when his leg already hurt?

'Sadie?'

She shook herself. 'He was in the window of a barber's shop, of all places, and it was love at first sight. I begged my grandmother to let us take him home.' She'd never been a child who asked for much, but she'd wanted that rocking horse so fiercely, she'd cried. She could still remember the scolding she'd received. She'd hadn't asked for anything that had really mattered since, until last month.

'I take it you were met with a stern refusal.'

'Of course.' She worked hard to keep her voice light. 'I don't even know if it was for sale. And, as I was only seven, I had no notion how expensive these guys could be.' She pressed her hands to her heart. 'Hence began a lifetime of unrequited love.'

She rolled her eyes. Unrequited love seemed to be the theme of her life. *Not any more.* She very gently moved the horse on its glider mechanism. It moved smoothly, as if someone had taken great pains to oil it over the years.

'In your line of work, you must've come across other such specimens?'

'A couple.' She rose to examine the saddle and stirrups. 'But none of those were for sale either.' The tail was as thick and lush as the mane and, while the paint had faded over the years, it wouldn't take much to bring this guy back to mint condition.

She stepped back, hands on hips. 'This fellow is in excellent condition, Enzo. He's beautiful.'

'If you want him, Sadie, he's yours.'

He said it so easily, as if it was nothing. She jerked round. 'No! You can't do that.'

'He's mine. I can do what I please with him.'

Enzo was extraordinarily generous, but she shook her head. 'Mr Darcy wouldn't be happy in my pokey little flat.' The pokey little flat she'd packed up and no longer rented—not that she'd told anybody that yet. 'Think how happy he must be here, with all this room to run around in.'

A rather delicious frown settled on his brow. 'I don't know if you've noticed, but Mr Darcy is an inanimate toy.'

'But don't you think it's fun to imagine all these toys coming to life when we're not watching, and having lives and adventures of their own?'

His mouth opened; he closed it again and frowned.

'Well, I do.' She led him back to the central aisle. 'And you're not going to rain on my parade.'

'Wouldn't dream of it.'

'Gallantly said!'

He really was making an effort. She sent him a grin and he blinked, as if it had taken him off-guard. Given her bossy brassiness of the previous day—and she still couldn't think of that without wincing—he probably was. They were both trying their best to be normal reasonable people. *Go us!*

She sensed he wanted to press the matter of the rocking horse, but when he opened his mouth, she leapt in first. 'I didn't come here to profit from you, either financially or materially, and it would offend me deeply to do so. I will not break up your collection, Enzo.'

His frown deepened. She frowned back playfully until a smile tugged at his lips. He might not think it at the moment with his broken heart—the thought of which had her own chest growing heavy—but one day he might have a little girl who'd fall in love with that rocking horse as deeply as she once had with the horse in the barber's shop. He'd be glad he still had Mr Darcy then.

They chose to browse different rows. The Lombardi collection was surprisingly eclectic, with toys from the 1980s sitting side by side with toys over a hundred years older. They eventually met back in the central aisle.

Folding her arms, Sadie turned on the spot. 'I don't think I'll manage to catalogue the entire collection in a fortnight.' Not if she was also doing all she could to cheer him up and get him out in the sun…where hopefully she could eventually talk him into the party Chelsea had her heart set on hosting. She wrinkled her nose in apology—whether for not being able to fully catalogue his collection, or because she intended to keep hassling him about the party, she couldn't say. 'I expect it will just be edited highlights.'

'You don't need to catalogue anything.'

'But I want to. You don't understand what a treat this is.' Besides, it would be handy for him to have.

He set his cane in front of him, rested both hands on it and bent slightly at the waist. His eyes were a deep, dark brown, and they had a slightly lighter halo around the pupil that fascinated her. It took all her strength not to lean in closer to get a better look.

'Why?'

She blinked. 'Pardon?'

'You said you didn't want to profit financially or materially. So why are you going to so much trouble for Chelsea… and for me?'

Oh.

He continued. 'Chelsea has this hare-brained scheme to throw me a surprise birthday party—something you clearly have reservations about as you *haven't* kept it a secret, and yet you're still rushing to do her bidding.'

He made her sound like a lackey or minion, when nothing could be further from the truth. 'There's no single simple answer to that.' She glanced at her watch. As suspected, she'd kept him up here long enough. 'I'm happy to attempt an answer, but maybe it's time to head down to the beach.' She glanced at the way his knuckles had whitened around his walking stick. 'Or perhaps the pool for a few lazy laps.'

His eyes narrowed. 'You don't think I can manage the path?'

'I've no idea; but, before you bite my head off, two things…' She held up two fingers. 'First, I don't want to be responsible for anything that might delay or inhibit your recovery. Second, are you the kind of guy who would recklessly race down that hill just to prove to some girl he doesn't give two hoots about that he's manly enough to do it?'

He eased back and blinked. 'I give two hoots about you, Sadie. You're a family friend.'

Her stomach scrunched up into a tight ball. *Ouch!* Enzo would never see her as anything more than his little sister's best friend, would he? He probably didn't even see her as a woman.

Do you want to explain those smouldering looks he's been sending you?

She rolled her shoulders. They didn't mean anything, not really. Enzo was mad at the world. The way Claudia had abandoned him had left his pride in tatters. It was only natural he'd want to reassure himself that women could still find him attractive.

She didn't care if he saw her as a woman or not. She wasn't going to resurrect that stupid crush she'd had on him. Nor was she going to let him shore up his male pride at her expense.

She folded her arms. 'I'm just saying that, if this is some male pride thing, then I want no part of it. I refuse to be responsible for you injuring yourself more. I'll just stay up here and do my lazy laps in the pool.'

His jaw worked; eventually he said, 'Would it make a difference if I told you I'd spoken to my doctor yesterday and he gave me the all-clear—on the proviso I take it slowly and rest at both ends?'

'Did you?'

'I might be proud, Sadie, but I'm not foolish. I've no wish to hinder my recovery. Shall we meet on the terrace in twenty minutes?'

She met him on the terrace a quarter of an hour later. He refused to relinquish the bag slung over one shoulder, gesturing for her to precede him along the path.

'If you stumble, I'll break your fall,' she chirped over her shoulder. 'Your own personal human-sized airbag.'

'Windbag, I think you mean.'

She snorted. *Look at him, being all teasing and relaxed, and the complete opposite of the grumpy bear from yesterday.*

She took the path slowly, but there was no denying the strain around Enzo's mouth when they finally reached the beach. She wordlessly took the beach bag from him and laid their towels out on the strip of golden sand. Once he'd seated himself, she handed him a water bottle and fished out the painkillers Luisa had handed her before they'd left.

He hesitated and then took one. She didn't say anything, and didn't tell him he'd done a good job. She feared anything she said would sound patronising. She also suspected that the difficulty of the descent had shocked him, and she had no desire to make him feel any more self-conscious.

Instead, she settled on her towel, drank deeply from the other water bottle—and drank in the view. 'Lord, Enzo, you're living in paradise.' Did he plan to make the castle his permanent home? She would in a heartbeat, if it were hers.

'Don't wait for me, Sadie. Go do your lazy laps, as I know you're dying to.'

'Ha! What you're really saying is, I look like I need cooling off. My face is bright-red, isn't it?'

Those stern lips twitched a little. 'Beneath the glow, you're still pale. A bit of sun will do you good.'

The water did look inviting. 'Aren't you coming in?'

His face immediately shuttered. 'No.'

Why not?

He closed his eyes, as if to shut her and the sight of the water out. Maybe he wanted a quiet moment to himself first, without her hovering. She'd hate that too; it set her teeth on edge. She didn't want to set Enzo's teeth on edge any more than she already had.

Leaping to her feet, she seized the hem of her T-shirt and pulled it over her head. 'If you're happy to wait for my answer to your earlier question, then…'

Dark eyes sprang open again. 'Actually, I'd like to hear your answer. I thought you were avoiding the question. I didn't want to press.'

His eyes widened when he realised she'd halted with her shirt halfway between waist and chin, leaving her midriff bare. Those compelling eyes darkened and travelled over her with a lazy thoroughness that had her skin sparking with instant heat. In this moment, Enzo *definitely* saw her a woman.

Her heart pounded in her ears and she tried not to groan, swoon or melt. She mightn't have a teenage crush on Enzo Lombardi any more, but there was no denying the man was darkly attractive, utterly compelling and smoking hot. Or the fact that she wanted him with every atom of her now very *adult* female body…

Enzo wanted to blame the exertion of the walk and a restless night for the barriers he felt dissolving between his beguiling house guest and him. But, despite wishing otherwise, if he was honest he found Sadie far too tempting with her lush, pursed lips, her glossy dark hair and those dancing hazel eyes. He had since the night of the summer ball nine years ago, when he'd kissed her.

Damn it, she was Chelsea's best friend. Even if she wasn't off-limits due to that unspoken code, he wasn't interested in pursuing any kind of romantic entanglement. Everything that had happened with Claudia was still too fresh in his mind.

Then stop staring at her as if you'd like to ravish her.

Except, somehow, that was impossible. Their gazes remained locked in some kind of silent battle—as if neither of them could look away. Her lips parted and a breath shuddered out of her. He was seized with a desperate urge to leap to his feet, pull her into his arms and kiss her until neither one of them could think straight. She stared at him as if that was exactly what she wanted too.

He remembered the taste of her—it had been sweet and addictive. He hungered for just the briefest taste again now...

Leap—you? With that leg of yours?

Swallowing a curse, he dragged his gaze away and slammed his sunglasses onto his face. He stared at the water, which was still, smooth and reflected back the perfect blue of the sky like a summer promise. In his chest, though, his heart dashed itself against storm-tossed rocks.

You'd probably fall flat on your face.

He was dimly aware of Sadie's ragged breaths, and that she'd smoothed her shirt back down, but she didn't move away. He hated to think what he must look like: grim; dark and forbidding; his scars a dark and vivid red. He must look an utter fright, a beast of a man. But she didn't move away.

'Enzo?'

Kiss her—you, with those scars?

It was the vision of his scars that hauled him back. What was he thinking? Sadie would see him as an object of pity, nothing more. He had scars enough to last a lifetime. He had no desire to acquire new ones—even if they were only to his vanity.

'Forgive me, Sadie. That walk was more taxing than I expected. Why don't you go for your swim while I rest for a bit, and then we can resume our conversation?'

Without waiting for her reply, he promptly lay back and placed his hat over his face—ostensibly to protect himself from the sun, but in actuality to ensure he didn't catch so much as a glimpse of Sadie's bare skin.

He counted to seven before he heard her move—clothes rustling and falling to the ground, soft footsteps in the sand moving away from him. The further away she moved, the easier it became to breathe. This attraction might be inconvenient, but he wasn't some hormone-riddled teenager. He was an adult and he *could* keep his reactions in check. Part of him hungered to join her for a swim—to be close to her effervescent sense of fun, to make her laugh if he could manage it, and just get out of his own head for a while—but…

Sadie hadn't flinched at the scars on his face, but the moment he removed his cargo pants he'd reveal the mangled mess of his leg. Not even Sadie would be able to pretend it was pretty. He didn't want to see horror and revulsion race across her face. He just…didn't have the heart for it.

Pushing the image from his mind, he forced himself to focus on his breathing. Eventually he found himself starting to notice the whispering of water against the shore and the melodic tweeting of the woodchats in the forest behind—easy, quiet, relaxing sounds. He frowned beneath his hat. This was…nice. Why hadn't he ventured outside sooner?

Lifting his hat a fraction, he dragged salt-scented air deep into his lungs. Hints of mimosa and jasmine seasoned the air—smells he associated with summer. The combined scents transported him back in time to a week he'd once spent with his mother, aunts and cousins at a modest seaside resort north of here when he'd been ten. The dramatic release in tension—of being away from his father and surrounded by kind, happy people who loved him—had been a revelation.

The sun warming his limbs, the scent of summer tickling his nostrils and the soft sound of Sadie splashing in the water—was that a light laugh he'd heard?—all had him letting out a long breath. The walk down had been arduous, but he *had* managed it. For the first time, he glimpsed a future in which he'd no longer be in pain, would no longer need his cane, and in which he'd feel hale and hearty once more.

Peace stole over him. He consciously relaxed his shoulders and jaw and concentrated on his breathing—a momentary surrender to the quiet, serenity, warmth and the scent of safety.

He came to, to find Sadie stretched out on her towel beside him—far enough away that he'd have to stretch out an arm to touch her—her eyes closed behind her sunglasses. She wore her T-shirt, but not her shorts. The T-shirt covered her to mid-thigh…

Don't look! He had no right to notice, let alone admire her curves.

'So…'

He started when she spoke, but another quick glance informed him her eyes remained closed, though a smile stretched across her lips.

'You're finally awake.' One eye opened and she peeked across at him. 'Do you know that you snore?'

'I do not!' He sat up. Did he? Nobody had mentioned it before. Reaching for his phone, he checked the time. *'Dio!'* He'd been asleep for two hours.

'Feel better?' She gave a lazy stretch, wriggling her back against her towel and clearly relishing the softness of the sand beneath. It filled his mind with forbidden images…

He slammed shut the vault of his mind. 'Much better.' He tested his leg—sore, but not too bad. 'I was grumpy after the walk down. I'm sorry.'

'I'm grumpy when I'm in pain too—the proverbial bear.'

She still lay back like a siren, her eyes half-closed, and he had to clench his jaw. He would *not* touch her.

'And I knew you weren't grumpy with me, Enzo, so it's okay. And you've given me all of this. How could I be anything but grateful?'

She sat up and his breath caught as her T-shirt lifted to reveal…more. She had long, shapely legs that made his heart pound and his mouth go dry. He'd bet they'd feel as silky as the water of the Mediterranean itself. 'I can't remember the last time I lay on the beach and…'

He dragged his gaze back to the view. 'Did nothing? Were lazy?'

'That's the one.'

'Did you enjoy it?'

'It was heaven.' She sent him a sidelong glance. 'Did you?'

He nodded. He felt like a new man, though he suspected the climb back up the hill would have him feeling like a grump again. Still; the fact he could feel this relaxed and this *well*—even if it was only momentary—was a revelation. Perhaps his family was right: perhaps he'd been brooding too much.

Admittedly, he'd had a lot to brood about, but so did the woman opposite. *Her mother has returned*…twenty-seven years after abandoning her. He made a vow to make sure Sadie had plenty of beach days over the course of the following fortnight.

Jumping to her feet, Sadie moved briefly out of sight before returning with a picnic basket. 'Luisa sent Guido down with our lunch, and with strict instructions that we're to leave the basket for someone to collect later. Apparently, if we do lug it back up the hill we'll be depriving someone of a swim. I suggest we do as we're told. It'd be bad form to deprive anyone of this.'

Sitting cross-legged on her towel, she opened the basket and examined its contents. 'Ooh, look at this.' She pulled out an antipasto board with cured meats, cheese and olives— enough to feed an army—along with a loaf of crusty sourdough bread and cans of icy-cold sparkling water. 'There are peaches and strawberries for after, and something else that looks wickedly sweet.'

He glanced inside. 'Sweet cannoli. I have a weakness for it.'

They attacked the food with gusto. Eventually Sadie gave

a satisfied sigh and rested back, her hands propped behind her as she lifted her face to the sun. 'There's something about being somewhere beautiful in nature that's tonic for the soul. No wonder you retreated here for your recovery, Enzo.'

And, yet, if Sadie hadn't turned up he'd still have been locked inside the castle walls, brooding on all the ways he'd been wronged.

'You're lucky to have this place. What are your plans for it?'

'I expect I'll sell it.' Her instant shock made him wince. 'I know it's beautiful, but this place is tainted with memories of my father and grandfather. The *castello* has been the family's summer residence since the mid-1700s—but, as far as I can tell, all of my ancestors were ruthless, selfish men. I've no desire to align myself with them or to revere their traditions.'

He had no desire to turn it into his own pleasure palace, or develop it into an exclusive hotel for the rich and famous. Instead, he'd sell it to someone who would probably do that anyway, but which would be none of his business. He would donate the proceeds of the sale to his mother's charity, so that people who'd been abused and exploited would get the chance to break free from their abusers. His father and grandfather would turn in their graves if they knew—a thought that brought him pleasure.

But he didn't want to talk about any of that now. 'I'm glad you're enjoying your time here, Sadie. My father and grandfather wouldn't have approved of you—an honest, hard-working woman with no family wealth or connections—and that gives me a perverse pleasure.'

She clapped a hand over her mouth to stifle a bark of laughter, her eyes dancing. His lips twitched. 'But that is not what I wish to talk about.'

'You want me to answer the question you posed earlier.'

Reaching into the picnic basket, she pulled out a strawberry and lifted it to her lips. Enzo dragged his gaze away, his pulse revving like the engine of a sports car. He made himself shake his head. 'I know why you go above and beyond for Chelsea.'

Sadie pressed the back of her hand to her brow, like some swooning pantomime heroine. 'Because she was the one person who stood by me when everyone else had forsaken me.'

He knew she hammed it up to make him laugh, but it had the opposite effect. 'Why do you do that?'

'What?'

'Mock yourself like that?'

'I was just being silly…funny.'

'Well, it's not funny.' He glared. 'It's like some awful defence mechanism to put yourself down before anyone else gets the chance.'

She scowled and fidgeted. 'Shut up.'

'I promise to not make fun of you—not about stuff that matters.'

'No, you'll just shout at me,' she muttered, drawing agitated patterns in the sand, and it was his turn to shift uncomfortably. 'Fine,' she huffed. 'You promised not to shout any more, so I promise not to do that.' She grimaced. 'Or at least, I'll try. It's a kind of second-nature thing.'

A chasm cracked open in his chest and he rubbed a hand across it to try and ease the ache that settled there. He might find the grown-up version of Sadie challenging and somewhat exasperating, but she'd been the loveliest of girls as a teenager. She'd deserved better from the adults in her life. He knew the same loyal heart beat in her chest now as had then—even if that chest was now distractingly curvy and beautifully formed.

Not looking!

'Anyway, back to the conversation. You weren't really asking why I'd go to so much trouble for Chelsea. What you really want to know is why I came here; why I thought all of this was such a good idea. And there are a couple of different answers to that.'

She lifted her sunglasses onto the top of her head so she could meet his gaze, so he lifted his too. It seemed only fair. 'Okay.'

'First of all, remember the no-yelling thing.'

Damn. That didn't bode well.

'The thing is, you see, the thought of you here on your own, in pain physically and emotionally—' she gestured to his leg '—because of that cow Claudia…'

Things inside him clenched at the mention of his ex-girl-friend's name, even as part of him wanted to laugh at Sadie's word choice. But why did she think he'd been in love with her? That had to have come from Chelsea. He fought a frown. Did the rest of the family think Claudia had broken his heart too?

'Well, I hated the picture that formed in my mind.'

His attention snapped back and his eyes started to burn. She pitied him. His hands clenched. *Was that* why she was here—she *pitied* him? He reminded himself about not yelling.

'The thing is, Enzo, you were so kind to me when I was a teenager and had that huge crush on you. And I've never forgotten it.'

His hands unclenched. He flexed his fingers. 'You knew that I knew?'

'Only in hindsight.' She rolled her eyes. 'I was far from subtle.'

She'd been delightful, though.

'You could've crushed me utterly, but you didn't. You were thoughtful and lovely. You were careful not to raise my hopes, but never ignored me or treated me like a nuisance.' Her delightful nose wrinkled. 'I'm sorry if I was tiresome or a bother, by the way.'

'You weren't. You were lovely, Sadie. And if you'd been a little older…'

She laughed. 'As gallant as ever, but we both know I never had a chance with you, not really.'

The memory of that long ago kiss rose in his mind again. Sadie had been lovely, and he had been tempted, but his mother had read him the riot act in a way she'd never done before. Her domestic harmony had been so hard won; he hadn't wanted to do anything to shatter it. So he'd toed the line and had promised to stay away from his stepsister's best friend. He hadn't done anything that might rock the boat and endanger familial relationships.

And yet part of him had always wondered…

No, it didn't.

'I've always considered you a friend, Enzo, and I thought that, if I could come here and be a friend to you the way you were once a friend to me…' One shoulder lifted. 'Well, I wanted to do that if I could. Also—' her nose wrinkled again '—you never did like surprises and, when I couldn't talk Chelsea out of a *surprise* party, well, given everything that's happened this year, I thought you might like it even less now.'

His heart started to beat too hard.

'I thought maybe I could help smooth things over for everyone somehow.'

Somehow, without him realising it, she'd achieved her goal.

It struck him then how well she knew him. He also realised in that moment that he was going to agree to the party.

CHAPTER SIX

SADIE KEPT HER gaze trained on Enzo's face as she spoke and tried to track the expressions flitting through his eyes; tried to interpret what the shifting muscles around his mouth and eyes signified. She released a pent-up breath; anger, fury and outrage weren't emotions she could identify.

That didn't mean they weren't simmering beneath the surface, though. And he'd become dangerously serious when her remit was to try and cheer him up. 'Maybe me thinking I could come in and wave a magic wand was a dreadful cheek. What's that saying about the road to hell being paved with good intentions? Mind you—' she gestured at the view '—if this is hell…'

She winked, and one corner of his mouth hooked up into one of those devastating smiles that had never failed to make her knees weak as a teenager. It wasn't her knees that were the problem now, but the fire threading through her veins that had heat pooling in unmentionable places.

For all that's fair and holy, stop thinking of Enzo in that way.

'You are aware that you rabbit on with some dreadful nonsense?' he said.

Maybe so, but the tension in his shoulders had drained away, leaving him looking more relaxed. She'd take that as a win. 'But, in the interests of full disclosure, there's another reason I came to Italy.'

His gaze sharpened, and she lowered her sunglasses back into place. She started to reach for another strawberry, but changed her mind. Her stomach had knotted.

'I'm all ears.'

She hadn't meant to tell him any of this, but it felt oddly deceitful to withhold it. 'I wanted, maybe needed, to get away from home for a bit.'

'Damn it, Sadie, that sounds serious. Why?'

She opened her mouth to make some flippant remark, such as, 'Oh, the Trials and Tribulations of Sadie's Life: Part Three, in four-part harmony', or some such nonsense…

His frown deepened. 'Sadie?'

She flashed him a quick smile. 'Sorry, just remembering my promise about not mocking myself. Sometimes it feels good to make light of the hard stuff—a form of letting off steam.'

'Are you sure about that?'

No, damn it, she wasn't.

'If that's truly the case, then mock away.'

But she'd lost the urge. She stared down at her hands. 'The thing is, Enzo, after the best part of twenty-seven years my mother has decided to return home and declares she now wants to be part of her family's lives.'

'She's *returned*?'

He sounded suitably outraged… 'Chelsea told you, huh?'

He swore. 'Only that your mother had returned, nothing more.' He scrubbed a hand over his face. 'I imagine it is…'

'Confusing? Confronting? Infuriating?' she supplied when he didn't continue.

'All of those things, *sì*.'

The steady strength in his voice and its underlying warmth helped to ease some of the burning in her soul, but that burning only settled behind her eyes instead, and she found herself blurting out, 'It's awful, Enzo. Horrible.'

Unable to keep her agitation in check, she leapt to her feet. Seizing a pebble, she hurled it as hard as she could towards the water—falling well short. Stomping down, she picked it up and hurled it again. This time it made a satisfying splash.

She started at a soft touch on her arm. Enzo stood there, offering her another pebble. She took it and flung it so hard, her shoulder ached.

'Remind me at some point to teach you how to throw properly.'

The wry tone had a reluctant smile tugging at her lips.

'Tell me what's so horrible about it.'

'Besides the fact that she dumped me with her parents and never contacted us once in twenty-seven years?' She thumped her hands onto her hips, finding it oddly disconcerting to be the object of such a concentrated gaze.

'Such behaviour is hard to forgive, *si*.'

It was. And yet she'd been prepared to, except… 'I just don't like her.' Maybe it was due to their history—or *lack* of history. 'She hasn't offered any explanation for why she left all those years ago, and she certainly hasn't offered an apology. She's just waved it all off with, "I had things I wanted to do with my life", as if that makes it all right.'

She frowned at the far horizon. 'There's something hard about her. She's totally self-centred.' Her heart gave a sick kick. 'I think the real reason she's returned is she's run out of money, and now plans to live off my grandparents' generosity.'

'How have they taken this turn of events?'

She threw her hands in the air. 'They're beside themselves with joy.' For the first time in her life, she'd witnessed how they looked when they were truly joyful, and it had cut her to the marrow that she'd never managed to generate even the tiniest flicker of that in them in twenty-seven years. 'They've

welcomed her with open arms. They've done the whole "fat-
ted calf" thing. I know I sound bitter, but...'

She was so worried about them!

His gaze felt like a living thing on her skin, making it
prickle all over. 'What *aren't* you telling me?'

His perception took her off-guard and she had to swallow
before she could speak. 'For one of the few times in my life,
and probably the last, I kicked up a fuss and made a scene.
I haven't done that since the rocking-horse incident. I've always done my best to be agreeable and undemanding; *pleasant*. Because despite my grandparents' lack of joy—' *former*
lack of joy, she added silently '—they're good people and they
never asked to be lumped with me.'

'Sadie...'

He halted when she lifted a hand. 'I'm not feeling sorry
for myself, over-dramatising or mocking myself, Enzo. It's
a statement of fact. Unpalatable, perhaps, but...'

He rubbed a hand over his face. 'I apologise for interrupting.'

She managed a smile. '*That* was a ten-out-of-ten apology.'
Blowing out a breath, she stared out at the water. 'I told Verity—that's my mother—that her parents deserved an apology...and so did I. I said I understood a phone call might've
been awkward, but how hard would it have been for her to
send birthday cards or a Christmas card every year to let us
know she was still alive? I told my grandparents Verity had
been selfish and untrustworthy and that I was worried she'd
take advantage of them *again*. I asked them to be careful and
remain on their guard.'

'What happened?'

'Verity laughed in my face.' She rolled her eyes. 'Which I
suppose I should've expected. I don't think she has any real
scruples. My grandparents, though...' She kicked at the water,
sending an arc through the air, the droplets sparkling in the

sun. 'My grandparents told me that I'd either have to accept Verity into our lives or they'd have nothing to do with me.' They'd demanded she *apologise* to Verity.

'*Dio!*'

And then he said a very rude word that had her blinking. His anger made her feel both better and worse.

'They've loved her all her life. They've missed her and grieved for her for the last twenty-seven years. It makes no sense, but the heart wants what the heart wants.' And their hearts craved Verity.

'I'm sorry, Sadie.'

She was too.

'How have things been left?'

She ground her palms on her eyes. She pulled her hands away and clenched them at her sides. 'I've told them I want nothing to do with Verity. I told them that, if they ever need me, they only have to call. I told them I'll always be there for them. But that embracing Verity...' She shook her head. 'That's a step too far.'

Was she being selfish?

'What did they say to this?'

A lump lodged in her throat and it hurt to swallow. 'That I wouldn't be hearing from them.' She pounced on another pebble and hurled it. 'I feel like I've abandoned them, though. I've left them alone with a...*wolf*!'

A strong arm drew her in close to his side, and for a moment she let herself lean against him and let his strength filter into her.

'Your grandparents are neither naïve nor stupid.'

Except when it came to Verity.

'They're adults—old enough to make their own decisions and to live with the consequences. It's admirable that you wish to save them from pain, Sadie, but that's a choice they have to make for themselves. You can't make it for them.'

Enzo smelled like a forest—cool and woodsy, with a hint of something dark and green, like pine. She fought the urge to snuggle closer. He felt like rest, respite and safety.

'But I also understand it doesn't make it any easier.'

With his arm around her, she no longer felt so alone. She rubbed her cheek against the soft cotton of his T-shirt, relishing the feel of him beneath it. 'I was thinking of ringing them once a month—just to check in and see how they're doing. I mean, there's no guarantee they'll take my calls, but...' She squinted up at him. 'What do you think?'

'Keeping the lines of communication open and letting them know you're there for them if they need you?' His arm briefly tightened around her. 'It's a generous thing to do. It demonstrates how Verity should've behaved for all of these years.'

He thought she was generous...

Her gaze traced the line of his jaw across to surprisingly sensual lips and her mouth went dry. She imagined those lips lowering to hers... A pulse inside her kicked to life. She imagined Enzo kissing her—the two of them shaping their lips to one another's and deepening the kiss into something fierce and passionate. Rest, respite and safety fled. In their place burned need and hunger.

A gasp escaped her. His gaze swung down, raking over her face with a ruthless precision that tore through all her pretences. Those dark eyes rested on her mouth, darkening further. Hunger, fierce and intense, flared through them. His arm tightened. Her pulse went wild. He was going to kiss her...

The arm slipped from her shoulders and he took a step back.

Sadie blinked. *Oh, God. Oh, God. Oh, God.* She did what she could to rein in her raging pulse.

'*Sì*, Sadie, ringing your grandparents once a month is more than many people would do in your situation.'

She forced her mind to the conversation, pretending her body wasn't on fire for him. 'Thank you.'

He frowned at the water, his eyes narrowing and his nose wrinkling. 'It makes me ashamed of myself.'

She jerked round, pouncing on the conversational lifeline he'd thrown to her. *'What?'*

'My family want to throw me a party and I'm acting as if it's the crime of the century. *Oh, woe is me.*' He pressed the back of his hand to his brow the way she had earlier, and she had a sudden insight into why he hated her self-deprecation. 'If Chelsea has her heart set on throwing me a surprise party...' He rolled those wonderfully broad shoulders. 'Rather than bellyaching about it, I ought to be grateful and submit with grace.'

A weight slammed down on her shoulders. 'And here we now are, on the road to hell.'

His brows lowered over his eyes. 'What do you mean? Why do you say this?'

'You, me and Chelsea—we're all in a bind of our own making, aren't we, due to our good intentions? Me wanting to help Chelsea and you; Chelsea wanting to help you and me; and now you're feeling guilty and feeling obliged to help me and Chelsea.'

That piratical brow lifted. 'And you think us all wanting to help each other is putting us on some figurative road to hell?'

'There are so many good intentions ricocheting about the place, they're like balls in a pinball machine! Or should that be gold paving stones?' She and Chelsea were forcing him to have a party he didn't want. That suddenly seemed terribly unfair.

'You're wrong about my sense of obligation, Sadie. I made the decision about the party while you were swimming—before you told me what had happened with your grandparents.'

She loved that he didn't mention Verity. That he'd dismissed her as the non-entity in Sadie's life she actually was. It was her grandparents' reaction that cut her so deeply, their hearts she feared for. But none of that made her believe him. He was being as gallant as ever, that was all. The weight on her shoulders grew heavier.

'You don't believe me.'

It was a statement, not a question. She glanced away from penetrating dark eyes and then started. 'Your stick is getting wet!'

'Does that matter?'

'It does if it's not waterproof.'

'I think you are once again trying to change the subject.'

So what if she was? The fact remained that they were wading in ankle-deep water and she wasn't sure how that had happened—had it been her agitation or his? But the salt water was probably doing nasty things to his cane—even if it happened to do lovely things to her over-heated flesh.

'While you were swimming, I forced myself to relax—consciously,' he said, ignoring her concern about his cane. 'You know the drill—unclench your jaw, relax your shoulders, breathe deeply.'

She found herself fascinated with the way his mouth formed the words. There was a decisiveness to the way he moved and spoke, but an innate sensuality to the shape of his lips. She knew from experience the devastating power those lips contained…

Once! He kissed you once!

And yet she'd never forgotten it. No kiss she'd had before or since had ever eclipsed it.

During that last summer she'd spent with Chelsea's family, Chelsea's father had announced he was throwing a ball in honour of Chelsea and Sadie finishing boarding school. Sadie could only stare at him when he'd told them. *She* was going to a real, live ball! It had been the most gobsmackingly glittering affair. Glamorous people had filled the ballroom, looking gorgeous; the champagne had flowed; waiters had circulated with the fanciest canapés she'd ever seen. There'd been a band and dancing. She remembered the lights, the laughter, the warmth...

Late in the evening, she'd retreated to the edge of the dance floor to stare at it all, determined to fix it in her mind forever.

'Enjoying yourself?'

That voice had immediately filled her stomach with a million fluttering butterflies. *Enzo.* 'It's amazing. I'm having a ball!'

They'd laughed at her accidental pun, but then his gaze had roved over her face and he'd shaken his head. 'Your hair...'

She and Chelsea had been fussed over by hairdressers and beauticians all afternoon. Her hairdresser had suggested a new cut, and on the spur of the moment she'd agreed. Her curtain of shoulder-length hair had been cut short, making her eyes look bigger and enhancing her cheekbones. She'd gazed at her reflection afterwards in wonder.

She'd touched it. 'Do you like it?' Her voice had grown confusingly breathy.

His eyes darkened. 'You look beautiful.'

The way he'd looked at her, she hadn't been able to utter a single word.

With a low laugh, he'd shaken himself. 'Why aren't you dancing? I've noticed you've not lacked for partners.'

Maybe it was the new haircut, all those glittering lights or the fact the night was nearly over, but she'd found herself saying, 'Why don't you ask me to dance?'

He held out his hand and she didn't hesitate. She'd always dreamed of dancing with Enzo, just once. The moment he pulled her into his arms, all the teasing lightness fell away, replaced with something far more exciting. 'I haven't been able to look away from you all evening.'

His words thrilled her. She lifted her chin, desperate to appear polished and poised, but their eyes locked and she couldn't look away, couldn't hide how much she wanted him. An answering hunger flared in his eyes and her heart stuttered. Enzo *wanted* her...

In a manoeuvre that thrilled her to the soles of her feet, he waltzed her behind a curtain to a private nook. He didn't release her, he just continued staring at her. She stared back. For the last five years, she'd dreamed about this man. Had he finally noticed *her*?

His eyes filled with an odd mix of fierceness and tenderness. 'I find myself aching to kiss you, Sadie.'

Her heart thundered so loud, she was sure he must hear it. 'I wish you would.'

His lips swooped down then and claimed hers in a devastating kiss that curled her toes. Wrapping an arm around her waist, he pulled her more firmly against him and she flung hers around his neck and kissed him back with inexperienced enthusiasm.

He stilled, and she worried she'd done something wrong, but then he kissed her again, slowly, teasing her tongue into a dance with his, teasing her to open herself up to him more fully. That exploration—the thoroughness of it and their delight in it—had a foreign heat gathering in her blood, a storm of sensation threatening to overwhelm her.

She needed more! And he gave her more until she was nothing but burning, writhing need, pressed so tightly against him that she could feel how much he wanted her too.

'Dio!'

Enzo lifted his head and she wanted to cry out a protest, but the sounds of the ballroom filtered back into her consciousness. They stared at one another, both breathing hard. 'This is not the time or the place for me to kiss you like this. Meet me in the garden tomorrow at ten.'

She nodded and, with a final kiss on her palm, he melted back into the crowd. Not a single moment in her life since had ever felt so full of possibility.

Sadie dragged her attention back to the present, her heart thundering. *Dear God.* What on earth was she doing, remembering that kiss? It had come to nothing then and it'd come to nothing now.

Shoving her shoulders back, she searched her mind for the thread of their conversation; what had they been talking about…?

'You relaxed…?' she said.

Enzo fought a frown. There was a funny edge to Sadie's voice that he couldn't account for. Was she worried about this party being forced upon him? He set himself to easing her mind.

'*Sì.* I started noticing the birds chattering away and the feeling of the sun on my skin.' Some of her curious tension eased. When she glanced up, he released a slow breath. 'There was a scent on the air that hurtled me back twenty years to a summer holiday I'd had with my mother's family. My father wasn't present and it was…joyous, peaceful. I remember feeling surrounded by people who loved me.'

Her face went soft. 'That sounds lovely.'

It had provided his mother and him with some much-needed respite. 'We needed it. At the time my parents' marriage was particularly rocky and my father had a way of shouting—so savage and brutal. He'd loom over my mother and…'

She gripped his forearm, her eyes wide. 'Oh, Enzo, that must've been terrifying.'

He stared down at that small yet surprisingly strong hand, her touch unexpectedly comforting. When his gaze lifted, she blinked, and the gold flecks in her eyes seemed to pulse. For a moment it felt as if time itself had slowed. Bright eyes lowered to his lips and his heart surged against his ribs. Small teeth sank into the plump ripeness of her bottom lip and need seared though him.

Sadie pulled her hand back and a chill chased through him. What he felt for Sadie was madness. He would *not* indulge it.

'Was your father physically violent?'

She didn't look at him; she stared at the ground, at her feet, instead. He gritted his teeth and counted his breaths, trying to pretend his body wasn't on fire for her. 'He didn't get the opportunity. During one particularly torrid argument, I intervened—pushed him away from her and yelled at him to leave her alone. I was twelve.'

Wide eyes lifted and she asked, 'What happened?'

'My mother—realising what a detrimental affect their fighting was having on me and how toxic it all was—decided enough was enough. She left my father that afternoon.'

'Good for her!' Sadie's chin shot up, as if she was proud of his mother. 'And good for you.'

Warmth spread through his chest. It didn't dislodge the prickle of desire, but it helped temper it.

'Life became smoother then. The courts decreed that my parents share custody. But it was easier to deal with my father when my mother wasn't there.'

The glance she sent him said she didn't believe him.

He shrugged. 'So when I was lying on the beach and recalled that week with my mother's family…' She looked him square in the eye. He held her gaze. 'It reminded me that there can be strength and comfort in having the people you love around you.'

He clenched his hands, fighting the temptation to hook a hand behind her head, to swoop down and capture her lips with his. Her actions, if not her words, had made it clear she didn't want that to happen, even if he'd started to sense that she too fought an unwanted attraction to him. She'd have her reasons for wanting to keep her distance and he'd respect that.

Maybe it's the vile scars on your face.

He ignored the ugly taunt. That voice sounded too much like his father's, and he'd always made it a point of pride to take an opposite position to his father's opinions—prejudiced and biased as they were. The one thing his father hadn't been was progressive. Sadie wasn't like his father—she didn't care about his scars.

He wasn't like his father either. He would *not* attempt to seduce her. Nor would he try to convince her to indulge in a fling when she didn't think it in her best interests…his back molars ground together…regardless of how much he might want to.

Seducing Sadie should be the last thing on his mind. He needed to convince her they weren't on some imagined 'road to hell' of her making. He wanted to convince his family he was doing well. 'Remembering that long-ago summer holiday had me rethinking my desire to keep everyone at a distance. Seems a little stupid now, if you want the truth.'

That had her shaking her head. 'There's nothing *stupid* about you needing time to adjust.'

Perhaps not. Still, while the scars that Claudia had left him with would last a lifetime, his family shouldn't pay the price for that. 'I'm well on the road to recovery; I'm gaining strength every day. It's true I'm still self-conscious about my scars, and the fact I need to walk with a stick for the foreseeable future, but my family have already seen my scars. They saw me when I was in hospital and my leg was in traction. But my face is no longer swollen beyond recognition, my cuts and bruises have faded and at least I'm walking, even if it is with a cane—all of that will be an improvement to them.'

A frown continued to lurk in the hazel depths of her eyes. Planting his walking stick between them, he leaned on it with both hands. 'If Chelsea is worried enough to send you here, that means she's picked up from her father that he's worried, which means my mother must still be worried. If having a party will stop them all from worrying, then I will gladly have one.' He leaned closer, catching her eye. *'Gladly.'*

Her hands went to her hips. 'You're amazing, you know that?'

He straightened at her words. Odd, but for a moment he'd felt as if he could fly. He gestured to the path instead. 'You ready to tackle that again?' He might as well harness this strange energy while he could and use it to his advantage.

'Okay.' She clapped her hands. 'Let's do it.'

'What film are we watching tonight?' Enzo asked after another of Luisa's delicious dinners. For once, he'd cleaned his plate.

They moved through to the drawing room and he halted when he saw his father's collection of military memorabilia had been replaced with his grandmother's scent bottles. He stared at the new display, his jaw slack.

Beside him, Sadie fidgeted. 'You did say if I found the perfect spot… If you hate it, I'll move it first thing tomorrow. I just thought…'

'No.' The display of scent bottles somehow eased the hard, aggressive edges of the room, much like his grandmother's presence had when she'd been alive. 'It's perfect.'

Continuing through the drawing room to the sitting room beyond, he found himself frowning. It had taken on a new life with Sadie here—nothing glaring or obvious. She had a fondness for colourful cushions and cosy throw rugs. She'd made the sofa look like a little haven of holiday goodness. His chair now sported a fat cushion that looked oddly inviting, as if she hadn't been able to resist providing him with a spot of comfort and colour too. The thought made him smile.

'I'm afraid I've taken a few liberties, ordering some things online for this room. I hope you don't mind.'

He didn't know what it was about those amber flecks in her hazel eyes, but they could make him clench and melt at the same time. 'Not at all.'

'As for what film to watch tonight... I expected this to be a democratic household—uh, castle. I'm happy to take it in turns.' She stuck out a hip. 'If you're up to the challenge.'

He couldn't back down from that. He immediately sifted through his DVD collection. He could choose something modern—perhaps with an actress who also had beguiling eyes—or stay on theme with another older film, maybe even another Audrey Hepburn movie.

'Roman Holiday.' She'd love it even more than last night's film.

'Another I haven't seen!'

He might consider Audrey Hepburn beguiling, but his gaze repeatedly returned to Sadie during the film rather than re-main on the screen. Her reactions to the lead characters' antics and dilemmas captivated him. Every time she laughed and happy-sighed, an unfamiliar warmth spread through his chest.

Internally, he rolled his eyes. Evidently he'd been hiding himself away from the rest of the world for a little too long. He'd never expected life to return to normal—not prior-to-the-accident normal—and he didn't now, but he'd started to sense that he could create a new normal.

Perhaps it was time to make a start: to return to Milan and work; to stare down the aggressively curious until he stopped being a novelty. Just as had Hepburn's character in the film, he'd had his time out. He could return to the world of work and duty, if not renewed then at least rested and ready.

The thought startled him. Sadie had been here for two and a half days and she'd already turned his world upside down.

He wondered if she knew what an impact she'd had on him, just like Gregory Peck's character had on Audrey in the film.

When the film finished, Sadie turned to him. 'An excellent choice, Enzo. So fun.'

He fought a frown. He'd expected her to be more enthusiastic and gushing. 'But?'

She mocked-glared. 'They fell in love. They were perfect for one another. They should've ended up together forever!'

Her words made him smile. 'You're still a romantic, then? But can't you see they came from different worlds? It would never have worked.'

She blinked and eased away a fraction, even though he sat in his arm chair and she'd curled up in a corner of the sofa.

'But meeting each other, spending time with each other, had a significant impact on their lives—made them better people. Don't you think that has a beauty and power of its own?'

'I suppose.' She clearly wasn't convinced.

'But?'

She stared at the now-blank TV screen, her eyes far away. 'But in two years' time they'll meet again after it's discovered he's the secret prince of a neighbouring kingdom.'

He couldn't help but laugh. 'Or it's discovered she's actually a commoner and is therefore free to marry whomever she pleases.'

'That could work too, but only if the new royal person is lovely.'

'And then *that* monarch could meet a commoner who changes his or her world for the better.'

'Or if the new monarch is a rotter…'

They bounced around increasingly ridiculous scenarios until they were both laughing.

'*Roman Holiday* was an excellent choice, Enzo. I'm going to have to put my thinking cap on to try and top it.'

He looked forward to her next choice.

'I've also been thinking…'

He glanced back to find she'd uncurled her legs from beneath her, her feet now planted firmly on the floor and hands pressed together. Was she about to spring some new and unwelcome plan on him? Should he be worried? 'About…?'

'I don't like lying to Chelsea.'

It hit him then that Sadie didn't like lying full-stop.

She leaned towards him. 'The upside is, if Chelsea knows that you know about the party, then you get a say in the party prep.'

She was trying to get them off that good intention road to hell, and her generosity melted some of the hardness inside him. She'd be the one to take the heat in this particular scenario. Yesterday, he'd accused her of taking away his autonomy, but here she was, trying to give it back to him—and not just giving it back, but handing it to him on a gem-encrusted golden platter. She'd called him extraordinary earlier, but she was the extraordinary one.

He had no intention of causing a rift between Chelsea and her but he couldn't deny the pull of having a measure of control over the party. 'What if I told Chelsea I'd overheard you and Luisa discussing the party and confronted you with it? It's only a little white lie, but one that will save everyone's face.' And should cause zero trouble.

She bit her lip. 'That could work. And it's in the spirit of the endeavour.'

He couldn't explain why, but the fact they were now conspirators lifted his spirits. 'And will you help me throw a party that my family will never forget?'

Her entire face lit up, and that was worth whatever sacrifice he'd just made.

CHAPTER SEVEN

THE FOLLOWING DAYS took on a pattern. Sadie catalogued the toy collection for a couple of hours each morning and then she and Enzo headed down to the beach. The clifftop path was clearly a challenge, but Enzo simply gritted his teeth and got on with it.

She admired his determination. And the strength of the powerful muscles developing in his thighs. And the breadth of his strong, broad shoulders. And the piercing power of his eyes…

And. And. And. She found so much to admire in Enzo, it sometimes made her dizzy. It was *platonic* admiration, though. Maniacal laughter sounded in the back of her mind. Fine, okay, it was lustful ogling, but any hot-blooded woman would feel the same.

She'd learned not to make small talk when they reached the beach, but to leave him be to catch his breath. He might not be the snarling, snappy grump who'd greeted her on her arrival, but she didn't want to push her luck. Enzo had donned a gallantly good face about the party and she wanted to make the trial of that easier, not harder.

He didn't swim—perhaps the walk down and back was enough to test his leg—but she silently willed him to remember that long-ago holiday when he'd been a little boy and to…

What? an inner voice mocked. *Look forward to the party?*

She bit back a sigh. If only. What Enzo was no doubt looking forward to was the party being over. And her being gone.

If she thought she'd noticed heat in his eyes once or twice, it was best to ignore it. Nothing could happen between them. They were from two completely different worlds. She wasn't going to put at risk the future she was building for herself.

Shallow creature that she was, though, part of her exulted every time that brooding gaze darkened and lingered on her. It made her want to throw caution to the wind. But then his gaze snapped away and all the reasons why it would be a bad idea rushed back.

She couldn't forget what had happened nine years ago, the morning after the summer ball. Racing down to breakfast, she'd passed his mother's sitting room and had overheard Isabella mention her name.

'What are you doing, Enzo, with Sadie?' Her heart had stopped; so had her feet. 'This must stop! Sadie is not from our world. She doesn't have the resources to negotiate the world you come from.'

She hadn't stayed to listen to any more. She'd fled. She'd thought Isabella liked her. She'd thought the family considered her an equal, not the second-class citizen the girls at school had thought her. To discover that wasn't the case...

She'd buried her face in her hands. In her desire to be loved and to belong, had she misread the family's regard for her? Nausea had churned in her stomach and she'd had to take deep focussed breaths to fight a growing sense of panic. Would Enzo do as Isabella asked? she'd wondered. Would he...?

Her mind had frozen. She'd become nothing more than a bruising, aching throb. *Give him the benefit of the doubt.*

Enzo had met her in the garden as planned, and with her every atom she prayed he'd defy his mother's injunction. Instead of kissing her, though, he'd shaken his head and a dark chasm had opened up inside her.

'You're lovely, Sadie, but I fear the romance of the ball went to our heads. It feels deceitful to lead you on. For the next few years, I need to focus on my business, while you ought to be focussing on university.'

'I see.'

'My life is in Italy, while yours is here in Australia.'

They could work around a long-distance romance, Sadie thought. If he wanted to…

'I'm not looking to tie myself down,' he'd said.

So he didn't want to. She'd simply nodded and said, 'Very well.'

He'd turned and walked away and her heart had shattered into a million little pieces.

She'd cut short the rest of her stay—told them Pop was sick and Grandma needed her at home. She'd never told Chelsea about the kiss. That was the last summer she'd ever spent with Chelsea and her family. She'd been eighteen—an adult. It had been time to stop relying on the charity—the pity and kindness—of other people.

Don't let your guard slip now. She would *not* let Enzo break her heart a second time.

In the evenings, they watched films. She countered *Roman Holiday* with *Notting Hill*, which had made him laugh. His next choice had been *The Princess Bride* and hers had been *Crazy Rich Asians*. Afterwards, they curled up on their separate seats with books or laptops before retiring for the night.

In the afternoons, they went their separate ways. Sadie to restore some project that had caught her eye just for the fun of it, or to read the journals she'd found in the attics, which led her down rabbit holes of their own.

And Enzo to…who knew? Rest? Work? Have some alone time? She'd love to lure him outside the castle walls and end this self-imposed exile, but didn't know how to broach the subject. Part of her was reluctant to risk the harmony they'd forged. Maybe pushing him to have a party was enough. Still…just to explore the village on the opposite hill would be something.

A knock on the doorframe of the drawing room had her swinging around from the work space she'd set up on the table beneath the bay windows. She did her best to temper her surprise. 'Enzo!'

'Am I disturbing you?'

'Nope, I'm just tinkering. Come and see.' She held up a miniature wind-up robot. 'I've been trying to fix this, but the proof will be in the pudding. Let's see if I've been successful.'

Winding it up, she set it down and then clapped her hands as it lumbered down the length of the table, arms and legs moving in tandem. Enzo grinned. The grin remained in place when his gaze lifted back to hers.

Heart-thumping and vein-throbbing immediately commenced. Of all the things that were ridiculously attractive about Enzo—and that list grew longer every day—it was his smile that held the most power. When he smiled properly, he did it with all of himself, and it never failed to knock her off her axis.

'You fixed this?'

'The wind-up mechanism just needed some TLC. As do these ones here.' She gestured at the two tin figures partly disassembled in front of her. Glancing up at him, she pursed her lips. 'It's not hard. Would you like to give it a go?'

'I, uh…' He held up his hands. 'These are…'

Beautiful?

'Big and maybe clumsy. What if I break something?'

She cocked her head to one side. 'There's a quote I love, or maybe it's a social media meme; I can't remember. But it goes like this: "what if I fall?" And the response is, "Oh, my darling, but what if you fly?" Whenever I'm intimidated, I recite that and it gives me heart.'

She'd been using it *a lot* lately.

She gestured to the toys. 'There are no guarantees. The mechanisms are old. There's every chance they'll crumble the moment we touch them.' She leaned in closer and drew in his glorious woodsy scent. 'But I'll let you in on a little secret—if that does happen, I can order replacement parts. I believe I have several in my work bag already.'

That made him smile again. *Don't stare.* 'Or, we could strike gold like we did with this robot here and they'll magically come to life again. The only way to know is to give it a shot.'

'I'm game if you are.'

'Pass my laptop over and I'll get it out of the way.'

He did as she bid, but the movement woke her computer from its sleep mode. She'd forgotten to close the app she'd been working in and a document she'd been going over earlier sprang to life.

Notice of Resignation: Sadie Beckett.

Swallowing a squeak, she leapt forward to snap the lid closed and move the laptop to the coffee table where it could safely hide all her secrets. Her heart pounded. Had he seen the document? Would he ask what the hell she was doing with her life?

But, when she turned back, she found him studying the disassembled toys, his brow pleating as he tried to work out how they all fitted back together. Letting out a slow breath, she returned to the table and set him up with the necessary tools then walked him through what to do.

Eventually they put the toys back together. Holding their breath, they wound them up and set them on the table. A ballerina on a pedestal twirled for all she was worth, while a flamingo flapped its wings and bobbed its neck.

Swinging to each other, they high-fived, grinning madly.

'You need to visit the artisan centre.'

She blinked. 'The what?'

'Some artisans in the local village have formed a cooperative—an artisan centre—in a renovated stable yard. You ought to visit before you go home.'

Her heart thumped. 'Would you take me?' She clasped her hands beneath her chin and prayed he'd say yes.

His face shuttered and her heart nose-dived.

The resistance rose through Enzo immediately.

Why? Was he really that reluctant to show his face in public?

Yes.

But he couldn't shake off the sight of the resignation letter he'd seen when he'd moved Sadie's laptop, and the way she'd snatched her computer from him… His every instinct had warned him not to say anything.

Why had she resigned? Was she unhappy in her current position? Was it because of her mother, or her grandparents?

Chelsea hadn't mentioned any of this. Did she know, or was Sadie keeping it from Chelsea because she was pregnant and didn't want to worry her? His hands clenched.

'Never mind. It was a silly suggestion.'

He hated the way Sadie's face deflated. She was making huge changes in her life and who did she have to offer her support? The people who should be supporting her had turned their backs. He silently called them every bad name he could think of.

She pasted on a big smile. 'What kind of artisans are there?'

'No toymakers, but there's a jeweller and a violin-maker.'

'A violin-maker!' She made it sound like the most amazing thing in the world.

Half an idea formed.

What if I fall?

Oh, but my darling, what if you fly?

'There's a shoemaker and a potter. And a candlemaker too, I think.' It had been a long time since he'd visited the village. He stared at the toys they'd just mended. She was doing all this work when she didn't have to. He thrust out his jaw. 'Yes. I'd be honoured to take you to see the artisans, Sadie.'

He wasn't sure who was more surprised by the offer—Sadie or him. She swung round from where she'd started to pack away her tools. 'Yes?' she checked, as if to make sure she'd heard him correctly.

'*Sì*, I will take you into the village.' Or, at least, he'd have Guido drive them. His leg needed more rehab before he could drive. She continued to stare at him as if he'd shocked her speechless. Rather than making him self-conscious, he found himself fighting a laugh. 'It is a KPI you can tick off in your report for my family—get Enzo outside the castle walls for an afternoon. You can write something like, "while not exactly garrulous, Enzo was polite and played well with others".'

Myriad expressions flitted across her face. 'Was that… *a joke*?'

'*Sì.*'

A slow smile spread across her face, to become an enormous grin, and then she started to laugh. She laughed so hard she had to hold onto her makeshift work bench to remain upright.

Something inside Enzo shifted. To see Sadie so utterly delighted electrified him. He wanted to do it again and again. 'Come, we'll go now.'

'Wait, what…*now*?'

'Do you wish to give me time to change my mind?'

'No.' She bit her lip. 'But do I have time to change? These are my work clothes and I look a fright.'

She looked delectable, but he couldn't say that. A funny ache took up residence in his chest. She was supposed to be on holiday, and clearly viewed this little jaunt into the village as a treat. If she wanted to fuss a little… 'Of course.'

'I only need ten minutes.'

'Take half an hour.' That would give him a chance to make the arrangements with Guido, and perhaps he would change his clothes too.

'Oh, Enzo, thank you!'

She hugged him, a quick, exuberant squeeze that was over before he had a chance to respond. He watched her dash from the room in the direction of the stairs, his heart thumping against the walls of his chest. It was such a small thing, taking her into the village, and yet it brought her so much happiness. He couldn't find it in himself to regret it, even if people did look at his scars and recoil. Or, worse, respond with pity. He ground his teeth together. He *could* do this.

The drive into the village took only fifteen minutes. Sadie leaned forward in her seat to take in as much as she could. On the spur of the moment, Enzo directed Guido to drop them at the piazza rather than the artisan centre. He would indulge her curiosity and delight. She'd earned it.

She stared around the square, with its quaint fountain and tubs of flowers. She stared as they negotiated tiny alleyways and took steps that led further up the side of the hill, opposite to the one on which Enzo's castle was perched. She stared at the landscape that opened up around them.

While Enzo did his best not to stare at her. She wore a red sundress dotted with white daisies and a pretty pair of sandals, and she looked the picture of summer. He was glad he'd taken the trouble to change into a pair of tailored navy trousers and a casual button-down shirt in a striking shade of earthy brown. The way her eyes had briefly flared when she'd seen him in them had made things inside him purr with satisfaction. *Not* that he was focussing on that.

'The village is amazing,' she breathed.

Was it? He tried to see it through her eyes: the cobbled streets that lent the village a mediaeval atmosphere; the warm, golden hue of the stone houses; the avenues of olive and cherry trees; the pots of rosemary and sage that scented the air; the cheerful chatter that drifted from the tavernas and restaurants as they ambled past.

Actually, it *was* charming.

'Don't frown.'

He shook himself. 'I forgot how much I liked this place. I used to escape down here whenever my father became too much.'

'Did you have a favourite haunt?'

'Several.' There was a taverna where he'd always been welcome to join the other patrons in a game of cards or dominoes, and a tiny restaurant that had served wholesome homely meals which had somehow provided him with more than physical nourishment.

He waited for her to demand to hear more—to ask him to take her to these places—but she didn't. His eyes narrowed. Why not? Was she using some dastardly form of reverse psychology?

Enough with the suspicions!

Sadie wasn't being manipulative. She was probably doing all she could to be on what she saw as her best behaviour. She was probably thinking she'd already demanded too much of him today.

Damn it! Why couldn't her grandparents see what a gift Sadie was?

The moment they reached the stable yard with the artisans in their individual workshops, Sadie went into transports of delight. She bought a beautifully tooled leather diary from the leather-maker, a new straw hat from the hat-maker, earrings, candles and a new pair of shoes. She bought tote bags from the bag-maker to carry them all in.

Eventually, he said, 'Sadie, you do *not* need a violin.'

'No, but…maybe I need a new hobby.'

'How do you propose we carry all of this back down the hill?'

'Oh.' Her face fell.

'We can come back another day. You don't have to buy everything now.'

Which immediately cheered her up. 'It's such a treat to see all of this, Enzo. Thank you.'

He wrestled with himself for two-tenths of a second. In truth, though, he'd probably lost this particular fight days ago. 'Would you like to stay on in the village for an early dinner? There's a little place I know…'

Her entire face lit up. 'Yes, please!'

They ate in the tiny courtyard of his favourite restaurant that had a view of the countryside. The proprietor greeted him like an old friend. As others had done today, the man surveyed his face and nodded. There was no pity in his eyes, not even sympathy. It was just an acknowledgement, and Enzo found that was something he *could* bear.

Sadie took a sip of the local Vermentino he'd ordered and her eyes fluttered in appreciation. 'Delicious!' Mischief flashed across her face. She touched her glass to his. 'To ticking off KPIs.'

He tried not to grin too widely at her teasing.

'You're really well liked by the locals, Enzo.'

Her words made him blink.

'It must be nice to be back.'

'I…' He hadn't realised how much he would enjoy it. 'Yes.' He sipped his wine. 'You know, Sadie, I could see you in a little place like the artisan centre, working on your dolls and toys.'

It was her turn to blink. But then she pasted on a big, fake smile. 'You know what? I can too. But not quite yet—the time isn't right.'

Why not? She'd just resigned! Surely there couldn't be a better time?

'So.' She propped her chin on her hand. 'Have you had any thoughts about the kind of party you want?'

He bit back a groan.

'Because I've had oodles.' She bounced in her seat. 'Make me your party planner!'

'You *want* to be my party planner?'

'I've never planned a party in my life! It must be the best fun.'

A giant throb settled at the centre of him. *Damn it.* 'Fine! You can be my party planner.'

She gave an excited wiggle. 'Okay, how many people were you thinking of inviting?'

'Hmm... Mum and Stephen, Chelsea and Dominic...and you and me.'

She folded her arms and waited. When he didn't add any additional guests, she shook her head. 'That's not a party, Enzo. It's a dinner reservation.'

A scowl lowered through him.

'Remind me why we're having this party,' she ordered.

'To make my family happy. To stop them from worrying about me,' he said grouchily.

'Do you really think a dinner party of six is going to convince them you're well on the road to recovery—physically, emotionally and vocationally?'

He rolled his shoulders. 'Fine! How many extras were you thinking of?'

Behind the hazel of her eyes, he could see her mind racing. 'What about the cousins, aunts and uncles who were on that long-ago summer holiday?'

He sat up a little straighter. *Okay, that could work.* 'It would be like a mini family reunion.' His mother would love that. 'Very well.'

'And what about your besties? They'd be hurt to be left out.'

'You're like a dog with a bone. How about we just focus on eating our food?'

Which, luckily, chose that moment to arrive.

'You can give it some thought and get back to me. You don't need to decide today.' Sadie picked up her cutlery and gave one of those happy shimmies. 'This looks delicious! Thank you for today, Enzo. It's been wonderful.'

She sent him such a smile that he almost found himself almost agreeing with her.

CHAPTER EIGHT

ENZO FOLLOWED SADIE into the pool house the following afternoon. 'You think I should have a pool party?'

'Absolutely! But we don't want it looking like this.' Her hands went to her hips. 'It's awful! It's like a Las Vegas show hall.'

Her nose wrinkled, as if she'd stepped in something nasty, and a laugh pressed against the back of Enzo's throat. Guests didn't enter this pool house and wrinkle their noses. They pushed their shoulders back, assumed bored expressions and hoped some obsequious tabloid photographer was lurking in the shadows and that they'd find themselves in the society pages of some sophisticated magazine in the near future.

Memories of parties he'd been forced to endure here as a teenager flitted through him—his father and grandfather had held court like entitled pashas. The male guests had sized up Enzo and told him he had a lot to live up to. The women had flirted and sometimes touched him, making it clear they'd love to bed the Lombardi heir.

He'd learned early how to extricate himself from the clutches of the predatory and the insatiable, the social climbers and the scandal mongers. Perhaps that was why he'd always found Sadie's schoolgirl crush on him such a panacea—it had asked nothing of him, had expected nothing, and she'd been so darn sweet. Part of him—a secret, hidden part—had half-wished she'd been three or four years older. Maybe then...

Don't be daft. Schoolgirl crushes by their very definition were immature—built on daydreams and fairy tales, all rainbows and unicorns. They weren't designed to withstand the harsh realities of a messy world.

Yet knowing Sadie, spending summers with her as a part of his mother's new circle, had prevented him from becoming too jaded. He'd loathed his father's world, but had come to see it as just one tiny corner of the world. The world his mother had carved out for herself had been an altogether different one. There, he'd been able to find peace, acceptance and an innocence that had soothed his soul.

He recalled his mother's reaction when he'd kissed Sadie that one time, and winced. She'd called him into her sitting room the following morning...

'Sadie is an innocent. This has to stop! She's not from our world. She doesn't have the resources to negotiate the world you come from. Four years may not seem like much of an age difference to you, but there's a world of difference between eighteen and twenty-two. Think of all you've experienced in the last four years.'

He'd wanted to argue, but couldn't. He'd spent the previous four years at university—a time that had defined him and had helped him choose the future he'd wanted. And yet he'd found a connection with Sadie that previous night that he'd ached to explore further.

'This has to stop! Your father and grandfather would eat her alive.'

Her words had chilled his blood. Sweet and vulnerable Sadie would have no armour against their sophisticated barbs and mockery, their malice. And he'd known he wouldn't always be there to protect her.

'And if you're only toying with that lovely girl—delighting

in her hero-worship of you to boost your own ego—then that would make you no better than your father.'

Nausea had churned in his stomach. Was that what he was doing?

'Young men can be reckless and thoughtless, but I raised you better than that.'

He'd sworn to never follow in his father's footsteps.

'She is your stepsister's best friend and is as dear to her as either you or I. If you were to cause Sadie pain, it could cause a rift between you and Chelsea that we might never be able to mend. And, Enzo, is a brief flirtation worth that?'

He'd wanted to argue that maybe it wouldn't be brief, but Sadie had been only eighteen. She'd had her whole life in front of her. What right had he had to influence her life at that time? *None.*

He'd shaken his head. *'No.'*

He'd never been able to forget that kiss, though. It had been full of hope and wonder. It sure as hell hadn't felt wrong. But beneath the surface innocence a shocking and bright carnality had lifted its head and roared to life, shocking him with its intensity. It was all he'd been able to do at the time to step away before he'd lost his head.

'Enzo.'

He snapped to, something in Sadie's voice informing him it wasn't the first time she'd called his name. 'Sorry?'

'You were miles away.'

He tried to get the raging of his pulse under control. 'Merely remembering the parties I was forced to endure here. Why, I wonder, did I toe the line rather than refusing to attend?'

'It was probably easier to grit your teeth and submit for a couple of hours than get into a fight with your father.'

Where possible, Enzo had avoided drama, temper tantrums and ugly displays of emotion—especially when it had come to his father. It had been oddly satisfying to keep an unemotional distance between himself and the older man. It had infuriated his father. As Enzo hadn't openly defied him, though, there had been little he could do about it.

As soon as Enzo had come of age, and after his grandmother had died, he'd cut all ties with his father, making it clear how much he loathed him and his lifestyle. He'd expected—*hoped*—to be disinherited. There'd been no money left—only debts and the castle. He wondered if that had been his father's revenge—forcing on him this place that held only bitter memories.

It *had* provided him with a retreat when he needed one, though.

He shook himself. 'Come, Sadie, let's chase those less than salubrious memories away. Describe to me your vision for this party.'

'You're making my day, Enzo.'

She feigned swooning, and her silliness chased his moroseness away.

'First of all, we need to move all of this ridiculous furniture out of here. You must have a shed somewhere we can store it.'

'We'll throw it.'

She stared down her nose at him. 'That's a waste. Sell it.'

'So I can stumble across it at some party I attend in the future? No, thank you.'

'Then donate it to an orphanage or a women's shelter or a nursing home where you won't stumble across it. Where people will use it and enjoy it.'

He grinned. 'That is a brilliantly devious plan.' His father would turn in his grave.

He raised his hand and she high-fived him without hesitation. Was it his imagination or did her breath hitch as their palms made contact? Their gazes caught and a primal surge of heat gathered in his veins. If he kissed her now, would she kiss him back the way she had when she'd been eighteen?

Sadie snapped away before that vision could fully form in his mind. Her chest rose and fell, and his heart thundered in his ears. She wanted him; he was sure of it. He did his best to keep his voice even. 'So we get rid of all the furniture. What then?'

'We go retro.'

He had visions of tall potted palms and elegant colonial-style furniture. It would be an improvement.

Sadie made a frame with her hands, as if she were a photographer. 'I'm thinking geometrical patterns and primary colours; futuristic furniture and lava lamps; inflatable bubble sofas and silly pool toys...'

His jaw dropped. '*1960s* retro?'

She danced on the spot and silently screamed. 'Oh, go on, Enzo, say yes. I know it's silly and probably dreadfully unsophisticated, but think how much fun it would be.'

Was this the kind of party she'd wished for growing up? An ache started up in the centre of his chest.

'Can you imagine the looks on everyone's faces when they see it? They'll be beside themselves. There'll be fun, boppy sixties surf music belting from the jukebox—'

'A jukebox?'

'There *has* to be a jukebox.'

The crazy thing was, he *could* see it. His mother would clap a hand over her mouth to temper her laughter; Chelsea would probably spin on the spot until she was dizzy. Everyone would have a ball. In fact, they'd be too busy having fun to quiz him too closely. Nothing would symbolise his recovery more than the party Sadie described.

'We must have a huge bowl of fruit punch,' he said.

'And serve pizza.'

Resting his cane against a table, he moved more fully into

the pool house and turned three-hundred-and-sixty degrees, imagining what it could look like.

'Believe me, Enzo, nobody can be sad when "Yummy Yummy Yummy" by Ohio Express is belting out of the juke-box.' She stuck her nose in the air at his raised eyebrow. 'I know what I'm talking about. I found a bunch of vinyl records in an attic once. Utter gold.'

'How much did they fetch?'

Sadie moved beside him to stare into the water of the pool, the surface reflecting the light back to make patterns on the walls. 'Oh, they weren't worth anything. The owner wanted to pay me to get rid of them. I convinced her to take fifty dollars for them. They were worth every penny.'

She'd bought them? He couldn't help but laugh.

She clapped her hands. 'That's beside the point. What do you think—shall we do it? Shall we throw a 1960s pool party?'

'*Sì.*' He recalled the resignation letter on her laptop and was careful to keep his shrug casual. 'Perhaps it's time for a career change. You could become a party planner.'

'I doubt it'd be as much fun if I was being paid for it.'

The sparkle in her eye, and the flush in her cheeks—her sense of fun—was somehow infectious. She was doing this for Chelsea and his family. For him. Obligation didn't weigh her down, though. She embraced the task with joy, despite all the other stuff happening in her life.

The last of his resistance to the party drained away in the face of her generosity. Reaching out, he squeezed her shoulder. 'Thank you.'

'Thank *you* for indulging my party planning fantasies.' She turned in his hold. 'I…' Her words petered to a halt at whatever she saw in his face.

'I'm even starting to believe I too will be transformed by…' He gestured to the room and frowned. 'What was the name of your song—"Yummy Yummy Yummy"?'

She nodded, but he suspected she was only half-listening as her gaze roved over his face.

His pulse picked up speed. 'You have breezed into my *castello* and now I can't remember why I was so cranky. You want to sprinkle a bit of fairy dust around and…'

'And?'

'I find myself at a loss to tell you how truly grateful I am.'

He didn't just see the way his words melted her, he felt it beneath his hand as her shoulder softened. His fingers, tender but hungry, curved around that shoulder and he ached to explore all of her—to run his hands down the length of her spine to her hips, to pull her in close and mould her to him. To feel her tense up again with an entirely different sensation.

Gritting his teeth, he ordered himself to behave, but for the life of him he couldn't let her go; he couldn't make his fingers uncurl from around her shoulder. 'Sadie, thank you.'

She pressed trembling fingers to his lips. 'No, don't. I'm so happy to be here, Enzo. I…'

He kissed her fingers. He didn't mean to. But his free hand lifted to hold her fingers against his lips and he pressed a kiss there—pressed a kiss to those sweet, elegant, *generous* fingers.

She gasped, as if his lips charged her with electricity, which was exactly how it felt—a charge racing from her fingers to his lips and then to his groin, the entire surface of his skin tingling and heating.

When she didn't move away, he did it again, his tongue darting out to taste her. Her scent rose up all around him—fresh, floral and more potent than alcohol. Her lips parted and her breathing grew ragged, but it was the hunger in her eyes that sent exhilaration racing through him. He doubted she was aware of it, but the fingers of her free hand gripped his forearm as if to help her remain upright.

'Enzo…'

His name emerged husky with need and he slipped an arm around her waist and drew her close, the press of her breasts against his chest the sweetest torture. 'You are beautiful, Sadie. And I'm tired of pretending I don't want you when my every atom craves you.'

She swallowed and nodded. She stared at his mouth as if hungry for his kiss, and he was more than happy to sate that hunger. Slowly dipping his head towards hers, her mouth lifted towards his as if in anticipation. He paused to relish the moment…

She blinked. 'But…'

He froze.

'Oh, God. We can't!' Sadie pushed away, panic streaking through her eyes. He let her go immediately but he'd forgotten exactly where they were, where they were standing. She took another step back.

'Sadie!'

He reached for her, but it was too late. Comprehension dawned over that beautiful face as she windmilled wildly before falling backward into the pool.

CHAPTER NINE

THE COLD DASH of water should've shocked Sadie to her senses, but the water wasn't cold enough for that. She wished it was January and the water frigid. She wished this water had the ability to dispel the hard, insistent ache beneath her breast bone…and other parts of her body.

But, as she gazed up at Enzo and blinked water from her eyes, all she could think was pulling him into the water too and having her wicked way with him. Thank God he wasn't wearing a business tie that she could reach up, wrap around her hand and…

Frustration ground from her throat and she flounced— had she ever flounced before in her whole entire life?—to the wide, shallow steps and stomped back onto dry land.

Enzo handed her the thickest of fluffy towels and for some reason that only fed her temper. If he laughed…

What?

She buried her face in the towel. If they laughed it might dispel some of the tension that had her wrapped up tight; might turn that near-kiss into something silly and trivial rather than something freighted with the weight of the world.

'Sadie…'

She lifted her head.

'Would it help if I threw myself into the pool as well?'

She let out a careful breath. Maybe they could pretend that moment had never happened. 'I'm tempted to say yes, but…'

Being soaked to the skin would plaster his T-shirt and chinos to his body like a second skin, and his body was already distracting enough. With a shake of her head, she set about drying her hair.

'We need to talk about what just happened.'

Damn it! 'Okay, fine.' Okay and fine *were not* what this was. 'But not here in Liberace's palace. This place is like the set of some terrible 1980s TV series like…like *Dynasty*.' Angsty drama wasn't the vibe she was aiming for.

'If you want to get out of your wet things first…'

Sadie led the way outside and flung herself down at a table on the terrace, angling her face to the sun. Closing her eyes, she gestured vaguely in the sky's general direction. 'I'll dry off soon enough.'

He hesitated and then sat too. 'Very well. First of all, if I misinterpreted your wishes and reactions just then, Sadie, I humbly apologise. I—'

'We both know you didn't misinterpret them.' *More's the pity.* She'd wanted him to kiss her. But she'd pulled back for a reason—a reason that hadn't gone away. She slanted a glance in his direction. 'That was a ten out of ten, by the way.'

Her words didn't lighten the moment. He didn't smile.

'Then may I ask why you pulled back? You looked *horrified*.'

She sat up a little straighter. 'You don't think I did it because of your scars, do you?'

He shrugged, but she recognised the turmoil burning in the dark depths of his eyes, and bit back a sigh. 'It wasn't because of your scars, Enzo.'

Her gaze travelled to the thick red scar bisecting his forehead. 'This is probably a dreadful thing to say, but I like your scar.' It took all her strength not to reach out and trace it with her fingertip.

'You *like* it?'

'It's official, right? I'm going to hell.' He continued to stare and she did her best not to fidget. 'I honestly and truly wish you hadn't had to go through the pain you did to acquire that scar. But…it hooks up your eyebrow in this particular way.'

She tried to demonstrate, trying to mould her eyebrow into the same shape with her fingers. 'I can't decide whether that look is teasing or sneering, but either way it's totally…' To say 'compelling' would give too much away. 'Intriguing,' she settled on instead.

He continued to stare and she shifted on her seat to glare out at the water. That view ought to be soothing—all sparkling sea and soft sky framed by cliffs and verdant forests— but she doubted anything could currently soothe her. 'Given time, your scar will thin and fade and become even more artistic.'

'Artistic?'

'Yes! And it's probably wrong on so many levels, but it's how I feel, and you wanted the truth. I didn't pull back from kissing you because of your scars, Enzo; I can assure you of that. I pulled back because…'

Her glare became a scowl and she kept it trained on the view rather than turn it on him, no matter how much she might want to. He couldn't help feeling the way he did any more than she could, or any more that her grandparents could about Verity. He leaned across the table, as if hanging on her every word, and it was horribly heady.

Don't let it go to your head.

'I pulled back because Claudia broke your heart and I am *not* going to be your rebound fling.' She deserved better than that. And, for the first time in her life, she'd started to see that maybe she deserved better in other areas of her life too.

He swore. 'I knew that would come back to bite me on the butt.'

It was her turn to blink. She tried to raise an eyebrow—

unsuccessfully—so pushed it up with a finger. Finally, he smiled, and her heart pitter-pattered. 'You want to explain what you mean?'

'I mean Claudia *didn't* break my heart. I should've corrected you when you assumed it on that first day, but I was too busy being grumpy.'

'But…you went so pale when I mentioned her name. Then when I told you how I got over my crush on you—in the hope it might help you get over Claudia—you scoffed and said it wasn't the same thing.'

He sent her an incredulous stare. 'You were referring to Claudia? I thought you were referring to me not being able to walk properly, and my scars, getting over the accident and how much my life had changed.'

Her jaw dropped.

'And I did not *scoff*. You've completely misread the situation.' He frowned. 'You've had this from Chelsea, right? She thinks Claudia broke my heart?'

Sadie didn't say anything, just shrugged.

'Well, you can tell her my heart isn't broken and that I'm actually glad to be rid of the woman.'

A weight lifted, like magic, easing the tension in her shoulders, her chest and her jaw. Settling back, she tried to fight a smile. He hadn't been in love with Claudia… She wanted to high-five someone.

The view acquired a new sparkle—all that summer magic shimmered with promise.

'What nobody knows is that I'd broken off with Claudia the previous week. It had been amicable enough, or so I'd thought. When she asked if I'd still escort her to a charity ball her grandmother had organised, I agreed.'

Because he wouldn't want to leave her high and dry, Sadie thought. Because he was a good guy. His other words filtered into her consciousness and things inside her started to tighten again. The accident had occurred on the way home from that charity ball.

'You said you *thought* it was amicable…which implies you were mistaken?'

'Wildly mistaken.' His lips twisted. 'A fact I discovered when I drove her home that evening.'

She went cold all over. 'What happened?'

He dragged a hand down his face. 'Damn it, Sadie, I wasn't going to mention any of this.'

'Too late.' The shadows in his eyes made her chest ache. 'You're going to have to tell me what *this* is now.'

Blowing out a breath, he tapped a finger against the table before straightening. 'During the drive home she wanted us to get back together, and outlined all the reasons we were good together.'

Sadie sucked her bottom lip. 'But you didn't agree.'

'What I'd forgotten to take into account was the fact that Claudia has rarely heard the word "no". Her father is a transport magnate and her parents have indulged her every whim.'

'But you couldn't be bought or brought to heel.'

'Correct.'

She stared at his scar and acid burned a path through her insides. 'She caused the accident.' Her heart pounded with big, hard, bruising thumps. 'She caused the accident,' she repeated, thinking she might be sick.

Dark eyes met hers. 'Inadvertently, yes.'

Her lungs started to burn.

'She lashed out at me—physically.'

'She *hit* you?'

'We were on a particularly dangerous piece of road and it took me completely off-guard. She had this hard little clutch bag and walloped me right here with it.' He pointed to his temple. 'And then tried to undo her seatbelt, presumably to get into a better position to keep hitting me. I had my hand over hers so she couldn't release the catch, so I was driving with one hand when she hit me again with that damn clutch. I lost control of the car, though thankfully I'd managed to slow down, so we didn't hit the tree at full speed.'

Her heart pounded in her throat. 'You could've gone over the cliff! She could've killed you both.'

He turned grey. '*Sì*. It has taken all of these months for that vision to stop waking me in the middle of the night.'

The darkness in his eyes had a lump lodging in her throat. Reaching across, she slipped her hand inside his. 'I'm sorry, Enzo. That was a truly terrible thing to go through.' She squeezed the life out of his hand, but he didn't seem to mind.

'I know it's an ugly story, but…'

'Why haven't you told anyone?' Why hadn't he made it public?

She found her hand suddenly empty and she nursed it in her lap, trying to rub away the feel of him. She needed to find a way to control the inconvenient feelings that gripped her whenever Enzo was near. There might not always be a convenient swimming pool to hurl herself into.

Enzo might not be nursing a broking heart, but he was in no shape for any kind of romantic entanglement. He needed rest, respite and a friend. Not the drama of a temporary love affair.

Would it be temporary?

Of course it would! As Isabella had pointed out nine years ago, Sadie would never fit into Enzo's world. The only thing that had changed was their ages, not their circumstances. He'd agreed with his mother then and he would again now.

When she'd left Australia, Sadie had told herself she was through with not measuring up, with not being *enough*. She wasn't going to let Enzo make her feel less again now. He mightn't mean to, but she was building a new life—a good life—and she wasn't going to put that in jeopardy.

Nor would Enzo want her to. The best the two of them could manage was something along the same lines as *Roman Holiday*. Her mind started to race.

That has merit.

Stop!

'Claudia did not emerge unscathed from the accident, Sadie.'

She dragged her attention back to the conversation. Claudia had broken her arm and fractured her collarbone. She'd suffered numerous cuts and abrasions—though not as seriously as Enzo.

'She suffered too. It seemed mean-spirited to point a finger in her direction—unnecessarily dramatic. She knows she caused the accident and will have to live with that knowledge for the rest of her life. That is punishment enough.'

He was too gallant. 'You should tell your family.'

He swung back, a frown on his face.

'They'll respect your desire for secrecy, but they love you, Enzo, and deserve to know what really happened.'

'You think that they will see it as an indication that I'm getting better.'

He *was* getting better, even if he couldn't see it for himself yet. 'I do.'

'Very well. When they come to this dreadful party, I will tell them the truth.'

She feigned affront. 'With me as your party planner there won't be anything dreadful about it. This party will be *superb*.'

One side of his mouth hooked up. '*Sì*, of course.'

He stared at her so long it took a force of will not to hunch her shoulders or snap, 'What?' at him.

'You backed away earlier under false pretences. I'm not searching for relief from a broken heart. But I cannot now help think your actions were wise.'

His words left her feeling hollow and she couldn't work out why when he was merely verbalising her own thoughts.

'I'm not in the right frame of mind to embark on a romantic liaison, no matter how exhilarating it might prove to be. For the next little while, I need the quiet life.' His lips twitched. 'And one thing you no longer are is quiet, Sadie.'

His words surprised a laugh from her. 'True.'

'And, while some flings end well with gratitude and affection on both sides…'

'Some don't,' she finished. 'And we'd rather chop off our right hands than do anything that might strain our relationship with Chelsea.'

His head rocked back. 'If she thought I had taken advantage of you…'

'Or I of you.'

His face grew grim. 'You are very beautiful, but I cannot…'

'Ditto and ditto.'

He leaned across, took her hand and squeezed it, and it felt as if he were squeezing her heart. 'But you are a very good friend, Sadie Beckett. One of the best.'

'Ditto,' she forced past the lump in her throat.

She leaped up, forcing him to release her. 'Now, you'll have to excuse me. I'm going to get changed, and then I have a party to plan.'

But, for the rest of the day, *Enzo thinks I'm beautiful* played over and over in her mind, making it feel as if it were her birthday and Christmas combined.

Sadie was a lark rather than an owl, and Enzo found himself settling into the same patterns and rhythms. He found it oddly soothing.

Her presence could be felt everywhere: in the way Sadie hummed when she worked on the toys; in the way curtains were flung open to let the sun pour in; in the way their movie club competition could make him smile at odd moments. Their last three movies had been *Pretty Woman* for him, *Sabrina* for her and *My Favourite Wife* for him. That last film had so delighted her, he'd felt like king of the world.

Since *Roman Holiday*, he'd been careful only to choose films with happy endings. The lines around her eyes and mouth had started to ease—the comedies were working their magic.

He suspected they were working their magic on him as well. Or was that Sadie herself? All he knew was that, when he was around her, he didn't feel broken any more.

He glanced up at a tap on his office door to find the object of his thoughts standing there.

'Sadie.' He gestured her into the room.

'Am I interrupting?'

A week ago he'd have snapped at her, or muttered something such as, *interrupting is your middle name*, but now he shook his head. 'I'm going over financial records and praying someone will interrupt me.'

'"Interruptions R Us" at your service.' She took a seat and waved a hand at his computer. 'Don't you have people to do that?'

'*Sì*. People more qualified than me, too, but it's good business practice to know what is happening in my own company.'

'Huh.' She blinked. 'So young and yet so wise.'

The admiration in her eyes had him shifting on his seat. 'It's a task that requires concentration and, since the accident and my concussion...'

What on earth...? Why was he telling her this? *Well, as you've told her practically everything else...*

'Oh, I didn't consider that.' She planted elbows on his desk, chin in hands. 'How's it going?'

'As boring as ever.'

His words made her laugh and he found himself grinning.

'What do you have there?' He nodded at the parcel she'd brought with her. She sometimes brought down some treasure from the toy collection to share. He suspected he enjoyed her delight more than the novelty of the items.

'Treasure, of course.' She dimpled at him. 'Is that coffee I smell?'

It was in all the little things—rather than asking if she could help herself to coffee from the pot on the sideboard, she'd not so subtly suggested he get her one. She didn't treat him with kid gloves, she didn't treat him like an invalid and she certainly didn't treat him like an abomination who needed to be endured. Nor did she act as if she was his lackey, which sometimes was the reaction his wealth and success engendered in others—as if those things made him worthy of deference.

His family never did, and he was glad Sadie didn't either. It was a healthy reality check. It was probably part of her overall plan to get him 'party ready'. Rather than resenting it, he found himself appreciating it. He knew she enjoyed cataloguing the toy collection, and he knew she appreciated being away from Australia, but he wished he could help her in a more significant way.

You could ask her about her letter of resignation.

Or he could mind his own business.

He gestured they move to the arm chairs, and he poured their coffees. He set a mug in front of her and took the other chair, trying not to inhale her beguiling fragrance to deeply.

Damn it. Inhale as deeply as you can. You only live once.

As long as inhale was all he did.

Handing him a velvet box, she grinned and wriggled as if she couldn't help it.

He lifted the lid, and inside on a bed of silk was the pocket watch he'd taken such a fancy to. Lifting it, he once again relished its weight. The gold gleamed beneath the overhead lights.

Opening the cover, his jaw dropped. 'It's working!' He stared at the watch. 'You fixed it!'

She danced in her seat. 'It was tricky and I needed to order some parts in, and I probably should've sent it to someone with more expertise in the area, but yes—it's working again.'

He'd treasure it—even though it was a relic from one of his hideously dastardly forebears.

'It's a beautiful watch, Enzo. Thank you for giving me the chance to work on it. I've also been reading those journals and they've proved enlightening.'

And now she was going to ruin the moment. He set the watch carefully back in its box and braced himself. 'More thieves and tyrants and exploiters of the weak and innocent?'

'Your great-great grandmother did a bit of a potted history of the family. While there was one rather awful landowner that you wouldn't have left your unmarried daughters unchaperoned with…'

He rubbed a hand over his face. 'Let me guess, he was murdered in his sleep?' A fate he no doubt deserved.

'It said he died of the palsy at the age of fifty-two, but his grandfather helped to fund an important university in the region, and not only donated generously to scientific research but also to the arts. The younger grandson, Felix, followed in those same footsteps.

'You also have an ancestor who was part of a diplomatic envoy to Ethiopia. There's a great-aunt who helped found a religious order. Plus there have been numerous civic leaders who've made improvements to their local villages. There's even a couple who were part of the resistance in the Second World War.'

His jaw dropped.

'That Count your father was always so proud of… He actually denied the title before it was fashionable to do any such thing.'

His father had loved bragging about his aristocratic lineage. 'No way!'

'Yes way. The Lombardi name isn't cursed, Enzo. There are some true heroes among your ancestors. It's just unfortunate that your grandfather and father weren't of their number. But, from what I've been reading, your father and grandfather are the exceptions to the rule, not the standard.'

He didn't know what to do with the information.

'So you can use that watch with pride. You're one of the good guys—a hero, not a villain.'

'You've been watching too many romantic comedies.'

She laughed. 'Now, if you really want to get back to your financial reports…'

'I don't.'

'Excellent!' She leapt up. 'Then I want to show you something.'

He found himself on his feet before she'd finished her sentence. A voice in the back of his mind warned him not to look so eager. But, not only had this woman fixed an antique watch he'd had an immediate affinity with, she'd presented him with a different version of his family from the one he'd always held in his mind. One he didn't have to be ashamed of. So, if Sadie wanted to show him something, he'd damn well see it. Not with impatience or bad-tempered grace, but with enthusiasm.

And pleasure, he realised when she dragged him out to the pool house. He'd been banned from venturing anywhere near it for the last week on pain of death. He'd seen the army of delivery drivers arrive over the course of the week, though.

With a flourish, she gave a resounding, 'Ta-da!' and threw open the door.

He headed inside, but stopped mid-stride. *What on earth…?* Sadie had transformed the place!

Rather than crystal and gold-gilt furniture, he was now surrounded by the futuristic furniture of the 1960s. There was an enormous rainbow-patterned bubble-sofa suite, a tan lounger and a selection of chairs in hot shades of tangerine, lemon and lime. Fat cushions in crazy geometrical patterns were strewn about in a riot of brown, orange and avocado. Lava lamps rested on moulded acrylic tables, and disco balls hung where the chandeliers had once been.

He tried to take it all in. 'How did you manage this in a week?'

'I'm a woman of action.' She stuck her nose in the air and pushed her shoulders back, but it thrust her chest in his direction. He stared, his mouth going dry, an instant hunger roaring through him. With a squeak, she immediately slouched again and crossed her arms.

Get a grip. He lowered himself to the nearest plastic banana lounger, pretending to gaze at the room while he focussed on getting the throbbing and fire back under control.

She perched on the edge of a futuristic purple cube that could be used either as a seat or a table. 'What do you think?'

The room. Look at the room.

He did, and when it eventually came back into focus he couldn't get over the transformation. He gazed at the surfboards on the walls, the carnival-style pizza stand at the far end of the room and the jukebox. 'How did you manage all of this in such a short amount of time?'

'Luisa and Guido. They're magicians! They arranged an army of helpers. And one can source anything online these days. And as you'd said money was no object…'

He didn't care what it had cost. This place had been a source of misery to him all his life. But now it looked…*glorious.* He fought an urge to lean across and press his lips to hers in gratitude.

'What do you think?'

His mind raced a hundred miles an hour. 'I think that this party is going to be a great success.'

'Of course it is.'

He even started to believe that he could manage more than the appearance of fun. It struck him in that moment that Sadie was due to return to Australia in a few short days. Every atom rebelled at the thought.

She drummed her feet on the floor. 'I'm going to shake you soon if you don't tell me what you *actually* think.'

'It's just my mind is racing with plans I never thought I'd be contemplating.' He stood and she did too. 'Ten out of ten. I love it, Sadie; I think it is wonderful.'

Her entire body sagged as if his words had melted her. As if his enthusiasm were a super-power. She pressed both hands over her heart, her eyes going misty.

He made a spur-of-the-moment decision. 'Can I ask a favour?'

'Absolutely.'

The generosity of this woman astounded him—it was unhesitating, unstinting. Again, it took all of his strength not to reach across and press his lips to hers. It had nothing to do with gratitude this time, though, and everything to do with dancing hazel eyes, a mischievous mouth and the memory of a long-ago kiss.

Her gaze lowered to his mouth and she moistened her lips. He could've groaned out loud. *Keep things light. Don't go there.*

He dragged his gaze back to her eyes. *Keep them there.* 'Would you consider staying on a little longer and helping me redecorate the castle?'

Her head rocked back. 'I'm not turning your castle into this!' She gestured at the pool house. 'This is great for fun and frivolity, but not for living in up there.' She waved vaguely in the direction of the castle.

'You've performed a miracle. You've made this a place I no longer hate. Not only can I see myself having fun here, I can…' He frowned. 'I could almost imagine a future here.'

A breath whooshed out of her.

'There are rooms in the castle I avoid because they remind me of my father and grandfather. It never occurred to me that it would be possible to erase that and replace it with…' He didn't know what word to use. Hope? Fun?

Comprehension dawned in her eyes. 'With something positive and lovely?'

'Sì.'

Hauling in a breath, he made a snap decision. 'Forgive me, Sadie—I will speak plainly, because I think we can help one another. I accidentally saw your resignation letter when I moved your laptop the other day. Please stay on at the *castello*, at least until after the party. That's only two weeks away. It will save you having to return. It will also give you a chance to spend some time on new job applications, if that's your plan, while also helping me come up with some decorating ideas. What's more, there'll still be beach time, and a chance to watch all the rom-coms you want.'

She stared at him and he swallowed. 'You're helping me find my feet again, Sadie, and I am not yet ready to let you go.'

CHAPTER TEN

He'd said… She…

Don't tackle the man—kiss him!

Which was exactly what she wanted to do. But she needed to rein in her *enthusiasm*. If she was silly enough to do something stupid, like fall in love with Enzo, he'd break her heart. She hadn't been good enough for him nine years ago and that hadn't changed.

She dragged in a breath. Fine; she wouldn't fall in love with him, then. *Simple.* That didn't stop temptation winding around her, though. Taking a step closer, she peered into his face. 'Do you mean that?'

'Yes.'

His eyes glowed with equal measures of defiance and sincerity. She feared she had stars in hers. She *wouldn't* fall in love with him. He *wouldn't* break her heart. At the moment, though, he was helping to heal some of the fractured places inside her. 'Thank you.'

'Don't thank me, Sadie. I'm the one who should be thanking you. I'm glad you came here to shake up my world.'

He moved a step closer until they were only inches apart. Reaching up, she pressed her hand to his chest. 'I can thank you for being kind, can't I?'

He laid his hand over hers. 'Kind? I was horrible!'

She pressed her hand more firmly against him and a shudder rippled through him. *She* did that to him. *Her.* Air hissed between her teeth as the power and potency of that big male body flooded her senses.

She managed a shrug. 'You were a bit grumpy, but that was understandable. Life has sucked ferociously recently. But, when you found out life hadn't exactly been a bed of roses for me, you were kind, and generous.'

His fingers traced a lazy path from her fingertips to her forearm and she wanted to stretch, purr and…bite him. She swallowed against the raw need that clawed through her. She wanted to sink her teeth gently into his flesh and watch his eyes darken with the same desire that flooded her.

'Why the frown?'

The rasp of his voice lifted the fine hairs on her arms. It took an effort to focus on the conversation rather than the fantasies playing through her mind. 'Your generosity has made me see the lack of generosity in other areas of my life.' She stared at the hand covering hers. 'I've always had to change to win my grandparents' approval—to not be *too much*. To not be too noisy, to not ask for a birthday party, to not play music or pin posters of boy bands on my bedroom walls. To not demand too much of their energy or time. I've started to see how small I had to make myself.'

Since living on her own, she'd learned to stop living so small. But somewhere along the way she'd forgotten how to dream big. 'I deserve better,' she murmured. She deserved the same generosity from them that she'd given.

His knuckles brushed across her cheek. 'You deserve the very best life has to offer.'

With Enzo, she could be as *much* as she wanted. It was so damn freeing. That didn't mean either the castle or the prince were on offer, though.

Maybe not long-term.

Her gaze lowered to his mouth and she recalled that long-ago kiss. A kiss that had rocked the foundations of her world.

She hadn't known a kiss could make her feel, and *want*, so much. She wanted to kiss him again now to find out if she'd imagined it; if she'd somehow exaggerated the power of that kiss in the intervening years.

She nibbled her bottom lip.

A groan left Enzo's throat and his hands went to her shoulders. She thought he meant to put her away from him. Instead those fingers curled around her shoulders as if they didn't want to let her go. 'Don't look at me like that, Sadie.'

The rasp of his voice grazed across all her fine nerve-endings and she lifted her gaze. The hunger in his eyes emboldened her. 'Why not?'

'Because you want the full, fairy-tale happy ending. You don't want *Roman Holiday*.'

Wait—what*?*

'I meant what I said the other day. I'm not currently equipped for romance. I'm not looking for love. I don't want the complication or drama that love involves. To be brutally honest, I couldn't think of anything worse.'

And yet he hadn't moved away. '"Forever love" doesn't feature in my future at the moment either, Enzo, if that's what you think I'm looking for.' She frowned up at him. 'My priority is building a new future. Love would be a distraction— a displacement activity.'

She wanted the foundations of her new future to be strong—she wasn't going to rely on anyone else, especially a man, to help her create that. The people she ought to have been able to trust had let her down. From now on she'd rely only on herself.

'Once my life is looking how I want it to, I might turn my mind to love—children might be nice eventually—but at the moment? No.'

His jaw went gratifyingly slack, as if her words had punched the breath from that big body of his.

'I am, however, rethinking my initial reaction to *Roman Holiday*. I'm definitely seeing its appeal.'

The pulse at the base of his jaw pounded. He wanted her with the same intensity she wanted him and she had to fight the impulse to reach up, cover that pulse with her mouth and lathe it with her tongue. 'I'll let you in on a little secret. My life is a bit of a mess at the moment.'

'Not a secret,' he murmured, his gaze raking her face and neck, then down to where her chest rose and fell, leaving a heated path of need in its wake. 'While mine is a total mess.'

'It's not as bad as you think.' She placed both hands on his chest and spread her fingers, feeling the power of his muscles beneath them. Very slowly she ran them up to his shoulders, relishing their width and strength; watching in fascination as his eyes darkened and pupils dilated. 'I don't think either one of us is in the market or headspace for falling in love. Yet I want you and you want me.'

'*Sì.*'

His nostrils flared. She had a feeling he was drinking in her scent and that thought had her nipples beading to hard, aching points. 'It sounds uncomplicated.' She tried to keep her voice steady. 'We're friends who want benefits, but we also have each other's best interests at heart.'

She didn't want either of them making false promises, but that didn't mean there could be *no* promises. She burned to make love with Enzo, but she didn't want him looking at her with shadowed eyes tomorrow. 'Maybe we need to give each other some assurances first.'

His hands moved to her waist. 'No temper tantrums.'

Her pulse picked up speed. 'Agreed.' She wouldn't throw some Claudia-sized hissy fit—not in a million years. 'We don't let this affect Chelsea.'

'Agreed.'

She stood on her tiptoes until his mouth was in reach. 'Kindness and generosity.'

'Done. But you've forgotten something.' One side of his mouth hooked up. *'Fun.'*

His breath teased her lips and a hot rush of exhilaration filled her veins. 'I can do fun.' She moistened her lips. 'Is it okay if I kiss you now?'

His answer was to claim her lips with his in a lazy, thorough kiss that had her smiling at the relief of it. His hands slid into her hair, holding her still, and his mouth slanted more firmly over hers, his tongue teasing and tantalising, sparking need *everywhere*, melting parts of her that ached for his touch.

Her hands clenched in the material of his T-shirt and she arched against him, seeking relief, revelling in his hardness against her softness. A moan was pulled from the very depths of her. *This...* She wanted *this*.

When he lifted his head long moments later, they were both breathing hard. She hadn't exaggerated that former kiss—not in the slightest. Enzo's kiss was every bit as potent and mind-blowing as she remembered.

Pulling his wallet from his pocket, Enzo extracted a foil-wrapped packet. 'If you'd prefer the comfort of my king-sized bed, Sadie, tell me now.'

Her reply was to turn, walk to the door and lock it. When she turned back round, she slowly made her way towards him, divesting herself of her blouse, bra then her shorts as she went.

His gaze darkened, but when her fingers went to the waistband of her panties he shook his head. 'Let me unwrap the rest of you.'

With unhurried strides he moved towards her, dragging his T-shirt over his head and tossing it off to the side. All that gleaming, manly flesh had her breath hitching. Reaching out, she traced a scar on his chest and another on his bicep. 'Do they hurt?'

He shook his head.

Reaching forward, she traced the scar on his chest with her

tongue. He stiffened and groaned, before cupping her breasts in his palms and brushing her taut nipples with his thumbs.

'Oh!' She arched into his touch and he gave her a satisfied smile. The pleasure was so exquisite, it almost hurt. Pressing her hands to his and halting the slow torture of his thumbs, she pushed her breasts against his hands more fully which had another, 'Oh,' choking from her.

'I thought I'd exaggerated the kiss we shared when I was eighteen—made it out to be bigger and better than it could actually have been in reality. But I didn't. You're going to completely undo me, Enzo.'

'And you me. But, Sadie, I promise we'll enjoy every moment. Do you trust me?'

'Yes.'

Their mouths crashed back together and they explored each other with their hands, their mouths and tongues. When Enzo finally rolled a condom onto himself and joined their bodies, they both paused to relish the moment. But then he moved. He'd kept her on the edge of orgasm for so long that after three long, slow, deep strokes her muscles clenched around him. Her body bowed up to meet his, fingers digging into taut buttocks, and she cried out his name as wave upon wave of pleasure crashed, pounded and pulsed inside her, flinging her outside herself to a place she had never been before.

When she finally had the strength to open her eyes, she found him watching her with a strange smile playing across his lips. 'You are beautiful.'

Their lips met in another intensely discombobulating kiss and she felt beautiful. For a tiny moment in time, she finally felt enough for someone, and it felt so damn freeing she wanted to throw her arms wide open to hug the entire world.

Enzo had always made her feel that she was enough. Except for that one time…

But then he did something that made her body quicken

for him again. Her eyes flew open to meet his. He grinned, and it was so full of mischief and delight that she couldn't help grinning back. She pushed away that long ago memory. That was in the past. Now, they'd share some uncomplicated fun—soothe and bolster each other until they felt ready to face the world again. She was no longer that silly schoolgirl with stars in her eyes.

Instead you're a grown woman with stars in her eyes.
They're not stars. They're hot, burning embers of passion...

Much later, they lay on the sofa, their hands drifting over each other's bodies—sated, satisfied and probably a bit smug.

Enzo glanced down at her. 'You never got round to answering me. Will you stay a little longer—at least until the party?'

Did he really want her to stay? Now that they'd made love, for him perhaps that itch had been scratched.

He twisted a strand of her hair around his finger and tugged on it gently. 'Let me guess what's going through your mind right now.' That piratical eyebrow lifted and she could've swooned. 'Enzo might be having second thoughts and wishing he hadn't made that rash request...*si*?'

Was she really that transparent?

'Let me assure you, nothing could be further from the truth.'

She eased away from him a little to settle on her side. He mimicked her pose, turning to face her fully.

'I meant what I said, Sadie.'

She believed him. Enzo had uttered too many hard truths since she'd arrived at his castle. If he'd changed his mind, he'd have said so. Not in a mean or angry way, but he wouldn't lie about it. He was too tired and still too raw from all that had happened for such lies.

'However, I understand that you may not think staying another fortnight a wise investment of your time.' Lifting her hand, he pressed a kiss to her palm. 'I'm hoping, however, that's not the case.'

Vulnerability stretched through his eyes before it was promptly blinked away. Something in her chest stuttered.

'Did you think I would use and abuse you and then leave?'

'Not abuse, no.'

She wondered if he'd realised that he'd placed her hand over his heart. The slow, steady beats beneath her palm soothed her.

'But you think it's within the realms of possibility that I'd have my wicked way with you and then ride off into the sunset without so much as a backward glance?'

'You don't think that's a possibility? Sadie, I know you are no longer that schoolgirl who had a crush on me, but—'

'I *don't* see you as some kind of trophy, Enzo. You're not an item I want to tick off some fantasy bucket-list. You're...' How to describe it? She sat up and then wished she had a bedsheet to tuck around her. She felt too naked. 'You're my friend, and you're also an amazing lover. This thing that we're doing...'

Rising, she grabbed his T-shirt and dragged it over her head. He remained stretched out, totally comfortable with his nakedness. Her mouth went dry. Oh Lord; why shouldn't he be? He had the body of a Greek god.

'This thing that we're doing...?' he prompted.

She returned to sit on the side of the sofa. 'I've never had a fling with a friend before—never done the friends-with-benefits thing—so this is all outside of my experience.' She met his gaze. 'But I have a great deal of affection for you.'

His eyes grew wary.

'And I think you feel the same way about me.'

'*Sì.*'

That wariness deepened and it had an ache throbbing to life inside her. Did he seriously think she'd do some kind of 'Claudia' number on him?

'I feel you have my back, Enzo, and I certainly have yours. I want you to enjoy your party; I want your family to stop worrying about you. And in terms of bucket-list fantasy items—redecorating a castle is right up there. So, yes, I would love to stay. I'd love to do more of…this.'

She gestured to the ridiculous bubble-sofa. 'If that's something you're interested in too.'

Enzo's wariness drained away. 'That's the part I'm *most* interested in.' He waggled his eyebrows like some pantomime villain, making her laugh. For a moment he'd been worried that she'd declare her undying love for him; would point to the intensity of their love-making as proof of a deeper connection. He could've wept when she hadn't. She'd meant what she'd said about not falling in love.

It didn't change the fact that their love-making had been intense.

That didn't mean anything. They were both going through a lot. It was bound to manifest itself intensely when they found an outlet. But Sadie was right: he wasn't a trophy and neither was she. She was more than an outlet too. She was a true friend. He just needed to make sure they stayed on the right side of the imaginary line they were negotiating.

'I'm glad. Though I feel I'm gaining more from the arrangement than you.'

She gaped at him. 'Summer, castle, Mediterranean, beach, sun…' Her arm gestured wildly in all directions, then her hands dropped to pleat the hem of his shirt. She looked delectable in his shirt. He should encourage her to wear his shirts at every possible opportunity.

Reaching out, he stilled her fingers. 'What is it?'

She wrinkled her nose. 'One of the reasons remaining here is convenient is the fact I have a job interview next week in Rome. So maybe you can also lend me Guido to take me to the train station on top of all of the Mediterranean, sun, beach and castle stuff…?'

He sat up. 'You're applying for jobs in Europe?'

'Yes,' she said in the smallest voice.

If she moved to Europe he might see more of her… He rolled his shoulders. And, that could be nice.

'Do you think I'm being an idiot?' she blurted out.

'What? *No.* Why would I think that?'

'Because it seems an over-dramatic response to me wanting to put some distance between myself and everything that's happened back home.'

When she put it like that…

'But, the thing is, I've kept my life small in lots of ways because of my grandparents. Not that they've asked it of me, so don't think that.'

He had a feeling she'd have loved it if they *had* asked it of her. An ache settled in his chest—a big, purple bruise of an ache. How could they not see what a wonder this woman was and treasure her like she deserved?

'So I've never considered living anywhere other than Melbourne, just in case they ever needed me. Being close at hand seemed the least I could do after they were forced to raise me.'

'They should have taken joy in you, Sadie; treasured having you in their lives, instead of making you feel like a duty.' His hands clenched. 'You shouldn't feel so beholden to them. It is Verity who owes them.'

'I can't help the way I feel.' She shrugged. 'And family can be complicated.'

Huffing out a breath, he nodded.

'What my grandparents care about is having my mother in their lives. They couldn't care less where I live.' She pressed her hands together. 'As much as I wish that were otherwise…' she slid a glance in his direction '…it also frees me up in some rather exciting ways.'

Sadie didn't waste time feeling sorry for herself; she concentrated instead on forging a new plan, a new shape for her life. It shamed him.

'You have a funny expression on your face.' Her brow crinkled. 'Should I be worried?'

He pointed to his face. 'Not a funny expression—*admiration*. For you; I think what you're doing is brave and wonderful.'

If her eyes went any wider, he'd be able to fit a castle, the sea and all of summer inside them. 'Tell me what you most want to do with this freedom of yours.'

'I'd like to see more of the world. To live in a different country for a while and experience life in a brand-new place.' She let out a long breath. 'I want to not be found lacking for once.' She was silent for a moment. 'I want a new start. No baggage.'

He wasn't sure if that last was possible… 'No regrets. Live life to the full?'

A smile spread across her face. 'Exactly.'

'It sounds like an excellent plan. Chelsea will be thrilled that you're moving closer. Tell me about the jobs you're applying for.'

He listened as she outlined the position at the auction house in Rome that she was being interviewed for, and the two jobs in London she'd applied for—one a museum position and the other as a toy restorer at an antiques centre.

She made no mention of starting her own doll hospital. Had she really given up on that dream? 'You've been busy. On top of cataloguing the castle's toy collection, dealing with a grump like me and planning a party, you've been applying for jobs and turning your entire world upside down.'

'Yet there's still been time to amble down to the beach every day to soak up some sea and sun. It's been heaven. And in case you haven't noticed, Enzo, you haven't actually been grumpy recently.'

He blinked. He hadn't just stopped snapping and snarling, he hadn't *felt* like snapping and snarling. He'd continued to put up some token resistance about the party for form's sake, but parties had never been his thing. When he thought of parties, he thought of the extravagant affairs his father had thrown.

He glanced round the pool house. His father would never have thrown a party like the one Sadie had planned. Like Sadie, Enzo could make new memories. If he had the courage.

'Don't make a liar of me now, Enzo.'

Her words were light, but he sensed the concern threaded beneath them. Dragging his gaze back to hers, he sent her a rueful smile. 'Not returning to grump mode. Just trying to trace the evolution of me holding my surliness in check to no longer actually feeling surly.' It had happened without him realising it. That was Sadie's doing.

She shook her head, as if she could read his mind. 'You were already on the mend before I arrived. You've been healing for some time, but I expect it hasn't felt that way. You've been in constant pain for months, but the pain has been easing, yes?'

'I…' He frowned. 'Yes.'

'Look…' she gestured '…you didn't even bring your stick down with you.'

He glanced around, searching for it. Hot damn!

'I don't care who you are; not even Mother Teresa could be cheerful when in constant pain.'

'Sadie, will you please stop downplaying all you've done? I retreated here to come to terms with the accident, but in reality all I did was nurse my sense of injury—and wallow!' *Pathetic.*

She sent him one of those 'school ma'am' looks. 'Stop beating yourself up. You're coming to terms with all of that now, aren't you? So come up with a plan for your life going forward, while doing some fun things like lying on the beach and refurbishing your castle.'

'And having a party?'

'Now you're getting the hang of it.'

Then she yelped and started flinging his clothes at him. 'Luisa is on her way down with lunch!'

Chuckling, he slid into his trunks and chinos while she slipped her capris back on. 'Keep my shirt.'

She wouldn't have time to wrestle with her bra. Reaching down, he picked it up and slipped it into his pocket to save her blushes, though he suspected Luisa wouldn't be fooled for a moment.

Later, over lunch—a delicious chicken pasta salad, crusty bread and sliced fruit—he turned Sadie's suggestion over in his mind. What did he want his life to look like going forward? He had the money to live his life any way he wanted. What did he want to do with all that freedom?

He knew one thing for sure—he wanted to look forward to his future with as much relish as Sadie looked forward to hers.

The next two weeks passed in a haze of golden summer fun that was reminiscent of that long-ago summer holiday Enzo had enjoyed as a boy. He and Sadie walked down to the beach every day to swim, lie in the sun and soak up the serenity. Every day that walk became a little easier.

They pored over ideas for refurbishing the drawing and dining rooms, along with the master bedroom suite. And, in doing so, he started to imagine living at the castle. He could work remotely if he wanted. He didn't have to base himself in Milan and go into the office every day. Even if he did want to go into the office, it was only a two-and-a-half-hour commute. Or he could leave his company in the capable hands of his senior management team and turn his mind to a different project.

Like what?

Ideas turned in his mind. Unlike his father, he'd love to leave a legacy behind that made a lasting impact—a *good* impact.

While this time with Sadie might remind him of that long-ago childhood holiday, there were now some far more adult activities on the agenda. He and Sadie couldn't get enough of one another. With unspoken agreement, he spent the nights in her bed, where they learned the shape of each other's bodies with an intimate detail that utterly delighted him. He loved knowing the spot on her hip that had her melting when he kissed it, and making the air between her teeth whistle when he kissed her nape.

He loved how she could slide a finger down his spine in a manner that made him hard in an instant, and the way she gently sank her teeth into his lower lip in a way that turned him on but also made him smile. And he loved waking up with her warm body curled against his, and loved the way her lips curved into a smile as she woke and blinked sleep from her eyes.

Had a fortnight ever passed more swiftly?

He woke early on the morning of the party to find Sadie already awake and gazing at him. 'Ready for the onslaught?'

His immediate family was due to arrive early afternoon and would stay for the weekend.

'Not quite yet.' Reaching for her, he kissed her with a hunger that roused an instant and equally fervid response. They made love with a desperate intensity, as if trying to cling to the idyll they'd carved out for themselves.

Nothing had to change, he told himself as he drifted off into a gentle slumber. Once everyone had gone home, Sadie could stay a little longer. She could stay until she found a job.

CHAPTER ELEVEN

THE MOMENT SADIE clapped eyes on Enzo on the landing, she had to clap a hand over her mouth to stifle her laughter. In denim flares and a shirt in an eye-watering psychedelic print—and with the top three buttons undone—he looked as if he had just walked out of Woodstock or off the set of the musical *Hair*. 'You look amazing!'

He struck a pose before flashing a grin that made him look younger. A throb bloomed to life at the centre of her. *That* was how he should always look—young, carefree, *happy*.

Those dark eyes moved over her, his lips turned wolfish and she started to throb in an entirely different way. She'd modelled herself on the movie character Gidget—complete with a Hawaiian shirt, hotpants and her hair pulled into two bunches.

'You look as cute as a button—all sweet and wholesome— and I'm now dying to corrupt you.'

He moved in close and her breath quickened. He hadn't touched her yet, but her every atom had come alive, burning for him. His mouth lowered towards hers. It hovered there, their breaths mingling...

'Lorenzo? Is that you?'

They snapped apart as his mother's voice rose from below. The family had arrived the day before, and they had agreed to meet in the drawing room before walking across together to the pool house. Sadie remained out of sight in the shadows, sagging against the wall, waiting for the strength to return to her legs while Enzo moved downstairs to greet his mother.

She heard their shared laughter, registered their voices retreating in the direction of the drawing room and closed her eyes. That had been close. She and Enzo had agreed to keep their fling a secret. They didn't want the pressure of outside judgements. This thing between them, though temporary, was lovely. And just theirs.

Hauling in a breath, she pushed away from the wall, only for her gaze to connect with Chelsea's, her friend peering over the balustrade from the landing above. Oh, lord, had Chelsea seen…?

She made herself smile. 'Look at you in your mini-dress and GoGo boots. You look amazing!'

Chelsea didn't smile back. Instead she moved downstairs as fast as her pregnancy bump would allow her. 'You're *sleeping* with Enzo?'

Damn it. She met her dearest friend at the bottom of the landing and took her hands. 'Please don't make a big thing about this Chels. We—'

'How can I not? I—'

She pressed a finger to Chelsea's lips. 'Enzo and I are having fun, nothing more. We're both young and…well, in case you've not noticed, I've never really let my hair down.'

Chelsea snorted, as if that was the understatement of the century.

'But I have here, and it's been glorious. It's helped me in ways I couldn't have imagined. And me being here has helped Enzo too.'

Chelsea ignored the latter part of Sadie's statement. 'Helped you how?'

She hesitated. 'He's made me realise I deserve more from my grandparents…and from my life. He's made me realise I shouldn't be settling for second best—that it's not my job to be a consolation prize.'

'I've been telling you that for years!'

'Yeah, but you're biased. And, while I know Enzo and I might be "having some fun"—' she made air quotes '—he's nothing if not brutally honest.'

Chelsea's posture unhitched a fraction and a twinkle lit her blue eyes. 'Well, I have to say, you don't look brutalised.'

Nope, she felt all loved up.

Her friend's eyes turned contemplative then, and Sadie set about shattering that ASAP. 'This thing is temporary; we've both been very upfront about that. We're at points of change in our lives, and just finding a bit of comfort in each other. But that's all this is, Chels.'

'All?' Chelsea didn't look convinced. 'You've always had a soft spot for Enzo.'

Reaching out, Sadie took her friend's hands again. 'I promise not to do anything to hurt your brother.'

'It's not Enzo's heart I'm worried about.'

Chuckling, she slipped her arm through Chelsea's and started them down the next set of stairs. 'I'm a big girl, Chels. There are no schoolgirl crushes here. And guess what? I'm hoping to move to Europe. I've two job interviews next week—both jobs are based in London.'

'No way!'

Chelsea lived in Oxford and, as hoped, the news diverted the conversation into safer channels. Before they entered the drawing room, Sadie eased them to a halt. 'Enzo and I were hoping to keep things secret. We don't want any hullabaloo.'

Chelsea's sigh was audible, but she nodded. 'Your secret is safe with me.'

She squeezed her friend's arm in thanks.

Once assembled, the family moved en masse to the pool house. Exclamations of delight sounded as they took in the

1960s furnishings, the jukebox and pinball machine. Sadie had decorated the individual tables with an assortment of mass-produced toys from the 60s, 70s and 80s, many of which she expected the guests to remember from their own childhoods, all sourced cheaply online.

She grinned as Dominic headed straight for the pinball machine while Stephen pounced on a yo-yo. Isabella lifted a viewfinder to her eyes while Chelsea grabbed a cushion in a crazy geometrical pattern and swung back to Sadie with a silent scream. Sadie asked the wait staff to circle around with glasses of champagne and the first playlist began belting from the jukebox as the other guests started to arrive—an upbeat mix of the Beach Boys and 1960s bubble-gum pop.

The party was a success. Who knew forty people could be so rowdy? There was laughter and dancing; some people swam while others played the games Sadie had spread around—Pick-Up Sticks, Hungry Hippos and even Twister. The pinball machine remained in constant demand.

She'd planned to stay in the background, not draw attention to herself, but Enzo wasn't having any of that. He introduced her to the people she didn't know—not as his party planner, but as his friend. He danced with her and made sure she had something to eat. When she made noises about checking on things behind the scenes, he told her that Luisa and her army of staff had it all well in hand and to enjoy herself instead.

He glared when a cake appeared. 'I didn't know there'd be a cake,' he shot out of the corner of his mouth.

'It's a birthday party.' She kept a smile on her face. 'There was always going to be a cake. That *shouldn't* surprise you.'

'I don't want cake,' he grumbled.

'Then don't eat any. Just blow out the candle and make a pretty speech.'

Which had him huffing out a laugh, before she blended back into the crowd.

He blew out the candle and a rollicking version of *Happy Birthday* rose up around them. He endured it with an odd mix of exasperation and affection, before motioning everyone to be quiet. 'I'd like to thank all of you for coming tonight and making it a celebration to remember.'

He stared into his champagne. 'As you know, this has been something of a turbulent year for me.' His gaze searched the crowd, settling on Sadie. 'But tonight marks a turning point.'

She swore to God her heart performed a triple somersault with a fancy twist. She couldn't have dragged her gaze away from his if her life had depended on it.

'I was initially resistant to the idea of a party, but I'm pleased my resistance was overcome. I want to give a special thanks to Sadie Beckett, who made tonight happen and who transformed the pool house into this vision you see before you.'

Dominic called out, 'Three cheers for Sadie!'

A lump lodged in her throat as the pool house rang with their cheers.

After Enzo's speech, she was swamped with people who wanted to find out where she'd sourced everything, from the furniture to the toys and the caterers. She noted that, as the crowd around Enzo thinned, his mother took his arm and led him out through the French doors to the patio outside.

When the cake had been sliced, Sadie seized two plates to take out to them and had almost reached the door when she heard Isabella say, 'What are you doing, Enzo?'

'What do you mean?'

'You know exactly what I mean. What are you doing with Sadie?'

Her insides scrunched up so tight, it hurt. She immediately turned and walked back into the midst of the rowdy festivities. She had no desire to eavesdrop on Isabella's objections to the situation; no desire to hear rehashed all the reasons Isabella considered her an unsuitable match. Nor did she have any desire to hear Enzo make light of their relationship.

Why not?

She didn't know. Maybe because it would cheapen what had happened between them.

What's to understand? You're having a hot fling, nothing more.

But it felt like so much more. She frowned…and *that* didn't bode well.

'Look what I found on one of the tables!' Chelsea held up a Hawaiian themed Barbie doll dressed in a hula skirt. She crushed the doll to her chest. 'Please tell me I can keep her.'

'She's all yours.' Handing Chelsea one of the plates of cake, Sadie settled with her at a table to catch up on the gossip.

Sadie blinked when a knock sounded on her bedroom door. She clicked her bedside light on but, before she could slide out of bed and grab her wrap, the door cracked open.

'It's only me.'

Enzo!

'Come in.' She kept her voice low. She hadn't expected to see him tonight. A dizzy rush of delight had her grinning and holding the covers open to him.

He didn't need a second invitation. Closing the door quietly, he moved across the room with a lithe masculine grace, and more than a hint of determination, that made her realise how much his leg had improved during this last month. Sliding in beside her, he waited until she killed the light before pulling her close.

'Tonight was a triumph.'

'Ah, but did you enjoy yourself?'

'The party was wonderful.'

She gave a low laugh. 'It's entirely possible that I embraced my role as party planner with more enthusiasm than necessary.'

A strong hand smoothed the hair from her face with a gentleness that had her eyes prickling. 'Thank you, Sadie, for not giving up on me; for convincing me to go ahead with it all.'

She opened her mouth, but before she could speak he covered it with his own in a warm, reverential kiss that deepened into something so intense, she found herself drowning in the scent, sound and touch of him. Greedy hands tugged at the scraps of clothing in their way, and they joined their bodies in a frenzy of need. She didn't know where that need had come from, but found herself completely incapable of resisting it.

She needed Enzo…*now*. Wrapping her legs around his waist, she drew him as close as she could. She came with a force that shattered her. Enzo swallowed her cries as he too came with a power that left him shuddering in its wake.

They lay there, breathing hard and staring at the ceiling. She turned her head on the pillow to find him frowning. Had that shaken him to the core as well?

She made herself smile. 'Happy birthday, Enzo.'

The frown cleared, his hand finding hers beneath the sheet. 'You're a witch.'

'A good witch, I hope?'

'I like it better when you're wicked. But, *sì*, a good witch. You come here and cast your spells and make everything better.'

She melted to warm toffee. Holding his gaze, she swallowed. 'I hope your mother didn't give you too hard a time.'

His brows shot up. 'You saw…?'

'I was bringing you out cake when I heard her ask you what you were doing with me.'

'Ah.'

'At which point, I turned round and returned to the party.'

He lifted his head from the pillow and mock-glared. 'Why didn't you come and rescue me?'

She stared at him for a long moment. His eyes were bright

points in the darkness, reflecting the light from the stars outside the windows. 'I heard her objections after you kissed me nine years ago. I didn't need a repeat performance.'

'You heard…?' He sat up, a frown settling over his face.

With a super-human effort, she kept her voice steady. 'The morning after the ball.'

'She—' He broke off. 'Tell me exactly what you heard back then.'

She sat up too. She didn't want to make a big song and dance about it. It *was* nine years ago. 'Only her say it had to stop. *It* being us.'

'And then?'

The weight of his stare burned through her, but she couldn't lift her head to meet it. 'She said, "Sadie is not from our world. She doesn't have the resources to negotiate the world you come from".'

Isabella had witnessed their kiss and her disapproval had sliced right through Sadie's soul. *Sadie is not from our world…* Those words had tormented her ever since. Once again, she'd been found wanting. Once again, she hadn't been enough.

'Oh, Sadie.' Enzo pulled her into his arms.

She couldn't resist the warmth or the proffered comfort, but she didn't want to hear his rationalisations or explanations. 'It was a long time ago. It doesn't matter now.'

'Of course it matters. I wish you'd eavesdropped a little longer. Then you'd have heard what she was really worried about—that you were too young. She was worried my father and grandfather would eat you alive: those were her exact words. And she was right—they'd have been unforgivably awful. Not just rude, but spiteful. They'd have sought out your vulnerabilities and played on them. She said you deserved to be treated better than that, especially as you were so young.'

'Hold on.' She eased away. 'She was *worried* about me?'

'You see, she'd had to put up with their ugliness for so long. She didn't want to see another young woman victimised. Especially not one she was fond of.'

Her jaw dropped. Isabella *hadn't* thought her deficient and not good enough. She'd wanted to *protect* her.

'She was also worried I was toying with you and would break your heart. She told me, if I did that, I'd be no better than my father.'

Ouch! That would've hit him hard.

'She made me see the rift I could cause in the family if I did hurt you—Chelsea would never have forgiven me.'

Sadie slumped against the pillows.

'She never disapproved of you, Sadie. Not then and not now. Once again, she's worried I will hurt you.'

Reaching out, she took his hand. 'That's not going to happen. I know you're not interested in falling in love. But, just so you know, your sister witnessed our near-kiss on the landing.'

He rolled his eyes ceilingward. 'Of course she did. What did you tell her?'

'Kept it light. Said we were both just having some fun—promised not to break your heart.'

'Which is pretty much what I told my mother.'

'Then I told her I was moving to Europe and that moved the conversation on.'

He sent her a sidelong glance. 'I told my mother you'd performed a miracle—that you'd turned me from someone who was cranky and snarly into someone fit for company again.'

'You *didn't*!'

'I did.'

That shouldn't make her so happy. 'I told Chelsea you'd made me realise I was worth more than the scraps my grandparents tossed to me.'

'*So* much more.' His nostrils flared. 'I also told my mother you've made me feel strong again.'

He felt strong again…

She tried not to grin too widely; tried to shrug insouciantly. 'I did tell Chelsea we were brutally honest with each other.'

'I should've mentioned that too.'

Moonlight lit the room and she could see the way his pupils dilated and contracted. He cupped her face. 'You're beautiful.'

He made her feel beautiful. 'I hope you're not tired, because I'm sending you what I'm hoping is my wicked witch, seductive smile.'

'It's working,' he growled. And then he kissed her.

Afterwards, Sadie lay awake for a long time, staring up at the ceiling, a horrible suspicion starting to take hold. This had started to mean too much to her: Enzo telling her how wonderful she was; how she deserved the very best life had to offer. Her heart gave a sick kick. Was she in danger of falling in love with him?

A frigid chill slid between her ribs. She *couldn't* do that. He'd made it clear love didn't feature in his future—*very clear. That* wasn't going to change. She needed to pull back. Her pulse started to hammer. She couldn't repeat the same soul-destroying patterns that she had with her grandparents. She couldn't.

Right. She needed to focus on the future. She needed to get ready to embark on that future. Her tenure at the castle was temporary. It was time to stop putting Enzo's needs ahead of her own and choose an end date.

None of those assurances made her pulse slow. She hadn't fallen in love with Enzo. She *hadn't*…

From a long way away, a voice sounded through her: *liar.*

The party, and the weekend spent in the company of his family, lightened something inside Enzo. But it didn't stop him from breathing a sigh of relief when they finally left. Things could now go back to normal with Sadie and him.

There shouldn't be *a normal with Sadie. There shouldn't be a normal with any woman.*

Claudia had laid bare something that had been crystallizing in his mind for some time. The women he dated were mostly cold and calculating, but he never discovered that until it was too late. Why could he not see through their disguises? He was no longer prepared to deal with the tantrums, the fits of pique, the sulking, or the outbursts. He would *not* turn his life into the same kind of battleground that his parents' marriage had been.

He'd always been a solitary creature. The thought of living alone didn't cause him any particular pangs. But Sadie had made him see that he could enjoy a fling—especially when the boundaries were agreed upon at the outset. Besides, Sadie wasn't just *any* woman. She was a friend.

Something had changed since the party, though. She'd become… Quieter wasn't the right word, nor was reserved, but he'd catch her biting her lip and staring off into the distance, a frown on her face. The moment he said her name, she'd shake herself and send him one of those big, mischievous smiles, but they no longer had the ability to put his world to rights. And he didn't know why.

'Did someone say something to you at the party?' he finally demanded. 'Or over the weekend?' *Heaven forbid.*

'Like what?'

'Something to upset you.'

That snapped her to attention. 'What? *No.* Enzo, your nearest and dearest are good people. Why would you think any of them would say something mean to me?'

'I said plenty of mean things to you when you first arrived, but I'm still a good guy.'

She eyed him up and down and gave a careless shrug. 'You're alright, I suppose.'

Which had him barking out a laugh, before scowling. 'You're not considering going back to Australia to abide by your grandparents' conditions?'

Her chin hitched up so fast, it should've given her whiplash. 'Absolutely not!'

He let out a breath.

'I hope they'll eventually see they can have a relationship with me that's separate from Verity, but I'm not going back to beg for whatever scraps they'd feel duty-bound to offer me if I did agree to toe their line.'

Reaching out, she took his hand. 'You've shown me that I'm worth more than that.' A funny expression flitted across her face, but it was gone again in an instant. 'I'm sorry if I've been preoccupied. I've been thinking about these job interviews I have coming up.'

She had two online interviews this coming week. If they went well, she'd progress to in-person interviews in London. Waiting on the threshold for a new life to begin had to be exciting, but probably nerve-wracking too. Her preoccupation made sense, yet that didn't stop a kernel of unease unfurling inside him.

At night, though, they made love with an intensity that infused him with joy. And something less intense but somehow deeper—*contentment*. A month ago he could never have foreseen this, could never have imagined it. He felt as if he'd been handed a miracle, and he wanted to pay tribute to that miracle.

'I've made a decision about my future,' he said.

They were down at the beach and Sadie's head spun round with flattering speed. 'What kind of decision?'

They lay on their towels, drying off after a swim, and the sand shifted obligingly beneath him as he turned to his side and propped his head on his hand. 'About what I'd like to do going forward.'

She was stretched out on her tummy, wearing a red bikini that he itched to peel from her body. She peered over the top of her sunglasses at him. 'Don't keep me in suspense.'

'I have all of this.' He gestured around. 'A castle, extraordinary grounds and a beautiful beach. It's too much for one person.'

She sat up, giving him her full attention. 'And?'

'I've been making enquiries—talking to people in the know—and I'm going to open it up during the summer for disadvantaged children to come and have a holiday.'

Her jaw dropped. She pulled off her sunglasses, her eyes wide. A lump lodged in his throat when he recognised the emotion reflected there: *admiration*. 'What an utterly perfect thing to do.'

He did his best to swallow the lump.

'To give a child the chance of a once-in-a-lifetime holiday—like the one you had when you were ten...'

And like the one she'd given him this summer.

She clasped her hands beneath her chin. 'To make something so positive from this place... What's the saying—making a silk purse from a sow's ear?'

He started to laugh—a simple chuckle that grew until he fell back on his towel, gripped with huge belly laughs. Eventually he sat up again and met her bemused grin. 'Sadie, in nobody's language can a castle ever be considered a pig's ear.'

'Pfft.' She waved that away. 'I'm glad you're not going to sell all of this to some cold-eyed tycoon who'd fill it with expensively hideous things simply to prove how successful he is.'

A man like his father? No. Instead Enzo would leave behind him a legacy he could be proud of. He'd reshape the future of the castle using his earlier forebears' examples—the ancestors Sadie had told him about. He'd never have known about them if she hadn't done her digging.

'It's an incredibly generous thing to do.' Sadie reached across to briefly clasp his arm. Before he could place his hand over hers, though, she removed it. It shouldn't have given him pause—she'd been leaning at a funny angle—and yet he couldn't shake off a sense of unease.

He tried to shrug it away. 'I have all of this through an accident of birth. It feels right to share it.'

'I don't doubt that you'll enjoy every moment of this new venture of yours.'

He suspected she was right. 'If you hadn't reminded me that I had the means to live my life in whatever fashion I wanted, I'd have probably returned to work in Milan and continued making a lot of money developing property.'

It was not that he wasn't proud of his company; he'd worked hard to make it a success, though it was naïve to believe he'd not had help. He'd had a trust fund, his family name and an excellent education. His father might've been a miserable excuse of a man, but Enzo had been gifted all the advantages to ensure he could make a financial success of his life.

'But it would've been mindless.' And his company deserved better. So did he.

'You're ready for a new challenge now.'

'*Sì.*'

'I wish you every success with your new venture, Enzo.'

She said the words as if she was saying goodbye and things inside him tightened. 'Will you come and visit when I have my first contingent of holidaymakers?'

'Of course!' But her smile was worryingly bright.

His heart thumped. 'Have you made some decisions about your own life too?'

'I...'

'Come,' he said when she hesitated. 'I've told you about mine.'

'What?' Her lips curved into a mischievous grin. 'Like an "I'll show you mine if you show me yours" thing?'

That smile, the twinkle and her teasing, made everything okay again. 'Absolutely.'

'But I feel as if we should wallow for a little longer in your plans. Imagine the children laughing and running on the beach, the sound of their feet pounding up the stairs in the castle, the way they're going to saturate the pool house with their shenanigans.'

He gave a mock groan. 'There will be water fights, will there not?'

'Bound to be.' She rested back on her towel and placed her sunglasses back on her nose. 'I'm seeing cream teas on the lawn… There has to be cake—lots of cake—and games of cricket.'

'Cricket is a game I do not understand. Football, however…'

'Football followed by gelato.'

Perfetto. 'And movie nights.' He'd enjoyed his and Sadie's mini comedy festival.

'And bedtime stories.'

He stared at her, but her eyes remained hidden behind her sunglasses. 'Bedtime stories?'

'Yeah. Didn't your mother read you bedtime stories when you were little?'

She had, and he'd loved it. He settled back down. Sadie hadn't had bedtime stories, birthday parties or hugs and laughter. His chest burned. 'It will be idyllic. I will make it one of the best times they have ever had. A memory to hold close.'

'Just as you have for me.'

Glancing across, he found a smile curving her lips. Reaching out, he took her hand and squeezed it. What a gift this woman was.

She squeezed it back, and he told himself that nothing was different; that all was still right with the world…

Enzo led Sadie out to the terrace and removed his hands from her eyes. 'Okay, now you can look.'

She opened them and her mouth formed a perfect 'O'. 'Ooh, Enzo! This looks utterly wicked.'

'When you mentioned cream teas on the lawn, I realised how remiss I'd been. Not once had I offered you a decadent afternoon tea on the terrace.'

She kinked an eyebrow at him. 'I promise you, the one thing I haven't been during my stay is hungry.'

The words were uttered with a wicked twinkle that made him grin. He held out her chair, poured the tea and served her a huge slice of cream cake. She took a bite and moaned in appreciation. '*So* good.'

'I feel as if I'm redeeming myself.' He tucked into his own slice of cake. 'And I am also hoping to now worm from you your plans for the future, after having wallowed so comprehensively in mine all morning.'

'Ah.' She set her fork down and reached for her tea. He couldn't help feeling she was fortifying herself. 'I'm pleased to report that I have face-to-face interviews for both positions that I applied for in London.'

'This is not a shock. You're wonderful, and any employer would be lucky to have you.'

She twinkled at him, but something about it had him frowning. 'On the spur of the moment, I also applied for a job I thought I'd have no chance of—a position as a researcher on an antiques-restoration TV show—and I have an interview for that one now too. My fingers and toes are crossed!'

'This is excellent news!' A cloud passed over the sun,

though—metaphorically speaking, as there wasn't a cloud in the sky. If she was offered one of these positions, their time here would come to an end.

Still, it would be several weeks before she would start a new job. They could relish what time they had left. 'I'll organise us flights to and from London.'

She shook her head very slowly. 'I've loved every moment of my time here, Enzo, but it's time for me to stop my dillydallying and finally embark on this new life of mine.'

Dillydallying? He blinked. Was that all he'd been to her—a dalliance?

It was what you agreed. It's what you wanted.

He nodded, frowning. It was.

Have you changed your mind?

The memory of his parents' constant fights rose in his mind. His heart gave a sick kick as he recalled how Claudia had lashed out at him. He ground his teeth together. *No!* He wasn't going to put himself through any of that again.

CHAPTER TWELVE

'Nevertheless, there's no need for you to make any hasty decisions, Sadie.'

Sadie nearly choked on her cake. The one thing she hadn't expected was for Enzo to encourage her to stay longer. She'd already over-stayed her visit by an extra three weeks. She thought he'd be…well, not exactly delighted; while she'd tried to create some distance between them during the day, she'd been powerless to do so at night. Nights continue to be tangled limbs, breathy sighs, sweaty bodies and ecstasy, followed by a deep and profound peace when Enzo wrapped her in his arms as she drifted off to sleep.

So, while she hadn't expected her news to delight him, she'd thought a big part of him would be relieved. She couldn't read the expression in his eyes. 'What makes you think my decision is hasty?'

He gestured at her cake, encouraging her to continue eating, but thoughts of leaving here, of leaving Enzo, had her appetite fleeing. It had become starkly clear to her over the last few days that her attempts to emotionally distance herself from Enzo were doomed to failure. She'd fallen in love with him—utterly, completely and *pointlessly* head-over-heels in love with him.

She needed to leave. Staying here would be self-defeating. He didn't want love in his life. Wishing and hoping otherwise wouldn't change that. She deserved more. She deserved better. Enzo himself had pointed that out on more than one occasion.

'You've not yet attended these interviews. You don't know if you will be offered a position.'

Her hands and jaw clenched. Did he think she wasn't good enough?

'Sadie!' He snapped out her name and she glanced up to find him glaring. 'I expect you will be offered *all* of these positions. I also think, until you decide which job you want, it makes sense to base yourself here. When you know where you're going to work, you can then find a place to rent.' His brow pleated. 'Does this not make sense to you too? This way, you will only be moving once.'

As she'd only brought two suitcases with her, moving wouldn't be a problem.

'And if you stay longer…' He sent her one of those slow grins that turned her knees to wet spaghetti. 'We can continue to enjoy the sun and beach, among other things.'

And that was the problem. She'd been enjoying it all too much. Enzo had come to mean *too* much. And she was now in a bind of her own making. 'You and I have always been brutally honest with one another, yes?'

He frowned. 'Are you going to be brutal now?'

She laughed. 'I promise I'm not.' She wasn't even going to be honest, though he didn't need to know that. 'Enzo, I've started enjoying all of this too much.'

His frown deepened. 'What do you mean?'

'We promised to keep things fun and light and drama-free.'

'Is this not what we have done?'

On the surface, perhaps, but things had also been unexpectedly hot and heavy. It had taken her off-guard. She didn't even have the heart to berate herself for falling in love with him. In hindsight, it seemed utterly inevitable. She'd loved her time here; loved her time with him. She refused to regret any of it. But she could no longer hide from the fact that pain loomed in her future—a lot of it—and to remain here any longer would only hurt her more.

If Enzo had taught her one thing, it was that she deserved better—that she should never settle for being second best. She deserved more than the few scraps of affection he was currently capable of giving.

'Sadie, is that not what we've done?' His voice sharpened. 'Dear God, please tell me… Have you…? You haven't developed *feelings* for me?'

Lifting her chin, she shook her head, proud of herself for not wincing at his horror. 'No.' It was a bald-faced lie, but she'd promised him she wouldn't fall in love with him. She'd promised him to keep things drama-free. She might've broken that first promise, but hell would freeze over before she broke the second.

'No, Enzo, but we also promised to keep things temporary, and I fear that if I stay much longer I'll develop more permanent feelings for you.'

She met his horrified gaze—his beautiful, horrified gaze—and her heart pounded so hard, it hurt. 'Now, if that's something you're interested in exploring…'

He shot away from their little table so fast, she felt as if something vital had been physically torn from her chest. With all her heart, she wished she could laugh at the expression of horror plastered across his face, but she couldn't. Not when her heart lay at her feet in a million tiny shards.

The pain starts now.

She dug up a smile from somewhere. *Keep it drama-free.* 'That's a no, then.'

'Sadie…'

'There's nothing to apologise for, Enzo. This holiday has been every good thing—a ten out of ten. But I think it wise for me to pack my bags and leave in the morning. And don't worry—we'll keep in touch. I can't wait to let you know which job I choose, if I get them, and where I end up calling home. Next time you're in London, we'll catch up over dinner or something, yes?'

'Yes.' The word croaked out of him, and it was all she could do not to drop her head to her hands.

'In the meantime, I'm going to finish my cake.' She shovelled cake into her mouth, feigned a moan and sent him a thumbs-up, gesturing that he too should finish his cake. She'd read somewhere that people comfort-ate because the physical act of eating helped reduce stress.

Not working...

But, look at her, keeping things drama-free. *Go me!*

He took his seat again, sending her a funny look—half-wary, half-unconvinced. 'We need to go back to being friends without benefits *immediately*!' He stabbed a finger onto the table.

A dastardly part of her couldn't resist teasing him. 'What? You think I'm going to fall head over heels in love with you in the—' she glanced at her watch '—next sixteen hours?'

He rolled his shoulders. 'Of course not! I just...'

'Chill, Enzo. No drama, remember? We promised.'

His mouth worked. 'Are you accusing me of being dramatic?'

She waved her fork through the air. 'If the cap fits...'

She finally finished her cake. *Thank you, God.* 'Look, everything is fine. We go back to being friends, no harm done.' She set her fork down on her plate. 'It's no big deal, is it?'

'None at all,' he managed through gritted teeth, though he didn't finish his cake.

'We should have a final film night, though—with popcorn,' she added, in case there was something to the comfort-eating hypothesis. She grinned. 'And I have the perfect movie for us.'

Roman Holiday!

Enzo glared down the long drive as Sadie's car disappeared. He'd offered to take her to the airport himself—had almost insisted—but she'd rejected the idea so completely, he'd let it drop.

He growled. He should've insisted.

Maybe it's easier for her this way.

That was the reason he'd refrained from insisting. He'd do anything to spare her pain.

She said she hasn't developed feelings for you.

Yet, when he'd made it clear he had zero interest in pursuing anything longer term, she hadn't been able to hide the flare of pain in her eyes.

Confronted with the same horror, wouldn't your feelings have been hurt?

Damn it. He should've been kinder. He should've said something gallant: *if there's anyone who could make me change my mind, it's you.* He should've said something to make her laugh and accuse him of flattery. But he hadn't, and his reaction had made her feel bad about herself. He'd give anything now to go back and change that, do better.

Despite her assurance otherwise, had she developed feelings for him? Had he inadvertently hurt her? And, if he had, how could he fix it?

You can't.

Then how could he lessen the damage?

Another growl emerged from deep in his throat. *He couldn't.* The best he could do was stay away and hope she hadn't been lying—hope she hadn't developed feelings for him. He didn't want to stay away, though. He wanted to check on her. If he didn't, who else would?

She doesn't want you checking on her.

Which made him growl again.

Damn it! Last night she'd made him watch *Roman Holiday* again. Now he couldn't get the damn movie out of his head. What on earth had he been thinking, giving it ten out of ten? He'd give it a big, fat zero now.

Turning on his heel, he set off for the kitchen. He needed strong coffee and something sweet, such as a slice of Luisa's panettone.

He halted in the doorway when he found Luisa standing at the bench, wiping tears from her cheeks. '*Mio dio!* What is the matter?'

She glanced around with a start.

'Sorry. I did not mean to startle you.'

She waved that away. 'Your Miss Sadie left me a gift.'

She wasn't *his*.

'And a thank-you note…' She reached for a pretty card with an image of a mug of steaming coffee and a big slice of cake on the front. 'For feeding her "such splendidly and utterly de-lectable treats". As if it's not my job and what I'm paid to do.'

'You went above and beyond—serving all of her favourite things. You made her feel special, and I appreciate it, Luisa.' She'd been wonderful, as had Guido. The other man had will-ingly put himself at Sadie's beck and call, always happy to help her move some heavy object or other in the attics.

Luisa held up a pair of pretty opal earrings and a sheet of folded paper. 'She left me her favourite pavlova recipe and told me it would have Mr Stephen swooning.'

'I will look forward to sampling it as well.'

'I shall miss her.'

'Yes.'

The castle seemed oddly empty without her. He might miss her, but their affair had always had an end date. Per-haps that end date had come sooner than he'd anticipated, but it was what they'd agreed. He had no intention of changing the rules to explore something deeper with her. Too many women in the past had turned from warm and charming into angry balls of rage when he couldn't be what they wanted. He wasn't sure he'd be able to stand it if Sadie were to turn on him like that. It would be safer to keep his distance and ensure that never happened.

He helped himself to coffee from the pot.

'Can I get you anything else, Enzo? Biscotti…?'

'No, thank you.' His stomach had gone too hard and tight for food.

Taking his coffee upstairs, he strode into the drawing room, but had no idea what to do there. He turned round, headed for his office instead and sat at his desk. He didn't turn on his computer, though. Instead, he stared at the wall opposite. His coffee went cold.

An hour later, he shot to his feet and strode back through to the drawing room, glaring at the table sitting beneath the bay windows. It seemed wrong that Sadie no longer sat there, tinkering away with some toy or other, her clever fingers working their magic and bringing the toy back to life.

Like she brought you back to life?

Sì. Her presence had dragged him out of the doldrums.

Are you going to fall back into them now?

Absolutely not!

He lifted his gaze to the view. The beach! *That* was what he'd do. He'd go and sit on the beach and swim a little, as he and Sadie had done. Just because she was no longer here didn't mean he couldn't still enjoy the routine they'd created.

Forty minutes later, he found it impossible to wipe the scowl from his face. The beach had lost its magic. Without Sadie, the sun didn't shine so brightly, and the water wasn't as invigorating. Even the sand felt lumpy and hard.

'Rain, damn it,' he muttered, staring at the cloudless blue sky. Rain would suit his mood more than this summer perfection.

When he retired for the night, he found a little parcel on his bed. His heart picked up speed. Inside were the clockwork figures he and Sadie had restored—the twirling ballerina and the flamingo. The accompanying card read:

Put these where you'll see them every day, to remind you to be playful, to have fun. Life is for living (to the full!), Enzo, but it's also for chasing one's dreams. I'll never forget my time at the castle. Sadie xx

Enzo spent the next three days trying to come up with a different routine—one that didn't remind him of Sadie. He swam laps in the pool first thing every morning. He spent his days working on his 'summer at the castle' project—getting two national charities onboard and finding qualified people to administer the programme. He spent the evenings in the drawing room reading the journals Sadie had brought down from the attic. But, while the routine was different, she was always on his mind.

And he spent far too much time winding up those clockwork figures and watching them twirl and dip. During the day, he kept them on her table in the drawing room where he could see them. He took them up to his bedroom when he retired for the night. He wound them up and watched them until they ran down and then wound them up again. It was while he was in the act of reaching for the twirling lady on the fourth morning without Sadie that the truth finally hit him.

He thumped down into the nearest chair, staring out of the bay windows to the lights glittering on the water below. He'd spent so long worrying about Sadie's feelings and Sadie's heart that he hadn't stopped to examine his own. All this aching and yearning…

His mouth went dry. He missed her. He missed her in a way he'd never missed another soul before in his life. With every fibre of his being, he wanted her here with him.

His mind raced and so did his heart.

He *loved* her.

He sat with that for a long moment. The women he'd dated in the past had lied about who they were; they'd hidden their schemes and greed behind charming veneers. Sadie hadn't tried to be charming. Not once.

Leaping to his feet, he seized the clockwork figures before moving across to his DVD library. Grabbing a bag, he dropped selected DVDs into it and then raced upstairs to grab his passport.

Sadie might not have feelings for him, but she'd indicated she'd be open to exploring and deepening their fling into something more. In letting her go so easily, he might've lost his chance with her, but there was only one way to find out. And he wasn't going to let her go without a fight.

'Yay!' Sadie mumbled, leaning against the wall of the lift as it whooshed her down to the foyer of the fancy London high-rise where she'd had her interview. *They'd love to offer me a position with the company.* Her shoulders slumped. *Great.*

She ought to be jumping with joy. Instead, she scowled as the lift doors opened to let her out into the grand foyer that was all marble and glass, and reminded her of the pool house back at Enzo's castle. She'd thought when she'd been driven away from the castle that she'd be able to compartmentalise her pain—put it in a box marked 'Enzo' and somehow keep it separate from her new life. She trudged across the foyer. What a joke! Missing Enzo overshadowed everything.

She walked about in a fog, as if a dark cloud had descended over her—one that not only refused to let the light in, but threatened to suffocate her—which made it impossible to feel happy about something as trivial as a job offer.

You still have to eat. You still have to pay the rent.

'Shut up,' she muttered.

'The interview didn't go well, then?'

She slammed to a halt and fixed her glare on the man

in front of her. A man who looked a lot like Enzo. She saw Enzo *everywhere*. Usually it was some broad-shouldered, dark-haired Adonis moving through the crowd ahead of her, whom logically she knew wasn't Enzo. But it never stopped her pulse from racing or hope from gripping her heart.

Reaching out, she pinched his arm.

'Ouch,' he said mildly, a piratical brow lifting.

She started. Oh, God! It really was… *'Enzo!* What are you doing here?'

'Why did you pinch me?'

'Just making sure you were real.'

A slow grin hooked up one side of his mouth. Her heart started to thud. In her grey fog, had she given herself away? It was all she could do to not stamp a foot in frustration. She'd worked so hard to save face during her last day at the castle. To blow it now…

She hitched up her chin. 'And, in answer to your question, the interview went very well, thank you.'

Hold on. He was *smiling.* If she'd given herself away, he'd be running as fast as he could in the other direction.

'So that pinch…' He ignored her statement about the interview. 'Are you saying you've missed me?'

She didn't have the resources for light, flirtatious banter—not this week. She folded her arms. 'What are you doing here, Enzo?'

Something in his face gentled, and he reached out as if to touch her cheek, but pulled his hand back at the last moment. 'I came here to tell you that I love you.'

She blinked and leaned towards him. 'I beg your pardon?'

'I…'

A crowd of people exited the lifts, accidentally jostling them. Taking her arm, Enzo led her across to the bench that ran along one wall where people could set up work stations or simply sit and watch the busy street outside.

Had he said...?

Surely not?

He settled her on a stool and then opened his briefcase. Pulling out a package, he unwrapped it to reveal the vintage clockwork toys she'd left for him. 'I'm in danger of wearing these out. I spend most of my nights winding them up and watching them again and again—hours on end. I watch them in an effort to try and recapture the fun and magic of when you were at the castle.'

A lump lodged in her throat.

'I went into a panic when I thought I might've hurt you. I couldn't think of anything worse. It drove me out of my mind.'

The lump promptly deflated. Her gaze dropped to her hands. 'That's guilt, Enzo, not love.' She didn't want his guilt and regret. She didn't want those things tarnishing the happy memories they'd shared.

'Which is what I thought too. Until I realised I was hiding behind that, too scared to face the truth.'

Her heart started to pound too hard and too fast, despite her warnings for it to do nothing of the sort.

'The truth is that I love you, Sadie. You taught me to embrace life again. You showed me how glorious that could be.'

Her hands twisted together. What she wouldn't give for his words to be true... But *that* was gratitude. And she didn't want his gratitude any more than she wanted his guilt.

'But when you left, I felt in a worse place than I had been before your arrival.'

She stiffened.

'And yet in a better place too, because you'd helped me dream a new dream and I still had it, even if I didn't have you.'

The lump surged back into her throat.

'That dream is worthy, and I mean to see it through, but I've lost my enthusiasm for it. And you want to know why?

Because you're not there to share it with. My life now feels like it's fifty percent less because I don't have your dreams to cheer for. I want your dreams in my life, Sadie. I want to celebrate your successes and be there when—' he gestured to the lift '—things don't go to plan.'

'I was offered the job.' Her voice sounded as if it came from a long way away. 'I've been offered all three jobs I applied for.'

'Then why aren't you happy?'

She raised her eyebrows, letting them speak for her.

He gave a decisive nod. 'I love you, Sadie, though clearly I have yet to convince you.' He suddenly scowled. 'And, just so you know, the ending to *Roman Holiday* is terrible. I can't believe you made me watch it again. It's a dreadful movie.'

'It's a brilliant film!'

He waved a finger beneath her nose. 'Our love story does not have to end in that way.' Seizing his briefcase, he pulled out a stack of DVDs. '*My Fair Lady*, *Pretty Woman*, *Ever After*, *Notting Hill*.'

As he said their names, he pushed each DVD into her hands. She stared at them. These were all Cinderella stories. Was he asking her to be his Cinderella? Her heart pounded, fit to burst.

'You indicated you'd be open to deepening our relationship. Please tell me that's still the case. Our love story can end like these ones if only you'll give me the chance to prove that to you.'

If only she'd give him the chance… Did he mean it?

Her heart lodged in her throat and pounded there. 'You were adamant you didn't want love in your life. You swore that you didn't have the resources to deal with the drama a relationship involved.'

Taking the stack of DVDs from her, he set them on the bench and perched on a stool, pulling it closer so that his knees bracketed hers. Reaching down, he took her hands. 'All my life I've been confused about what love looks like. My mother claimed to love my father—but all I saw was bitter arguments and fights and my mother crying.'

She squeezed his hands. She couldn't help it.

'And then Claudia claimed to love me, but lashed out in such a physical way…and with such terrible consequences.'

Acid burned her stomach. Claudia's actions could've killed him.

'It has made me equate love with turbulence and fury and upheaval. I did not want any of that in my life.'

She didn't want any of that for him either.

'But then you came to the castle with all of your sunshine and smiles and teasing.' He frowned. 'And, when we argued I was the dramatic one, not you, you didn't throw temper tantrums. When you considered yourself in the wrong, you apologised.'

'So did you.'

He stared at his hands. 'My mother might've loved my father, but he didn't love her. He didn't treat her with respect. He flaunted his lovers; that's what their arguments were about. My father wasn't capable of loving anyone but himself. You, though, do respect me.'

'Yes.'

'As for Claudia… Hers was the temper tantrum of someone too used to getting their own way, not the act of someone who loved me. *You* do not throw temper tantrums.'

Her throat thickened and she had to swallow.

'And then you made me watch romantic comedies and…'
She leaned towards him. 'And?'

'Those movies demonstrate characters becoming *better* people because of love, not worse. They might behave badly during the course of the movie, but then they find the courage to change and make whatever sacrifices are necessary to win their loved one's heart.'

The words he uttered made beautiful and logical sense… But could she trust them? Could she trust *him*?

'I've realised that the women I've dated in the past—women I thought were charming and lovely—were lying about who they were and putting on a performance. They were hiding their true selves behind pretty veneers. But you don't do that.'

'No.'

'I didn't believe anyone could bring out the best in me, but you did. I'm a better man for having you in my life. The question now is…do I bring out the best in you?'

Of course he did.

'And can you face your fears for me?'

She stiffened. 'What fears?'

'That you're not good enough. That you don't belong in my world.'

Her face grew uncomfortably hot.

'You ran, Sadie, rather than tell me the truth. You ran. You didn't stay and fight for me—for us.'

'I promised I wouldn't fall in love with you. And I promised there'd be no drama. I did *not* promise you honesty.' She moistened her lips. 'I didn't mean to break the first promise, so I did everything I could to keep the second one. When I checked to see if you were open to taking things further…'

'I shut down.'

'You didn't just shut down, Enzo, you looked sick with horror, and I didn't want to be the cause of so much distress. Confessing my love wouldn't have brought you joy. It would've brought the exact opposite. And I figured you'd been through enough.'

'Confessing your love…?' He touched a hand to her cheek. 'You really love me, then?'

She stared into that beautiful face, those steady eyes, and the dark cloud surrounding her slowly evaporated. Enzo *loved* her. Not only did he love her, not only did he think her enough, he thought her *extraordinary*.

A smile stretched across her face until she thought she'd become all smile and nothing else. An answering grin stretched across Enzo's. Slipping off her stool, she moved into the circle of his arms, looping her arms around his shoulders. 'I love you, Enzo. I can't promise you a drama-free life. But I can promise to walk that drama beside you.'

His hands settled on her waist and he pulled her closer. 'If you're beside me, I won't even notice the drama.'

Oh, Lord, this man could melt her to a puddle with his words and the heat in his eyes. Reaching forward, she covered his lips with hers and kissed him with all her heart—with all her hope and love. He kissed her back with an intensity that stole her breath.

When they eased apart, they were both breathing hard. His eyes glittered. 'Where's your hotel?'

'Not far.'

'*Dio!* We need to go shopping first. I brought nothing with me except…' He gestured to his briefcase. 'And I'm not leaving you now. Not even for a day to collect my things from the castle.'

She wanted to float up to the ceiling, happy dance and kiss him again. 'You're not afraid I'll run away again, are you? I promise not to do any such thing.' She leaned against him, relishing the strength of that big, masculine body. 'Instead, I'm going to make your life so full of fun and laughter and love, you're going to have to pinch yourself to keep making sure it's real.'

Enzo smiled down at her. 'I do not think you're going to run. But as one of the heroes in one of those movies said— when you realise what you want your life to be, you want to start that life as soon as possible. My life feels as if it has started today. And I am not going anywhere.'

She simply stared, letting the magic of his words wash over her.

'Now, how does this sound? I can work remotely, so when you decide which of the jobs you want to accept, we'll buy a place of our own. One you will love and...'

She pressed her fingers against his mouth. 'We already have a home we love. You always knew what I most wanted to do—to set up my own doll hospital. With your help, I could do that.'

It was time to stop being so afraid.

His eyes glowed. 'I love you, Sadie. I'm yours—heart and soul.'

'That's a nice line,' she whispered.

'I've been practising.'

His smile filled her vision. 'Take me home, Enzo.'

'That's a better line,' he said, before kissing her with a fierceness that made her toes curl.

Lifting his head, he took her hand in his. 'Let's go home.'

* * * * *

If you enjoyed this story, check out these other great reads from Michelle Douglas

Tempted by Her Best Friend Billionaire
The Venice Reunion Arrangement
Secret Fling with the Billionaire
Tempted by Her Greek Island Bodyguard

All available now!

MILLS & BOON®

Coming next month

FOR BUSINESS... OR PLEASURE
Joss Wood

'Everybody loses their breath when they first walk onto the veranda.'

Instant recognition stiffened her spine and caused her heart to flutter, then shudder. That voice...deeper, darker, more compelling, it was the same one that painted compliments on her skin, whispered dirty, delightful suggestions against her lips. Calla felt her knees weaken and clenched her fists, telling herself she couldn't pass out, couldn't gasp or sway or act like a fool.

What was she supposed to do? Say?

Biting down hard on her lip, she half turned and, as casually as possible, slipped her Audrey Hepburn glasses onto her face, hoping the gesture would give her a couple of seconds to gather her composure. But how was it that her sexy bartender was standing on the terrace of Judah Reyes's luxury St Croix house...

Unless...no! Unless he was the owner, the CEO...

No. Way.

Continue reading

FOR BUSINESS... OR PLEASURE
Joss Wood

Available next month
millsandboon.co.uk

COMING SOON!

We really hope you enjoyed reading this book.
If you're looking for more romance
be sure to head to the shops when
new books are available on

Thursday 26th February

To see which titles are coming soon, please visit

millsandboon.co.uk/nextmonth

MILLS & BOON

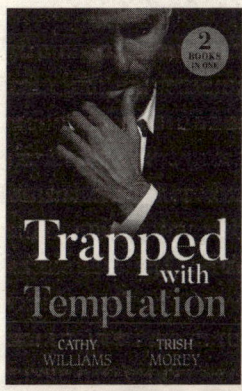
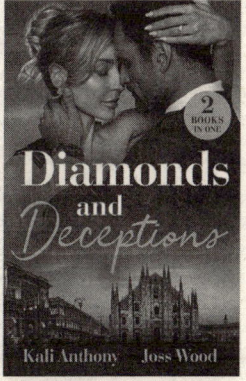

LET'S TALK
Romance

For exclusive extracts, competitions and special offers, find us online:

f MillsandBoon

X @MillsandBoon

⊙ @MillsandBoonUK

♪ @MillsandBoonUK

Get in touch on 01413 063 232